The Light of Amsterdam

DAVID PARK has written seven books, most recently the hugely acclaimed *The Truth Commissioner* which was awarded the Christopher Ewart Biggs Memorial Prize. He was the winner of the Authors' Club First Novel Award, the Bass Ireland Arts Award for Literature and thrice winner of the University of Ulster's McCrea Literary Award. In 2008 he received the American Ireland Fund Literary Award for his contribution to Irish literature and has also been awarded a Major Artist Award from the Arts Council of Northern Ireland. He lives in County Down, Northern Ireland, with his wife and two children.

'The humanity of Park's writing is such that even at the most prosaic of moments, unique insights quiver into life' *Guardian*

'Like Jane Austen and E.M. Forster, Park sets his characters a moral examination . . . a very good novel indeed' Allan Massie, *Scotsman*

'There are few other writers who could write so plaintively about lives of quiet desperation. It may be plain chant but the language makes this novel sing' Mary Morrissy, *Irish Times*

'[Park's] books are packed full of understated glory, of tenderness and of truth. This new book is quite something. It's about marriage and children and fear of children growing up and the moments of treasured joy between parent and child that the child might not even know. It is also, as always, about the small glories and epiphanies that light up all our lives . . . I can't recommend this book enough' *Daily Mirror*

'Park is more than merely a fine writer with a great deal to say – as if that were not sufficient. He is an astute storyteller whose vision is sustained by instinct, intelligent observation and a sense of responsibility' Eileen Battersby, *Irish Times*

The Light of Amsterdam

DAVID PARK

BLOOMSBURY

LONDON · NEW DELHI · NEW YORK · SYDNEY

First published in Great Britain 2012
This paperback edition published 2013

Copyright © 2012 by David Park

The moral right of the author has been asserted

Bloomsbury Publishing, London, New Delhi, New York and Sydney

50 Bedford Square, London WC1B 3DP

A CIP catalogue record for this book is available from the British Library

ISBN 978 1 4088 3154 0

10 9 8 7 6 5 4 3 2 1

Typeset by Hewer Text UK Ltd, Edinburgh
Printed and bound in Great Britain by CPI Group (UK) Ltd, Croydon CR0 4YY

MIX
Paper from
responsible sources
FSC® C020471

www.bloomsbury.com/davidpark

For Alberta

In others' works thou dost but mend the style,
And arts with thy sweet graces graced be;
But thou art all my art, and dost advance
As high as learning my rude ignorance.

William Shakespeare, Sonnet LXXVIII

One

THE INK WAS BLACK, the paper the same shade of blue as a bird's egg he had found a week before. In their balanced elegance the capital G and B mirrored each other. Unlike most of the soccer signatures he collected which were largely indecipherable hieroglyphics – the bored scribbles of fleeing stars – this name was readable and perfectly formed. He knew instinctively that it wasn't a fake and Thomas Bingham who harboured no interest in football hadn't asked for a payment, other than an unspoken acknowledgement that through living in Cregagh Estate he had access to important people and so, if only vicariously, was also an important person. He had always assumed that it had just been big talk when Bingham said he'd get it for him, that it was only one of those self-aggrandising promises boys shake up like a lemonade bottle and release with the empty froth of their words.

George Best's autograph. Where did it go? Where was it now? On a Saturday morning, a lifetime later, he stood waiting at the top of the Cregagh Road close to the estate and wondered how you always lost the things over which you should have taken more care. It would mean something to have it now and he patted the empty pocket of his overcoat as if to check whether by some transubstantive miracle memory might have realised it into a physical reality. But there was only emptiness and as he turned again to look down the road that ran from the city to the Castlereagh Hills and comfortable suburbia, the panelled sky hung grey as if hammered out of tin with the only visible colour the distant yellow of the shipyard cranes. It was an hour before the cortège was due but already the road was lined on both sides and then just after 9.30 a.m. it did what didn't seem possible and the sky darkened even more, almost as if the waters of the lough had flowed into the city. He wondered again why he had come and felt a sense of confusion edged with embarrassment. It had the same uncomfortable feeling of emotional meltdown, the collectively generated hysteria of sentiment, that had prompted all his joyful cynicism about Diana's farewell.

He tried to justify his presence by telling himself that it was about respect, that it was about memory, because unlike most of those around him he could claim to have actually seen him play and not just the jaded pastiche of his final years when his legs had gone. Saw him at Windsor Park for the price of a bus fare by simply going to the turnstiles, searching for a sympathetic face and asking to be 'lifted over'. Overhead a helicopter relentlessly shredded the air while motorcycle outriders patrolled the road constantly checking the route was clear. What was it he remembered? The heady, sweet-sour, swirling narcotic of nicotine and beer? The collective howl and roar of a predatory, almost exclusively male crowd, a fierce living creature swaying on the terraces, anticipation bursting from its throat every time he touched the ball? The fear in the eyes of those who had to mark him as foot on the ball he struck his matador pose, signalling them forward to their public humiliation? All of them left the pitch with heads spinning and, having had a transfusion of the twisted blood, glad their ordeal was over. No, it was something else that brought him there, something to which he couldn't give a name.

It was raining now and people were putting up umbrellas but no one risked losing their place in return for shelter. Every few minutes heads collectively turned as a whisper spread that the cortège was coming but all that arrived was more rain, insistent and indifferent. All colour had leached from the sky and then in the distance from the entrance to the estate they heard the clapping start and knew it was finally on its way, the applause being passed along both sides of the road getting louder as the cortège moved slowly through the morning gloom. A green-flag-draped coffin. Despite the rain George's son in the following car kept his window down and acknowledged the crowd. And then, as quickly as it had come, it was gone, the applause a fading echo along the route of this final journey. In its wake the road looked suddenly startled, its grey, wet-slicked surface brightly spangled by the strewn flowers that had been thrown in the path of the hearse.

He stood in the steady slither of the rain for a few moments fiddling with his coat as if making the necessary preparations for his own journey. Letting the crowds slip past him he stayed facing the road and he was glad it was raining, glad that it might just disguise the tears that had started and which he was desperate to prevent. He didn't even know why he was crying. He hadn't cried since childhood – not even the night Susan told him she was leaving him – so it was a strange and unsettling sensation. Perhaps it was for George, perhaps it was for the past. For everything that gets lost, for all the things with which you should have taken more care. And then as he tightened his collar he blinked

3

the tears away because despite it all, despite everything, he guessed that he was crying for himself and knew that was a good reason to stop.

The whole city was a giant wake. They were bringing home their favourite son and determined to give him a send-off of which they could be proud. Now most would go back home with their families and watch the official ceremony at Stormont on television but he didn't want to return to the flat, thinking that this was something that needed to be shared, and so decided to head over to his local bar and view it there. It was on the big screen and he watched it with the other punters, glad now to be a little distanced from it by the drifting fug of smoke, the smell of dampness rising off wet coats, the clinking salute of glasses and the general clumsy attempts at reverence that soon slipped into maudlin tributes and competitive reminiscences. But it was not a city where reverence ruled easily and soon there was a commotion further down the bar when some hard-bitten cynic, who somehow had already managed to drink too much, suggested George had wasted his talent and it would have been better if someone else had been given it, some-one who would have taken better care of it. Then swivelling on his seat he taunted the simmering bar by asking what George had in common with the new West Link motorway, and after raising his glass to his audience told them that they were both blocked by midday. Then the shouting and recriminations started and the exchanges were heating up dangerously until Sam the bar owner informed the dissent-ing voice that he was no longer welcome and to a volley of cheers suggested that he should take his business elsewhere.

Some of his own emotional confusion was beginning to slowly seep away but as always when things get shaken and tumble around inside, like cargo in stormy seas, back in calm waters everything has been displaced and so when he returned to the flat and saw the red message light on his phone, he still didn't feel fully familiar to himself. He knew it would be from Susan who, despite three months of official divorce, remained, in his head at least, irrevocably his wife and for a second he thought of phoning her, telling her it was all a terrible mistake, that he still loved her, that George would want them to get back together, but he knew it would only be true in the crazy disorientation of the moment, that the shifting plates opening up some fault-line of his need would soon settle back into place and what might be true in the heated confusion of the present would be a lie in the cold new light of day.

'Alan, I need you to come over. There's something we need to talk about.'

He slumped into his chair, then leaned over to the stereo and set the stylus on Dylan's *Blood on the Tracks*, let the old familiar sound wash over him in an effort to restore his equilibrium. Always vinyl, even with its dusty patina of imperfections and scuffs.

Susan's need had not declined since their separation and if anything the phone always made it seem more insistent, more statutorily binding, and of course she had him on tap because he was the defaulter, the unfaithful one, and that residual guilt they both knew he felt meant he was always available for small acts of contrition. These might involve hedge cutting, emergency DIY or financial contribution, but as often as not recently they had focused on their son Jack who at the age of sixteen had belatedly and unexpectedly sailed into the maelstrom of adolescent upheaval, who after a quiet and inconspicuous childhood had become windblown, wind tossed, and whose increasingly fragile foundations threatened to be submerged by whatever darkening and unfathomable waters now swirled inside his head. A couple of poor reports at school in this his important GCSE year, a couple of detentions for posting an inappropriate picture of one of his teachers on Bebo, an unfortunate incident involving the breaking of an elderly neighbour's window with a golf ball and the appearance of a relatively small amount of cannabis in a bedside table – he supposed in the greater scheme of teen trauma it didn't amount to very much but these weren't the real things they worried about. It was more the sullen retreat into self, the isolated slide into some remote world governed by shifting and inexplicable rules that required the wearing of only black clothing, that the menu of what he ate had incrementally reduced itself to a core of about five items, that the computer was the ventilator, the dialysis machine, the heart defibulater that kept him alive, the mechanism that allowed him to go on breathing when everything else appeared to have been discarded as meaningless. All his room emptied as if memory, or the past, was a weight round his neck, piled into black bin bags and dumped with ruthless efficiency. Only his mother's surreptitious salvage had succeeded in preserving a few items. And there were, too, the scratches on his arm which to their embarrassment the school had noticed rather than them. Thin little red scratches on his lower arm that he had inflicted with the edge of a protractor and for which he wasn't able, or for which he was unwilling, to give any rational explanation. Self-harm was fashionable, the school had reassured them, it didn't always mean anything, but naturally all parties were to keep an eye on it. Their interview was kept low-key, counselling for Jack was offered, which he refused, while they tried their best to hide the tumbling terror they both felt.

The past was simple. But one day you were searching in rock pools or kicking football in the garden and the next it was all gone, airbrushed from history and replaced by a monosyllabic, non-committal, non-communicative vagueness that suggested a gaping space had opened up inside, that the hard drive had been rewired, reprogrammed and you didn't have the password to access it any more. He listened to Dylan's 'Shelter from the Storm' – it usually made him feel sad in a happy way but this afternoon it just made him sad. And of course Susan predictably had regularly dumped the blame on him, on his one and extremely pathetic infidelity. So it was the break-up of the family, the divorce, the loss of faith that had sent their son spinning off into some catatonic cyberworld on the edge of the universe. It pained him to think of the times he had attempted to follow him, to reach out and pull him back into whatever might constitute his personal happiness, only to be rebuffed at the frontier with the coldness of the dead-eyed, brainwashed border guard.

So if his summons was about Jack it would be a wasted journey. He didn't have any answers except a vague and unconvincing reiteration that it was a phase he was going through, one of a million such adolescent journeys and which sooner or later he would come out of, and if not be his old self again exactly, then someone at least they could recognise and even have a conversation with, exchange pleasantries about the weather or plans for the weekend. He thought, too, of George's son confronted with all that outpouring of love for his father. How did that make him feel? It was not Susan's gift of guilt now he opened, which he knew was counterfeit and unfair, but his own which was more crushing because he believed it came stamped with the hallmark of truth. There was no outpouring of love for him, no public or personal achievement that a son might see and have it shape his view of his father. In stolid middle age and with a predictable and plodding job teaching in the city's art college, what fires might spark his son's evaluation of his father? What was there to admire or emulate, what shared language to speak? And why did he have this permanent feeling about his own life that he, too, was going through a phase, a phase that seemed to have no ending, but which in his imagination was the precursor to something better? Something, however, that recently seemed less and less likely to arrive.

He looked round his flat, the one-bedroomed hidey-hole he rented after his eviction from the family home and the half-hearted attempts to soften its bleakness only seemed to signal how far short they fell. So the black and white portrait of John Lee Hooker, the Dali poster of melting clocks and the three of his own abstract paintings – one of which had a damp patch in a corner, a consequence of Susan's banishment of them to the garage a decade earlier – seemed like futile gestures that only drew attention to the very condition they were supposed to remedy. He wondered what the most accurate description of his living quarters was – it wasn't a bachelor pad or an apartment, it wasn't a gentleman's residence or a den but just a tired space above a flower shop that existed on the edge of shabby. His eyes rested on the folded portable bed, the one he had bought for Jack in anticipation of when he would sleep over and which had been used twice. He had slept on it himself more and more, usually those times when his own bed seemed only to signal its emptiness and he needed the momentary comfort of a narrower, smaller place. It also helped sustain the illusion that where he found himself was a temporary setback, a brief diversion into a siding before he returned to the main line for the continuation of his journey to some better destination.

He knew that the future journey would not involve Susan and part of him believed that his infidelity was not entirely unwelcome to her as it provided the justification for his dismissal and was merely the event that galvanised her into an action that had been brooding in her mind for some time. He put the bullet in the gun and she fired it. And there was a new man on the scene to set the seal on the permanency of their separation. Bloody Gordon. He couldn't think of Gordon without prefacing the name with a term of abuse and although he was prepared to acknowledge that jealousy was the spark that initially fired his judgement, it had burned more intensely and purely the more he got to know him. Gordon the small-time builder of extensions and roof-space conversions, Gordon with his suntanned muscular arms who couldn't wear any kind of shirt unless it had an alligator or a polo player on his left tit. It was as if Susan was kicking sand in the face of how he liked to see himself and had taken a wild swing on a vine through the jungle and thrown herself into the arms of someone who didn't do art, or read books, and who permanently had a copy of the *Sun* folded on the dashboard of his white van above the steering wheel like a proud proletarian flag. Gordon who listened to AC/DC and Metallica and was five years younger than Susan. Gordon who was good with his hands – why didn't she just come right out and say that he was red-hot in bed and in comparison made him look like an undersexed wimp? The solace he tried to take in his intellectual superiority was thinning in spiteful synchronicity with the thinning of his hair and if at the back it still rested at an artful and slightly rebellious length below his collar, there was a melting polar cap at his crown that he monitored in the mirror on a weekly basis. In spiteful contrast Gordon sprouted hair from every possible part of his body: he had a Michael Heseltine hairline that started low on his head and swept back like the thickest of hedges where all sorts of wildlife – foxes, rabbits, birds' nests – could hide undetected. It fell out from his always open shirt like tumbleweed in an abandoned Wild West town; it swathed his forearms. He remembered the story of Jacob who deceived his blind father by covering his arms with animal skins to get the blessing and started to think that the hirsute Gordon had stolen his.

He wondered what their daughter Caroline thought of him. Away at university in Scotland she had less time to form any strong opinion but he fervently hoped she disliked his replacement before telling himself that he was being selfish, that if he had been so committed to happy families he wouldn't have strayed one night in October when false faces and municipal firework displays were the order of the day and somehow, and for reasons he didn't fully understand, he had succumbed to temptation, only to find that what held the tantalising prospect of passionate excitement fizzled out almost instantaneously like a damp squib. A Master's student he was supervising. A mature student thankfully. A ceramicist. He had felt it coming for weeks – the needing advice, the enjoyment of his praise, the way that being together subtly left him feeling slightly different, in some vague but pleasant realignment. So maybe it wasn't about future possibilities so much as nostalgia, a rediscovering of what had been lost. Late at night in the studio. She was rolling clay, slapping and stretching it with an honest vigour and a simple determination that made him stretch out his hand and touch her hair. That's all he did, all he would have done, except she was in his arms and kissing him with an urgency that took his breath away and before any part of his brain could engage with the moment she was pulling him backwards on top of the table, on top of the clay. Afterwards – one of several embarrassments created – there was a pressed print of the moment. But a print of what? Passion? Loneliness? Stupidity? He still didn't know and it was followed by nothing else. Nothing was ever fired or formed beyond that brief, breathless encounter where two strangers stumbled against each other. Afterwards he did what he thought was the gentlemanly thing and inflated her marks and they parted wishing each other well with an unspoken understanding that they would never see each other or mention this thing ever again. Ships in the night they sailed steadily on.

So why then had he felt the necessity of telling Susan? Why in hell did he tell her? Well, of course, there was the usual tongue-loosening prompting of shame – the hair trigger of guilt – but also, if he was entirely truthful, a self-destructive desire to suggest that he was still someone that someone else could want, in a way she no longer did. None of it mattered really because before he had finished his genuine expression of abject remorse and appeal for forgiveness, she had dismissed all such present or future pleas and sent their marriage to Death Row.

He made himself a cup of tea and let the record finish, complete with its occasional crackle and one large jump, before driving over to the house that he still thought of as his home. But at the front door he rang the bell and waited, the obligatory humiliation that attended every visit and marked him as a temporary visitor, a guest whose welcome or unwelcome status was linked entirely to the reason for his arrival. And he couldn't just call in on a whim or to collect something – everything had to be prearranged. He couldn't even be a father except by appointment. Only the absence of Gordon's van lightened the moment as he waited for admission through the door that he had personally painted a very beautiful vermilion but which she had dismissed as pillar-box red.

'Thanks for coming,' she said, opening the door and then walking back down the hall, leaving him to follow. She had pulled her hair back tightly in a ponytail and she hadn't got her face on. Perhaps he imagined it but she seemed to have lost a little weight. There was the smell of soup cooking. Homemade soup – already he felt vulnerable. Lentil soup no doubt, thick with chicken or bacon, and served with baguette and proper butter. If it was a softener, a bribe for what she needed him to do, she was already halfway home. She still hadn't faced him and was stirring the soup, adding a little black pepper with an elegant shimmy of her fingers.

'Did you watch the funeral on television?' he asked in an attempt to make conversation, an act that still felt shockingly strange after the intimacy of twenty-two years of marriage.

'No, I've been busy. Sorting stuff out.'

She didn't elucidate about what stuff had preoccupied her and as she hadn't watched the funeral there wasn't an obvious topic to talk about. He wasn't going to tell her that he was one of those attending because he knew she would take it as further evidence of his supposed mid-life crisis and collapse into a dangerous and unpredictable state of emotional chaos.

'How's Jack?'

'Who knows?' she said, turning to look at him for the first time. 'You need a haircut,' she added in a low voice as she inspected him and then, perhaps remembering that she no longer had proprietorial rights, stirred the soup again. 'He's in his room. Appeared for breakfast about an hour ago. Then disappeared.'

'And how are things?'

'With Jack? Just the same. Who knows? He hasn't said half a dozen words in a week.'

'Is he still going out with Jasmine?'

'Think so. She was here last weekend.'

'That has to be good for him?'

'How do you work that one out? The girl never speaks either and she's dyed her hair jet black with purple streaks. She's wearing it over one eye like a patch. Gordon thinks she's a Goth but when I asked Jack he nearly did his nut as if I'd insulted her.'

It pleased him to hear that Gordon had got something wrong even though he knew it was irredeemably childish. 'So is it Jack you wanted to see me about?' he asked, but she looked at him as if he hadn't been listening and already the tone of her voice suggested that whatever he had to say would at best be wrong and at worst an insult in its unfathomable depths of stupidity.

'It's not all about Jack and I'm tired living my life worrying about my children. If I'd known there was this much worry I swear to God I wouldn't have had them.'

'Is it Caroline? Has something happened to her?' Already his mind was frantically freefalling through the nightmares of pregnancy, date rape, examination failure.

'No, it's not about Caroline. Alan, just for once this is not about our children. Why can't it be about me? I'm a person, too. And right now I don't feel great.'

She stirred hell out of the soup and he knew, he just knew, it was cancer. He held the edge of the table with both hands as if standing in the dock, because he was guilty, he was the one who'd brought it on, and all their friends and their two children would blame him and hate him for ever. One crazy, selfish act had released the spores that had infected her and there was no way back. And he'd just asked her if she'd seen the funeral!

'I'm going away, Alan,' she said, turning to look at him again, her face steamed and shiny.

He staggered to his feet. 'Susan! Susan! When?'

'Next weekend.'

'Next weekend?' God, she must have kept it a secret for a long time. Or else it must have advanced very quickly.

'There's an easyJet flight. Back late on Sunday. It's only a two-and-a-half-hour flight.'

They were sending her abroad for treatment. And a bloody easyJet flight. Cut-price cancer care, low-cost lymphoma. He would write to the newspapers. He would go to Stormont, confront the minister at his desk.

'I'll come with you.'

'Alan, what are you talking about?'

'I'll come with you – you can't do this on your own,' he insisted. 'It's only right.'

'Alan, what are you on about? Have you been out on the town last night? Gordon's coming of course. He's part of this.'

He fell back in the chair. He was to be replaced by Gordon right to the end and he winced at the sharpness of that hurt.

'Why didn't you tell me before?' he asked, conscious that his sense of grievance was insensitive and unreasonable but unable to shake off the unfairness that one poor press into clay was going to blank out over twenty years of marriage, every one of those years crammed full of a shared intensity of life that still felt real and not just yellowing pages pasted in some scrapbook.

'We've been thinking of it for a while now but it's a big decision and I need to talk to you about it. It'll involve selling the house.'

She was going to marry Gordon. Her final throw of the dice. There wasn't any time now for holding back so he said, 'You're going to marry Gordon?' trying to stop incredulity seeping into his voice.

Setting the wooden spoon on a saucer she came and sat at the table, staring again as if inspecting him. 'Alan, is there something wrong with you? You're not listening. I'm trying to tell you something and you're not listening so if you could just be patient and take this in I'd be very grateful.'

But his fear and eagerness had no capacity for patience and he blurted out, 'You're going into hospital? Why do you have to go abroad?'

He watched her place both hands to the side of her face, shake it and simulate a scream. Then she reached out across the table and took both his but it was a gesture of restraint, holding them in the way a parent might the hands of a wayward child whose absolute concentration was required.

'Alan, I have no plans to get married to Gordon as of yet, and I am not going into hospital.'

'You don't have cancer?'

She shook his hands slowly from side to side as an emphasis to her words. 'I don't have cancer though why you thought this I don't know. I haven't done my face but I didn't think I looked that rough.'

'You look beautiful,' he said before he had worked out whether it was a good thing to say or not, but as soon as he said it he felt like a little boy, a needy little boy, and she dropped both his hands and sat back in the chair, quizzically screwing her eyes into narrow slits while she scrutinised him.

'You're scaring me now. So please stop saying things that aren't true and don't make sense and just listen to what I have to tell you. Can you do that?' He nodded as above their heads there was the low rumble of a guitar riff. 'Now just sit back and, without interrupting, try to listen and take in what I'm saying.'

He was still a child, a child about to be told a story by his mother, so he sat up straight in the chair and hugged the comfort he suddenly felt from knowing that she hadn't got the big one.

'For some time I've been thinking that I'd like a change of direction, that I'd like my life to go a different way. Even before what happened. I just never said anything. I don't want to plod on like I've been doing. So are you ready for this? I'm thinking of going to live in Spain. I'm thinking of opening a guest-house. I've been looking for somewhere suitable for some time, an older place that with Gordon's help I can do up and renovate. Are you with me?'

He was with her. She hadn't got cancer and wasn't marrying Gordon, only maybe going into business with him. It was better, he told himself. So he nodded encouragingly but forced himself to say nothing despite the stream of questions flooding through him.

'We've got an estate agent looking for a suitable place and something's come on the market. It's not far from Alicante but it's up in the mountains away from the crowds. He's sent email photographs of it. It looks a bit run-down at the moment but we're going to fly out and take a look at it, see if it might fit the bill. Gordon might be willing to invest some money in it, buy a share, but at the very least he would take on and supervise the work.' She stood up again and stirred the soup. 'I'd rather buy the place outright myself but to do that I need to get my share from this house. So what do you think?'

He didn't know what he thought but there was still the residual relief that she wasn't going to die, and however far away Alicante seemed it was still closer than the silent swathe of eternity so in response he uttered some bland sentiments of approval that appeared to please her.

'I'd like to put the house on the market reasonably soon. We need to get it valued but the way the property market is right now, we could get a really good price and there isn't a huge amount of mortgage left to pay off. You could use your half to buy somewhere better as well. I know it's a bit out of the blue but what do you think?'

'It's a bit of a shock. Out of the blue like you say but if it's what you want. I suppose you're sure, that you've thought it through,' he said, looking at his hands to avoid her eyes that had turned into lie detectors. She sat down opposite him again and he would say yes to anything she wanted. 'What will we get for this place?'

'Manleys' went for four a month ago. But it had a conservatory. Still we must be close enough to that sort of money.'

'Four? Manleys' went for four hundred thousand? Remember what we paid for this place and how we struggled those first couple of years when the mortgage rate went up?' But he could see that she didn't want to do nostalgic reminiscence so he focused again on the future that now felt unpredictable, ready at any moment to veer off in some direction outside the realm of his imagination. He was desperate to find something to hold on to; something stable that he might set his feet on and enable him to look about without this feeling of freewheeling, freefalling through unknown and uncharted worlds. 'And what about the children? Have you told them yet?'

'I've told them, and Caroline, who is hardly a child, has no problems with it.'

'And Jack, what about Jack?'

'Jack,' she said, letting their son's name hang in the air and there was a lengthened vagueness in how she pronounced the single syllable. 'As always Jack is a bit of a problem. I don't know what he thinks and probably he doesn't know what he thinks either. But I wouldn't even consider going until after he's done his GCSEs. Then I suppose it's his choice – he can come or stay. Stay with you. That would be possible, wouldn't it?'

'I'd have to find somewhere better. But I suppose I could do that with my share of the house.'

'The thing is I need you to look after him, not this weekend coming but next when I'm flying out to view the property – just the weekend. That's all. You can do that, can't you?' Then she tightened the screw. 'And you haven't spent that much time together recently.'

Not this weekend but next? It suddenly clicked. 'Shit! Susan, I'm away that weekend. I'm going to Amsterdam to see Bob Dylan. I've got the concert ticket, booked the flights. You're definitely talking about not this weekend coming but next?'

She looked at him as if he was worse than her worst concept of useless and put a hand to her forehead as if a sudden migraine had just stabbed her. 'Alan, the one thing I need you to do. There's nowhere else I can leave him. You have to have him. I need to see this place. I have to go to Spain. We can't leave him here on his own – you know that.'

He owed her. He owed his son. 'I'll take him with me,' he said, following the spurt of his own words with surprise. 'I'll get him a ticket, book the flights. He can come with me for the weekend. His passport's still valid, isn't it?' She nodded rapidly and dropped her hand from her brow. 'But will he come, Susan? Will he come to Amsterdam?'

'He has to, he just has to, and that's all there is to it. I'll talk to him, try to explain. When you think of what we do for him and have done over the years, it's hardly too much to ask. He'll have to go.'

But as he listened to the insistence of her words he knew she was trying to convince herself and he cautioned, 'Don't put it to him like he's obligated to go in case he puts his back up. Just say that we'd really appreciate it if he'd come. That he might enjoy it. That it's somewhere he's never been.'

'That's something else I can't understand. Right now you could offer Jack the Grand Canyon, the Great Wall of China, and he wouldn't be excited or even interested. I'm tired tiptoeing round him, trying to anticipate things, guess his mood. I'm weary of it and I'm not going to let him spoil my chances of doing something that's really important to me.'

He was about to reach out and pat her hand but stopped himself, instead offering, 'I know: it's not easy but everything will work out right. And maybe a weekend with his dad won't be such a bad thing?'

'Bob Dylan?' she asked, her eyes widening with uncertainty. 'Is he not dead? Why does it have to be Bob Dylan? He's not going to want to go to a Bob Dylan concert.'

'He can't keep going much longer. Wanted to see him before it's too late. I'll talk to Jack. He'll come.'

Just as he was beginning to feel a sense of something shared, of an unspoken ease with each other that he'd almost forgotten how comforting it could be, there was the sound of a key in the front door and then it opening.

'It's Gordon,' she said, standing up, and as she touched the side of her hair his heart kicked repeatedly as if a hard stone had been skimmed over it, as he understood she had realised that she hadn't her face on but even in that concern he saw a lightness seep into her features and he swallowed, tasting a bitterness, the intensity and pain of which shocked him. Then instead of fading away it was increased by the realisation that Gordon had an automatic access that was denied to him. The keys to the kingdom.

'All right, Alan?' Gordon said. There was a green alligator on the left tit of a pink shirt – he thought of these logos now as the mark of Cain – and it felt as if his wife's suitor took up a lot of the kitchen's available space. He didn't have the need of a jumper or coat even though it was raining. 'That smells good,' he said, peering into the pot but thankfully didn't kiss Susan or touch her in any way. 'That was some send-off today. Some crowds. And the florists must have cleaned up. They were throwing flowers like there was no tomorrow. Did him proud.' He sat down and clunked a large bunch of keys on the table. 'Did you watch it on TV, Susan?' But she gave the same answer as before and in the face of her indifference he directed his thoughts to his other listener. 'Some show then. Though what entitled the politicians to stick their arses in the frame, I don't know.'

'It was a nice touch when they went outside and invited some ordinary punters into the service.'

'Nice touch,' Gordon concurred, sniffing the air. 'Is that soup ready yet?' he asked, shuffling sideways on the seat to look at Susan. As he did so he revealed a glimpse of a gold neck chain. She told him that it would be a little while yet and it felt as if he was in a scene from *Ghost*, watching over the life from which he had suddenly and unexpectedly been ripped. He remembered there was a scene with clay somewhere in that as well. And sex. 'Some great stories going the rounds about George.' And then Gordon proceeded to tell all the hoary old favourites that had been told a million times about drinking Canada dry and the hotel waiter who, bringing the champagne and seemingly oblivious to a Miss World sprawled on the bed amidst the casino winnings, asked where it all went wrong.

He listened politely and pretended to smile in all the right places. Gordon was a talker, a man with opinions on everything. Someone, too, who knew the price of everything and it seemed as if he absorbed too much of the room's oxygen. He had started to feel suffocated, breathless, but he listened patiently and sometimes when Gordon said something particularly stupid he tried to catch Susan's eye to see if it had registered but there were no clues to be found in her face. Then Gordon leaned back on his chair puffing out the tumbleweed on his chest through the open neck of his shirt and became philosophical.

'What I don't understand is why in this country we always produce stars who are completely screwed up, out of their tree on booze or just barking mad. There's George, there's Alex Higgins – did you get a glimpse of him at the funeral? Like a walking skeleton – he could have fitted in the box as well. He's spent his life fighting with his own shadow – do you remember the time he told Dennis Taylor he'd get him a head job? Jesus! And Van Morrison! A genius, no two ways about it, but the ultimate grumpy old man. They say he's the pop star all journalists hate to interview.'

'It's a mystery, Gordon.' One of many mysteries and none so great in his mind as how this man had come to sit in his kitchen, make love to his wife and be about to launch into some business scheme that could take her to a new life in Spain.

'And, Alan, you're an art man. What about Van Gogh? Another genius but cutting off his ear – what's that all about?'

'I think it was something to do with a woman.'

'A woman? Makes sense. They can go on a bit. But you learn to shut it out. Isn't that right, Susan? No need to cut your ear off.' She didn't answer but instead searched in a drawer for something, her hands rattling the cutlery loudly. 'So what do you think of this Spain idea?'

He was about to answer with a passing attempt at optimism when Jack suddenly appeared in the doorway holding his guitar at his side. 'Hi, Jack,' he said, raising his hand slightly. Jack nodded and looked at them as if he had just seen a lynching mob, or as if the kitchen – his kitchen – had been taken over by dangerous aliens.

'All right, Jack?' Gordon asked and there was a muted, mumbled response that might or might not have been a 'hi' and then he was gone, his bare feet whispering him back down the hall to the front room. A few seconds later there was the sound of a television.

'Alan,' Susan said and, standing directly behind Gordon who was about to start talking about the price of houses, nodded at him. He understood and got up, silently pointing in the hypothetical direction of Jack to explain his departure as Gordon launched into a story addressed to the empty chair about how developers were buying houses with big gardens, knocking them down, building apartments and then making a killing. Even after he stood up and walked away the story continued and he was suddenly afflicted by the idea that Gordon was some sort of carpetbagger, not just a cuckoo in the nest, who saw the chance of shady property deals and had not so much got his eye on Susan as their valuable house. Perhaps he'd soon be saying that he knew someone who would be interested in their property and how they could save estate agent fees on a private sale. But then his attention focused on his son who was curled up in an armchair, feet tucked under him with his black guitar resting across his lap.

He sat opposite him in the chair that had always been his own favourite. Jack didn't look at him which allowed him to take him in. He seemed a little older but still not much more than a child. His collar-length hair was black out of a bottle with the strength of its colour accentuating the paleness of his skin. His eyes were blue but sometimes like today they seemed paler, as if they had been faded by the sun. When he glanced down at the guitar, strands of hair slipped forward and curtained one of his eyes but he didn't flick them away or push them back with his hands that were thin-fingered and neat, papery and delicate in their skin. He was wearing black jeans and a black T-shirt. His arms were also thin and at his wrist he wore a little leather bracelet. The red bangles of scratches were slowly fading. He tried not to look at them but couldn't stop his eyes returning again and again.

'How are you, Jack?' he asked.

'Fine,' he said as his fingers lightly brushed the strings.

'That's good.' Fine was a core word in his son's personal lexicon. It meant nothing, gave nothing away but painlessly fulfilled the obligation of communication. It was also a word used to avoid any form of commitment, that allowed the speaker to stay safely inside whatever world it was he felt safest in. Fine reached out to no one, provided no hook on which to hang a question, and gave no encouragement for further exploration. So everything was fine. Always fine. But for the moment all he could think to say was to repeat, 'That's good.'

He watched his son pluck one of the chords with two fingers as if he was pulling back the string of a bow. On the television was a programme about Amelia Earhart's disappearance and old men were giving their theories about what had happened to her. Jack glanced at the screen from time to time but mostly his eyes rested on the guitar strings.

'So how do you feel about your mother's idea of going to Spain?'

'Don't know,' he said, glancing briefly at him.

'Do you think you'd like to live in Spain or stay here?'

'I haven't thought about it.'

He told himself that he had to resist saying all the things that were springing to his lips, all the things that were the obvious commonsense things that begged to be said and which he was being invited to say – it's time you did think about it because it affects you and sooner or later you're going to have to make an adult choice that could shape the future course of your life – but he knew if he did, he would sound like a schoolteacher and saying what was expected of him would only confirm that what he was saying was nothing at all. So carefully and without any trace of sarcasm in his voice he simply said, 'Fine,' and when Jack looked directly at him he didn't make eye contact but stared at the television. They sat in silence for a few seconds that felt like a very long time and he imagined some future programme where old men offered their opinions about what happened to him. Just disappeared one day. Living on an island off the west of Ireland where he paints abstract paintings no one wants to buy. Went to Spain where he services swimming pools. Grew so weary that he couldn't lift his head up any more. Who would know? Who would care?

He glanced at Jack who was waiting for some homily that wasn't coming. The advantage was momentarily with him and knowing that in this game, intensity or passion were the illegitimate children of commitment, he tried to project a sense of casual indifference. It wasn't easy because he knew that sooner or later love would blow it out of the water.

Love was the unavoidable spanner in the works, the thing that stopped you walking away and made your pretence of calm control a hopeless lie that ultimately would force itself free from the heart and into the words you didn't want to use. Had he imagined it or were Jack's eyes sharpening into focus? He strummed a chord with the first sign of vigour, the sound trembling in the air between them. It felt as if he was flying a plane over foreign and perilous seas. Thick cloud everywhere. He needed somewhere to land. There was writing on the inside of his son's forearm. Black spider writing like Chinese calligraphy on the white paper of his skin.

'You know your mother's going to Spain for a weekend to look at some property? She wants you to stay with me. Just until she gets back.' He paused and tried to anticipate what was coming.

'Why can't I stay here?'

'Because she'd worry about you and probably wouldn't be able to get on with what she needs to do.'

'I'm sixteen, Dad. I can look after myself.'

'Of course you can, Jack. We both know that.' He was pleased to hear the word Dad but nervous at the rising indignation in his son's voice.

'I don't need looking after. I'm not going to starve or anything.'

'I know, Jack. But listen to me. Your mother's got herself a dream – it may come to nothing or it might: I don't know – but she needs to see if she can make it real and we both owe her, owe her big time, and we need to do whatever we can to help her check it out. And it's only a weekend. What do you say?'

Jack said nothing and instead shuffled into a new position on the seat. Even for a teenager who had made a unilateral declaration of emotional independence, guilt was still a heavy trip and he was pondering it, poking it with a stick the way you might poke a dead animal to check if any life persisted. Push on while the clouds reveal the possibility of land.

'And, Jack, I have to go to Amsterdam. We can both go. It's a great city – a young city – and I think you might really like it. Just for the weekend. We'll stay in a hotel.' He didn't mention Bob Dylan – didn't want to risk the wheels coming off just when there was the possibility of making a landing. 'What do you say?' No answer. 'For your mother's sake.'

Jack curtained his face with more hair and plucked a single string. 'I'll think about it,' he said, then reached out for the remote and flicked the channels.

'Thanks, Jack. Your mother'll really appreciate it.' He stood up, keen to make an exit before the dice had a chance to throw against him, but something made him pause and ask what the writing said on his arm.

Jack glanced up at him and then, as if opening a book, revealed the white page of his skin. 'It says, "People are shit". It's the name of a song.' And then he closed the book and flicked more channels.

Back in the kitchen Gordon was about to tuck into the soup that had been set in front of him. Against the pink flag of his shirt the bowl looked small and white. There were little bits of potato and bacon cresting the steaming surface like sharks' fins.

'What did he say?' Susan asked, her nervous hands hidden inside a tea cloth.

'He says he'll think about it. I think it'll be OK.'

She saw him looking at the soup and her relief made her ask if he'd like to stay and have some. But he lied and said he'd better be going, that he had a few things to do. She nodded and smiled a thanks then came to see him out. They paused outside the front door which he discreetly touched briefly with his fingers and because she was standing on the step he had to look up to her.

'We don't need to put the house on the market yet but it would be good to get a valuation, see what we're talking about.'

'That's fine,' he said, thinking that if life could be divided up and shared as easily as the price of a house then everything would be simple.

But on this funeral day as he drove slowly and reluctantly back to his flat he sensed only the infinite complexity of what stretched ahead of him. He thought about the soup, knew how much he wanted to stay, even in a house where he wasn't fully loved. He thought of stolen blessings and the mess of potage that awaited him and, irrespective of what he had brought on himself, couldn't help but feel cheated out of things that were rightly his. He drove past council workers removing barriers and traffic cones, their yellow jackets luminous against the day's shadows. Windblown flower petals frittered up like confetti. George was starting out on his journey by now. He felt shut out, too, by his own son. If he would let him be his father there were so many important things that he could tell him, things that might help him face full-on the relentless storm of life. People are shit. Yes they are Jack, but some aren't and even the ones who are have some part of them that isn't, just as those who aren't have some part of them that is. As he drove he talked to his son, told him that nothing was simple. Except to the stupid and the dangerous. So, Jack, don't be frightened of uncertainty and confusion, it's our natural state. And as he headed along the embankment beside the dark skein of the river suddenly there was a single rower sculling the water, his oars twisting little curlicues of white. He pulled the car over to the pavement, got out and stood watching as the oarsman slowly disappeared into the dusk. He was taking George home. After all the public pomp and show of ceremony, the eulogies and the flowers, he was taking George home. If he were religious he would have said a prayer for safe crossing, a prayer for all their coming journeys, but instead he simply bowed his head for a moment then watched as the silent wake slowly disappeared and the street lamps began to sheen and smear the dark surface of the water into some new tremble of light.

Two

A T THIS EARLY HOUR of the morning the city still belonged to those whose job it was to prepare and dress it for the coming day, but as the light stretched itself awake they emerged from office blocks and stores already decorated for Christmas, lighting their cigarettes and setting out in small groups towards bus stops or pick-up points. Karen raised her collar and shivered then turned to see what was keeping Lisa and Pat. Huddled together with their heads almost touching they were trying to create a shelter from the wind that would let them light their communal cigarette. A post-office van with its lights on full beam hurried past, its exhaust a smoker's throaty cough.

'This street is a wind tunnel,' Lisa complained, as the lighter spluttered out again.

'What's the point?' Karen asked, hunching her shoulders. 'Marty won't let you smoke in his taxi. He told me off last week for eating a packet of crisps.'

'He's not here yet, is he?' Lisa said, clicking a furious Morse code on the lighter. 'I think this is empty and I need a fag. He's getting like an old woman about the taxi. He'll be putting up net curtains soon.'

Karen went and stood at the edge of the kerb looking for a sighting of their lift. At the side of the City

Hall yellow-windowed buses were already pulling in and discharging their dark silhouettes. A council cleaning lorry with huge, whirring circular brushes was scouring the opposite side of the road. On the front grille was pinned a bouquet of plastic daffodils. She let her toes move out over the kerb's edge and held herself in balance.

'Here, one of those would get your work done pretty quick,' Pat said, pointing with the still-unlit cigarette at the vehicle. The driver waved his hand in greeting.

'Here, girl, I think you've clicked,' Karen said. 'It's freezing. Where's Marty? Should you phone and see where he is?'

'Here he is,' Lisa said, taking her cigarette from Pat and slipping it inside her pocket.

The three women bunched up tightly at the side of the kerb as if waiting for rescue from a sinking ship and then as the taxi stopped they clambered in with Karen in the front and the two others in the back. The car smelled of air freshener.

'Home, Marty, and don't spare the horses,' Pat told him, snuggling into the seat.

'You going back to bed?' he asked.

'Here, is that an offer?' Lisa said. 'Because you're talking to the Three Musketeers and what one gets the rest has to get.' The other two women laughed as they angled their heads to the grey wash of city streets.

'I never mix business and pleasure,' Marty answered.

'You should try it some time,' Lisa said before asking if she could smoke.

'No you can't – you know you can't.'

'And I'm in a hurry because I've four kids about to wake up looking for their Coco Pops and me to get them out to school,' Pat said, 'and after that there's a day's work to be done.'

'I phoned the daughter this morning,' Lisa informed them, holding the unlit cigarette under her nose as if she was a connoisseur smelling a cigar. 'Gabrielle's still cutting her teeth and keeping them up half the night.'

'You phoned her again? You're pushing your luck,' Karen said. 'If the supervisor catches you it's the sack.'

'They wouldn't sack you for phoning your daughter?' Marty said as he weaved into a bus lane.

'They would, Marty, when your daughter lives in Australia,' Lisa answered, and as the other two women laughed she put the unlit cigarette in her mouth. 'And don't worry, I'm not about to light it. Wouldn't want your wee palace smelling of anything as disgusting as fag smoke.'

'Here listen, Marty, have you heard about Karen?' Pat paused for dramatic effect.

'She's not won the lottery on the sly, has she?' he asked, glancing at her before turning to give two fingers to a BMW that had cut in front of him.

'I wish.'

'She's going to Amsterdam, next weekend. What about that?'

'You are not! Can I come?'

'Girls only, Marty, her daughter's getting married. They're having their hen party in Amsterdam.'

'Can I still come?' Marty asked. 'I'll chaperone you, keep an eye out for you. I've always wanted to go to Amsterdam.'

'Marty, these girls would eat you alive,' Lisa said. 'Chew you up and spit you out in little pieces.'

'It's not going to be like that,' Karen insisted, without conviction. 'And I've never even been on a plane before. Had to get a passport as well. A night out in Belfast would be a lot less hassle, if you ask me.'

'You only live once,' Marty ventured, 'but anyway I'd rather go to Thailand. The boss goes once a year, says it's the business. Brings home these counterfeit cigarettes that he tries to sell all the drivers.'

'And does he take his wife?' Lisa asked.

'Never mentions her. I don't think so.'

'Didn't think so either and sooner or later he'll bring home something besides phoney fags,' Lisa said, pretending to smoke the cigarette and blowing imaginary rings through the exaggerated pursed circle of her lips at Marty watching her in the mirror.

They dropped Pat off first and then Lisa who told them she was absolutely gagging for the fag as she lumbered wearily out of the car.

'That one's barking mad,' Marty said as they drove off.

'She's all right. Likes a laugh, that's all.'

'Do mothers go on their daughter's hen do?'

'That's what I asked but she wants me to go and it's coming up to my fortieth and it's supposed to be a treat for me as well. I got tired arguing. Sometimes it's easier just to go with the flow.'

He nodded as if he understood. Then he looked at her for a second as they reached her house. 'Any chance of a cup of coffee, Karen?'

She smiled at him before saying, 'Sorry, Marty, there isn't and there's never any chance. Remember, never mix business and pleasure.'

'No harm in asking.'

'No, no harm and you have a good day,' she said as she closed the door.

When she got in the house everywhere was dark and quiet. Going into the kitchen she put the kettle on, warming her hands against its sides as she stood waiting for it to boil.

Shannon wasn't up yet and wouldn't be for another half an hour so this was her time, when she had breakfast and rested before the demands of the day imposed themselves once again. Sometimes if she was very tired she would go to bed still in her clothes for a couple of hours but there was always the danger of slipping into a deep sleep and being late for work in the care home. After she had dropped a piece of bread into the toaster she emptied her pockets into the biscuit tin she kept in a cupboard. Today she had only brought four paper clips, two red and two yellow. She added them to the others, the pencils and pens, the rubber bands, the little memo block in lilac, the tiny bits and bobs that no one was ever going to miss, and let her hand lift and sift through them like sand. Why she bothered to bring them she wasn't sure when the other women only thought of secreting more useful items like toilet rolls and dusters or the odd wad of photocopying paper and would laugh at her if they knew. Kevin the doorman always looked at them on their way out as if he'd like to search them, and not out of pervy pleasure, but because he hated the idea that someone might dare to filch something from his little kingdom.

She stole other things. But they couldn't do you for looks. So when she did the desks she always studied the photographs, sometimes holding them close as she pretended to dust. Held their family snapshots. Children in Disney World. Children coming out of the sea in black wetsuits and carrying bodyboards. Engagement parties. Groups of people leaning into each other around restaurant tables with their glasses raised to the camera as if it was their best friend. Young mothers cradling newly arrived babies. She was familiar with it all – their mugs with funny slogans and little desk ornaments; their postcards from around the world; their paperweights and their yellow Post-it notes to themselves, reminders of phone numbers to be rung and dental appointments that had to be kept. And everyone's desk declared that it was a happy little personalised kingdom but always willing to join in others' laughter. There were a couple of exceptions of course and she thought of McClean's desk with its absence of any such softeners or revelations of personal life, his recent attempts to stop smoking – the store of nicotine chewing gum – and the ripped lottery tickets in the waste bin. His habit of sticking spent gum on the underside of his desk. She'd like to talk to him about that, as well as how he managed to get Tipp-Ex on his phone. From time to time he left her an unwanted present of fast-food containers or dregs of coffee in polystyrene cups from which he had always crumbled little bits and dropped them into the coffee. Why didn't he get a nice mug with a snazzy slogan? She had started to think he was divorced, that he had slipped into slobbishness due to the absence of a loved one. But perhaps there never was a loved one.

Because she wasn't stupid she knew that the photographs couldn't all represent perfect lives and that people only took them to preserve the moments when they were most happy, but she still couldn't help thinking that they lived in some world that was distant from, and different to, hers. Lives which weren't built on struggle and which gave access to higher levels of reward than she had ever been invited to share. And if there was this world, then there had to be a key, some membership card that gave admittance, so she studied their faces closely in the hope that the answer might be written there. Sometimes she told herself that it was all about luck – an accident of birth – and that made her feel better but at others she thought it was down to passing examinations and intelligence, to knowing the right information and the right secrets.

She curled into an armchair and had her tea and toast. She didn't want to go to Amsterdam. It was far too much money on top of everything else and even if the wedding was going to be modest in size there were still a lot of expenses to be met – both their outfits for a start, the cars, the flowers and the cost of the buffet afterwards, even though his family was going halves. She tried to add it up as she did at regular intervals and each time got a different sum, always getting confused about what cost per head they had agreed on. A meal and a few drinks afterwards would have done the hen night and they were spoilt for choice for eating places. Every five minutes there was a new one opening in the city. She'd heard people say the Red Panda was classy and she'd always fancied one of those meals with all the courses that they put on a wheel.

After a while there was the sound of the bathroom and she knew that Shannon was up and starting the process of putting on her face, getting herself ready for the day ahead. What her daughter spent on make-up would pay for the wedding twice over – working in Debenhams and then giving them back half her wages, despite the discount. She had a lovely face – she told her that all the time – so why did she insist on plastering so much slap on it? There were heavy footsteps on the stairs and when the door opened it wasn't Shannon but Wade.

'Morning, Karen,' he said, straightening and tightening his tie.

'I didn't know you were here,' she answered, irritated that her daughter hadn't told her.

'We got in late. I'd had a few so I just stayed.'

'Right. Better not to drink and drive.' But he wasn't really listening to her, instead combing his hair with his hand and checking that he'd got his mobile phone in his jacket pocket. 'Do you want some breakfast?'

'No thanks. Haven't got time. I'll get some later. Don't want to hit the traffic.'

And then he was gone. She cupped the tea with both hands but the heat had gone out of it already. Why was she so cold today? She couldn't afford to get sick right now. She might even have to take a few extra shifts at the care home if she wasn't to end up in the poorhouse. And then it was Shannon coming down the stairs in her full-length dressing gown with the hood and her half-pinned-up hair tumbling everywhere in an avalanche.

'Why didn't you tell me that Wade was staying over? I didn't know he was here.'

'It wasn't planned. We got in late and you were sleeping. I was hardly going to wake you up and tell you,' she said as she poured breakfast cereal into a bowl.

'You look rough, girl.'

'Thanks.'

'And can you afford to be out mid-week? Better to be salting that money away towards your deposit.'

'Mum, give us a break. We only had a few drinks.'

'Every penny counts. And another thing, you let him have it too often and too easy and he'll start taking it for granted.'

'Mum, please. I'm trying to have my breakfast. Don't talk like that – it's disgusting.'

She watched her daughter assemble the pathetic little arrangement she considered a breakfast but after their conversation about Wade she was reluctant to criticise her again knowing anyway that it was a waste of time, because at the end of the day her daughter did things how she, and only she, thought best. So there was never really any chance of changing her mind about Amsterdam or any of the other ideas about the wedding that seemed to spring from magazines or what some of her friends thought was the classy way to do things. Although she knew it was wrong, she couldn't help thinking of her own life, of being dumped before a wedding had the chance to take place and when she was three months pregnant, and there seemed, to her mind at least, to be a connection between the naive expectations and lack of understanding of what was important, the mistaken energies invested in fripperies, with the likelihood of future failure. For a second she wanted to shake her by the shoulder and tell her that weddings were fairy tales, the happy-ever-after dreams of know-nothing children, and the more these dreams were allowed to grow reckless and unchecked the more likely there was a poisoned apple or a spell waiting to be cast. And she wasn't sure about Wade.

It was true he seemed to have a decent job and went each day to work in a shirt and tie, that he told them before long he was going to be manager of his branch of Carphone Warehouse. And while it was also true that his parents were decent working people who were putting a little towards the cost of the wedding, there was still something that she didn't feel certain about. Perhaps it would be the same with any boy Shannon wanted to marry, perhaps after what had happened to her she found it impossible to trust anyone because with men she believed that what you saw was not what you got and what you always wanted to get was your trust rewarded. Rock solid. She watched her daughter finish her breakfast almost as soon as she had started it, then drink the first of the endless glasses of water that she believed were essential for the maintenance of her complexion. A little water dribbled down her chin and she wiped it roughly but expertly with the back of her hand like a beer drinker might. It was a high-maintenance complexion seemingly requiring endless scrubbing and masking, steaming and moisturising. And now there was tanning as well, about whose cost she was persistently vague but which had become an important part of the image she wanted to project to the world, so it looked as if she was permanently just returned from a holiday in the sun.

So what were the chances of Shannon spending the rest of her life rock-solidly happy with Wade? Who could tell? But she'd be happier if she saw some shaft of energy illuminate his face more often, if he had more get up and go. If he even had more get up and didn't find so much satisfaction from being sunk in the settee with his pint of beer, his football on the television, his Chinese takeaway, his stomach already beginning to creep over his belt. If he wasn't so set in his ways. But then, she told herself, stuck in his ways made it less likely that he might ever have the desire to stray. To stray she imagined you needed energy and despite what he said about being earmarked for the manager's job she couldn't believe that there wasn't at least one of his colleagues who displayed greater commitment and drive. Someone who would pip him at the post every time until he gave up and slipped into indifference.

'What do you want for your tea?' she asked Shannon although at this time of the morning it was difficult to think of food or being hungry.

'Anything, so long as it's not fried or too heavy.'

'Right,' she said while wondering if it ever entered her daughter's head that some night it would be good if, even just once, she made her mother's tea. She put off thinking what form the tea might take, there would be plenty of time to decide, then watched her hurry back up the stairs to get dressed and ready for work. She returned to the teapot and poured herself another half cup but it wasn't warm enough and she didn't finish it. Perhaps she was being too hard on Wade and when her daughter eventually came back down the stairs she tried to compensate by telling her she had scrubbed up well and clearing both their breakfast dishes to the sink, but if Shannon noticed the gesture she gave no sign and instead leaned into the mirror above the fireplace, offered a frozen kiss to her reflection and concentrated on a final application of lipstick.

'Have a good day,' they said to each other and then her daughter was gone and the house was silent again but it wasn't something that she welcomed because now it felt as if into her daughter's wake flowed a tired predictability about the hours ahead. She was tempted to go upstairs and climb into her bed but it was a bed that would hold no vestige of heat and in whose still-unmade mess she would feel only a nagging guilt about her failure to do what had to be done. So she cleaned up the kitchen, washed the dishes and stacked them to dry, then splashed her face and tried to energise herself.

After she had changed into her green uniform she brushed her hair at the same mirror at which Shannon had stood. She could never see any of her daughter's face in her own although sometimes people said they looked alike, nor she told herself was she frightened about being forty. But putting down the brush she pressed her fingers to her cheekbones and stretched the skin, then raised her chin with the tips of her finger, offering her face to the mirror for its inspection. She assured herself she still looked young, that when she went to Amsterdam it wouldn't be obvious to strangers that she was Shannon's mother. There were faint circles under her eyes that were only noticeable under harsh light and a slight crackling of fine lines at their corners but the mirror wasn't unkind to her. Using her fingers she pecked at her hair, lifting strands and letting them fall. Her roots were beginning to show again and a couple of hairs were hinting at grey but she would get it done before the wedding.

When she arrived at The Rowans care home a florist's van was parking and a delivery man was getting out carrying a bunch of flowers that partially covered his face. 'In here, love?' he asked, momentarily confused about where the entrance was.

'Are they for me?' she asked.

'Sorry, sweetheart,' then as an afterthought, 'if they were for you they'd have to be roses.'

She rewarded him with a smile and then held the door open. Someone's birthday. Easier to send flowers than turn up in person. A reminder to reward their deep love with a lion's share when it was time to divide the spoils. Was it her imagination or did these old folk have birthdays more often than other people? Perhaps they were right that time flies, that when the clock was winding down the quicker it sped to its conclusion. When she entered the reception area she knew right away that breakfast was just ending. From the dining room came the clatter of cutlery and plates and the communal rasp of conversation straining and pushing at the edges until it eddied out in thin streams of disconnected sound like a radio station not properly tuned in. She wondered how old people could be so noisy. Was it the relief of being granted another day? It could hardly be an excited uncertainty about what it might hold because the smooth management of The Rowans necessitated that everything ran according to a preordained schedule. As she watched the flowers being handed over to Muriel on reception she glanced at the day's programme and saw that the afternoon had an art class timetabled. She wondered if they needed a life model and smiled at the pleasure the home's couple of men would derive from that experience. She knew already from the occasional comment or look that their blood still flowed. Flowed in the brain at least.

'Morning, Karen,' Muriel said, watching her sign in. 'Aren't these beautiful?'

'Who are they for?'

'Mrs Cunningham. Birthday. I hope we have a vase big enough.' She turned the bouquet slowly round and lowered her face into the cellophane-wrapped bouquet as if going to bathe it in the blossom. 'Beautiful smell, too.'

'Do you want me to take them up to her room?'

'No, it's all right, I'll take them into her in the day room. She'll enjoy them even better if everyone sees her getting them. You know what they're like.'

'She'll not like it if someone asks what age she is.'

'She's still letting on she's five years younger than she really is.'

'Maybe we'll all do that when the time comes,' she said as she turned to go to the store and pick up her cleaning trolley.

'Karen,' Muriel called after her and her voice lowered into something pretending to be a confidential whisper, 'Mrs Weldon would like to see you before you start work. In her office.' And she pointed down the corridor as if she didn't know already where the office was.

'What about?'

But Muriel only looked down at her desk and shook her head from side to side.

Her first thought as she walked slowly towards the office was that she was going to get her notice at the very time when she needed the money most but as she considered it she couldn't think why this would happen. The home was completely full so it was always a question of waiting for someone's estate to be eaten up by the cost of their residence or for a death to give admittance. She'd never had any complaints about her work. And then she thought that it was possible the cleaning had been farmed out to some new private company who would bring in their Polish and Lithuanian workers to do the job for half the money and be grateful for the work. She paused at the door and tried to stem her nervousness. Her eyes focused on a framed print on the wall, a picture of a thatched Irish cottage with purple mountains behind it sweeping to a sky where the clouds swirled and streamed. She knocked on the door and waited until she heard a voice telling her to come in.

Mrs Weldon sat behind her desk and beside her was a man she'd seen before but didn't know. He had a notebook and a pen.

'Come in, Karen, and have a seat,' she said, pointing to where she wanted her to sit. As she did so the phone rang but after answering it she asked for all calls to be held. 'This is Mr Jennings who's sitting in with us.' He smiled and raised his pen very slightly but didn't speak. There was a slight whorled sheen on one of the lapels of his dark suit as if someone had pressed a wet thumbprint into it. She felt increasingly nervous and, when asked how she was, mumbled 'OK' and tried not to show how anxious she was to discover why she had been summoned to an office that she'd only been in once in ten years when she had to ask for time off so that she could look after Shannon when she broke her arm in a playground accident.

'There's nothing to be worried about, Karen,' Mrs Weldon said, putting on her glasses as if she needed to be able to see her more clearly. She heard the words but knew they weren't true. It felt for a second as if she was in a police station and about to be interviewed about a murder. Her imagination printed out lurid newspaper headlines where she was accused of giving overdoses or smothering elderly patients who wanted her to help them die. She fiddled with her name tag as if to say that this was who she was and there must be some mistake.

'You've been here a long time, Karen, haven't you?' Mrs Weldon asked.

'Ten years.'

'That's right,' Mrs Weldon said, 'I've looked it up. Started just before me.'

She watched Jennings write in his notebook. There was a smear on one of the lenses of his rimless glasses that made her want to reach across the desk and polish it. After he'd finished writing he snuffled his slipped glasses back into place by crinkling his face. When he did this his eyes closed for a fraction of a second.

'You've always been a good worker and I don't want you to think that anyone is accusing you of anything. That's very important. No one is accusing you of anything but sometimes things happen and we are obliged to follow certain procedures. And I don't want you to think that you have been singled out because we'll be speaking to a range of staff in just the same way that we're speaking to you. Do you understand?'

Despite nodding she understood nothing and the longer she didn't understand why she was there the more frightened she felt. Mrs Weldon held a pencil at both ends parallel to her chest. She was overweight and as she leaned forward her dress strained a little across her heavy bust and under her arms, the material creasing like a series of cracks in plaster. She felt a growing sense of the unpredictability and danger that hovered over the room and which tempted her to confess to whatever was to be her crime so she could bring the experience to an end.

'Things happen in homes from time to time – it's inevitable, I suppose. But it's important that residents and their families have total confidence in us because that's essential to the success of what we do. You understand, Karen?' She nodded again then stared at his pen poised above the notepad seemingly impatient to write. 'So when something happens it's important we're seen to respond right away, sort things out.' She noticed the two framed photographs on the desk and wondered whose job it was to clean this room and what world the photos spoke of beyond the business of running the home. There was a pause and Mrs Weldon set the pencil precisely on the desk.

'Something's gone missing. A piece of jewellery. Quite a valuable item apparently. Have you heard anyone talking about this?'

'No.'

'It's a gold bracelet belonging to Mrs Hemmings. A present from her late husband. So obviously it's of sentimental as well as financial value. And we'd naturally be keen to find it.'

'And you think I took it?'

'No, Karen, that's not what I'm saying or even suggesting. I don't know what happened to it but I do have a responsibility to make enquiries and ascertain its whereabouts. But I'm not accusing you of anything and it's important you understand that.'

'It feels like it,' she said. 'And are you sure it's missing? You know how often old people claim to have lost something and then it turns up – you know that happens all the time. And sometimes they say they've lost things they never had in the first place.' She looked at them both, appealing to their sense of fair play, but their faces were closed, impassive, their eyes withholding either belief or suspicion.

'That's true and it does happen. Except, when Mrs Hemmings arrived here last year we itemised her valuables, even took photographs, and I've personally helped her look and can't find it.' She pushed a photograph across the desk. 'That's it. Have you seen it before?'

She held the photograph in both her hands and nodded. It was a plaited gold bracelet with blue stones at intervals.

'When did you see it last, Karen?'

'I can't remember, she wears it from time to time. She's shown me it. I know she likes it.'

'And when you clean Mrs Hemmings' room have you ever come across it?'

She watched the pen move across the page and saw the way he dotted his i's as if he was pressing home the confirmation of her guilt.

'I don't know exactly where she keeps it, perhaps in the drawers of her dresser. Does Mrs Hemmings say I took it?'

'No she doesn't. And no one's saying you took it. We both know that Mrs Hemmings is – how shall we say it? – a demanding lady. But she's fond of you and you probably get on better with her than anyone else on the staff. However, she does want her bracelet back and she's also the type who will make a very loud fuss if she doesn't get it. So is there anything you can tell us that might help us locate it?'

'I don't know anything about it. I haven't seen it and I don't know anything about it,' she said and looked at Mrs Weldon directly.

'So you're sure that there's nothing you can tell us that might help?' It was Jennings speaking for the first time. His voice was low-pitched and slow and in her ears sounded like an adult asking a question of a child but she wasn't a child and after the questions petered into silence she decided that she'd had enough so she stood up and told them that she was sorry but she couldn't help them. She took a step towards the door then turned to face them again.

'Do you want me to work today or not?' she asked.

'We want you to work as normal,' Mrs Weldon said. 'Just carry out your schedule and I would be grateful if you wouldn't talk about this to anyone else. Better just to keep everything that's been said private. Just between us, for the present at least.'

She closed the door behind her and for the second time that day shivered a little as she stepped into the corridor. She felt cold again and for a moment she thought of handing in her name badge at the desk, going home and climbing back into bed. Only the thought of Shannon's wedding and its spiralling cost prevented her. Loading her trolley with fresh towels and bed linen she wheeled it to the lift, irritated as always by the squeaking wheel which was bent a little and prevented it running smoothly so she had to steer it forcefully to stop it veering to the left. Clive the caretaker/handyman had promised to take a look at it for her but never seemed to get round to it. She experienced a growing sense of anger that he could make her a promise but not keep it. As she wheeled it past reception Muriel was pretending to be busy with paperwork.

So she had stolen a bracelet. Everyone probably knew and thought so by now. Nothing happened in the home big or small that it didn't course through the communal circuits like electricity and, in a place that consisted mostly of a dull waiting, nothing gave more pleasure than a sudden surge of shocking gossip. She imagined the residents in the day room, where they were now confined for the next hour while their rooms were done, passing the story from mouth to mouth, their grey-haired heads leaning in conspiratorially to each other, liver-spotted hands held flutteringly like fans across their mouths. Like Chinese whispers, who could guess the elaborate embellishments that would be added as flawed hearing and malice warped the words into some new shape? She hated them all a little as the squeak of the wheel beat in time with the pulse of her rising anger.

When she came she had thought this would be a good place to work, full of kindly old souls who would be grateful for the comfort and service their money had finally brought them. But while it didn't cater for those with dementia or serious illness and was clearly at the top of the price range and supposedly offering some independence of living, now she thought of it as the home of the bitter, the unhappy and often the deserted. Nothing ever satisfied, nothing ever fully lived up to the expectation they had of what their money entitled them to. So it was as if they were on a cruise ship and some aspect of their accommodation or entertainment schedule had fallen short of what the brochure promised. Individual and collective complaining – there wasn't a week went by without someone organising a gripe about something – was also their way of asserting their dignity, their self-image of being strong people who couldn't be put upon. Each and every one of them thought of the staff as working personally for them. And that was to say nothing of the rivalries amongst the women, the constant struggle, in a world where everything was designed to give equal treatment, to hold on to notions of superiority and class. To be better than someone else. To have more money. To be more independent. To be more loved by their relatives.

Relatives. That was a laugh. Couldn't get a space in the car park at Christmas, Easter and Mothers' Day and the rest of the year you could land a plane in it. And the more they didn't come, the more they compensated by talking about their sons and daughters, their nephews and nieces, their grandchildren who had all just finished university and were doing terribly well. But no one ever asked anything about her or her child who wouldn't have enough money when they were old to stay for a week in a place like this.

No one except Mrs Hemmings. She paused at the door of her room. Perhaps they should have asked someone else to clean it and suddenly it seemed like a trap where when she went in there would be a stash of money sitting on the dresser and if she were to touch it the secret camera would capture it all on tape, alarm bells ring and her guilt would be established for all the world to see. But when she entered everything looked as it always did with the shelves slightly buckled by their books and classical CDs; the desk with laptop and papers; the fat, mirrored wardrobe that contained the vast array of clothes, most of which would never be worn again but would never be thrown away or sent to the charity shop the living side of death. And the dresser that kept the jewellery box, the letters, the personal and legal documentation, the photograph albums. On the walls hung the two landscapes and the framed panoramic black and white photograph of staff and pupils standing in tiered rows.

She knew everything in the room intimately because she was Mrs Hemmings' most frequent visitor and because there was little that she hadn't been shown or been given to hold. Mrs Hemmings, a former headmistress of a Belfast grammar school for girls, was used to having people listen to her so in the absence of pupils or staff, she talked to her, felt it her duty to teach her things. So as usual and in breach of all the home's regulations that Mrs Hemmings refused to accept applied to her, she appeared in the doorway, dressed as if about to go out to a meeting of her Board of Governors.

'Morning, Karen,' she said, still standing at the doorway, uncharacteristically hesitant. 'I'm not in your way, am I?' It was a question she had never asked before and when she answered no in reply she didn't stop cleaning to look at her.

There was a moment's silence and then she lifted her face from straightening the bed cover and said, 'I didn't take the bracelet.'

'Karen, Karen, what has Weldon been saying? Because if she's accused you of taking it I'm going to see her right now. The one thing I told her was that you were above suspicion. Made it crystal clear but as you know the woman has problems listening. But I can assure you that I don't think for a second that you had any part in this.'

'She didn't say outright that I took it but I felt she was thinking it.'

'My dear, that's Weldon's problem – she doesn't think. We've both known each other for a long time and I'm a good judge of character. I know the people I can trust. And I can tell you that there's a number in here that I have serious doubts about. I just wonder what sort of vetting system they have in place – if any.' She came into the room, stepping elaborately over the vacuum-cleaner lead as if it was a major obstacle, and sat on the swivel chair at her desk, then turned to face her. 'There aren't even any security cameras outside in the grounds or at the entrance. And perhaps she's forgotten that incident last year when someone walked in off the street and stole a handbag.' She brushed something from her trousers and then eased them up slightly over her knees the way an old man might do. She was wearing pop socks that finished too soon and which exposed the white flesh of her thin shins, mottled like the breast of a thrush. 'And I wouldn't say this to anyone but I have my doubts about Clive. He came in here about a week ago to change a

49

light bulb and he had a good look round. Taking things in, and he has the keys to every room, I'm sure.' She swivelled from side to side in her chair for a second then stopped and gripped the armrests, the ridged tendons on the backs of her hands tightening and the blue veins inking up in the light that was slanting in from the window. 'Let's put this business about the bracelet to one side – I hardly ever wore the thing, to be honest.' She turned to face her desk and reached for her reading glasses. 'Stop for a second and come and see. I've a piece in the paper today. Come and look.'

It was part of their daily ritual and one of the reasons it took twice as long to clean her room as anyone else's. She set the vacuum down and stood behind her, looking at the computer screen as Mrs Hemmings scrolled down. After years of writing letters to company directors and politicians about various shortcomings in their offered services and having received for her efforts nothing more than standard, impersonal and unsatisfactory replies, she had now discovered the ability to post replies to newspaper articles and the capacity to share her views with the world at large. So almost every day she posted or emailed her views on a range of subjects.

'Here we are,' she said, leaning back in the chair and making the leather squeak. 'It was an article about the examination system – the usual sort of rubbish.' There was her paragraph and as Karen scanned it she recognised similar phrases to the ones she had read so often – 'As someone who has spent her life in education at the highest levels . . . What your writer fails to understand about education is . . .'

'Very good,' Karen said after a suitably polite interval.

'I don't know where they get these journalists but it's obvious they've never stepped foot in a school since they were children. Really, it's embarrassing some of the stuff they write.' She swivelled forward again. As she spoke Karen smelled her musty breath, the breath they all had whatever the mints and washes used, the smell that always made her think of rotting leaves in winter. Stepping involuntarily back she flicked her duster vaguely in the air as if she might have seen a cobweb. Then she went into the bathroom and started to spray and clean, finding relief in the scented chemicals. Mrs Hemmings was still talking but she turned on the taps and drowned out the words because now she didn't want anyone else's voice inside her head. There was a long, thin grey hair in the sink that she swirled away and the mirror above the washhand basin was pitted with misdirected hairspray which smeared when she rubbed it. She pushed the bathroom door almost closed and sat on the toilet but even then she could hear the high-pitched complaint of the computer printer. Something else she would have to take away and read for her education, for her improvement, because Mrs Hemmings thought of her as her last pupil and told her that she had the potential even at her age to make something of herself.

To make something of herself. She thought of the words as she flushed the toilet, sprayed and wiped it. Only more words she didn't fully understand. Part of her wanted to shred them like paper and scatter them to the air but what if just maybe there might be some possibility of something better happening to her? Knowing the right things, meeting the right person, being given the answer to the code. She remembered the way the city looked in the first light of the morning, brooding and hung-over from the night before, how the coldness seemed to thicken and coarsen the skin and seep into the bones, the way buildings were half lit, doormen locking the entrances after they left. It was always waiting to give itself to others, wearing its polished and pretty face for the ones that were only thinking of stirring from their sleep as she headed home. And perhaps she was to blame for the way that Shannon sometimes was, because she hadn't given her an example, something to aim at in her own life. Taking off her rubber gloves she dropped them into her plastic carrying bucket then washed her hands, her eyes fixed on the bottles and creams on the shelf under the mirror, all of them loud with their promises about rejuvenation and anti-ageing, their ability to hide blemishes. She tidied them and replaced a lid thinking of Shannon and the money she spent on her appearance and it made her look at herself in the mirror for the second time that day. Almost forty and nothing made. She tried to tell herself that bringing up a daughter on her own took all her time and energy but didn't succeed. Sooner than she wanted to think she would be old, the breath in her mouth stale like the leftovers from yesterday. She thought for a second that she saw her future face coming towards her in the mirror and turned away and as she did so noticed the crumpled dressing gown hanging on the peg behind the door with one arm pushed inside the shoulder. Instinctively she pulled it free then straightened and smoothed it flat. She felt it inside the pocket, recognised the shape almost immediately and, slipping her hand in, found it under a letter, its cold hardness nestling snugly on a bed of crumpled tissues.

'Almost finished, Karen?' The voice made her start. She understood right away what had happened. Taking a bath before bed she'd dropped it in her pocket and forgotten about it. So it had been stolen. She was about to shout when the words stifled in her throat. The bracelet was beautiful, almost perfect, with its twisted band like plaited hair and its small blue stones. She thought of the desks and work spaces she had cleaned that morning with their trinkets and desk ornaments, the people in the photographs she looked at every day but who had never seen her or knew who she was. There was the sound of footsteps. It was Mrs Hemmings walking towards the bathroom door and in that second she took it all – the bracelet, the letter and the crumpled tissues – and dropped everything into her bucket and covered them with the duster and her cleaning cloths.

'I'm not that messy,' Mrs Hemmings said, smiling. 'Am I?'

'I'm a little slow today,' she answered without looking directly at her.

'Well look, Karen, I've printed out some must-sees in Amsterdam. You mightn't have time to do everything but who knows? Now make sure you get to the Rijksmuseum above all and see the Rembrandts – don't try to see every-thing, there's too much. I've printed some info about *The Night Watch*. And then there's his house and Anne Frank's house of course. It's all here.'

'I'll have to see what Shannon and the other girls want to do as well.'

'Of course but it's such a wonderful city that you don't want to miss out. It's a real opportunity to see things,' she said, pointing her reading glasses at the window as if the city was just beyond. 'Think of me stuck in here for another weekend. But I've decided I'll not under any circumstances participate in any more of those inane so-called entertain-ments Weldon thinks up. Quite frankly they're an insult to the intelligence.'

For a second she thought Mrs Hemmings was going to ask to come with her on the trip so she pretended to read the pages she'd been handed but the moment passed and ended when they thanked each other. She watched the older woman sit down at her desk and put the arm of her glasses in her mouth while she contemplated once more the words she had given to the world. Then as she left her the final sound from the room was the rapid, insistent pecking of her fingers at the keys, until slowly walking away it was gradually replaced by the squeak of the broken wheel and the endless babble of far-off voices.

Three

SHE FELT HEATEDLY SELF-CONSCIOUS and whatever way she considered it could find little dignity in this initiation. So as the young man blathered on about the respective machines and what they would do for her heart and her cardio-respiratory system, she thought only about why they felt the need to have so many mirrors in a place where people like her presumably came because they didn't like the way they looked. As he pointed out dials and adjusting mechanisms she furtively glanced at herself, once again thought herself ridiculous at the age of fifty-four to be wearing sportsgear whose very newness identified her as a novice, a supplicant striving for the physical blessing of her body, a blessing that had been denied her for more years now than she cared to remember. She wondered why she hadn't been given a female member of staff to show her how things worked and why it had to be this young man who she imagined must see it as a chore, akin to the constant testing of the water in the turquoise pool and the allocating of towels to guests, or any of the other mundane requirements of his job description. And in the mirror she couldn't see other people like her but young women with hard angular bodies that seemed to pulse and pump with a hatred of something and wanted to pummel the machines into submission and whose behinds were so tightly sculpted in black lycra that they looked like perfect little plums.

She wondered why she had to endure this public lesson and then remembered it was a requirement of every new member and to do with insurance. Presumably if she hurt herself or did some deep personal damage she alone would now shoulder the blame. The young man was called Paul and he called her Marion as if they were lifelong friends and he saturated her with instructions and facts that she couldn't possibly absorb so she constantly had to nod to show that she was taking it all in. He had a little twined coloured wristband and the tips of his hair were flecked with blond like a paintbrush that had been lightly dipped in gold leaf. He was talking about building things up, about taking everything gradually, of finding what she was comfortable with, and she wanted to tell him that she'd found that out a long time ago and none of it had anything to do with her body. She didn't believe in miracles and so despite the fervour of those all around her, including the young woman who ran ever faster towards her own image in the glass in what looked like a desperate attempt to meet the person she wanted to be, she did not believe that whatever she performed in this place would remap the landscape of her body. She was a formed continent, and only her dignity felt a sense of erosion as he led her to some kind of rowing machine and made her sit on the seat with his hand on her shoulder.

Before they were married, when he was still courting her, Richard took her out in a rowing boat one Easter Monday in Portrush. He just assumed he could do it, the way he could do everything he put his hand to, and when she laughed at his incompetence, at their first circular motions, he got a little peeved and then embarrassed. His pride was hurt and it made him try even harder until he found the knack. All these years later it felt as if he was punishing her as she pulled at the handle and her seat scuttled forward and a young man told her that she was doing well. He was patronising her with his praise and she longed for the whole initiation to be over so she could find anonymity in a quiet corner.

'I think that's about everything for the moment,' he said eventually, putting his hand under her elbow as she inelegantly levered herself back to her feet. 'Is there anything you'd like to ask, anything you want to know about?'

She looked at him and for a second she wanted to ask if there was anything about her at all that he might possibly have found attractive, if during their time together, when he was standing close and touching her arms or shoulders, there was even a moment when he felt aware of her. But behind the bland functionality of his smile she saw an impatience in his eyes and knew that there was somewhere he'd rather be – probably joking with the young girl at reception as she studied her text messages and swapping stories about what they'd done at the weekend. The girl with the blonde hair and the tiny diamond on the side of her nose that shone like a spot of moisture or a snowflake frozen into hardness and who, too, possessed that sense of cold confidence.

After he was gone she looked at herself in the mirror as she sat on a cycling machine and pedalled slowly, never getting any closer to where she wanted to be. She still had the brightness of her eyes, she told herself, and the blessing of good teeth and healthy hair. Tilting her head so that her neck tautened the small fold of flesh under her chin she pedalled a little faster as if the increased speed might slip away some of the pounds that had settled on her hips and which also cushioned the thin hardness of the seat. She tried to look elegant as she pedalled, straightening her back and seeking to maintain a steady rhythm. She hadn't been on a bike since she was a teenager and as she stared at herself in the glass, encouraged by the fixed way those around her did the same, she searched for any sign of that girl she once was.

A group of them had ridden along the coast to Groomsport where one of the girls had a family caravan. It was warm that summer's day and she remembered the red patches on her knees where the sun burnt them. She must have been wearing shorts. Not like these black legging things she had on now that stopped at the ankles and thickened her legs even more. She recalled herself in a series of photographs. The four girls – they always thought of themselves as like the Four Marys out of the *Bunty* – linking arms outside the cara-van door, a chorus line about to do a high-stepping dance. But if there were four of them in the photograph who was taking the picture? She didn't know. On the beach, Susan standing on her head with Hilary holding her legs. The Four Marys. Tiptoeing in the sea, squealing at the cold lace of the water embroidering their feet. Lillian dead now from breast cancer; one living in America out of touch except for the Christmas card that had come every year for thirty years with the couple of sentences that told of children's marriages and the birth of grandchildren; one divorced and on her second marriage and still living close by but whose life never seemed to cross her own.

A lot of water under the bridge, a lot of years. Everything getting added on like rings in a tree. Your life getting bigger and heavier with possessions. Growing more branches, spreading more roots. How could it be possible to stay the same and not also become part of that growth, the ever-increasing weight of solidity that made a life established and permanently fixed? Two sons, both in good business careers, a daughter living in France, a home that had more rooms than they could ever use and a business that provided for everything they needed. Her legs were already sore but she cycled on, remembering all those trite sayings that linked pain with gain. And perhaps she deserved the pain for not fighting hard enough to hold on to that young girl. For letting herself go. For not struggling enough. She looked at her hands, the blue veins beginning to rise like flooding rivers, her knuckles creasing into deepening whorls, the two rings that seemed old-fashioned in their clumpy design. He never wanted a wedding ring, always turned his nose up at any idea that a man might wear jewellery. So he never wore a ring and she supposed it made him feel more of a man in just the same way that he would never carry an umbrella or push one of his children's prams in public.

And this present – and she can't even begin to think of it as a present – of a year's membership of this swanky fitness and leisure complex was filled with unanswered questions and once again it confused her that a man who could speak so directly in business continued to be someone unable to express himself openly in other matters. So was he telling her that she'd let herself go and needed to pull herself together? Was this his way of expressing his disappointment? She stopped pedalling and freewheeled through the uncontrolled spin of her thoughts. Time had been kinder to him. Barely heavier than when they got married, with even the grey seeping through his hair giving him a sense of dignity, of gravitas, and it struck her as unfair that a man who loved his food more than she did should be effortlessly able to burn off every calorie that crossed his lips. The energy he put into the garden centre and a round of golf a week seemed enough to keep him trim and fit-looking. A handsome man. He was slowly leaving her behind and at this thought she lowered her eyes from the mirror and started to pedal again. But she had touched something unintentionally with her hand and now it was harder and harder and she was pedalling uphill and in her mind she couldn't believe she was ever going to catch up.

Afterwards the changing room provided an even worse torture. She undressed slowly in the poor privacy of a corner, sheltering half-heartedly behind a towel as if she was on a holiday beach, trying not to look at the young woman who had stepped out from the shower area and with no trace of self-consciousness or embarrassment strutted towards her locker. She was showing off her body and she tried not to give her the satisfaction of letting her see her glances. But she'd already registered enough to know that everything was toned and tight and she had a tan that left the only whiteness on the tips of her breasts as if someone had delicately pressed champagne glasses to them. Let her have three children, she thought, and see then where her firmness goes. Work hard to raise a family and make a business a success and see then how everything slips into softness and unwanted abundance. She waited until the young woman had her back turned and was fully focused on getting dressed before walking quickly to the showers with her towel wrapped round her like a cocktail dress.

As she stood under the water she hoped that she would have gone before she'd finished showering and her heart sank as she realised that this was an experience that Richard would expect her to repeat at least once a week and possibly even more. A man who liked to get value for his money and perhaps he would judge that not only by the frequency of her visits but also by the physical change he saw in her. At first he might enquire if she was enjoying it and then she imagined him asking if it was doing her any good, as if he'd paid for a course of private medical treatment. What would she say? How could she tell him the truth that he had wasted his money, that it was going to cause her nothing but embarrassment to come here? She was not going to change into this young woman who preened and paraded herself in a peacock display of perfection. And then she hurt herself by thinking how pleased he might be if she did.

The water splurged and splashed over her and she held her face close to the shower head as if it might soothe away the burn of that thought. A man who enjoyed women, what enjoyment had he found in her over these last years? Perhaps if she worked really hard on these machines change might be possible and then he might look at her as he did a very long time ago. A lifetime away and she was glad it was so rare now because when it happened it felt no more than a momentary need, like food that had to be taken to prevent dying of starvation, or not much more than an itch that had to be scratched. And she suspected that she played no real part in it any more, so she was only involved because she was there as she always was and she couldn't talk to him about it because she was frightened that if she did they would both use words that might shake whatever scaffolding held together the life they lived. The water was warm and she let it fountain over her hair and down her back as her hands clasped her stomach which felt both empty and full. Soon, she thought, he would cheat on her. With one of the customers perhaps but more likely with one of the Polish girls they now employed in the planting sheds. She believed it hadn't happened yet but wasn't sure and didn't want to think about it. There was the age difference but he was a handsome man who knew how to make people laugh and his money and the employment he provided would sooner or later minimise this difference and, for a little while at least, be no longer important to some lonely and vulnerable girl who cried each night for home. She knew that he cared enough about her to be discreet and not humiliate her, that he would take whatever it was he needed and then return to the normal cycle of his life.

It was the waiting she hated most. It was the waiting she found unkind. If it were possible she would tell him to get it over with and put it behind them. Perhaps she should do it to him first and somehow equalise the pain but the thought was as ridiculous and repugnant to her as making this place part of her life for at least a year. She had no interest in it, no desire left that had much to do with the body, and now thought the world would be a simpler place if it didn't exist, this strange, inexplicable thing that happened between men and women and about which she had no real understanding. Perhaps this was one of her failings and a selfishness on her part that she should have done more to remedy. But who could you talk to about such intimacies, to whom could you reveal the inner life of a marriage? Another generation perhaps, with their internet blogs that laid out the secrets of their lives like so many clothes taken from their wardrobe and spread on the bed for the world to inspect. She could never do it, so whatever happened must only happen inside the privacy of her head.

She turned the water off and listened. There were no other sounds from the changing room except the piped Christmas music and the hum of pipes and spin of extractor fans. Perhaps she would be lucky in this at least and have the place to herself but she sheathed herself tightly in the towel, took a deep and involuntary breath and then walked slowly back to her locker. The young woman had gone, the only traces of her, wet footprints on the tiles and the scent of the perfume that she'd sprayed. So quickly she changed, not caring that little spots of dampness seeped through her blouse and made it look as if she'd just come in from the rain. Then packing her things away she went to the mirror that filled the wall beside the entrance and switched on the hairdrier. She brushed and dried, pushing her hair back into shape, and all the time tried to tell herself that she felt some benefit from the exercise. A mother with a toddler came through from the swimming area, the child shivering a little until he was wrapped in a large white towel that had an image of Spiderman climbing a skyscraper. She rolled him in the towel as if coating him with flour and about to bake him in the oven. Watching them in the mirror made her remember how it was with her own children, sad just for a moment that they were grown up and no longer needed her to hold them in her arms, no longer looked to her for their protection or warmth against the cold. The child was puffing air as if blowing up some invisible balloon and he wore a little red and white swim cap that when taken off revealed a flattened bob of blond hair. She looked at herself again in the mirror and, seeing her face was still red from the heat of the shower, applied a little moisturiser to try and calm it. Perhaps she should think about changing the colour of her hair, nothing too dramatic or risky but something to lighten it or even just add highlights. A change, something unexpected. Too stuck in her ways, too stuck in her comfort zone. That's what they'd say if she was the subject of one of those makeover programmes that were on every channel and every night. They made it look so easy, like a fairy story where magic dust was sprinkled and wishes granted. But she didn't know where or how to start, and more than anything dreaded looking sad and desperate, advertising to the world what insecurities had driven her to an attempted transformation. And anyway she didn't believe in fairy stories and perhaps belief itself was the prerequisite for such miracles.

At the desk on the way out the girl was still studying her mobile phone while Paul was flicking through a collection of CDs. They both looked up as she passed and smiled. The girl said, 'So you survived then,' and her voice was friendly and warm. The light glittered the diamond.

'See you soon,' Paul said and she answered yes and walked off down the corridor wondering what they were really thinking. The new CD was put on and as she pushed the front door open she heard the opening bars of some tune she vaguely recognised but couldn't name.

So this was his birthday present to her. A year's subscription to the leisure complex, a year's opportunity to get herself in shape. And of course a weekend in Amsterdam. It wasn't exactly the best time of year from a business point of view so she was surprised he'd organised it because after the lull of November they had the Christmas trade to deal with – the decorations and lights, the rows and rows of poinsettia plants, the increasingly tacky and Americanised items and of course the trees themselves. Apart from the horrible, gaudy artificial ones there were the real ones, some rootballed for replanting, the rest specially grown in the sustainable woodland they'd planted five years earlier with the help of a grant and which allowed them to supply other outlets as well. Perhaps it was because he was now so confident that the place could be managed by Alex, who had been with them almost from the start, that allowed their absence and she wondered if there might be a possibility of a longer summer holiday for the first time in their marriage. She had always wanted to go to Italy – perhaps a hotel on Lake Garda or a villa somewhere in the countryside.

When she arrived back home Richard wasn't there and she assumed that he was out locking up for the evening. The house felt empty and still. She told herself that she should find him and say that she'd enjoyed her first visit, describe how plush everything was and let him know that his money had been well spent. So she dropped her sports bag in the utility room in front of the washing machine and headed out the back door and along the floodlit passage-way that linked their home to the garden centre. She passed the huge polythene tunnel frosted by the whiteness of the light. From inside, the red glow of heaters looked like the eyes of animals peering out at her. In the third one there was a light on and she saw her husband's giant silhouette thrown against the skin of the tunnel, his arm raised and moving as if he was conducting some invisible orchestra, but although she strained to catch his voice she heard nothing but the hum of electricity and the far-off sound of passing traffic. She squirmed through the plastic flap and saw him standing with a rolled-up catalogue in his hand and heard the laughter from the two girls who were sitting at the table potting up seedlings. For a second, lost in the sound of his laughter, he didn't register her presence but then followed the gaze of the two Polish girls to where she stood watching. The girls lowered their eyes to their work again as if they were servants in the presence of their mistress. They should be going home by now, if the small terraced house that five of them squeezed into could be called home. She had tried to brighten it for them and felt a little better about it in that they only charged them a very nominal rent. There were so many stories about exploitation and she was determined that no one would ever have grounds to level that accusation at them. They were reliable workers and for the most part good girls but they never stayed long, the realities she supposed never quite matching up to their dreams.

'These girls should be going home,' she said, hoping that her face had been drained of some of its redness. 'I can drive them.'

'It's all right,' he said, dropping the catalogue to his side. 'They've just been finishing off some stuff and I said they could have their tea with us. We can send out for some Chinese if you like.'

'It's all right, I'll make something,' she said, wondering why his capacity for generous gestures usually entailed more work for her. 'I'll stick something in the oven, but it'll be nothing too wonderful, girls.'

'Thank you, Mrs James, but please don't go to any trouble,' Anka said and Celina nodded her agreement.

'It's OK, girls. It'll be about half an hour.' She was about to turn away.

'So how did it go?' he said, but he shouldn't have done it in front of them because it felt as if it should be something only they shared.

'Good,' she answered. 'I'll tell you later. I'll get the tea on.'

'Do you need any help?' he asked, stepping towards her for the first time and both of them knowing that his offer was only a polite gesture.

'No,' she said, looking at him just long enough to tell him that he should have asked her first before the invitation was given, and as she walked back to the house she strained to hear if there was any more laughter but there was only the frosted silence of the night.

She didn't begrudge two girls far from home a hot meal but felt a little resentment that her husband would get the credit for it and in the minds of the girls the kindness would be his. Emptying her new sportsgear into the washing machine she hoped he wouldn't talk about the gym over the meal and imagined the blonde-haired, blue-eyed Anka and the equally slim Celina with her hennaed bob of hair and almond eyes looking at her the way women do with each other, weighing her up, evaluating her strengths and weaknesses. She threw some chicken breasts into the oven, opened some pasta and searched in the cupboard for a jar of good-quality sauce which she hoped would disguise the basic nature of the meal. She remembered the sound of their laughter and felt again her exclusion. What was the joke? Why did they stop laughing when she entered as if she was the schoolteacher returning to the classroom who expected to find only quiet work?

The central heating had come on a couple of hours earlier and with the heat of the oven the whole house seemed too warm. Perhaps the thermostat was set too high. She bent over the sink and splashed her face with cold water then set the table, momentarily confused as to whether to use the very best plates and cutlery or the workaday set, but decided on her second-best set because it was important to make a good impression, even if the meal was unspectacular. She wondered what proper Polish food was like – there were some shelves in the supermarket set aside for it and in the library there was even a new section with Polish books. Perhaps they could have gone to Krakow for the weekend instead of Amsterdam but at least they'd been once before and would know their way about a bit. And the hotel looked nice. She had looked it up secretly on the internet and was impressed by what she saw. She didn't understand why he still insisted on using a travel agent to book everything when she could do it in a matter of minutes. But then he didn't trust the internet and still refused to use it for banking, talking about it as if it was a television screen which anyone could switch on and watch the same thing as you. She'd tried to persuade him but with no success and so she'd never even bothered to tell him that they were having broadband. If she was truthful with herself she would have had to admit that her knowledge gave her a sense of advantage, a skill that he didn't have, and there was a frequent playful satisfaction when she was able to supply him with some piece of information that had eluded him, or find a price for something he was thinking of buying. It even pleased her to see him eat a meal, oblivious to the fact that its ingredients were part of a grocery delivery she had ordered online.

He came in the back door, the two girls hesitating a little until she invited them in with an exaggerated sweep of her arm. They smiled self-consciously and still loitered at the door until she showed them where to sit. She was about to offer them a cold drink when she saw him opening a bottle of wine and rummaging in the wrong cupboard for glasses. She pointed to the right one with her fork and then declined the offer, worried that her face would flush again.

'There you go, girls,' he said as he handed them the too-full glasses. 'It's good to be in the heat.'

'It's not really that cold for this time of year,' Anka said.

'Colder at home?' he asked.

'Much colder,' she said, sipping her wine and then licking the taste from her lips.

There was a silence that extended slightly too long and she tried to think of something to say. 'It doesn't feel like Christmas,' she offered but the words led nowhere and she turned back to the cooker.

'You'll be looking forward to getting back home,' he said, holding his glass towards them as if he was offering a toast.

'Yes, it will be good to see our families again,' Celina said. 'Will you see your family?'

'Judith is coming from France but Adam and Colin have their own children now so they'll spend Christmas Day in their own homes and we'll meet up on Boxing Day.'

'That will be nice,' Celina said, holding her glass close to her cheek. 'Why do they call it Boxing Day?'

'I don't know,' he said, looking towards her for help but she didn't know either. 'Maybe because that's the day families get fed up spending so much time together and begin to fight.'

She would Google it later. It seemed a bit stupid not knowing about their own customs. He was drinking his wine too quickly and suddenly she realised that he was nervous. Why should he be? She turned and looked at the two girls, wondering which one he found the most attractive. It was probably Anka, she decided. She was more conventionally pretty than Celina and as she smiled at both of them she noticed that the blue of her eyes was light and washed-out, almost the colour of faded denim, and she imagined she saw a sadness there as if some hoped-for happiness had slowly leached away.

'What were you all laughing at earlier?' she asked, half-turning as she continued to stir the pasta. There was no immediate answer and she saw them looking at each other in confusion. Perhaps they laughed together so often that it wasn't possible to remember. Perhaps it was something secret and private that they didn't want to share. About her and the gym?

'I don't remember,' he said and because she didn't believe him she reminded him that he was driving afterwards and like a child he immediately set the glass down. 'Do you remember, girls?'

'You told us about the man who bought his wife an iron for Christmas with petrol tokens and she hit him with it,' Anka said.

What age was she? She couldn't remember although the information was on the computer in the office. Twenty-eight perhaps. Young but not young. By that age she was married and a second child on the way. She tried to imagine herself living in a foreign country, earning not very much money, but couldn't do so and using a pair of oven gloves opened the cooker door to inspect the chicken. A rush of heat enveloped her and she pulled her head back for a second before lifting out the baking tray.

'Do you need any help?' Celina offered but she thanked her and said everything was fine. Testing the chicken with a fork she decided that it was almost cooked and added the contents of the sauce jar. No time for marinades, no time for anything sophisticated. She opened a salad bag and emptied it into a bowl and remembered to put out a bottle of salad dressing and some leftover coleslaw. The phone in their home office rang and Richard rolled his eyes before going to answer it.

'Don't be long,' she told him, 'I'm almost ready to serve.'

Anka said something to Celina in Polish and it made her nervous. She wished now she had taken a glass of wine. The sadness in Anka's eyes worried her. Perhaps she would try to find happiness in some way that she wouldn't normally do, perhaps she would clutch at straws, disorientated by loneliness and the strangeness of where she found herself. She wanted to turn and tell her that it wouldn't make her happy, that she should think of going home and starting her own family, that it was time she found a man to spend her life with. For a second the words half-formed but then they blurred and she knew if she were to speak they would tumble out in a confusion that might be misunderstood and, even worse, offend, and she would not offend even a woman she thought might sleep with her husband. She tried to focus only on serving the meal. Making the plates look as good as possible.

'It's not much, girls,' she said as she laid the plates, but they contradicted her and told her it looked lovely and for a second she was pleased by what seemed like the sincerity of their gratitude.

'It was a rep,' Richard said, returning from the call. 'Think they could find a more convenient time to ring.'

'I suppose they think they're sure to get you,' she said, setting his plate on the table and then stepping back to blow a thin stream of air against her face.

'Looks great,' he said. 'Eat up, girls.'

She watched them start to eat and for a second she had no appetite, thought of excusing herself, but just when she felt she was no longer needed he stood up and pulled back her chair in invitation. She lifted her plate and was reminded that he had always been kind to her. Kind and generous. The kindness was quiet and unfussy but a constant on which she had always relied and never taken for granted. What right had she now to imagine it would dry up and torment herself with doubts about what went on inside his head? She glanced at him to see if he was looking at the girls but he seemed focused on his food and for a while they all ate in silence until someone succumbed to the need for speech and they chatted about inconsequential things.

She pushed her own food unenthusiastically around the plate but was pleased to see the pleasure with which everyone else was eating. She would have to go on a diet again if this gym thing was to be seen to produce any tangible effect.

'So you're going to Amsterdam,' Celina said, looking at her over the top of the wine glass.

'Yes, just for the weekend,' she answered, not quite sure why she thought the news shouldn't have been shared so soon.

'Very nice,' Celina said, setting her glass back on the table. Her nails were short but had a thin dark rim where she had pressed them into compost. 'I would like to go to Amsterdam.'

'It's a beautiful city,' she told her. 'We've been once before.'

'And did you see the girls sitting in the windows?' Celina asked, giggling until Anka glanced at her companion like an older sister.

She shook her head and stared at her plate to hide her embarrassment, then Anka said something quietly in Polish and the silence suddenly stretched and strained.

'No we didn't see that,' Richard said, coming to her aid, 'and what I remember was visiting museums and flower markets. And the trams. Nearly getting knocked down by a tram. You didn't know where to look. Trams and bicycles flying at you from everywhere.' He poured some wine into the girls' glasses and glad of the excuse she got up from the table, found herself a glass and held it out to her husband.

'Just half a glass,' she insisted and then as if giving him the opportunity to drink some more asked, 'Would you like me to drive the girls home afterwards?'

'You're OK, I'm not drinking any more and there's a couple of smoke alarms I need to fit.'

She stared intently at him as he carefully poured the wine but he was concentrating on what he was doing and didn't look into her eyes. She didn't want him to take the girls home, she wanted him to stay there with her but she had given him the opportunity twice and he'd refused it. She would not try again. So instead she cleared the table and started to make coffee. Anka helped her and suddenly she asked herself would it be such a terrible thing if it was this young woman who knew the proper way to do things and who would have no need or motivation beyond the moment, who would let go again and probably be embarrassed enough afterwards to find a job somewhere else or take a flight home? As she handed her a plate their fingers brushed lightly for a second. Then she suddenly felt as if she might cry and so she excused herself and went to the bathroom where she sat on the toilet and dabbed her eyes with tissue before gradually pulling herself together again. In the mirror she couldn't see anything clearly because everything was fogged and smeared inside her head. She washed her hands and didn't look at her reflection.

The table had been fully cleared and the plates loaded into the dishwasher when she returned. A cup of coffee sat on the table ready for her and she was momentarily irritated that Richard had used assorted mugs that looked ill-matched and ugly.

'Why didn't you use decent cups?' she asked more sharply than she intended but before he could think of an answer Anka told her that the coffee was very nice and then both girls thanked her for the meal. 'You're welcome,' she said. 'It wasn't very much.'

She looked at Anka and for a second their eyes met. It felt that just in this moment everything about each other was known, that all their secrets were laid open – it was what happened sometimes between women – and then they both turned away and the moment closed over once again.

Something had been shared but she didn't know what it was or if it could ever prove stronger than whatever personal need pressed against the pale skin of this girl with faded-blue eyes. And what did any of it matter if everyone was still alive and you still had the strength to keep on going? So perhaps these were things that just happened to you along the way like illness and bereavement and you did your best to get over them and struggle on. She just didn't want any mess, no unpleasant and embarrassing residue clinging to them, so if it was to happen let it happen cleanly and quickly and let them both move on and if they might never be exactly where they were before, let them do their best to refind whatever balance it was held them together.

When the girls had finished their coffee he told them that he'd drive them home. She was glad that he didn't offer them any more wine and that he hadn't drunk any more. When he went off to fetch the smoke alarms and his toolbox she looked at the bottle and was momentarily tempted to finish it off after everyone had gone but tried to strengthen her resolution to dedicate herself, if not to abstinence, then at least to moderation. The girls left by the kitchen door to go and fetch their coats. She heard them chatting in Polish as they walked out into the floodlit corridor. Standing at the glass she looked at how the harsh light bleached Anka's hair almost white. For some reason she thought they looked like prisoners making their way back to their cells for the night. She felt sorry for them in their struggle to make a better life. She didn't think she could be as brave, told herself that she had never been brave, so this thing that she was planning to do seemed like it belonged to someone else and she wondered if she would find the strength to see it through.

He came back with his equipment and thanked her for the meal.

'It was nothing,' she said but stopped herself adding that more warning would have been good because suddenly she realised that one of the things she liked about him was his capacity for generosity and as he started to zip his coat said only, 'Be careful.'

'I will. The roads are always full of madmen this time of year and if they don't get you then the traffic cops are hiding in every hedgerow with their hairdriers.' He spoke the words without looking at her but, as he finally pulled the zip close to his chin, met her gaze. 'Are you all right?'

'I'm fine,' she answered, forcing a half-smile.

'You didn't take too much out of yourself?' and he was studying her more carefully. 'You need to build it up slowly.'

She answered only by nodding and then, as he stood weighing her up, she pretended to busy herself with the dishes.

'I'll not be long,' he said.

'Be as long as you like,' she said without turning round because if she turned round she might ask him not to go at all and then she didn't know what answer he might give.

'An hour at the most.'

It felt like he was trying too hard, too anxious to gain her permission. And perhaps ultimately that was what it would take – her unspoken but tacit approval. She understood that now. It was what she must do, she told herself. How much would it take out of her? Would it leave some yawning chasm opening up to then flood with hurt and bitterness? She didn't think so. It was the waiting she couldn't bring herself to bear. This was the best way.

'Come outside a minute,' he said to her as he paused at the door.

'To see the girls off?' she asked.

'Just come outside for a second.'

She followed him to the front of the house where the two girls were standing beside the four-wheel drive. Celina was wearing a long scarf that seemed to endlessly spiral round her neck and fingerless gloves in the same colour. They looked as if they had been hand-knitted. Electric light left yellow transfers on the bonnet of the car. Behind the windscreen it looked as if fog was pressing against the glass.

He appeared in the lighted doorway. 'Stand beside the girls, Marion,' he called and as she did so the three of them looked at each other with confusion. It was as if he was going to take a photograph but she knew that wasn't possible. The wind was beginning to nip her cheeks and she shivered.

'Da da!' he said loudly, his voice a rising descant of boyish pleasure, and they looked up to see an illuminated Santa Claus climbing the chimney, then endlessly reversing and repeating his journey. The girls clapped their hands and squealed a little. His smile stretched from ear to ear. 'So what do you think?' he asked and she heard the childish need in his voice as Celina said, 'Very good,' over and over. Then she started a little as she felt Anka's hand rest on her shoulder.

'You should go in now,' she told her. 'You have no coat and the night is cold.'

She nodded and walked towards the lighted doorway. Did it feel like a kindness? Did it feel like a younger woman trying to preserve an older, frailer being? He stood aside to let her pass and although she didn't look at him she knew he wanted her approval but the only word she said was 'Anka'. She walked on down the hall and then turned to face him. 'Anka is a nice girl.' He stared at her with the same uncertainty she'd seen a few minutes earlier.

'Yes, so what do you think?' he asked.

'Whatever makes you happy,' she answered and then closed the study door behind her.

The computer started up and as she waited she could hear the car driving off. She checked her emails first of all but it was the usual concoction of spam with offers for beauty products, special phone and insurance deals and even someone asking if she was looking for love. She deleted them all and then started searching. It surprised her at first but it shouldn't have because there was nothing it seemed in the world that was not available if you had the money to pay. So the nature of the goods was really neither here nor there. She wondered for a moment about those who fell in love on the internet, puzzled a little about what cybersex might consist of and then looked at the faces scrolling across the screen. The faces were the most important because she had to find the right one and quickly she discarded anything tacky or vulgar. Discretion and decency were what she was looking for but at first it seemed that she must be the only customer for these commodities. And of course, not too young. Now she'd managed to narrow it down to three or four but was constantly changing her mind. She imagined she had the ability to see characters in expression. There was too a variation in price but the cost was not particularly important and would not be the crucial factor in her final choice.

Perhaps it would snow at Christmas. Perhaps her daughter would finally produce a boyfriend when she returned for the holiday. She had all her family presents mostly bought. Many of them online of course. But how would she feel afterwards? After it was done. She would cancel the gym membership. That at least would be a relief. By then he would understand and everything would be all right. Her fingers flicked over the keys. Soon she would shed the burden and everything would be light again. She thought of herself as a young woman with sunburnt knees paddling in the sea with her friends, heard once more their squeals of pleasure as the water plumed against their thighs. Remembered the way the sand seemed to slip away beneath her feet as the waves foamed and burbled between her toes.

Four

M ONDAY MORNING IN THE college was similar to Friday afternoon in that the demarcation with the weekend blurred and was vaguely defined and just as at the end of the week the students slipped away, so at its opening there was rarely a full complement before lunchtime. No lectures were ever scheduled for this period and those students who lived in the city were slow of movement and thought, as if unable to fully throw off the legacy of whatever excesses their weekend had enjoyed. Those who had gone home to have their clothes washed and to empty their parents' fridges and wallets drifted back in ones and twos, often carrying their bags, and spent what was left of the morning drinking coffee and listening to anyone who had a story to tell.

It used to be a time he enjoyed, a quiet interlude before the pace quickened. If not a time exactly when he got things done, then at least a period when he was able to potter about, consider the week's possibilities and gird up his loins so to speak. But that of course was before the meetings started, the endless timetabled, minuted meetings of department and faculty that were supposedly designed to transform the once leisurely and gentleman's game of teaching into a professional process complete with measurable outcomes.

So targets and evaluation, performance indicators, were the names of the game now and with an inspection looming there was an ever greater intensity of hysteria and policy documents piling up in his in-tray like a snowdrift. He'd only scanned a couple but already they were threatening to avalanche and slide across the surface of his desk.

He supposed the inspection was the reason that Stan Stenson had asked to see him at such an early hour and formally by memo. They went back a long way and had started teaching at the college within a year of each other but, unlike his own career that was successfully built on an inherent lack of ambition, Stan's had grown steadily until he seemed to have responsibility for a whole host of things. He liked Stan but didn't envy him his elevation. In fact he often felt sorry for him as he watched him shuffling paper and knew that whatever was the tide of useless, bureaucratic flotsam and jetsam, it always washed up first on his desk.

He knocked at the open door – he never assumed anything based on their friendship too overtly – and saw his head of department scrawling in red pen over a scree of paper. It was still surprising to see him beardless and short-haired, Stan who once looked like a Belfast Ginsberg and who as a young man thought that the purpose of art was to shock and disturb. As he was wordlessly signalled into the room he couldn't help thinking of Samson with his locks shorn. So there would be no more howls or radical gestures against the Belfast bourgeoisie. It came to all of them in one way or other so he didn't condemn him for signing up but it did allow him to feel a momentary sense of moral superiority until he was forced to admit that his own reluctance was probably due to a natural and self-preserving indolence rather than principle.

'Come in, Alan, have a seat,' Stan said, throwing his pen down in a dismissive gesture.

'Doing your head in?' he asked, thinking it was important he established a sympathetic sense of unity against the common enemy. 'Don't envy you.'

'Have you read the Dean's proposals about the proposed new modular course?'

'Haven't reached them yet. It's on my desk.'

'You need to read it because it affects you: it affects all of us.'

'In what way?'

'You need to read it, Alan, before you end up teaching stuff you don't want to in ways you don't want to.'

'Is that why you wanted to see me, Stan?'

Stan picked up the pen, threw it down again and leaned back in his chair, making it squeak in protest. His eyes blinked and then gazed at him in a fixed way.

'How's things, Alan?' he asked.

'What do you mean?' The personal tone was ominous. It felt suddenly as if he was in a doctor's surgery and the second he told the doctor he was hale and hearty he would be confronted with the indisputable and irrevocable revelation of a terminal illness.

'I mean, how do you feel things are going?'

He thought of his son and said, 'Fine.' He wished Stan would stop staring at him so intently.

'You know we need to talk soon about your staff appraisal?'

'That time again? Well we won't get too worked up about that, will we?' he said, remembering the previous year's experience that seemed to be nothing more than a bit of form filling.

'We might have to, Alan.'

'Have to what?' he asked, staring at the dark palimpsest of beard on his head of department's lower face that threatened to seep through the ageing surface of his skin and re-form its former glory.

'Get worked up about it. Everything's changing here, Alan – if you ever actually read anything that's sent to you or lifted your head up and had a look about, then you'd know that.' He picked up his pen and held it this time like it was a syringe. 'This can't be a rubber-stamp job any more. There are certain issues I have to address with you and I'm afraid we need to come up with convincing answers.'

'What issues would those be?' he asked, not entirely sure he wanted his question to be answered.

Stan loudly clicked the pen and it made him think that he was about to inject him with a truth serum.

'Well perhaps it might be no bad thing if I flagged them up for you, gave you time for a considered response.' He paused, stared across the desk through to the outer room. 'Shut the door, Alan.'

So it was this bad. It was shut-the-door bad and for a second he considered running away while the door was still open. When he sat back down on the chair it groaned in complaint. Stan was leaning closer across the desk and when he spoke his voice had dropped and the sudden sense of intimacy shrank the room even smaller until he felt claustrophic and struggling for breath.

'There's been complaints.'

He immediately thought of his moment of madness. Was she complaining about her marks – hardly possible since he'd been entirely and imprudently generous? Was she complaining about his performance? He was certainly no expert but in times of deep and inexplicable emotional need, performance didn't seem particularly crucial. Surely this, too, hadn't fallen prey to the vocabulary of performance indicators and success criteria?

'Complaints?' he repeated, attempting a tone of mild curiosity.

'From some of the students.'

The bitch. He'd lost a marriage out of it and she'd printed herself on a slab of clay in a way she hadn't intended then got marks her mousey little gimcrack pots didn't merit. The world didn't know how to be fair any more.

'Listen, Stan, if it's about that MA student I'd just like to say . . .' But he couldn't actually think of what to say and so he was almost relieved when Stan held up his hand like a policeman stopping traffic.

'It's not about the MA student and right now if there was a problem there I'd rather not know about it so let's just focus on the problems I do know about.'

'Fair enough,' he said, thinking it good tactics to appear open and relaxed about whatever was coming.

'There's been complaints from a series of students and, before you ask, I'm not able to give their names at this stage of the,' he hesitated, 'proceedings. I can summarise them best as falling into three categories. One: not giving a reasonable allocation of individual time to each student and not being available for guidance to final-year students when needed. Two: being insensitive and overly dismissive about work you don't like. And three: not turning up for some scheduled seminars and tutorials.'

'And I'm to face these complaints without knowing my accusers?' he asked, momentarily believing that attack might be the best course of defence.

'Listen, Alan, take my advice – don't dramatise this and don't for God's sake get on a high horse. And, believe me, you should be grateful that there are no names attached to the complaints because if there were, it would be formal and we wouldn't be able to chat about it in my office.'

'So I should be grateful that I'm accused of stuff without knowing my accusers.' But already he could think of a full range of potential point-the-fingerers. 'I don't think I missed that many tutorials – perhaps a couple when I had the flu.'

'Alan, I'm speaking to you as a friend as well as the person who's supposed to manage you, I don't wish to trawl through all the various issues but I do need you to take on board some basic points and reflect on the need to implement them. The first is that things have changed in here and out there as well.' He swept his hand in an all-encompassing movement. 'You need to register that more clearly than you have done to date. They're all paying good money and as soon as they do that they believe, rightly or wrongly, that it entitles them to certain things and our time is one of them. They've come from a system that spoon-fed them and pushed them through every exam they ever faced so they need to feel that assurance of personal support.'

He went to say something in reply but was faced with the traffic-controller's hand again and he fell obediently silent and sat a little higher in his chair to show that he was paying attention.

'This might stick in your throat – it might even stick in mine – but it's the way it is and if you can't face up to it you're only going to get more grief than you want. And you can't sneer at their work or tell them it's no good.'

'But what if it *is* no good?'

'Tell them how to make it bloody better and do it with sensitivity so that they're not here in my office crying or having a hissy fit. And if you want my private opinion there's one or two out there who have the potential and the knowhow to cause us all real trouble, who should be told they're the next Damien Hirst or Tracey Emin if it keeps them off our backs.'

'You think I'm a dinosaur, Stan, don't you?'

'You're old-school, Alan. And there's a lot to be said for that but we let other people take over and perhaps you should think about your contribution to that and now they want the game played by different rules. And although you haven't worked this out there isn't a nice quiet corner for you to hide in any more. And I suppose in some ways you are a dinosaur but I tell you this, Alan, you have a choice – evolve or face extinction.' He leaned back in the chair, making it squeak again, and his face had reddened as if he'd just finished blowing up a balloon.

'Well listen, Stan, I appreciate your honesty and I'll try to shape up, toe the line.'

'Don't take the piss. Just do what you want but know that we're in a system where there'll be consequences and I don't want to lose someone I know is a good teacher.'

The kindness of the compliment affected him more than any of the other words and he didn't want to give his old comrade any more problems so he said nothing but nodded to show he'd understood. He stood up but Stan signalled him to sit down again.

'We might as well kill two birds with one stone here. I have, I'm afraid, one final issue to raise with you and one which has caused some awkward questions down the corridor. You haven't had a show in more years than I can remember. But more importantly than that you haven't published a piece of research in the last couple of years and with this inspection in the pipeline we need everyone to make a contribution. Research will be one of the things that affects our final score. So do you have anything on the go at the minute?'

He felt an obligation to his old friend and perhaps out of guilt for the grief he had caused him, or perhaps just out of impulse, he suddenly heard himself say, 'Well actually I have an article I'm working on – it's about Van Gogh and Gauguin and the period when they shared the house at Arles. I'm analysing the work – the precise chromatic range – in relation to immediately earlier and later paintings and showing how this period of physical intimacy affected their colour choices, how there was a kind of chromatic symbiosis.' He couldn't help smiling because he was pleased with his imagination and because it struck him as a pretty good idea.

'Don't take the piss, Alan.'

'No seriously, Stan. I think I can get a publisher.' He saw that his head of department was still unconvinced so he tried to clinch it by saying, 'Actually next week I'm going to Amsterdam to complete some research.'

One of Stan's eyebrows curled slightly but his face remained stonily impassive. 'I look forward to reading it. And I can pass this piece of news on to the Dean?'

'By all means,' he said, slowly pushing himself out of the chair. 'And thanks, Stan, I appreciate your help and I'll do my best to take on board the things you've said.' For a second he thought of offering him a handshake but Stan was leaning back in his chair rubbing the point of his chin as if he was sanding away the press of stubble.

Five

'YOU CAN'T BE SERIOUS, Shannon,' she said, pointing at the two costumes splayed across the bed. 'I can't wear that.' She looked at her daughter who was standing hands on hips, all her admiration evident in her posture.

'Of course you can. Just go with the flow, Mum. You'll look great. It's out of Elliott's costume shop – the real thing and it's not tacky or anything. It looks great.'

'Look at the length of the skirt,' she protested, measuring it against herself. 'It's far too short – I can't wear a skirt this short at my age.'

'You've great legs – you can get away with it. Just wear thick tights and your suede boots and, Mum, you're going to Amsterdam – no one's going to know you, or ever see you again. It's just a laugh.'

'There'll be plenty of laughs, all right, but I don't want people laughing at me all weekend.'

'Mum, it's a hen party. Everybody always dresses up and it could've been something worse – like schoolgirls or tarty nuns.'

'But Indians, Shannon. Why Indians?'

'I think it looks great. Look at your top with all the beading and put your feather on,' Shannon said, handing it to her and nodding encouragement as if she was talking to a child. 'In fact try on the whole costume.'

'Should I not keep it till we get there?'

'Till we get there? We're travelling like this.'

'We're getting on the plane dressed like Indians?'

'That's the whole idea of it – that's what happens on a hen trip.'

She slipped the skirt over her jeans and for some reason didn't want to undress in front of her daughter. 'Well, if I have to do it, let's see you in yours.' She was glad when Shannon took hers across the landing into her bedroom.

'And take those jeans off,' her daughter called. 'And try to get in the spirit of it, Mum, or you're not going to enjoy yourself. It's only a bit of craic.'

As she changed she couldn't imagine that the weekend would hold much enjoyment for her and while she was initially flattered to be asked, she now held serious doubts about the whole trip, not least because she was increasingly conscious that she'd never been in a plane before, a prospect which caused her deep anxiety. She stood in front of the mirror and saw a ridiculous Indian squaw in imitation buckskin decorated with plastic beading.

'Put your headband on, Mum,' Shannon insisted as she entered. She of course looked tall and willowy as if her outfit was a designer label. 'Well how do I look?' she asked in the way she only ever did when she already knew the answer.

'Like a catwalk Indian. How does this thing go?'

'Give it here – you're putting it on back to front. The feathers go at the back.' Her daughter stood behind her peering over her shoulder at the mirror. She was smiling and then she rested her hands lightly on her mother's shoulders, stooping a little as she did so in order to catch more of her reflection.

'You look great. And, here, don't forget your hatchety thing.'

'I think it's called a tomahawk. Where does it go?'

'In the waistband. Tuck it in like that.'

'A handy thing for a woman to have on her. And you're telling me the other girls are going dressed like this? They're turning up at the airport like this?'

But her daughter was preening herself sideways to the mirror while pressing her dress smooth with the palms of her hands and when she spoke it was to say that she was going to ring Ellie to tell her the costumes were cool. She listened to her daughter's excited feet on the stairs and wondered if she would jump the bottom two steps the way she always did on Christmas morning but guessed that age and the tightness of the skirt would prevent it. Turning to the mirror again she repeated the word 'cool' in a vain attempt to convince herself then sat down on the edge of the bed.

She had been saving for over a year for the wedding, had gone without in lots of ways – she'd hardly bought a thing to wear apart from a few pairs of tights and couldn't remember the last time she'd been out socially. She'd lost track, too, of the extra shifts she'd done in the home, had done so many that some of the girls said she should ask for a room. She'd dined off leftovers from the home and stuck every spare penny in the bank account she'd opened especially to pay for everything. It wasn't going to be the biggest wedding in the world or something you'd see in the pages of *Hello!* but it was going to be as good as anybody else's and she was determined to show the world that she had done right by her child despite everything.

She heard Shannon bubbling her excitement down the phone and did her best to share in it but the worry about money got in the way and she felt, too, an increasing frustration that so much of her daughter's own wages were squandered on things that had so little value. Her eyes caught the sheaf of papers that Mrs Hemmings had given her and picking them up she flicked through them but none held any meaning. What did Rembrandt or some painting mean to her? Anyway she would be lucky if she saw much more than the inside of some clubs or bars and, when she realised that, she felt again the pointlessness of the choice and the money wasted on a journey abroad. She sighed too when she thought of how she would have to look at the pages in more detail to be able to lie to Hemmings and make her believe that she had at least seen some of the suggested sights. It was true that she did harbour some curiosity about what it would be like to be in a foreign country but it faded when measured against the hassle of having to get a passport and money changed, and nothing that it could possibly offer would ever compensate for having to get into an aeroplane. She tried not to think about it but was unable to block out recurring images of the plane suddenly plunging out of the sky – it seemed to her to be totally impossible that something made from material as heavy as metal should ever be able to rise from the ground and hold itself aloft.

Shannon's voice was lilting and singing, sometimes giving little squeals of pleasure at what was being said, but as the call dragged on she thought only of its cost and despite her reluctance to feel mean couldn't help comparing it with her own purely functional use of the phone. She lay down on the bed and tried to curl herself into a little calm. Her fingers traced the cheap beadwork that felt as if it could all fall off at the first excuse and wondered how she was going to go to the airport dressed like this, only comforting herself by the belief that at that time of year she wasn't likely to bump into anyone who knew her. Lisa and Pat would think it all a good laugh and she understood she'd have to provide them with every gory detail of the trip and if it proved too uneventful, just as for Mrs Hemmings, she'd have to make stuff up. They'd wound her up about smoking dope and she'd countered that the candle table decorations for the wedding had already seen enough money go up in smoke without wasting more. Then she felt a little ashamed that she hadn't invited either of them to the wedding and had got herself in a state where she couldn't think of any guest except through the price being charged per head. But it was true as well that she was nervous about Lisa getting a few drinks in her and letting herself down as she had at last year's Christmas party. She wanted her daughter's wedding to be classy and dignified so she wasn't going to risk Lisa which meant she couldn't ask Pat. Mostly on her side it was just going to be Shannon's friends and then more people could come to the disco afterwards if they wanted. She looked again at the Indian dress and wondered if the outfit she had bought for the wedding was good enough. She hadn't shown it to Shannon yet and was nervous she might think it wasn't up to the mark. It was out of Marks & Spencer so there was still time for her to change it if it wasn't all right. Eventually she heard her daughter put the phone down and wondered if this was the right moment to show her but the possibility of it being criticised made her reluctant and happier to postpone it.

'Mum, don't get your dress creased,' Shannon said, and she got off the bed like a child who had been caught doing something wrong.

'It's fine. I'll hang it up in a minute.'

'You have to look your best for this weekend. I don't want you letting yourself down.'

So now her daughter was speaking to her as if the parent–child roles had been reversed and the irony of it irritated her. Then Shannon saw the printouts on the bed and lifted them before she could stop her.

'What's all this?' she said, scanning the pages.

'Just some stuff somebody gave me, stuff to go and see.'

'Mum, you're going on a hen party, you won't have time to go and look at this sort of thing. You'll be too busy having a good time to bother about all this and it looks a right bore anyway.' Dropping the pages dismissively on the bed she admired herself in her costume again. 'Are you sure this is a good fit?'

'It's perfect. You'd think it had been made for you.' She said the words as if from a script memorised through constant use. Then as her daughter changed her viewing angles she sat on the edge of the bed and watched her.

'Mum, will you check with the florist again today that the flowers are going to be right, that they've got the right colours? And the photographer – we still need to choose the album style. Can you phone him and ask when we can see them and make a final choice?'

The list grew longer by the day. She was growing a little weary of it and as soon as one thing was sorted something else sprang up. But she assured her that everything would be done and then as Shannon was about to go to her room and take off her costume, on impulse she asked her to wait a moment.

'Sit here a minute,' she said, patting the edge of the bed. 'I want to talk to you.'

'What about?' Shannon asked suspiciously as with an air of reluctance she joined her.

'Getting married is a big commitment and I just want to know that you're sure about everything. It's easy to get wrapped up in all the stuff that goes with a wedding and forget what you're actually signing up to.'

'Signing up to? You make it sound like we're going to war.'

'Well I could think of a few who would probably describe where they ended up as not far from it.'

'So, Mum, what is it you want to say?'

The impatience in her daughter's voice made her uncertain of the way forward but she rested her hand on her shoulder and asked, 'Are you sure about Wade?'

'Of course I'm sure – I wouldn't be marrying him if I wasn't sure. And you like him, don't you? You like Wade?'

'Of course I like him.' She wasn't sure how many lies or half-truths she had to give in exchange for one expression that revealed the truth of what she felt. 'And you're sure he'll look after you, keep you in the style you're used to?' Her attempt to leaven it with lightness felt as if it had missed the mark.

'He better do or he'll have me to answer to. Wade's a walkover – he does what he's told, Mum. There isn't anything to worry about.'

She wanted to tell her that with men there was always something to worry about but instead she reached her arm across her daughter's shoulder and pulled her close for a moment.

'Watch my dress.'

'Sorry. Go and take it off.'

'Do you think you could take the hem up a bit – just a temporary job?'

'Shannon, is it not short enough? You don't want to be coming home with a cold.'

'Just a couple of inches,' and she did her pleading little-girl voice.

'If I have to.'

Her daughter pecked her on the side of the head and then hurried off to her room, all her giddy movements sparked by her excitement. When she had gone she quietly pushed the bedroom door closed, then slipped off her own costume and put it on a hanger. She would shorten her daughter's dress and then secretly try to lengthen her own. When she placed it in the wardrobe her eyes focused on the suit she had bought to wear to the wedding, and touching it lightly she told herself that it would do the job, then turning back to the bed gathered the pages Hemmings had given her and stored them safely in a bedside drawer. As she moved across the room her eyes caught the ghost of her reflection in the mirror and for a second standing in her underwear and with feathers in her hair she wondered what she had seen.

Six

A S HE PARKED OUTSIDE the house he saw that the door was already partly opened in anticipation of his arrival but sensed that it was not an invitation to enter, so much as a means to aid a quick departure, and he was disappointed because he felt that this might have been an opportunity to achieve, if not a moment of intimacy, then at least a brief expression of shared parenthood, an affinity of sorts. He was taking Jack to Amsterdam, he was helping her out, even though it meant she was flying to Spain with Gordon. So it seemed like another small incremental step on his slow road to atonement and everything would be better for him if he were to receive even the briefest, most cursory recognition of his penance. And now Susan stood in the open doorway and as she turned her gaze back into the house without any acknowledgement he knew she was summoning Jack, packing him off to allow her to pursue some dream of another life in which he would presumably play no part.

She finally gave him a perfunctory wave but just as he was pondering whether to get out of the car Jack appeared wrestling a black plastic sports bag over his shoulder. He unwound the window as she went to kiss their son who didn't turn his face to her and so she ended up kissing the back of his head.

'All right?' he asked.

She nodded her answer and then he felt her hand resting lightly on top of his. There was still a pale groove where her wedding ring once was which he knew would fade completely in a little while.

'Thanks,' she said, 'thanks for taking Jack. I'm sure you'll have a great time and I'll be here when you get back.' Then moving her hand she lowered her head level with the window to ask Jack if he had remembered to lift his passport from the hall table.

'Yes,' he said, without looking at her, his voice layered with undisguised exasperation.

'Well, good luck,' she said, patting his hand again, and when he smiled up at her she rolled her eyes as if to say that he would need it, and as he started the engine he glanced once more at her but her face was closed and, despite his years of experience, he was unable to discern what she was thinking. So as he drove away he tried to hold her reflection in his side mirror and read what, if anything, was in her touch. He knew that he could still feel something in the sudden shock of that brief moment but didn't know whether it should bring him comfort or continued pain.

'So, Jack, you looking forward to seeing Amsterdam?'

'I'm not a child – I could look after myself for a weekend. I'm sixteen. I'm not afraid of the dark or anything.'

'No you're not a child, Jack, just a complete asshole who doesn't know how to take a mother's kiss,' he wanted to say but instead turned to look at his weekend companion. The hair was black, black as can come out of a bottle, and it made the paleness of his skin look like it had been pressed from snow. Snow that was cold and frosted. The hair was in a new style – bunched up and then slipping sideways as if a black ice-cream cone starting to melt. One thick strand curled like a question mark across the corner of his eye. There was something about him that smelled musty.

'I know you're not, I know you can look after yourself, but we're doing this for your mother.' This part was all right but then he heard himself say, 'It's important to keep her happy.' He pretended to concentrate on his driving and as Jack turned slowly towards him with scorn, he knew he'd just offered him the chance to stick a knife in his side. He winced silently as he anticipated the pierce of its words but his son's head returned again to stare out the side window, his hands momentarily raised to his ears as if he was posing for *The Scream*.

The only sounds were the hiss of his MP3 and the click of his fingers as he texted on his mobile phone. All the way to the airport. Just hiss and click. After a while he didn't mind any more because it took away the pressure of conversation and avoided the possibility of using up all the topics he had garnered in his head as potential connectors for the weekend. But the supposed connectors of flesh and gene – were these just biological figments of the imagination? Was there an inescapable and eternal bond that wasn't the product of DNA profiles? If it didn't exist, could parents and their children come to mutual agreements and advertise for replacements in the Get Connected pages of the *Belfast Telegraph*? And yes he was already becoming familiar with the syntax, their acronyms and their codes, their GSOHs, initially telling himself that it was merely the product of prurient amusement but already knowing that his sense of superiority was gradually eroding to be replaced by some deeper curiosity. And words that had started to hold the promise of some future connection weren't entirely

97

unpleasant. But perhaps in the future it would be possible to advertise a swap for your biological offspring for what might be better suited. How would it go? He penned it as he drove. 'Wanted: house-trained adolescent, no substance abuse, good academic ability, capacity to converse and socially engage. Ability to generate simple pleasure, and occasionally joy, essential.'

'So what do you think, Jack?' he asked quietly without taking his eyes from the road. 'You must think you could do better for a father, and maybe you could. So what would you ask for?'

But the only answer was the hiss and click of his son's fingers pecking the keys, sending messages through time and space. He imagined his conversation was with Jasmine – a curiously sweet-scented name for a girl whose appearance seemed to be designed to frighten, in her exotic and strange hybrid of retro-punk and Goth. How she must hate her name and he had already heard Jack refer to her as Jas. Jack and Jas go up a hill and do whatever they do but he can't imagine them even kissing. So what was being said now in this stream of truncated, abbreviated textspeak that winged its way through the ether?

'So, Jack, go on, tell me what you want, what you'd like your father to be?' he asked again and perhaps this time he said it too loudly, or out of the corner of his eye his son caught the movement of his lips.

'What?' he asked, prising free one of the earphones. 'What did you say?'

'I was wondering who you were listening to?'

'The Death Pixels,' he said then ended the conversation by letting the earphone slip back into place.

'That's good, Jack. The Death Pixels. Never heard of them but that's good too.'

He tried to imagine a father that Jack might want but couldn't construct it in his imagination and because he was unable to construct it, it meant he couldn't aspire to become it. It was presumably a given that he'd want a father who stayed faithful to his mother and who in the middle of his life didn't suddenly prove pathetically flawed and self-seeking. If that was a given then it was also true that children allowed you no life that wasn't at their behest and that they liked things, for better or worse, to stay in the same predictable place. He had come too late to realise that they wanted cornerstones wedged tight no matter how much they might rebel against the foundations which you sought to offer their life or the boundaries you tried to give them. And what sort of son would he want? As he drove through the city the answer was easy because it was set in his memory as sharp and clear as the early morning light on the beach, with the zing and zest of the waves lacing and crimping the sand as it pulled away, leaving the rock pools laden with the fruits of the sea. And the eight-year-old boy has a green net on a bamboo cane and a bucket and every pool is a brimming briny adventure where startled crabs scuttle from under their hiding stones when he turns them over and Jack squeals with excitement and fear at the size of this one. And in the momentarily clouded water it disappears for a second but he sees it and he's almost falling in as he tries to scoop it into his net. 'Go on, Jack!' he says and then it's half in and half out of the net but somehow he manages to bag it and slop it into the plastic bucket. 'Wait till your mother sees this!' And he's holding the bucket level with his head like he's a champion and they're laughing and into the laughter flows the light of the morning and the seeming promise of all that lies ahead. So stop the home movie just there – no need to roll it any further, just freeze-frame it, letting it become the future as well as the past. When his son still showed the tangy, sea-sprayed excitement of life on his face and everything was all on the surface with no hidden hinterlands and when he still valued a father's approbation.

They were on the motorway and making good time now that they'd escaped the Friday home-going traffic of the city. He glanced at Jack who was scrunched into the seat with his legs pulled into him. Black jeans, baseball boots and a black hoodie with the zip pulled up to his chin. With his black hair, like a thin stick of liquorice. In one hand his mobile phone, in the other his MP3. Passports to another world. He wondered what the Death Pixels sounded like. Taking the child he once was would have been fun and he constructed an imaginary programme in his head of bicycle hire, canal-boat rides, and the shared pathos of Anne Frank's house. A McDonald's Happy Meal, a visit to a toy shop and home again with stories to tell. Easy peasy lemon squeezy. At least he hadn't completely balked at Dylan, might even have seemed mildly interested. For that alone he was grateful even though it meant buying two new tickets on eBay at a totally ripped-off price and then partly offsetting the loss by selling his one for an equally exorbitant sum. That was Saturday night taken care of but it left the remainder of that evening, the rest of tomorrow and Sunday morning to accommodate. And just as he pondered the problems this presented he remembered with a shiver of embarrassment the unbelievably, inexplicably stupid guff he'd told Stan Stenson about an entirely imaginary piece of research involving Van Gogh and Gauguin. Stan had thought he was taking the piss and now, to prove he wasn't, he would have to come up with something even though he had no idea of how he was going to do it. He lowered his head towards the steering wheel in a squirm of shame then straightened when he saw that his son was staring at him. It felt like the Death Pixels were playing in his head and the only tune they played was a tune of pain. How could he have been so stupid?

They had to slow down as they entered a coned-off section of the motorway and for a second he thought he saw an Indian in the back seat of the taxi in front of them, a feather sticking up above the seat. He needed to pull himself together, needed to have all his wits about him if he was going to help them both get through this weekend. Perhaps there was another way he could escape the mess with his head of department, perhaps he could start to paint again, conjure up a small show in a local gallery. Perhaps even have it linked in some way he couldn't yet imagine to the work of the two painters. Surely anything was possible with a bit of invention. And when a short while later they were close enough to the airport to see a plane coming in to land and Jack squirmed in his seat to catch it, he blinked his eyes and saw instead a night café under a yellow canopy and a blue shock of sky, white spotted with a snowfall of stars.

After they got their overnight bags out of the car she watched her husband stopping to write the letter and number of their location on the back of his car-park ticket, then carefully place it in his wallet. It was what he always did, prompted presumably by a fear of not being able to find the car on his return, a fear of getting lost. He had been quiet on the journey to the airport and when he had spoken it had been about some aspect of the business, some small and to her inconsequential thing that they had forgotten to do. While he had driven she had tried her best to search his face, trawl the timbre of his voice for some sign that he had already been unfaithful to her. Sometimes she used the word strayed rather than unfaithful because she was able to conceive of it as a temporary loss of direction before the possibility of return. And she knew she would let him return and felt both the shame and what she supposed was the weakness of that. But only if it was private and without public humiliation.

As she watched him pat the wallet in his inside pocket to reassure himself that it was safely stored, she wondered how he could be so precise about so many things and uncommitted about others. So as he set off towards the terminal with the bag he had weighed and measured to ensure that it would meet the requirements for hand luggage, and as she followed him, there was a stirring of resentment. All she wanted was a steadiness, a personal and mutual equilibrium that didn't need her to strive for something, that didn't live on the edge of unpredictability. She didn't want to fight with the machines, didn't want to measure herself, didn't want to have her whole life weighed in the balance and found wanting by someone who didn't know anything about her. The trouble was that she had started to understand that there was no steadfastness or safety when you were dependent on someone else. She couldn't tell any more where love ended and the need for something that was akin to but more than security began, where you had evolved or regressed to a point where it felt as if you only existed in the affirmation of another.

'Richard, can you slow down a bit? You're going too fast,' she said, surprised by the irritation in her voice.

'Sorry,' he said, stopping to turn to her. 'Is that bag too heavy? Let me carry it.'

'It's not heavy, you're just in a bit of a rush. We've plenty of time. The flight doesn't go for another two and a half hours.'

'Sorry,' he said again. 'It could take extra time to go through security.'

'This is supposed to be a break,' she insisted, as if in an argument, 'and I don't want to be worn out before we even get there.'

'OK, we'll slow down. Let me carry your bag.'

'I can carry my bag, Richard,' she said as she strode past him towards the terminal.

Perhaps the whole idea had been a terrible mistake. It was a crazy time to be going away. It was a crazy idea, too, that she had let burrow into her head. How could she have been so stupid, so inexplicably cast adrift from the normal sensibilities of her life? As she entered the terminal she searched for some way to turn them round and abandon the weekend, thought even of saying she was taken ill but she knew she couldn't pull it off and that she didn't have the skills or capacity to deceive him face to face. She had also started to believe that if things were to tumble out into the open, they would spiral away in directions she couldn't anticipate or control.

'I'm the one who couldn't keep up,' he said as he set his bag at her feet. 'That gym must be doing you good. Perhaps I should join too.'

'You don't have the time,' she said, trying now to smooth the irritation that had previously edged her voice. 'And anyway you never put on any weight that I can see.'

'I've added a few pounds over the last while,' he insisted.

'Well they don't show. I seem to put it on for us both.'

'They don't show,' he said and smiled at her.

'Then it's not gym membership you need but an eye test. We better check in. Which desk is it?' As she turned to look she felt his hand lightly on her arm.

'Are you all right, Marion?'

103

'I'm fine, just a bit nervous about going away and leaving everything, I suppose.'

'There's nothing to worry about. We've got a good team around us. If I thought there was a problem we wouldn't be going. So try and relax, try to enjoy yourself – it's not that often we get the chance to get away.'

'So you really want to come?'

'Of course I do. And if you want to know I hate this Christmas period. When you're not selling plants any more but all that tacky stuff.'

They joined the short queue in front of the desk and suddenly she felt self-conscious as if somehow they looked different to everyone else. She tried to think of things to say as a way of hiding her discomfort.

'So you know it's a load of tat?' she asked.

'Of course. You'd have to be blind not to see that – all those flashing lights and blingy ornaments. It gets worse every year and you know what? The tackier it is the better it sells.'

'And the Santa Claus climbing our chimney – that's a piece of good taste?'

'It was just a laugh. And since I put it up I've sold at least a dozen and the last one was to a man who said he was driving by, saw it and wanted one just the same. The girls enjoyed it, didn't they?'

'I think so. When are they going home?'

'Week after next. Listen, Marion, I was wondering what you'd think of this.' He shuffled his bag forward with his foot. 'How would you feel about us taking everyone out for a Christmas meal, as a thank you before we close and they all go home?'

'Can we afford it?'

'On the year we've had I would say so and we've even sold three of those black fibre-optic trees since Monday.'

'A black tree at Christmas – it's not right. And they're terrible to touch – creepy, horrible. We shouldn't sell them, no matter how much money we make on them. People have no taste any more.'

'At least the needles don't drop. Are you looking forward to having Judith home again?'

They shuffled forward. 'I'd like to see her back home for good and a wedding ring on her finger. What happens if she meets someone in France and they settle there and we have to get on a plane every time we want to see our grandchildren?'

But there was no time for him to answer because they were next at the desk and she watched as he handed over both their passports and the booking form and gave the young woman the lightness of his charm. A black Christmas tree. She squirmed a little as she remembered the synthetic feel, the stupid blue fibre-optic lights, then smothered it with the thought of the large tree they would soon cut and bring to the house, where it would fill the room with a forest freshness, and how she would dress it with the decorations that owed little to fashion but instead represented the history of their family. The older bits and pieces, the things the children had made in primary school, the birds with the delicate, coloured tails, the favourite baubles that had been acquired in various cities and at different times.

After going through security he got them both a coffee and they found seats but it was as if they had run out of things to talk about and so they sat and watched those around them, glancing from time to time for news of the gate at which they were to board.

'Anka seems a nice girl,' she said suddenly, pressing the rim of the coffee cup to her lips.

'She's a good worker. They all are. Could teach some people here a thing or two.'

'Perhaps she won't return after Christmas. Perhaps she'll get home and decide to stay.'

'She'll come back,' he said.

'How do you know?'

'I just know.'

'Has she said something?'

'Just that she wants to raise as much money as she can and eventually start her own business.'

'Here or in Poland?'

'I'm not sure. She wants to open a florist shop.'

'She'll never make the money for that,' she said.

'I'm just talking off the top of my head now but I've been thinking about that. You know that the Clements are putting their flower shop in the main street up for sale? I was thinking, now just thinking, that it might be a good investment for us. And you wouldn't get a better person than Anka to manage it. I haven't said anything to her about it or anything of course. Just a thought, need to do the figures and all and hear what you think obviously.'

'And you haven't mentioned it to her?'

'No, of course not. So what do you think?'

'I think the Clements wouldn't be selling if there was a good profit to be made. There's not enough all-year-round money in it. Look at how many of them are selling other stuff – arts and crafts, jewellery, everything under the sun. And at the end of the day what do we really know about Anka?'

'She's a hard worker. And she seems an honest, straightforward girl. And if she has the ambition and the drive it could be a winner.'

She watched him take the lid off his coffee and then peer into the cup as if the future might be discerned there. She wanted him to look at her so that she might see what their future was. It was an idea he had clearly been hatching for some time but she knew already that she would never agree to it. A mistress was something else entirely. That was outside the realms of possibility. She was certain about that.

'But does she actually know anything about flowers? Does she know anything about what's involved in running a business? It all sounds a bit fantastic to me.'

'It's only an idea, Marion – I'm not suggesting that we're about to do it. It's only an idea. We shouldn't even be discussing this sort of stuff on a holiday.'

She watched him lift his eyes to the information screen and sensed he was embarrassed. He had spilled it out sooner than he intended and she believed he knew how unconvincing it had sounded. She swirled the remains of the coffee but already it had started to taste bitter and it was with a sense of relief she realised that it wasn't compulsory to finish it.

She knew most of the other members of the tribe but, still self-conscious, she tried to shelter at the edge of their excited meeting where hugging arms flailed and flapped like the wings of birds. There were a couple of girls she didn't recognise but most of the others were either longstanding friends or workmates of her daughter. They were squealing as they admired each other's costumes, Shannon doing a catwalk twirl and pirouette after the slightest encouragement, and she felt again that she was too old to be there and too old to be dressed as an Indian squaw. She was aware of people looking at them and even though she could see most of them enjoying the joke it did not ease her discomfort. She was also mindful that in a short period of time she would be on her first flight and that too made her increasingly apprehensive.

For a moment she thought of turning and running towards the exit but as she searched for it she heard her daughter say, 'Doesn't my mum look great, girls?' and Shannon's hand was on her shoulder, presenting her to the others. And then they were all agreeing and touching her costume admiringly as if she was a child in her new birthday dress.

'I'm too old for this, girls,' she said to hide the embarrassment of their collective attention but they shushed her into silence, reassuring her again that she looked great. Two young men strolled by eyeing them up, one of them saying something she couldn't quite catch, but in an instant Lorrie was telling him that she would scalp him except he hadn't any hair while the other girls whooped and made Indian war-dance noises by flapping their hands against their mouths.

Then they were heading off through security but they got no further than the desk at the entrance when she was stopped by the official checking their boarding cards.

'You can't take the hatchet on, love,' he said, holding his hand up to her as if she was a flow of traffic he was trying to halt.

'It's not a hatchet – it's a tomahawk,' Shannon said.

'I don't care what it's called, she can't take it on to the plane.'

'It's not real. It's rubber,' she said, taking it out of her waistband and stabbing the palm of her hand with it.

'It doesn't matter, love, what it's made of – you can't take it on a plane. You can't take any imitation weapons or such things on board.'

'It's not as if she's going to hijack the plane with a rubber tomahawk,' Shannon said and her voice was edged with the belligerence that she increasingly recognised as her daughter's response to what she didn't like.

'You shouldn't use that type of language and if you use it again I'm calling security and the only thing you're going to see is an interview room.'

'She's sorry,' she said, pushing her daughter forward with her hand. 'What will I do with it?' She offered it to him, handing it over by the plastic handle as if to avoid the possibility of injuring his hand.

'I'll store it here,' he said, still looking at Shannon as he took it. 'You can collect it when you return.'

'Thanks,' she said, smiling and submissively following his direction to which queue to join.

'What a jobsworth,' Shannon hissed at her. 'A little power and it goes to their head.'

'I suppose he has to do his job,' she said as she tried to read the instructions about what wasn't allowed in her hand luggage. All the focus on security only encouraged her imagination to construct doomsday scenarios that trembled her hand and made her conscious of her breathing. Then as she walked through the metal detector she thought of Kevin the doorman at work and how much he would enjoy this job and how he'd personally search everyone. She remembered, too, the photographs that she lifted each morning and suddenly she realised that she, too, was in a story that would end in a photograph, a photograph that would show her smiling and be just like the ones that sat on the office desks and served to tell the world that they had a life that existed beyond the daily grind. So perhaps it was a good thing that she had come, that these moments would give her admittance to whatever world existed for people other than herself. She thought, too, of Mrs Hemmings' missing bracelet and as she walked through the gate for a second she imagined that the alarm would explode into hysterical noise and the sound of rushing feet as hands stretched out to grab her and rush her away. But there was only the security guard waving her forward and a second later she was reunited with her possessions and focused on putting her suede boots back on and buckling the belt she had been told to remove.

'Hell's bells,' he said as he saw them filing into the departure lounge and knowing that Jack couldn't hear him nudged him with his elbow. 'Red Indians and they're getting our plane sure as anything. That's all we need – a hen party and probably half tanked already.'

'They're not called Red Indians.'

'They look like Red Indians to me.'

'They're called Native Americans.'

'You're quite right, Jack, but it's a bit academic and whether they're Red Indians or Native Americans they're definitely millies. And try to make sure we don't get seats anywhere near them or it'll be a long flight.'

'What are millies?' Jack asked, taking off his headphones for the first time since they had left home.

But as he thought of how to explain the word he knew it couldn't be done without appearing a snob or a misogynist or something it was better not to be in the eyes of your son so he just shrugged dismissively and pointed vaguely in their direction. 'Girls like these,' he said and then pretended he was studying the flight-information screen. Almost immediately he realised that Jack was no longer engaged with the Death Pixels and so in theory at least was available for conversation.

'So you and Jas seem to be getting on well,' he said, glancing at his son and tentatively exploring the possibility of a response but Jack merely and almost imperceptibly tilted his head. 'So what's she planning to do next year?'

'She's going to tech to do Theatre Studies.'

'Theatre Studies? That's good,' he said, although he didn't know if it was or not. Then asked, 'So she wants to be an actress?'

'I don't know,' Jack said. And he knew that if asked another question his son would put the earphones back in so instead he sank into his seat and watched the hen party on the other side of the lounge. It was the risk you took flying to Amsterdam on a weekend – stag parties, hen parties, lowlife in general – but at least it didn't come close to that nightmare of the sailing to Stranraer, when by the very worst of luck he had found himself trapped between rabid sets of Rangers and Celtic supporters who despite the police presence terrorised the boat with sectarian warfare.

'So, Karen, you work in an old people's home?'

'Yes and your name is Martina, so you work with Shannon.'

'That's right. And what's it like working in an old people's home? It can't be much fun.'

'Well it's not a bundle of laughs but you could do worse and it pays the bills.'

'Do they die?' Martina asked, leaning closer so that Karen could smell the drink on her breath.

'Sometimes but not that often. It's not a nursing home where people are ill.'

'I hate old people. Sometimes they come up to your counter and want you to make them up. I hate it when they do that. What do they expect? You can't work miracles. But at least they always buy the stuff afterwards.'

'I suppose they're desperate, Martina.'

'I suppose they are. I never want to be old. Your skin goes all leathery and dead.' She squirmed then leaned back again before saying, 'You've got great skin, Karen, for your age and all. Really, with a bit of highlighting you could do a lot for yourself. Does Shannon not look after you?'

'It takes Shannon so long to do herself that she's no time for anyone else,' she said, glancing over to where her daughter was laughing at something someone had said.

'Well, Karen, before this weekend is over I'll do your make-up so you won't recognise yourself.'

The thought of not recognising herself only added to her increasing feeling of disorientation. She had never been in an airport before and to be in one dressed as she was seemed intensely strange. If anything were to happen to her during the flight or the weekend itself she believed that she would never be reconnected to herself and be forever adrift in some limbo world. And suddenly she felt weightless as if the slightest breeze might carry her away. Martina was still talking but the words streamed past her and then into their slipstream came a voice telling them that boarding was commencing.

'What's the point of rushing? We'll only have to stand for ages. And anyway our number hasn't been called,' she said, laying her hand on Richard's arm to stop him getting up.

'If we end up beside those girls it'll be a long flight. I think they're already high as kites and we aren't in the air yet.'

'They're just out for a bit of fun,' she said, surprised to hear herself defending them. And suddenly she knew that she envied these young women. Their friendship, their laughter, their not having to care about anyone else. Perhaps she was a fool to herself to worry about so many things. For some reason she wished she was back sitting at her computer where she found a pleasure in looking at things without any of them ever looking back and where everything could be made to happen with no more than the click of a mouse and where she was the only one pointing. She clutched her magazine and watched as a scrimmage started near the gate. She flicked her passport open and studied her photograph. In another year the passport would have expired and she wondered if she could renew it online. The photograph wasn't so bad – she looked quite young and her hair was shorter than she wore it now. The Indians were still squealing and it made her think of the friendships she too had once shared and that day when they were the Four Marys and intoxicated with their freedom from parents and when a tiny caravan assumed the splendour of an exotic Eastern palace. They didn't need alcohol, would have giggled for ever if a boy had so much as glanced sideways at them. And feeling safe and not thinking of what days were to come or what they might bring and the water tracing the outline of their feet as they paddled and squealed like these young women. Sometimes, too, when they sat round the little pull-out table with cups of tea or cold drinks they would catch each other's eye and suddenly know they were playing at adults and pass their laughter at the ludicrousness of this from one to the other, until the cups threatened to spill their contents.

Richard stood up as if he thought there was a risk the plane would go without him and imposed himself in a space in the queue, then signalled her to join him. She thought of not getting up, of just sitting there as the thickening throng behind him carried him forward and out of sight. Of course he would turn and call her to come but she might not answer him and then it would all be too late. The sun had baked the inside of the caravan – was it really true that summers were hotter then? – and everything smelled like they were inside a cardboard box and there was the sweet – was it sweet? – scent of gas. It was a wonder they weren't all poisoned and then she thought of Lillian who died a young woman and left a husband and three children. What made it pick her out of all of them? Were the spores there even on that day? She wondered if at any time after she found out, did that moment slip into her memory because it was probable that she would think back over her life. Did she question why she was chosen and not them? She wondered, too, if when she did that she felt a bitterness. It was Lillian who always started the game where each in turn had to say who they fancied, after, on pain of death, swearing never to reveal the names to anyone outside the group. She will never reveal any of the names because she doesn't remember any of them, not even the one she confessed. Watching the young woman, who was probably the one getting married, showing her passport to the attendant, she wondered what was the name of the boy she loved and if he would prove worthy of that love. Then Richard was calling her again and, gathering her hand luggage and magazine, she went to join him.

She had to force herself up the steps of the plane, lagging behind the others. It made no sense to her at all. She associated flight with lightness, feathers, small things, so as she glanced at the plane she couldn't understand how such a thing encased in a metallic heaviness could ever rise into the air and then stay there. It seemed totally ridiculous, positively suicidal to be mounting these frail metal steps that clanged against her heart with every heavy tread that rattled and strained. She tried to keep her eyes on the heels of the person in front so that she wouldn't let herself take in the side of the plane, its black pouting engines, its heavy slabs of metal. In the doorway the stewardess smiled at her and she felt a moment of relief that she was stepping into an interior that seemed vaguely familiar. Perhaps it was the smell that reminded her of the offices she cleaned each morning, a strange mixture of the synthetic and the human, a sense too of a space that belonged to people who were no longer there.

She got stuck in the aisle behind a small man struggling to stow his bag in the overhead locker and when she eventually sidled past him she found herself separated from the tribe by other passengers. She was held up some more and when she reached her group it was clear that there were no free seats. She looked in panic for Shannon and when she caught her daughter's eye she stood up and looked around her, shrugged her shoulders and then pointed to a single seat a few rows in front. There was no choice about it and so after asking if the seat was free she tried to manoeuvre her bag into the small space that was left. She had to stand on her toes and then, remembering the shortness of her skirt, sank back on her heels.

'Can I help you with that?' he said and as she nodded her thanks he stood up and edged past her. She hoped it wouldn't take long and was suddenly conscious that all the people in the seats behind were probably staring at her. But he had to jiggle the other bags and as he did so she smiled nervously at the boy in the window seat who was looking at her but who turned his eyes away when she did so and busied himself with his MP3 player. His face was pale against the darkness of his hair.

'That's it,' he said, slamming the lid on the locker and slipping back into his seat.

'Thanks,' she said, squirming as she tried to free the safety belt she had sat on. 'There wasn't much room.'

She accidentally pushed her elbow into him as she finally released the belt. 'Sorry.' She felt flustered, claustrophobic, increasingly confined in some bad dream. 'Not much room.'

'Hi,' he said. 'Or should it be Hiawatha?'

'Hi. Hia . . . ?'

'Hiawatha – an Indian girl.'

'It's my daughter's idea. Nothing to do with me and I don't really know why I'm here,' she said, finally clicking the belt shut.

'Her hen party?'

'Don't know why we have to go all the way to Amsterdam for it or why I'm going dressed like this.' She tried to stretch her skirt towards her knees but there was little give.

'You must be close for her to ask you. This is my son Jack,' he said, pressing his son's arm until he turned his head and looked at her again. She raised her hand in greeting and got an almost imperceptible nod in response. 'I don't think he'll invite me on his stag night. He's listening to the Death Pixels.'

She didn't know what to reply but the stewardess was already asking for their attention and doing the safety drill. She watched intently, only glancing away to study the safety card. It seemed vital to remember how to tie the life jacket and where to locate the whistle. In her imagination she practised the brace position. Shannon should have kept her a seat – she didn't want to die beside a stranger. Even the card seemed an inadequate preparation for disaster, hopelessly imprecise with its arrows and cartoon illustrations. Her palms were beginning to sweat again and her mouth was dry. She thought of the photographs on the office desks and the lives they represented, of all the times she had wanted access to their worlds and how she had sometimes thought that they were barred to her because she wasn't clever enough, didn't have the right certificates. But now it struck her that perhaps her exclusion was a failure of courage. She couldn't step inside because she wasn't brave enough to leave behind what she was prepared to accept were the limits of who she was. People flew in planes every day – the girls at work said it was safer than being in a car – so why should she now be sitting in the tightening grip of fear? Perhaps the flight was her moment of initiation and if only she could endure it then everything would be opened to her. Her hands gripped the armrests as the engines started and the plane began to move along the runway.

She told herself that she was brave enough for this, had already shown how strong she was from the moment when three months pregnant she had read his letter telling her that he was leaving. Written in pencil on a page torn from a spiral notebook, the edges little curls of white that flaked away in her hand. So he wasn't ready to be a father, it had all been a mistake, it was better to put things right before it went any further, he was sorry but it was better to be honest. He had tried, really tried, but it was no use. Of course he hadn't told her that he had met someone else – she would find this out only later. It was a page taken from the book he used in his PVC windows business. He had made her a customer and was settling the account. It was a bill she had to pay and she told herself that she had met it in full, bringing up a child on her own, a child that he had never once made any attempt to see and had been happy when she had rejected his offer of a pathetic amount of money. Others had told her she was a fool, that she should have got legal advice and fleeced him for every penny she could squeeze out of him, but she wanted nothing from him, not even his money. To take it would have been to taint how she saw her child. There was no part of him in her daughter and she would not acknowledge any form of claim that the money might bring.

She pushed back into the seat and told herself that her bravery had already been proved, that nothing could be harder than that, that there was nothing to worry about. And the one thing she knew above all others was that no man would ever steal her trust, that she couldn't be fooled again. She tried to turn her head to see Shannon but it wasn't possible and then the plane was rushing down the runway and she had no thoughts for anything else.

He didn't like take-offs and landings. They always made him, even in his disbelief, utter a little prayer that he might be allowed to return safely to his family. Jack's head was fixed on the window taking in every second of their lift-off. He could glimpse enough to see that the world had suddenly angled and then the plane seemed to groan and shudder a little and he heard her say 'Shit' and then 'Oh my God' and her hand pushed against his and almost instantaneously their fingers gripped and knotted. He felt the force of her fear in her tightening grasp and as he turned to where she strained against the back of the seat as if trying to push herself through it he said, 'It's OK, it's OK, we're almost up. Everything's OK.' And then as they climbed he felt her hand slip away and she was apologising, her fluttering hands an embarrassed fan in front of her face.

'It's my first time,' she said. 'I'm sorry for being so stupid.'

'First time can be a bit scary but you'll be all right now. I'm Alan, by the way.' And he offered her his hand again and she shook it quickly but didn't give him her name. 'And you're . . . ?'

'Karen,' she said but she was glancing down the aisle and he knew she didn't want him to talk to her so he lifted the flight magazine and flicked the pages. A few seconds later she did the same and seemed to squeeze herself smaller and almost into the pages, plucking at the corners as she turned them. He bent down and in his bag found his copy of Van Gogh's letters to Theo. Perhaps his blurted fabrication to Stan Stenson had not been so foolish after all, perhaps there really was something credible that could be garnered from the idea. He needed of course to identify the paintings done just before Gauguin's arrival in Arles and then compare them with those after and try to make some connections between the two men's work. It wasn't entirely impossible that some symbiotic relationship might be detected, and at the end of the day what did it matter so long as he could find some journal to publish it and he did have an ability to spark the suggestion of profundity from rubbing a few twigs together? He believed the key to success was to assert things confidently and even if it evoked mountains of rebuttal he could claim that his provocative article had sparked a new intellectual debate.

He scanned a few of the letters, drafting grandiose sentences as he did so, and then flicking the pages his eyes caught a painting he hadn't seen in twenty years. It was *Old Man with his Head in his Hands* and, if his memory was right, painted shortly before Vincent's death. There was a shiver of recognition, a regeneration of the intensity of bleakness that he always felt in its presence. The old man's face was hidden behind his hands and he was dressed in blue peasant clothes as he sat slumped forward in a chair. The bare floorboards, the inability of the fire's meagre flames to kindle any consolation pressed home on the viewer – it was a picture that always frightened him in its unrelenting presentation of uncomforted human suffering. And although he tried to shrug it off the painting taunted him with a vision of a future he didn't want to contemplate. He thought of his flat above the florist's shop, of George's funeral cortège, of the single rower sculling through the dusk. Closing the book he slipped it into the pouch of the seat in front.

He always turned the flight magazine to the back pages where he perused what might be bought if he had the inclination and as always he pointed out particular objects to invite her scorn for their supposed rip-off prices. She was aware of a slight scrupulousness in him that was thankfully restricted only to business and if it was softened by his willing generosity to her, it was probably still the hallmark of every successful businessman. He knew what everything cost and sometimes she didn't want that but what was it she did want? A brief moment of moderate recklessness? A spontaneous gesture that put nothing important at risk? And after all they had worked so hard for what they had. She flicked the pages of the magazine and looked at a feature on trendy holiday spots. Why did they still work so hard, so hard that they felt guilty about taking a weekend off? And who would benefit from it all? Did they spend their lives married to work so that they could simply pass it on to their children, children who if truth be told she suspected of taking their numerous generosities a little for granted?

She shook her head dismissively when he asked if she wanted this or that. Every other thing he did irritated her now and she knew that she had to get control of it or the weekend would turn into a disaster whose consequences might prove destructive of all she still valued. She anticipated that he would order a drink or something to eat and then there would be all that smiling charm as he paid the stewardess. He had already discreetly studied their legs as they went about their business, no doubt had weighed them up and made a hypothetical choice. Perhaps a drink would be a good thing, a glass of red wine to help smooth the sharp edges of the tension she felt seeping through – she wasn't sure whether it was her head or her body or both. For a year she had increasingly felt the recurring presence of anxiety, a real and pressing anxiousness but vague and unpredictable in its comings and goings. If it got worse she would have to visit her doctor. But what if he were to ask her about the reasons for her anxiety? She would have to say she didn't know and in part at least that was true. And no doubt he'd be reluctant to dole out a pill but would probably tell her to get some exercise, to join something or to take up something like yoga, suggested cures that she knew were only likely to increase what she suffered from.

Suddenly a flower shop seemed not a bad idea, a flower shop not for Anka but for themselves. Why not think of downsizing, selling the garden centre that required so much constant year-long work and taking up a small business that wouldn't need half the time or commitment? They'd surely make enough from the sale to see them through and the shop would merely tick over, providing enough to meet their living costs. But then she remembered the house and realised that it would have to be part of any sale and that was something she couldn't contemplate so easily. It wasn't just their home, it was their children's home – where they came back to, where they would visit this Christmas. She felt that so many of the important elements of her life were ingrained in its fabric that to leave it would be to leave part of herself.

A shop where young women came with their mothers to choose their wedding flowers. She wondered when she would do that with Judith. If her daughter were to marry someone in France perhaps it would be his mother who would play that role and perhaps all Judith's life, its foundations and its future, would be established permanently far from home. She glanced at the magazine again which shrank Europe to two pages and where flight lines threaded countries seamlessly together. And of course there was always the computer which could send email and photographs and, although she didn't know how, she believed it was possible to talk and see each other if you had the right pieces of equipment.

'All right, love?' he asked, leaning his shoulder lightly into hers.

'When they come with the drinks, get me a red wine.'

'Do you want something to eat?'

'No, just a glass of wine.'

He nodded and leaned his head out into the aisle as if to check the trolley's progress. She closed the magazine and tried to imagine what flower arrangements she and Judith might choose for her wedding.

It was the second time that day that a woman had touched his hand and, while ultimately neither moment had been unpleasant, both had only served to remind him of what he didn't have. He hadn't even realised until after the split how fundamental a pleasure it was to be touched by another, no matter how briefly or simply, and perhaps it was something that transcended pleasure and was rooted in a deeper need. His own touch was a poor substitute and could not compare to the fleeting brush of a stranger's skin, even if it was the subsequently embarrassed hand of someone dressed as an Indian. He knew that she had shrunk into the seat so that no part of her touched any part of him and he felt sorry for her, wanted to give himself a kind of reference to reassure her, to let her know that he wasn't a predator who would try to exchange trinkets and glass beads for her favours. But he knew, too, that he was a little dizzy, a little vulnerable in his need, and he had felt it long enough to understand that it was potentially reckless and given to unexpected and unwise actions. He remembered with a wince the hopelessly naked print of his need on the clay and how everything had seemed to spiral out from that misjudgement, so no matter how pleasant her touch had been and indeed the knowledge that they had a landing to share, he wasn't going to let himself fall into that trap again. She seemed to have hidden in a still silence so he was surprised when he heard her speak.

'Have you been to Amsterdam before?' she asked, her head half-angled to him but her eyes looking at the seat in front.

'A good number of times – first when I was a student, and that's not yesterday.' She spread the magazine over the bareness of her knees. 'You've never been before?'

'No, never.'

'You'll like it. Everybody likes it.'

'I have a list of all the things I'm supposed to do but I don't think I'll get to see too many of them on this trip. Are you on a holiday?'

'We're going to see Bob Dylan in concert and look at a few paintings.'

'Is Bob Dylan not dead?'

'No, not yet but there mightn't be too many more opportunities.'

'And you like paintings?'

'I teach in the art college, for my sins, so I better say yes to that.'

It seemed that the last bit of information had silenced her and her hand smoothed the pages of the magazine as if she was ironing them. He felt a need to remove any remoteness his job might have created.

'My father always wanted me to be a painter and decorator. He was probably right – I'd have made more money, that's for sure.'

She smiled lightly and he wanted to ask her what she did but instead he fell back into silence and tried not to think about how in a few hours Susan would be flying off to Spain with Gordon to explore the possibilities of a new life. Would Jack go with her if she managed to set herself up in some business or would he choose to stay with him? But already he knew that if he opted to stay it would only nominally be with him and that considerations other than filial affection would prompt his decision. He glanced at the back of his son's head as he pressed his face close to the window and then watched as he started to take photographs with his mobile phone.

'What are you doing, Jack?'

'Taking photographs.'

'What of?'

'Just random photos – there were some lights out there a moment ago. Might get a shot of a UFO.'

'You think there might be a UFO out there?'

'It's pretty likely. There's been lots of sightings this month.'

'How do you know?'

'There's websites log them all. Sometimes they've got photographs. If they publish your photograph they pay you.'

'You don't think that might encourage people to fake shots?' he asked as Jack turned away from the window and, with a black slick of hair sliding over one eye, started to view the pictures he had taken.

'Dad, this is for real, not kids' made-up stuff. These guys

are experts so they're not going to be conned by half-assed pictures of Frisbees or stuff like that. Some of them have worked for the government so they know all about the cover-ups and about what goes on in places like Area 51.'

'Area 51?' He hadn't heard his son sound so animated in a long time and even if it was some half-baked fantasy he wasn't going to rain on the parade.

'It's a secret camp hidden in the Nevada desert where they store UFOs and aliens and do research on them without telling anyone.'

'You think they have aliens there?' He did his best to make his question sound sincere but didn't manage to carry it off.

'Yes, they do and even guys who were NASA astronauts know there's a cover-up. The government thinks we'd all panic or something if we knew.' He turned his head away as if he'd said more than he should have and stared out of the window again.

He didn't know what to say and what was worse he realised that he didn't know anything about what was spinning round in his son's head. Perhaps, too, the UFOs were his fault and he remembered the Sunday afternoon when he had been minding Jack and Caroline while Susan was making tea. They were young, sitting on the settee with him and watching *ET*, but somehow he had managed to doze off towards the end and when Susan had entered she found the two of them sitting crying at ET's impending death, uncomforted, while their father blissfully snored. Perhaps that was the moment aliens took up residence in his son's interior landscape. He looked at the glossy black clot of his head staring into the darkness. He had to say something, didn't want to let the moment slip away.

'Do you think they really landed on the moon?'

Jack looked at him as if checking he was for real and his eyes widened with what was obvious disdain.

'Of course they landed on the moon. Only complete idiots believe that it was all a con. And do you think the Russians would have let them get all that credit if it was? It's all straightforward, everybody apart from no-brainers knows the answers. The flag blowing in the wind when there isn't any wind is because it was attached to a spring which didn't open properly so it's not blowing, just crumpled. And the no-stars bit is because the camera speed couldn't record the tiny spots of light. Like you could fake it all in a studio. As if.'

As if indeed. He had been admonished if a little reassured to know that there were others out there his son considered no-brainers. It was clear that there were some conspiracies he signed up to but which ones these were and which he treated with scorn he was unable to say. It was just another of the many things he didn't know and he reflected on whether the end-product of the weekend would be to merely emphasise the absence of this knowledge. Then the lights dimmed and he settled back into his seat and wondered if the stranger on his other side would need a hand to hold when they came in to land.

Seven

H E INSISTED ON TAKING a taxi from Central Station
although she would have been perfectly happy to catch
a tram. She liked the trams, the way they surreptitiously
pushed you up against the mystery of other people's lives,
where you could privately observe intimacies of appearance and relationship. But although both their small cases
were on wheels and didn't require much lugging he said it
would be awkward getting on and off. He chatted enthusiastically to their taxi driver who told him that the weather
had been very mild for that time of year and if they were
lucky they might even see a bit of sun. But now it was the
city's lights that held her gaze as they blurred and coalesced
into a glitter of neon and Christmas decorations, a steady
pulse against the eyes. The lights were pretty, crystalline,
icing the streets in shivering spangles. She already sensed
the quickening power of the city, its streets and squares
crowded with people and not just young people, the way
it would be at home on Friday night, but all ages and all
ethnic backgrounds while the cafés and restaurants threw
warm yellow-yolked invitations from their open doors. So
much here, even in winter, was in the open and she understood this was the right place and the right time to do what

it was she had decided. How would he react? She didn't know and part of her didn't care because she couldn't go on living in the shadow of uncertainty. She had a right to her life and it was the first step to making it into the shape she wanted and not having to care about what anyone else thought. And she wasn't going back to the gym, was never setting foot inside its door again, and if he wanted he could cancel the subscription and claim some of his money back.

They passed Dam Square where the lights of a giant Christmas tree trembled slightly in the breeze so it looked as if the whole tree was lightly quivering, not from cold, but rather the way a young girl newly dressed in her finery might shimmer herself to the world. She thought of the four acres of Christmas trees that they grew at home. It had been wholly her idea and she had done the research about sustainability and government grants and it pleased her to think of all the trees people had loaded into the backs of cars, how even now her trees sat in front windows dressed in their filigree and baubles. Some Sunday mornings before he had even wakened she liked to walk through the grove and smell the scent that she always associated with Christmas. And there was another thing she would have to tell him before they went home which was that they had sold their last black Christmas tree. She didn't care about profit or how many people thought they were lovely. She wasn't superstitious but it felt as if they were inviting bad luck, even some unforeseen disaster, by overturning the natural order of things.

There were groups of people around the tree in the square and she thought of the one at home in front of the City Hall. It used to be one of the family traditions that on the night they closed for Christmas they would take the children into town to see it. So many of the traditions, so much of the excitement, evaporated with the absence of children, yet even now, for all her apprehension, she felt a momentary wakening of something that was tinged at least with a memory of what she had felt in the past.

'A good size of a tree,' he said, pointing at what she had already seen.

'Yes, a good tree.' He could keep the Santa figure climbing their chimney but the only trees would be hers.

'I hope they've got it well secured – there's a bit of movement in it. You know something, Marion – I've always regretted not going to the City Hall the time Bill Clinton switched on the Christmas tree lights. And Van Morrison played.'

'I don't remember you saying you wanted to go.'

'I don't think I did at the time, it was only afterwards I thought it was one of those things it would be nice to say you'd been at. Do you know what I mean?'

'You don't like Van Morrison.'

'I know but it just seemed special like a party you didn't go to and afterwards everyone tells you how wonderful it was. Do you understand?'

'Yes,' she said, her face angled to the city. They were in the Leidseplein already and the bars and restaurants were in full flow, the crowds deeper and more fluid, groups crisscrossing each others' paths and igniting the night with the sharp sparks of their voices. A party to which he never got to go. It was what he probably felt more and more, made acuter as each year passed and with them the sense of opportunities slipping away. But she knew now that she wouldn't let him think that she was the one to blame. He could go to the party if he thought that was what would make him happy. She would open the door for him and bid him go.

There was a tree too in the foyer of the American Hotel and laughter and noise flowed through the open doors of the bar and restaurant. Their room looked out over the Leidseplein but was efficiently sealed off from the noise so when she looked out it felt as if she was watching a film with no sound. They left their bags at the end of the bed and to hide her sudden sense of self-consciousness she walked about as if inspecting the room.

'Very nice,' she said almost to herself as she scanned its quiet elegance, with everything dressed in cream and brown.

'Very good. Worth the money. And a nice central location,' he said as if he needed a greater commendation.

Then a silence settled and she knew what they probably both felt was what all couples felt in a hotel room, no matter how long they'd been together – a charged sense of each other and an uncertainty about what had always been taken for granted. She went to the bathroom and surveyed its white-towelled, sanitised cleanliness and looked at herself in the mirror. But it was his face standing in the doorway behind her that she focused on.

'So what would you like to do?' he asked, pushing one hand against the doorframe in too deliberate a study of nonchalance. 'We can go for a drink, or get something to eat. Or just walk.'

'Let's get something to eat. Can you give me five minutes?' As he turned back into the room she slowly closed the door. Her bag with her make-up was still on the bed but she didn't want to go back out, so instead she lightly splashed her face and then sat on the toilet. He had turned on the television and she could hear the sharp-edged staccato of voices as he flicked through the channels. Now that she was actually here, however, she was filled with doubt. Perhaps the idea had been the most foolish thing she had ever dreamed up and so far from anything else in her life that she should have dismissed it as complete madness. There was still time to call it off. Time to go back to the way things were and yet she knew she didn't want that either. She had to pull herself together, try to think less about things, the way she assumed those people in the square below were able to do. She flushed the toilet and patted her face dry, then pressed the towel tightly to her face to enjoy its consoling softness.

'I don't think it's particularly cold but you should wear something warm,' he said when she came out. He was sitting on the end of the bed and continued to surf the channels as he spoke, then turned the television off and dropped the control dismissively. 'We can get Sky news and not much else.'

'Well, hopefully we won't be sitting here watching television,' she said, reaching for her make-up bag and lifting out a lipstick. She felt impatient to be out of the room and out of the hotel.

'I'll get myself ready then,' he said, pushing himself off the bed. 'What do you fancy? Chinese, Thai, Italian?'

She didn't answer at first and instead concentrated on putting on her lipstick then said, 'I don't mind really. Let's go – it's too warm in here.'

But when he started to look at the radiator she told him he could sort it out when they came back. She watched him putting on his coat and running a hand through his hair in what was all the grooming he ever seemed to need. 'You're keen,' he said, checking he had his mobile in the pocket of his coat.

'It's just being cooped up in the plane and everything. That's all and we don't want to waste the time.'

They shared the lift with a young Japanese couple who smiled and made space for them. She looked at the black glossiness of the woman's hair, and the angular perfect symmetry of the cut. When the woman moved her head her whole hair seemed to flow in perfect synchronicity. Both wore what looked like identical Burberry raincoats and on the woman's feet were white trainers and little socks with red bows on the side which were curiously childlike, and everything on both of them looked like it had just come out of a crisp box. She wondered what they thought when they looked at her and then about how long they'd been married and how long it would be before they had children. When the lift reached the lobby there was an embarrassed shuffling little ceremony about who should leave first and much smiling and nodding of heads.

Outside the hotel he paused on the steps and opened his map. She walked on and skimmed the top of the water in the fountains with her fingers. She wished that for once he would put the map away and just walk and see where it took them. She didn't wish to be bound by the fixed parameters that were the normal constraints of their lives. He caught up with her and she guessed he was no wiser for all his map reading. Offering her his arm he pointed vaguely across the square. Cautiously navigating the constant flow of flaring yellow-windowed trams and both lit and unlit bicycles, they passed the small ice rink where some children and their parents scored and hissed the neon-coloured ice. The side streets were garlanded with Christmas lights and they set off down one that was crammed full of restaurants but she didn't want to pick somewhere too soon and so she urged him on when he paused to look at menus. It felt as if the whole city was only starting to come into the life it wanted for itself and that the working week was being swept away in a coming together of friends. There was an open invitation in it and although she knew that they would never take it up, the very fact that it was also extended to them made her feel lighter.

'Look, there's the Indians!' he said, pointing to the bottom of the street, but she only caught a couple of their stragglers before they too disappeared. 'Getting a bit nippy for those costumes.'

But every other girl who passed them seemed to have snubbed her nose at the growing cold of the evening and was dressed in a skimpy skirt and low-cut top. A few wore light shawls but the only people in coats were those of their age. It served to divide them into spectators and participants. And she could see already that there were lots of people like them, just strolling and looking while behind the windows of restaurants and bars there was the rising tide of life.

'Are we going to eat?' he asked, teasing her with a little tightening of his arm.

'Are you very hungry?'

'I am if you are. I'm not really sure – you decide.'

Part of her complained privately when he decided things for her and part complained when he pushed decisions on to her. Perhaps she was too hard on him and as she glanced at him she was reminded of those things that she liked and as they passed another group of young women, dressed in a way that shouted their sexual attractiveness, it wasn't her husband she resented so much as these young girls who were so unrestrained in their assertion of themselves. She thought there was something insensitive about it to other women, women such as herself, and she wondered if it couldn't be done in a way that was less strident. But perhaps they would only come to understand that when they had grown older and time had left them with less to catch the eye of the world.

'If you don't mind I don't think I want to eat a meal in a restaurant. I'd just like to get something from one of the street vendors or in one of those little fast-food places.'

'Are you sure?'

'Yes, if it's OK with you. I don't feel like sitting down to a large meal at this time of night.'

'The night's a pup, girl.'

'It might be but we're not.' She glanced at him, suddenly curious. 'How do you feel?'

'What do you mean?'

'About your age?'

'I don't really feel any age, if that's what you mean. I feel fine, apart from my back complaining occasionally. But I'm careful about lifting things after I put it out that last time. How do you feel?'

'Getting a little older, I suppose.'

'Well neither of us is ready for our bus pass yet. So let's find you something to eat.'

They headed down a side street towards a canal and then she saw it, a small fast-food shop on the corner with some basic seating and a few Formica-topped tables. Apart from one customer at the counter it was empty.

'Let's go here,' she said, tugging on his arm.

'Marion, are you sure this is what you want? It's just a Smoky Joe fast-food shop. We could've stayed at home. Why don't you let me spend some money on you? It's supposed to be a treat after all.'

'Look, it's empty – tonight I don't want to go somewhere crowded and noisy. Let's just get a few chips.'

She could feel his lack of enthusiasm but led him on. The owner greeted them with a smile and a slight bow while they stood and stared at the gaudy photographs haloing his head. He wore a white shirt that made her wonder how he had managed to keep it white and on both his cheeks there was a fine fritter of ridged scars. Then she ordered two portions of chips, two cans of Coke, and paid the few euros. The owner smiled again, indicating that he was about to close when they asked to eat in, but seemed to change his mind and told them that they could stay if they wished. She assured him that they would take it with them but he held his hands across the counter as if inviting them to take a seat in his restaurant. They sat at one of the red-topped tables and he brought them their cans of Coke, plastic forks and napkins. He smiled all the time and then she watched him pull the front shutter halfway down preventing new customers entering.

'Tea at the Ritz,' Richard said.

But she was irritated by his words and wanted to tell him that a working man should respect another. The chips were brought in perfect little cones and he set salt and ketchup on their table and bowed his head again. There was something strangely perfect about it. Something powerfully real and true.

'You wouldn't be treated as well as this in the Ritz,' she said and suddenly she felt bolder and, turning to the owner who was clearing up behind the counter, asked him, 'What time did you start work at?'

'Eleven, this morning,' he said, rubbing the top of the counter with his cloth.

'A long day for you.'

'It's long,' he said, nodding and smiling.

'You have a family?' She felt free to be curious despite Richard's bowed silence.

'In Africa. One day they perhaps able to come here.'

'I hope so,' she said, thinking too of her own family who would soon assemble for Christmas. 'You go home often?'

'Two times a year.'

'The chips are very good,' Richard said, raising his fork in a salute, and some of her earlier irritation ebbed away. Then as the man started to brush the floor her husband asked if she thought he owned the business, but she wasn't sure. She said she hoped so.

'Some people have to work very hard,' she said and then there was a silence between them broken only by the voices of people passing outside.

'We've always worked hard, too. Do you remember what it was like when we were just starting out and working every hour God sent us? But it can't be easy being far away from your family. Being on your own. I wouldn't like it.'

It pleased her to hear him value his family. It pleased her to sit in this about-to-close little fast-food place and feel a sense of connection to someone whose name she didn't know and would probably never see again and to share an understanding about work and about family. Her simple food felt seasoned with something precious and she felt a sudden largeness of heart. She watched the man making his final preparations for closing but saw too that he wasn't rushing them.

'We shouldn't keep him,' she said and her husband nodded and gathered up the sparse debris of their meal and carefully placed it in a bin. It wasn't enough. 'Give him something,' she whispered.

'How much?'

She wished he hadn't asked. 'Twenty.'

'Twenty?'

'Yes.'

'Most expensive chips ever,' he said, slipping his wallet out of his pocket.

'Please, Richard. It was one of the nicest meals I've ever had.'

They stood up and thanked their host and then Richard went to the counter and handed him the money with a quiet discretion that met her approval.

'Good luck,' she heard him say as he tucked his wallet away. Yes, that was what was needed for them all now – good luck. Good luck and family. They bowed their heads as they dipped under the half-closed shutter and as they did so the lights went out behind them.

He searched for them as he always did when he arrived in this city but wasn't sure if the sense of exhilaration and anticipation was real or merely generated by memory. It was part of an increasingly blurred distinction between what belonged in the past and what continued to exist and more and more he found himself unable to discern which was which. There was no doubt, however, about what he had felt as a young man when he had first discovered the city as a student and it had nothing to do with drugs or sex. If anything it was almost Calvinistic, a heady intoxicating sense of freedom from the tyranny of real and imagined authority, of stumbling into a place where the tribal divisions of his home city seemed primitive and preposterous superstition. Let them all come to Amsterdam, let it be compulsory for every citizen to temporarily sojourn there and imbibe the knowledge that race and religion, colour and gender mattered little in the pursuit of happiness. Look at every street where every possible human permutation seemed to flourish and no head turned to stare or finger pointed. He was transfigured by the city. It was unlike anywhere he had ever been before. Despite his little money – he had slept out once in Vondelpark before the police had stopped it and he had been forced to find a hostel – he had felt himself momentarily part of something bigger and freer than he had ever known.

And there was the art of course. Enough paintings to last a lifetime and never be able to absorb them all. He had always thought of Amsterdam as a holy place and so it secretly irked him to hear others who knew nothing of its reality reduce it to some tawdry and cheap location for licence and excess. He didn't want stag parties to come here, he didn't want a hen party of empty-headed young women to disfigure its history and beauty with their raucous hedonism. If he were totally honest he didn't want to share it and instead wanted a Christ or a ruthless government cabal to drive the money-lenders out of the temple. So let the parties of stags and hens be taken from the airport and diverted to some simulation of their fantasy about the city. There was only one person he wanted to share its truth with and that was Jack. It might well have been foolish but he had started to think that this weekend could be the beginning of something better for them and that by bringing his son here the city might be able to work its power and free him from himself, or whatever it was that seemed to bind his spirit, and just perhaps it might stir his soul in the way that it had done for his father all those years ago. So as they left Central Station on foot, re-creating his very first journey, he glanced at his son who had already established a pattern of not walking beside him but about two paces behind his right shoulder that meant he had to twist his neck to see him, and was pleased to observe the curiosity and even a little trepidation in his eyes that surreptitiously scanned the throng.

He started to point everything out as they walked but there was no response and gradually he too grew silent and focused instead on where they might eat. There were so many things he didn't know about his son and they included his current basic likes and dislikes. But the problem of what to eat was easily solved. A cheeseburger in Burger King was what Jack wanted and if it wasn't exactly his own preference he could live with it. Despite being offered different types of restaurant, Jack had screwed his eyes up at them all before spotting the familiar signage branding the night sky. For some reason he had thought Jack might have turned up his nose at such a place, whether from concern about some multinational conspiracy to supersize the world or just from an aesthetic rejection of its menu, but he seemed reassured by its surroundings as if welcomingly reorientated by the familiar.

They joined a long queue and Jack gave him his order of a plain (the word plain repeated with emphasis) cheeseburger, medium fries and a large Coke. He asked if he wanted to go and sit down, keep them a seat, but he stayed resolutely on his shoulder, momentarily transformed into a dependent, slightly nervous child, and it wouldn't have surprised him at any minute to feel the tug of his son's hand on the hem of his jacket. In a few moments however the illusion of familiarity ebbed away and as they edged forward they both registered that the clientele was not what they were used to. There were tourists like themselves of course, but there were other individuals who looked poor and as if they might have spent the rest of the day gathering the requisite funds for this, their only meal, and others, some in pairs, who simply looked strange and unpredictable. Someone tried to ask money of them but they turned their heads away. And then three black youths with an exaggerated loose-limbed street swagger that made their bodies look as if they had been deboned, quivered like glinting fish along the queue and took up residence at the counter. The tallest and oldest held a hand up to the queue which might have been an apology but had more of an air of assumed authority. He tried to stop himself thinking in stereotypes, engaging in racial profiling, but the three youths made it difficult with their white sportswear that looked as if they had just stepped off a field in Philadelphia or Chicago and the bling round their necks and wrists and back-to-front baseball hats. Suddenly he felt angry, the anger of the compliant, lifetime queuer, at the selfish disrespect of the jumper. And it was brazen as they lolled against the counter and leaned into the serving area. The oldest one was talking to someone. Surely the staff would refuse to serve them. Surely security would arrive and sort it out but in a few seconds they were pointing and ordering. Something was overflowing in him. He didn't want to be treated like this.

'Hey, guys, there's a queue,' he heard himself shouting but his voice wasn't threatening and he believed it contained the correct degree of friendly reasonableness.

'Dad!' And this time there really was a hand tugging at his coat. 'Dad, don't, for God's sake!'

Heads in the queue and those on other sides were turning to stare at him. He wanted to suddenly reclaim the words, smother them in his throat, but it was too late, they were out, and in response he simply shuffled his feet and tightened his grip on the handle of his bag. The three youths were talking to each other and looking vaguely if not precisely in his direction and for a second he wondered if his accent had made his words meaningless, but then the tallest one and clearly the dominant of the trio was easing himself out of the slouch across the counter and theatrically straightening himself and eyeballing him, his mouth working in energetic contrast to the languid tempo of his body as he chewed on a little toothpick. He didn't return the gaze but stared straight ahead with his head up, something telling him from a David Attenborough natural-world programme that in the animal kingdom to display fear would only encourage attack. They continued to talk together and one of them was making a joke. A joke was good because already he was revisiting a whole library of newspaper headlines that involved people getting stabbed by strangers over similar and seemingly inconsequential interactions that resulted in a supposed loss of face, some unintended public expression of disrespect that sent fragile, insecure egos into total meltdown. And he had Jack with him. He had his son with him and five minutes after arriving in Amsterdam he might end up a headline in a newspaper. He started to imagine the Bebo/Facebook cybertributes, started to construct the opening of his son's funeral oration. That was if Susan even let him attend because she would blame him and she'd be right because who else was responsible?

He remembered the scene in *The Godfather* where the humble baker had to stand outside the hospital and keep his hand inside his coat to give the impression he had a gun and for a second he held his inside his breast pocket that contained only a boarding card, until it felt ridiculous. The tall guy was saying something and gesturing slowly as if he was asking someone not to block his line of vision. Perhaps they could both just turn, take their bags and quietly leave, but the thought of being humiliated in front of his son felt the sharpest pain of all. What was the guy saying? Then he made it out over the residual noise.

'It's an emergency, man. An emergency.' And at his words his two companions were snickering and one of them held his hand across his mouth to restrain the smile melting across his face. Then he turned back to the counter where his order was ready.

Jack tugged at his coat again. 'Let's go, Dad, we can get something to eat somewhere else.'

His son had given him permission to go and he was grateful for it but it was too late because the three queue jumpers were already moving towards them with their brown paper bags. With a hand behind his back he grabbed a handful of Jack's coat and pulled him to the inside of the queue and kept staring ahead and trying to make himself as tall as possible. In *The Godfather* the car with the would-be killers slows down and takes a good look at the solitary, momentarily plumped-up, inwardly shivering guard and then drives on. He wasn't sure whether to keep staring straight ahead or make eye contact, but something, and he thought it also came from a natural-world programme, told him that eye contact represented a challenge so he stood as nonchalantly as possible, as if pondering his choice of meal. When level the taller one paused beside him and he was smiling, the toothpick hanging out of the corner of his mouth like a wooden tongue. Holding the bag between their faces he repeated, 'An emergency, man, an emergency!' Then he took the toothpick out of his mouth and lightly, almost delicately, pressed his shoulder with it. Twice.

He heard himself saying, 'No problem, no problem.' Then they were gone and he shuffled forward with the queue, his eyes fixed on his feet. He was glad he couldn't see Jack but he felt his presence weighing against him and he thought of making a joke, of saying something flippant and dismissive to repair and break the silence that had oppressively settled around them. But nothing came to mind and so he asked Jack to repeat his order even though with everything else, with every movement of the queues, with every clink of money and snatch of conversation, it felt as if it was seared in his senses. When he spoke Jack's voice was dead and almost imperceptible.

'It's very slow,' Alan said eventually. No answer. 'I don't

know why they call it fast food because it's taking ages.' No answer. He had started to think that words might extinguish the fire but just when he needed them they became evasive and always out of reach like the wind wafting away a piece of paper each time you stretched for it. He pretended to hunt for something in his pocket. When they reached the counter he affected nonchalance again but he knew the girl was looking at him and he got confused when she asked him whether they were eating in. Jack said yes on his behalf and then they were weaving back past the queues searching for a seat and he was trying to strike a balance between the tray and the bag on his shoulder. To drop everything would be the crowning glory and he had a vision of his son publicly disowning him and disappearing into the night. He had let his son down, the way he had that sports day fathers' race when he had lost his balance amidst the jostling elbows at the starting line and watched prostrate as the other fathers disappeared towards medalled glory; the way he wouldn't go on the roller-coaster at Alton Towers because of his vertigo and his two children had been temporarily fostered by a Polish couple who afterwards gave them sweets and probably would have kept them with any encouragement; the way he had betrayed Susan.

'It's not a plain cheeseburger,' Jack said after they had found a corner seat and he was holding open the bun as if in a court and a jury needed to be convinced. 'It's not a plain one,' he repeated.

'I asked for a plain one. You were there, you heard me.'

'She mustn't have understood you.'

So this too was his fault. Suddenly he felt angry. He'd ordered his son a plain cheeseburger and they had given him something else. It wasn't right or fair the way they let people jump the queue and then gave people what they hadn't ordered. Something was bubbling up and, reaching across the table, he took the offending burger and stood. 'I'll get it changed,' he said but immediately Jack stretched out his hand and pulled him back by the wrist.

'It doesn't matter,' he hissed. 'It doesn't matter. Give me it back.'

He had already noticed how Jack almost whispered in public and it suddenly struck him that one of his son's greatest fears was of drawing attention to himself, an acute self-consciousness that probably made this whole episode his idea of hell. So reluctantly he gave up the opportunity to redeem himself by asserting his right to have what he ordered and sat down meekly, and with an unspoken apology rattling round his head watched his son meticulously scrape every vestige of salad and dressing free from his burger, as if clearing it of toxic waste. Then they ate in silence.

The first thing they did was drop off their bags in their hotel. Although she had never stayed in a hotel she knew that it was too grand a word for where they were booked. They had been able to walk to it from the station and some of the girls had used it before. It was somewhere between a hostel and a boarding house and the rooms had three or four beds jammed in so tightly that there was hardly space to move between them.

'We're only sleeping here, Mum, it's just somewhere to lay your head when you can't party any more.'

She nodded. At least there was a bathroom. There was a smell of food in the rooms and although there were No Smoking signs there lingered a sense that someone had done so very recently. A metal cupboard that clanged with hangers when anyone walked close to it was the only furniture.

'At least we don't have to get changed,' Shannon said. 'Just slip on a bit of lippy and we're off.'

The young women flounced in and out of the room, borrowing make-up and mobile phones, comparing money and generally unable to sit down or entertain any form of stillness.

'Your turn, Karen,' Martina said. 'I'll do you now. Come on, girl, let's get your war paint on.'

'War paint?'

'We're going to war, girl, and look out any man who gets in our way tonight,' she said, gently leading her by the arm towards the bathroom.

'They'll be lucky if it's only their scalps they lose,' Lorrie squealed and other girls were pairing up and applying stripes and circles to their faces in garish colours. Ellie's phone rang and before answering it she told them it was her boyfriend checking up on her but Shannon grabbed it out of her hand.

'Barry, you're looking for Ellie. Well she's not available and in fact the last time I saw her she was smoking blow with two black guys who said they could get her into films. You get yourself a fish supper and a video out of Xtravision. Nothing to worry about, Barry.'

Martina's hand was shaking as she joined in the laughter and she had to steady herself with a deep draw of breath before starting to apply the marks of war.

'I'm too old for this,' she said.

Martina, who considered herself an artist, pulled her head back and held it at an angle while evaluating her creation. 'You're never too old to party and if you say that one more time I'm going to tell Shannon her mother's a party pooper. There you go. Looks good?'

She stared at herself in the mirror and suddenly felt a little dizzy. She was in a foreign city, for the first time in her whole life far from home, and she was dressed as an Indian about to go to war. She thought of Mrs Hemmings, of the list of places she had given her, and wondered what she would say if she could see her.

'Looks good,' she said, thinking it made her look like not so much a warrior as an old tabby cat. All she needed was whiskers.

A queue had formed at the bathroom door and as she passed them hands blessed her with their approval but already she had decided that coming was an act of foolishness, an expense she couldn't afford, and if she wasn't careful she would end up as an embarrassment to herself and a hindrance to her daughter. Shannon was applying her own decoration, holding a make-up mirror in that familiar angled poise of her hand. The marks she made were light and designed to accentuate what already existed. And in that moment she knew that her daughter was too often absorbed by appearance. Not just in herself but in everything. The whole wedding, even though it was to be in a registry office, was planned out in meticulous and increasingly expensive detail, starting with an endless deliberation over the colour and style of invitations and spinning out through place settings and flowers. She thought of the wedding dress they had bought and part of her resented its cold elegant beauty and the fact that she herself had never got to wear one. Perhaps afterwards when they had gone on honeymoon she would be able to try it on without telling anyone. Just once to wear the dress. She thought too of Wade and wondered if he would prove worthy and she shivered a little at the instinctive inevitable anticipation of failure that she was unable to disassociate from all future relationships between men and women. She wanted to ask her again if she was sure, if she was really sure, but knew she couldn't. Shannon was moistening her lips, satisfied at last with how she looked. And she found pleasure in her daughter's appearance. If she had been unable to give her child all the other things that some children received, she had somehow managed to create a physical beauty. And in the absence of so much else, why shouldn't her daughter make the very most of what life had given her?

She wished she owned a camera that would take good pictures rather than the grainy, useless blur her mobile phone provided. She would buy one before the wedding and she knew that she would take one of the very best photographs with her to her early-morning work and leave it on the desks as she cleaned, moving it from place to place, letting it have a space with all the other photographs of family.

'Well, how do I look?' Shannon asked, clicking the compact closed and dropping it into her bag with the finality of someone who knew that the job was well done.

'You look great, love. Really great.' And something welling up inside her made her go and hug her, disregarding the surprise and bridling uncertainty in her daughter's body.

'Thanks, Mum,' Shannon said, patting her neutrally in the small of the back at the same time as she eased her body free from the embrace, then smoothed any creases the contact might have produced.

'Aww, isn't that nice?' Ellie said as she entered from the bathroom, her war paint shimmering and the two red circles on her cheeks making her look like a clown. 'I wish I was as close to my mother as you two. We just fight all the time.'

'Oh we can fight the bit out too,' she said, embarrassed by her own emotions. She was going to say something else but the other girls were coming out of the bathroom and she had to sidle into the narrow space between two of the beds to make room for them.

'Now listen up,' Ellie said as she stood on a bed, her heels sinking into its softness and making her legs look as if they were made of rubber. 'Let's get the rules clear. First, we get some food to put a lining on the stomach, then we hit the bars – starting with the Bulldog – and then a club. Rule number one: we stay together, no copping off with fellas.'

'But what if they're gorgeous and a millionaire?'

'A quick snog and no more – you can leave them your number. Rule number two: it's Shannon's night and nobody spoils that or they get dumped out of the tribe. Rule number three . . .'

'Go on, what's rule number three?'

'I can't remember so it must just be: enjoy yourself and party, party, party!'

Then, as everyone engaged in a communal wow-wow-wowing, she did a kind of war dance on the bed, her legs spongy and wobbly, her arms working like an automaton, until outreached hands helped her off and they were down the stairs and into the swirl of Friday night in Amsterdam.

By a show of hands they decided on pizza and ten minutes later, in a narrow restaurant-lined street where they ignored the invitations and proffered menus of keen-to-have-them waiters, they found an Italian place. At the door they were greeted by an older man in a black suit who looked them up and down and, clearly deciding that they were undesirables, foolishly asked if they had a reservation. His question was greeted with sniggering and then Lorrie piped up, 'Of course we have a reservation. And a very nice one too.'

'I'm sorry, ladies, we are fully booked tonight,' he said, shrugging his shoulders in a half-hearted simulation of an apology.

'White man speak with forked tongue!' someone called.

'Listen,' shouted someone else from the back, 'we don't want to eat in your poxy restaurant.' And then as they turned away there was the by now ritual wow-wow-wowing of the tribe as they struck out for a more welcoming venue.

They found it a few minutes later round the next corner and the staff were happy to slide tables together and rearrange furniture so that they could all sit together and, spurred on by the bottles of wine that quickly appeared, they started to flirt with the waiters, asking questions about the size of the pizza and holding up their hands as if to indicate measurement. She tried to enter into it, laughing along to hide her discomfort.

'You like a big pizza?' the young waiter asked.

'The bigger the better.'

'If it's too big we'll have to share it though.'

'No, I want it all for myself.'

'Could you show us how big it is?'

And on and on but she was glad at least that the waiters were well able for it, giving as good as they got and pouring glasses of wine and good humour, perhaps even glad of the break in the monotony. One of the girls sitting beside her who worked with Shannon and whose name she couldn't remember leaned into her and pointed out one of the waiters as gorgeous, asking her if she agreed.

'Yes,' she said, 'he's very nice and even nicer if he's the owner's son.'

'That's not very romantic.'

'I'm too old for romance.'

'Well I wouldn't mind letting him visit my tepee.' And then she laughed heartily at her own joke, shouting it across the table until she was satisfied everyone had heard it.

And so the evening unravelled, full of laughter and not enough drink yet taken to tip it over into anything other than the energetic pursuit of a good time. But already she felt it slipping away from her, as sometimes in her imagination she was watched over by all the people she worked with in the home and Mrs Weldon having all her suspicions confirmed and even Kevin the doorman scrutinising her for what she might have secreted about her being, even though all she had taken from the plane was the magazine and the sick bag. And the safety instructions card which she intended to memorise before she got the return flight. She thought too of the bracelet and the way Jennings had looked at her, so even though she was further away from home than she had ever been there was something that still tied her to the life there that she knew as hers.

After the meal she tried to shake it off as they made their way to wherever they were going, intrigued by the strangeness of the buildings and the tall narrow houses on either side of the canal that stood like bookends on Mrs Hemmings' shelves, but it was impossible for her to read what lives might live within them, either now or in the past. She liked the strangeness, too, of the people, especially the women on their bicycles, indifferent to everything but their own balance and direction and always in such a hurry as if there was some important moment in their lives that it was vital to reach. She knew people were looking at them but she felt hidden in the group and, even when young men made remarks, the collective energy of the response they received seemed to intimidate them and so tagging on the tail of the tribe afforded a protection and a chance to absorb everything that was new to her. She still wasn't sure if she liked it, tasting it gingerly on the tip of her tongue as she would some strange new food. But at least it didn't frighten her or make her feel threatened the way walking late at night in her home town might. There were too many people coursing through the city and it was as if the streets belonged to them rather than the buildings. So although she was a stranger to Amsterdam she could still feel at least a sense of this belonging. She stared wide-eyed at an older woman with long white streaming hair who rode her bicycle with two dogs in a basket attached to her handlebars and a man dressed in a business suit who carried a young child on the back of his. The clang of a tram made her jump and she felt that she needed to take more care if she were to avoid becoming a traffic accident.

They reached their bar and were met by a wall of booming bass noise at the door and inside was all metal and wood and packs of mainly males clustered round their drinks. Some of them cheered their entrance and shouted comments she couldn't make out. Taking residence at a couple of tables near the stairs they pooled money and started a seemingly endless supply of drinks which mostly she only half-finished while sitting on the edge of things and although she knew it was wrong she couldn't help falling into her customary habit of measuring personal expenditure by the time spent to earn it. And when the drinking games started she couldn't understand the rules or make out the instructions over the noise of the music and the din of conversation that seemed to rise and rise like a river in flood until the only way to hear anything was to hold your head above the flow and shout into someone's ear. Sometimes young men came over, their beer glasses cupped in their hands, and stood watching as if it was a spectator sport. Occasionally one would point with his glass and say something in what she assumed was Dutch and which sounded to her as if it came out of a gargling throat before it splintered against the barrier of teeth. The girls tended to ignore them but sometimes directed their banter towards them and as the night went on and the drink seeped over their restraint they became more sexually provocative, flirting with each other and with everyone who caught their eye. Some began to dance and the watching males sidled in amongst them like sharks amongst a shoal but they took delight in only dancing intimately with each other, their movements deliberately exaggerated and parodying of themselves as they simulated abandonment that was controlled by a knowledge of how they wished to look. She hadn't danced in public since she was sixteen at a school disco but despite her protests they dragged her to her feet and she did her best to pass herself, throwing her arms in the air and shimmering in a kind of slow slalom, trying to match the motion of her body to the beat she couldn't find and which was replaced by a breathless and insistent drill that provided no space for respite or elegance and which pulsed and fused itself with the pink and lime-green neon that seemed to wash over and through them like radiation.

She watched Shannon as she danced, one side of her face stippled by a pink light, eyes sometimes closed as if lost inside the music, and she envied her self-assurance, her confidence about how she looked, but then she remembered the work and cost that was constantly needed to maintain it and for a second closed her own eyes and tried to find some memory of who she once was when life appeared to stretch out in front of her and the doors of possibility still seemed open. She remembered the guy she had sat beside on the plane. The one going to see Bob Dylan. The one with the son who didn't say much and who took all the photographs out of the window. She had embarrassed herself but he had been good about it even when she had grabbed his hand. It had felt like a good hand. She thought of Marty who drove her home every day in his taxi and who every morning hoped she would ask him in for a cup of coffee and anything she was willing to serve up and wondered if she would ever get to feel so needy or so desperate that she would issue that invitation. She believed not but as she danced she saw herself again as that young girl moving just as self-consciously in the school assembly hall at the Christmas disco and how then she had believed that a life without love was no life at all, that the only purpose of life was to find love and hold it so tight it could never escape. She let her arms drop into a light embrace of herself, then contoured the outline of her body with wavy movements of her arms, and for a moment it seemed as if she was swimming into a warmer sea whose currents might be able to carry her to some better place. Perhaps it was what she had drunk. But it wasn't impossible, she told herself, and if she didn't have the education or the knowledge or the social connections to open the shut door, could it not be that love, some better love than she had ever known, might be the key to open it? She knew, however, as her movements slowed into a dream, that she had parts of herself which were damaged by the bitterness of her experience and she wondered if they might ever heal and allow the possibility of trust. She no longer heard the music as she danced and moved in tune only with the rhythm of what the future might bring.

Plans to move on came and went. Some had already consumed enough alcohol to ensure that they only wished to remain slumped on their seats, animated only at intervals to share some sobbing aspect of their lives, some tale of two-timing boyfriends or puppies run over by post-office vans, while the tepee-joke girl whose name she still didn't know grew increasingly belligerent and offered to fight anyone over some convoluted story involving her nephew, *The X Factor* and Simon Cowell. She herself hadn't drunk as much as the others but more than she was used to and was already beginning to think longingly of bed, certain that none of them had started work as early as she had, cleaning city-centre offices while they were snug under their duvets. She remembered how McClean's desk had looked that morning and the little spur of concern she had felt when she had seen it. He, or someone else, had tidied it and there was none of the personalised debris that was its customary decoration. But it hadn't made it better – if anything it had acquired a new sense of desolation like a house clearance after the owner has died. Perhaps he was being moved or perhaps he had left. But if he had it all seemed very sudden. She wondered how he would spend his Christmas and whether the imaginary and fragmented family she had constructed for him would manage to come together, however briefly, for at least Christmas Day.

The smoke, and although not an expert she guessed it was from more than just tobacco, was starting to sting her eyes and she went and stood in the street for a few moments. Veronica with the wild red hair and who had grown up a few streets from Shannon was there trying to get better reception on her mobile phone. The two feathers in her headband had slipped into tired and opposite angles so that it looked as if someone was holding their fingers in a V-sign behind her head.

'Just checking that Matt is coping with the kids and got them off to bed all right. Sometimes they play him up, take advantage, make him read stories until he's the one falling asleep. But I can't get a signal.'

'I'm sure they'll be fine. Be good for him to look after them for a while.'

'Well he moaned and groaned about it but he's a short memory. Seemed to have conveniently forgotten the golfing weekend and the weekend in Manchester to see United.'

'They all have short memories,' she said, stepping aside to let a large man past whose beard reached to his chest and seemed to hang like a curtain on the rings of his lip piercings. His muscular arms were inked in a complex latticework of what looked like hieroglyphics from some ancient parchment.

'I wouldn't fancy waking up beside him,' Veronica said, dropping her phone dismissively into her bag. Then she opened a cigarette packet and offered her one.

'One bad habit I've managed to avoid.'

Suddenly Veronica began to cry and she wondered if she had said the wrong thing. She was snivelling, one hand enfolding her stomach while the back of the other that held the cigarette dabbed her eyes so that Karen worried that the two things might come into fatal contact at any moment. Taking the cigarette from her she handed over a tissue she had found in her pocket while putting a consoling hand across her shoulder.

'There, there,' she said as if talking to a child. 'What's wrong, Veronica? What's wrong, love?'

Veronica shook her head from side to side as if this might be a better way to get rid of the tears. 'It's stupid, really, but I think I'm homesick. I'm not used to being away from the kids and Matt means well but he doesn't know all the wee things – how to do their breakfast the way they like it, how to mash it up so there's no bits; that sort of thing.' She reached out for the comfort of the cigarette. 'I suppose I sound really stupid – you won't tell the girls, will you? They'll think I'm sad.'

'I won't tell anyone and you're not stupid and not sad. It just makes you a good mother but we're only here for two nights – it'll fly in. And the kids will be just fine – they'll muck in and if nothing else it'll show him how tough it is being a full-time mum.'

Veronica had stopped crying and exchanged the soggy shredded tissue for her cigarette but continued to heave deep sighs.

'Take a deep breath. That's a girl.'

'Is my face a mess?' she asked, tilting it for inspection, the hand with the cigarette stretched out at an angle from her body, the two fingers holding it in a stiff V-shape.

'Veronica, all our faces are a mess so I wouldn't worry.' And then with the tip of a licked finger she tried to erase the smudge of mascara that to the casual eye might just have been part of the tribal markings. Veronica tried to smile but the corners of her mouth trembled a little so that it looked as if she might start to cry again.

'Let's go for a walk,' she said. 'I could do with getting my head showered – I don't know about you but that music's too loud for me. We can go back in a minute – no one'll miss us.'

She linked her arm through Veronica's and they set off across the front of the bars and round the nearest corner, the night air cool against their faces. 'So what ages are your kids now – I've lost track?'

'Ethan's third birthday is next week and Ella is five next Easter.'

'So Ethan was a Christmas baby?'

'We brought him home just before Christmas. It was really lovely, Karen, the tree up and all. It was like getting the very best present ever.'

A rising breeze made them lean into each other and lower their heads, oblivious to any jokes made at their expense by passers-by.

'You must be very excited by the wedding,' Veronica said, her tousled mass of red hair spuming up from under her headband. 'And I think it's very big of you to have your ex at it. Shannon's really pleased that he's going to give her away. After all this time.'

She stopped suddenly, her arm stiffening and restraining Veronica's forward movement. She felt as if she was going to be sick.

'My ex at the wedding? What are you talking about, Veronica?'

The sudden brake to her walk had caused her companion's headdress to slip and more of her hair seemed to spring free as if suddenly coursing with electric current.

'Rob's agreed to give her away,' Veronica said, her eyes and mouth opening. 'Shannon told us last week. Out of the blue, like. Oh my God, Karen, she hasn't told you.'

She unlocked her arm from Veronica's and turned back the way they had come. 'Perhaps it's a mistake,' Veronica called after her, 'perhaps I got it wrong.' She didn't reply but kept on walking and with each step she told herself that yes it had to be a mistake. It wasn't possible, not in a million years could it be possible. She felt sick and then something hardened and settled inside her, momentarily pushing aside everything except an anger that seared her throat with the words that wanted to score and scar the night. She glanced up at the sky and it was contracted into a deep blackness streaked with purple and spotted with the neon that dazzled and blurred whatever truth she tried to grasp. It had to be a joke, a bad joke. How could her daughter let herself be given away by a man who had already given her away all those years ago, who had walked out on his unborn child and never showed any interest in either of them? Her skin crawled with the thought of him taking Shannon's arm or even being at the ceremony and she shivered. Somewhere trailing behind, Veronica was calling to her, shouting stuff about perhaps being mistaken and not to tell Shannon that she had said anything. How many of the rest also knew? Shannon wasn't particularly close to Veronica any more – she guessed she'd only been asked for old times' sake – so if she knew, everyone knew. Even as her feet pressed the solidity of the pavement things felt as if they were crumbling and falling apart with each step, and it was as if she were to take away her anger then there would be nothing real at her centre to hold her together.

At the entrance to the bar two black-coated doormen momentarily barred her way, smiling as they asked if she had any dangerous weapons concealed on her body. Knives? Guns? Spears? She pushed past them as they laughed at their own joke, their shoulders rising and falling against the tight seams of their identical coats. For a few seconds the noise and lights made her lose her bearings. Everything in the bar seemed to have moved its position and been randomly shuffled but then she saw them and immediately her eyes picked out Shannon who to the compelling cheers of the other girls was drinking some pink-coloured cocktail in a frenzy of concentration, her face contorted by a distaste for its contents. Walking to the edge of the group she waited until the last dregs had been drained and the challenge passed to someone else before she caught her daughter's eye and signalled that she wanted to see her. Without explanation she gestured for Shannon to follow her to the toilets and only when in the narrow mirrored space did she turn to face her. Her daughter was brushing the back of her hand over her lips and still squirming from the legacy of whatever had been in her glass. As soon, however, as she saw the mirror she leant towards it as if to kiss it and delicately inspected her face with the tips of her fingers.

'Having a good time, Mum?' she asked, her eyes still searching for any damage to her make-up, and then shook and flounced her hair as if to stir its sleeping form back to life.

Part of her wanted to grab her by that same hair and hurt her in the same way as she was hurting but there was no pain she could inflict that would match her own and she tried to steady herself with one hand holding on to the coldness of a washbasin.

'How could you do it, Shannon? How could you do this to me?'

Her daughter smoothed the skin at her throat and she knew right away from her expression that she understood what she meant.

'Who told you?'

'It doesn't matter who told me because it wasn't you.'

'I was going to tell you before we went home. I wanted to find the right moment.'

'So go on, Shannon. Tell me now. I want to hear you say the words otherwise I won't believe it's true.' Behind her daughter's head someone had drawn a smiley face in red lipstick. The tap close to her hand was dripping. The basin had a web of fine cracks. Outside the music sounded like an incoming sea and for a second she felt as if she might drown in its riptide. 'I'm waiting, Shannon. I want to hear you tell me.'

'I've asked Dad to come to the ceremony. I should have told you before you heard from someone else.'

The word Dad was a hook tearing her open. She wanted to grab her and push it back down her throat and tell her never to let it pass between them again.

'How can you do this to me? How can you do this to yourself? After all these years what right have you to bring him back into our lives? And he's not your dad! A dad doesn't walk out on his child before she's even born. Have you forgotten that, forgotten everything?'

'He's changed, Mum. He's sorry about what happened.'

She felt sick, felt the tumble and loosening of it in her stomach as she realised for the first time that they had been in contact.

'How long have you been seeing him?'

'About a year. It happened by accident. We met in town one day. He knew who I was and said he often thought about me.'

'And you believed that? You believed everything he said. How stupid can you be, Shannon?'

'He's sorry about what happened. Knows he can't change anything but he'll come to the wedding if I want him there.'

'And what about me? What about what I want? Did you even for one second stop to think about that?' She waved her arm in the air and its reflection in the mirror made it look like the broken fluttering of a bird's wing as it tried to lift itself into flight.

'He says that he would have played a part in my life but you didn't want him to. And no matter what happened in the past he's still my father and I'd like my mother and father at my wedding. The way everybody else gets to do.'

She had deceived her. Deceived her for a whole year. 'The way everybody gets to do' – so she was to set aside everything he'd done so that she could make her marriage measure up to everyone else's. And in those words she knew what she had really always known but had chosen to ignore, that her daughter, this child of hers whom she brought into the world on her own and reared on her own, valued nothing but appearance and nothing even came close to matching that importance. She felt a sharp surge of shame that she had allowed her to grow into this and for a second wanted to put the bitterness of that knowledge into words that would shake her child into some better understanding of what she had become but even then in her anger she knew that it was no longer possible, that it was too late. Too late for all of them.

Ellie's voice came through the half-open door: 'Everyone all right in here?'

'Just give us a few minutes, Ellie,' she said, without looking at the bodiless face that had appeared in the doorway. She turned to the mirror but didn't meet her reflection and instead held the basin with both hands. It felt cold against the heat of her skin. She waited until the door had closed.

'I'm afraid, Shannon, that this is one thing you're not going to be able to have because if Rob's going then I won't be. So whatever way you plot and scheme this there's only going to be one of us there so you go ahead, take your time and make your mind up.'

'Why does it have to be like this? Why can't this be my special day? Why can't you just do this for me? You don't even have to talk to him or anything.'

She heard the whining, victimised voice adopted by her daughter, saw the practised expression of suffering of someone who has been hard done to by an unfair and malicious life, and all her anger flooded up and threatened to breach the trembling remains of her restraint.

'Mum, it's just one day.' And now she was pretending to cry.

Just one day. Not even one day, just about the time it took to write a scribbled letter on a page pulled from a spiral notebook. And it was doubly her fault. Firstly in her daughter's eyes because she thought that she had prevented her father having a relationship with them and secondly because she had let her daughter become something she was no longer sure that she could ever love in the way she had always done. They had both cheated on her, taken her for a fool for their own selfish purposes.

'I think you're being selfish, Mum.'

Something that couldn't be held back any longer coursed over and swept away all instinctive caution and before she could stop herself she had slapped her daughter's face with her open palm. For a second they stared freeze-framed at each other with shocked fierce eyes until a piercing wail broke the stunned silence. Her hand trembled at her side and she wanted at first to reach out and soothe the pain from her daughter's cheek but as she gently and tentatively raised it Shannon shrugged it away, her shrill child's cry subsiding into a lumbering sob. She softly repeated her name and if she had been allowed she would have poured out all her remorse and begged forgiveness but her anger flared again as she watched her daughter turn to the mirror to assess if any collateral damage had been caused by the blow.

'Selfish? When I'm the person working every hour God sends to help keep you in your style and saving every penny I make for this wedding so you can act the grand lady. Selfish? Shannon, you're the selfish bitch here and that's the truth.'

Suddenly she felt trapped in a grubby, ugly little room that was too small for all the feelings that wanted expression and where the mirrors seemed to reflect everything endlessly back into her so there was no release even after the words were spoken and she needed to be gone and breathing the cleanness of the night air before the anger inside choked the remaining life out of her. Brushing past her daughter and ignoring her sobs rising again into a wail she hurried through the bar aware that all the party sat silently with their faces turned towards her and she could see that

162

someone was standing attempting to comfort a weeping Veronica.

Outside she took deep breaths and tried to steady herself. Already part of her wanted to go back and make things right but a stronger part insisted that she had only told the truth. She wanted nothing more than to go home but instead found herself in a strange city, on her own and dressed as an Indian. Her costume had never felt more painfully ridiculous than it did in that moment and if there had been any way she could have torn it off and replaced it with her own clothes she would have grasped it with both hands but there was no alternative to trying to make it back to the hotel. She stopped in the penumbral light of a café and searched in her bag until she found the tourist map she had lifted from the foyer while they were checking in. Locating the station she realised that most of the roads stretched eventually back towards it and trying to stem her fear she started off through the streets that seemed even more full of people than when they had set out. People were looking at her, some were laughing at her, but she ignored them all and kept her head high and stared only straight in front, determined not to let the humiliation show on her face. Once she stopped to show her map to a young woman on her own who patiently took time with her, pointing the direction and smiling in a way that made her grateful for the kindness.

The walk slowly burnt the anger away but left in its place an emptiness in which echoed a confusion of other feelings that couldn't be controlled or shaped into comfort or meaning. She passed a group of young men, one of whom plucked a feather from her headband, but she kept walking and when they had gone she took the headband and threw it into a rubbish bin. Then into the hollowness at her core started a fear like the one she had felt when the plane was taking off, a fear that she was about to hurtle into a sphere where she was not supposed to be and where only danger and destruction awaited. What did she have but a daughter and whatever she had become was in part down to her, so to throw her away now was as impossible as throwing away some part of herself. Shannon would see how she felt and, even if she sulked and pouted, when it came down to a choice she would never pick someone who was little more than a stranger over the person who had cared for her and loved her. She was sorry she had hit her and then sorry that she hadn't done it years ago. Knocked some sense into her empty head. Knocked her on the right track while it was still possible and with a pulse of bitterness she thought of all the times when she was growing up that she had gathered the money to buy the right clothes, the right trainers, the latest this and the latest that, all of which enjoyed the shortest of shelf lives before their five minutes of fashion expired. All except the dressing gown. She had got it when she was about ten. Bright red with flowers embroidered on the pocket and collar. She had kept wearing it into her teenage years when her arms and legs stuck out and it just about met round her middle. Even when she stopped wearing it she had insisted on keeping it in the back of her wardrobe until years later and without comment she had cleared it out with more recent obsoletes and sent them down to the charity shop.

Reaching the hotel she went as quickly as she could through the entrance and up to her first-floor room. It wasn't good that she had to share but at least Shannon was in a different room and so whatever was going to happen would happen in the light of a new day when she hoped heads were cooler and things would somehow fit back together. He had turned Shannon's head the way once he had turned hers but he wasn't ever going to get a second chance to worm his way back into their lives. Surely she would be able to see that and when she weighed everything up she would understand where her loyalties lay. If she did this, then in time perhaps she could forgive what she thought of as her daughter's betrayal. It was also true that she could not now think of the man who had deserted her without something of him tainting her vision of Wade and already she doubted that he would ever be someone with the energy or eventual inclination to meet Shannon's inevitable expectations. At least the absence of a baby was something for which to be grateful and if they had any sense they would make sure one didn't arrive before they had got their home organised and the means to provide for it.

In the bathroom she started to scrub off the war paint and the damage of the night that made her face look like the crackled glaze on the inside of an old cup but couldn't look in the mirror without thinking herself back in the bar. She had never struck her child before and her hand still held the memory of slapping her face. She folded her costume and placed it in the bottom of her case. She would have no further need of it. Now she sought nothing more than to get into bed and to pull the sheets round her and seek to block out everything that had happened, try to fall into the deepest dreamless sleep and in the morning start to sort out the mess the way she did in her job. She felt cold and her body tried to shiver some heat into the bed but although she wanted to she would not let herself cry and so in the first night in a foreign city she burrowed her head into the pillow and tried to block out the drunken shouts of someone in the street below and the distant warning of a tram.

* * *

The mid-price hotel he had booked was in Spuistraat over-looking a canal and it was only after they had checked in that Jack realised he was sharing a room.

'Why can't I have a room of my own?' he asked, look-ing at the two beds and keeping his bag on his shoulder to suggest that he might not be staying.

'Two single rooms are much dearer than a double and it's only two nights.' For a second he thought of saying sarcas-tically that it would be more fun to share but he checked himself.

'Why are single rooms dearer?'

He sensed the potential of the issue to become a protracted one and already a little wearied by the strain of the journey he slung his bag on the bed nearest the door then sat on its end and considered his son's question.

'I suppose hotels know that single people are generally sad losers who'll pay whatever needs to be paid so they see it as a way of making more money. We each have our own bed – it's not as if we have to share.'

'Mum says you snore.'

He looked at Jack who still stood resolutely with his bag on his shoulder. His hair had flattened and died so that it looked as if he was wearing a black bathing cap. So Susan had no doubt itemised his faults to their chil-dren and he wondered if she had included his propen-sity to spill food down his front when he was eating, his tendency to leave traces of jam in the butter and his occasional inability to bring his amorous advances to a satisfactory conclusion. For a bitter second he thought of spewing out a balancing list for his wife, his ex-wife – that fact was going to take a very long time before it fully registered as a reality – but instead he simply said, 'I'll try not to.' And then he lay down on the bed, put his hands behind his head and stared at the ceiling in a gesture of exhausted surrender.

Without turning his head to look he heard his son's bag plop on to the bed and then the sound of him locking the bathroom door. So in the momentary calm he composed speeches he knew he would never deliver about sleeping in shrubbery in Vondelpark, about having no money, about never in the whole of his growing up having stayed in a hotel room, about how his first and only family holiday was in a caravan in Millisle. There was a vicarious pleasure in the unbridled freedom of being able to say what you wanted to your child without having to walk on the eggshells of potential regret at having inflicted some life-long trauma and given them reason to hate you that no sessions of therapy would ever cure. He had looked forward to seeing Bob Dylan for so long and now the experience was to be tempered by the need to accommodate his son's unpredictable and unfathomable state of being. He was grateful at least that it was getting late and soon it would be permissible to go to bed and in giving himself to sleep he would have to make no effort or worry about anyone else. And then with a pang of pain he remembered that Susan too would be sleeping in a foreign country but that she wouldn't be sleeping alone. Despite himself he started to think about things that he knew would only cause him pain and as Jack finished in the bathroom he wished he could so easily flush away the images that took pleasure in tormenting him. And so he was glad when his son emerged from the bathroom and he could turn his head sideways to look at him and say in sarcastically jolly-father style, 'Hi Jack, jimjam time?'

* * *

For some reason she had woken early and despite her best efforts couldn't make herself drift over again. She got out of the bed and went to the window. Richard slept on, his breathing steady and relaxed. He was wearing the new blue pyjamas she had bought for him in Marks & Spencer, still bearing the furrowed fold marks and smelling like fresh cotton should. The room remained too hot despite his attempts to adjust it and she regretted wearing the heavy nightdress she had chosen for the trip. She pressed her face close to the glass as if she might be able to absorb some of the cool morning air. Outside the light was milky, almost clotted as if it could be scooped in the hand and pressed to the mouth. She printed her fingers lightly on the glass and when she looked into the square below was surprised to see signs of life. Policemen hung around in relaxed mood beside their vehicle; bare-headed, arms resting on their black belts they stood watch as assorted groups of people made their way across the square, occasionally someone dropping behind to crouch over and light a cigarette, their arm raised level with their heads to act as a windbreak. She assumed they were returning from clubs but found it difficult to grasp how anyone could spend so many hours doing whatever it was they did. On the edges of the square council vehicles were cleaning and emptying bins. It was as if there was a secret life of the city that she had never glimpsed before.

She looked back at the bed but stayed with the coolness of the glass. A jogger with a dog on a lead cut a diagonal across the space below. A drunk was approaching the policemen but they stood impassively and then one waved him on and although she could not hear him, she could see that he was calling out and two of the drunk's companions returned to claim him and usher him on his way. A couple of girls wearing high heels and with cases on wheels appeared below crossing the road in front of the hotel, their cases bucking upwards when they hit the tram lines. Another troupe of young women in party dresses, although clearly together, cut a straggling broken line with the lethargy of their movements in sharp contrast to their stylish appearance. She thought how much their looks contrasted with her memory of herself and her friends. Would it be possible to organise a reunion of those surviving girls? She thought of poor Lillian dead from breast cancer and suddenly the young women in the square seemed sad vulnerable creatures, unprotected from what life might have in hold for them. So let them link arms and let them pull their shawls and flimsy jackets closer in the early light of morning if these things might ward off future danger. But perhaps her former friends would come together and find that their lives had moved on, what previously existed had faded, and that realisation would damage the memories they shared. One of the young women passing the policemen did a little pirouette and bow and got a salute in response.

She remembered the terror of her final-year school formal and the nightmare of waiting to be asked and only being saved by the complex machinations of Susan and Hilary who ran a kind of match-up service for lonely hearts. And then as she stared into the strange light she couldn't stop herself remembering what she didn't want to remember. It was sad and strange the way a thousand kindnesses might fade out of the memory while a single unkindness might remain untarnished for a lifetime. Once in the week before the formal she had overheard a group of girls in her year refer to her as Maid Marion and it was something that had managed to stay with her and despite all her efforts she could not erase. So that was how she was seen and if she had confounded them by marrying a handsome husband she had also paid the price a plain wife would always have to pay. But she was tired now of that insecurity and would have it no more in her life. It was time to give it up. For a second she glanced back at her sleeping husband as he turned on his side oblivious to her absence. How would he cope in the future? How would he come to terms with this change? That would be up to him. She thought of the young trees in the grove at home and of their scent as the early-morning light pressed them awake. They had more years of growing before their time would come and there was new planting to be done to continue the cycle. She wished more people would buy rooted trees and then replant them, but it was already clear that it was a wish that had little chance of being granted in an age where no one wanted any inconvenience and everything had to be instantly disposable. Sometimes in life patience was needed.

There was movement in the square below and she watched the policemen get into their vehicle and slowly drive away. The light was already beginning to nudge the day awake, a day when so many new things would happen, and suddenly shivering a little and not knowing whether it was from the cold or that knowledge, she went back to the bed, put her arm round him and tried to share his warmth.

Eight

S HE HAD PRETENDED TO be sleeping, lying with her face to the wall when the other two girls arrived back in the room, and in the whispers she heard no trace of Shannon's voice. Out of kindness they had undressed in the light from the bathroom and apart from one stumbling and almost falling on top of her, they had managed to get themselves into bed with as little disturbance as might be expected from two girls returning from a hen night.

When she woke in the morning she was momentarily confused about where she was and thought she had slept late for work but the unfamiliar seep of light through the poorly curtained window and the unusual combination of noises from outside reminded her of what had happened the night before. She sought at first to feel remorse but immediately her anger flared again and with it came an unchanged belief that she had been in the right and that her daughter had betrayed her in a way she could never have imagined possible. If she had been sure how to do it she would have gone home as soon as a plane could take her but understood she would have to stay until Sunday as planned. She didn't want to be there when everyone woke and knew also that there was little chance of anyone stirring before mid-morning at the earliest. The room was heavy with the stale smell of alcohol and perfume and one of the girls was snoring in a rhythmic rise and fall that already felt as if it was drilling inside her head. She knew she had to get up and out and if the prospect of spending more time on her own in a strange city intensified her already sharp sense of loneliness, it was to be preferred to staying in the mildewed tent of a room and then having the embarrassment of engaging with bleary-eyed, hung-over companions.

Showering as quickly as she could she checked to see if every trace of the previous night's make-up had gone and then dressed in the bathroom. At least her own clothes gave her some possibility of blending in and she would hopefully no longer be the focus of everyone's amused attention – the journey from the bar to the hotel had been the longest, loneliest walk in her life. She didn't want to repeat it. As she searched the pockets of her coat she found the list Mrs Hemmings had insisted on giving her but in truth she didn't care where she went so long as she was out of the hotel and in the cleanness of the morning air.

As she walked there was a comforting recognition of a city wakening itself into the life of a new day and, if it wasn't exactly the same, there was enough in common with what she encountered each morning at home to increase her sense of confidence. She walked with an assumed sense of purpose and told herself she didn't stand out or look much different from others. But the city did feel different and it wasn't just in what she physically saw but how inside her head everything felt rewired in some way that allowed new currents of sensation to course through her consciousness. She wasn't sure at first, exploring and still savouring the city like some new taste on her tongue, and then gradually there came an awareness that she liked it and with it came a sense that she was welcome as no one looked at her as if she was a foreigner or an affront to their sensibilities. So she didn't really care where she was going as long as she was walking and giving herself time to breathe and think about what must be done.

After a short hesitation and much looking in the window she went into a small bakery and bought a coffee and a bagel, surprised at how simple the transaction proved, that there was no confusion of language or incomprehension about what she was asking for. She told herself that perhaps a different country wasn't so big a deal as she had always thought, that really anyone could do it. Taking her coffee and bagel down a side street she stood at a railing overlooking a canal. The light was beginning to play on the surface of the water, teasing it with ever sharper reflections until the sky itself began to press its face against it. A barge went by, cracking wrinkles across the smoothness of its skin. She wondered if it was ever possible in the world to be anything other than on your own and whether that wasn't the best way to be. She had thought she understood Shannon and believed all of her daughter was encompassed by that understanding, so she was shaken now by the realisation that there was part of her own child that was unknown and secretive. And in that knowledge Shannon felt less like her child than some adult who had an independent life to which she was only allowed partial access. What else might be found in that secret life? On either side of the canal the houses looked stiff and formal, rich in history, rich in wealth.

When she had finished she walked on and kept walking until she crossed a bridge and passed the entrance to Vondelpark where a black choke of cyclists spluttered through the throat of the gates. She hadn't ridden a bicycle since she was a small girl and even then it was a sister's hand-me-down which she outgrew not long after she got it, her knees soon scraping the handlebars. Seeing a sign for the Rijksmuseum and remembering it was on Mrs Hemmings' list she followed it in a businesslike way because it seemed important to her to look as if she had a purpose to her journey. She hadn't been in a museum since Shannon was young, taking her there some wet Sunday afternoons in the winter when there was nowhere else to go, drifting round familiar exhibits and spending a long time in the shop and the café. But when she reached the Rijksmuseum she saw that there was no comparison in size to what she knew in Belfast. It looked more like a palace or a cathedral and for a second she felt intimidated but knew it was part of taking a photograph, even if it was only in her head, the type of photograph that decorated the desks in the offices and asserted themselves as evidence of a life being lived. So she waited patiently on a seat outside, near the kiosks that sold art prints and wooden clogs, and decided that when it opened she would go through the doors and look at whatever was inside and when she went back to work it would be one less lie she would have to tell Mrs Hemmings. And then slipping her hand in her pocket she took out the bracelet and studied it. Why had she taken it rather than simply slipping it back in the dressing-gown pocket where she had found it? It wasn't like any of the other stuff because its value was evident in every aspect of its appearance. She had never done anything like that before and she didn't understand it.

At first she wandered aimlessly in the museum, looking at the other visitors as much as the work, and in some of the galleries she found the formidable size of the paintings and their subject matter ugly and oppressive. It was too old and dead to her and the sitters seemed ridiculous in their plumed hats, wigs and elaborate costumes, their portraits all to do with money and show, and she couldn't pretend to find much that interested her. She wandered on, sometimes sitting on the seats and wondering what the other people saw when they viewed the same things as her, but she couldn't detect any outward sign that they had experienced some profound insight. Most like her simply drifted along, nothing holding their gaze for more than a few seconds, and then she wondered if she had hired the headphones whether that would have made sense of everything. Sometimes she came across a painting that told a story and she found things to like about these but *The Night Watch* meant nothing to her and seemed not much more than men with guns and spears showing off. She was glad to slip past its crowded audience and the guides pointing and explaining. But then she saw some quieter paintings which she thought were very beautiful and there was something strange about one in particular. It was a portrait of a woman and looked as if all the light was shining out of the painting and the light was so real that it almost tempted her to lift her hand and let it touch her skin. She didn't understand it and as she walked away she glanced at it over her shoulder to check whether the light had faded but saw that it was still there.

Moving on she found herself in front of a painting that made her stop and stand and stare for a long time, oblivious to the other viewers who stood on her shoulder or brushed across her vision. It was a young woman, dressed in a kind of blue smock, reading a letter that she held in both hands and it looked as if she was pregnant. Then she read how in 1691 when sold at auction the catalogue noted 'the changing light and dark suggest a splendid wellbeing'. They hadn't understood the painting, hadn't looked at the way the young woman held the letter tightly in both hands as if trying to keep her balance, hadn't seen the stiffness in her arms. She knew she was going to cry. She had to get away but she stood perfectly still, wanting to do what she knew she couldn't and reach out her hand and touch the figure in the painting, somehow comfort her for what she was reading. Instead she raised her fingers to her eyes and tried to stifle the tears that might come at any moment. Everything was loosening and falling away. A letter never brings good news, her mother had said, as if that supposed piece of wisdom was enough to impose a simple acceptance of everything. Her father had gone looking for him but came home angry and drained of colour saying she was better off without him and never all the rest of his life uttering a single word about what had passed between them, or if he had even found him.

Three months pregnant and the letter stuffed through the front door without an envelope like some local flier or cheap piece of junk mail. She'd already had the first scan and he'd come with her, taken an afternoon off work and driven her to the hospital in his van. The same van where the baby was conceived. Parked in the Craigantlet Hills, the city all sparkly and amber-beaded, spread below them like diamonds sprinkled on black cloth. He had a blanket which he stretched across the floor and they made love in the space cleared of work tools and debris from his last job. He was her first and if she didn't think it was true of him then she hadn't asked because everything was about the future and how together they might shape it.

She had been working in a bakery when he and his mate had arrived to fit new windows and doors. Right from the start when he had rubbed his hands as he inspected the counter display he was full of laughter and chat. She knew at once that he fancied her because he was happy to let it show and even exaggerate and play it up so she was never sure what was for fun and what was for real. He was about to go out on his own and set up his own business now that he had learned the ropes. Often when they went out they would walk along the seafront at Cultra – the Gold Coast, he called it – and while she looked at the sea he would look at the large expensive houses that faced it, all fronted by landscaped gardens, and he would try to get her to play the game of choosing which one they were going to own. It was only a matter of time because according to him the whole world wanted PVC and even in big houses like the ones they were passing who might turn their noses up at the idea of plastic, they were making ones that looked like mahogany and ones in Georgian style. It was guaranteed, a sure thing.

So he was going places and although he never said it openly it was clear that he saw her as someone who might share everything that was coming. And she didn't want to disappoint him or dampen his enthusiasm by telling him that none of it really mattered to her deep down so long as she had the richness of love. The night she had told him that she was pregnant every part of her was alert and sensitive to his reaction, searching his face for the truth of what he felt but even by then less sure of her ability to read what he could mask with a smile and lightness of speech. But outwardly at least he had welcomed the child and announced that they would be getting married and she had chided him for the assumption that he'd made and insisted on receiving a proposal. He'd proposed there and then and made a little joke of giving her a metal ring out of the toolbox and she'd worn it all that night as happy as if it was a diamond because the lights in the city below were bright as polished pearls strung on the current of the night.

The girl in the painting had no ring. Always postponed with some plausible excuse centred on the idea that he only wanted her to have the very best. So now as she stands in the hall of her parents' home with the light slanting across her through the front door coloured by the stained glass she too holds a letter in both hands. It's written on the paper he uses in his work and so he has made a business of her and her child. And he's not ready to be a father or to be married, as if his readiness is a requirement that must be met before he will allow himself to become anything other than what he is now. When she was a child she liked to press a clear sweet paper against the glass so that it changed colour. Turn the paper red or green. Turn it yellow or green. Magic the light. And of course he's sorry, so sorry to have let her down, but even this is his kindness because he thinks it better for this to happen now than later. She turns the letter over thinking there must be more on the other side but there's nothing and she wants to take it and press it against the glass, let the light shine through so she can see its true colours and try to understand it. The edge has little flecks and curls of white where it has been pulled from the spiral book he uses for his orders and there is the faint indentation of whatever was written on the previous page and now she wants to take the child that is growing inside her and rip it out and away from every memory of him. She wonders if there's still time and she sits on the bottom stair and listens while her father gets ready to do his taxi round. In the kitchen her mother busies herself in making his breakfast and as the smell of egg and bacon seeps down the hall she feels sick. Everything feels stalled in time. The girl in the painting is frozen too, always trapped in the moment amidst the darkness of the furniture and the heavy table fixed in front of her. There is a map behind her head. That's what's needed now – a map to show the way. She leans forward and angles her hand against the glass so that it colours a little of her skin and then she hugs the child that grows inside her and tells her that she's sorry and that she's no one now but her own and that they will only have each other. After time unfreezes, too, this young woman in blue will sit at the table and set the letter down for a moment as she tries to shape the words into meaning, because already they have sprung apart and become jumbled in her head.

Her father comes down the stairs and he's puffing a little because there's a hospital run to start his day and you can't be late for that and he says the traffic up round the Ulster is enough to give anyone a heart attack. She squirms aside to let him pass and turns her head to the wallpaper which is bruised and soiled by the years of hands that have helped themselves take the first step. Someone stands close beside her and it is her father's voice she hears and he's asking what's wrong over and over but she can't speak and then he takes the letter and reads it and calls her mother who comes out of the kitchen with a tea towel in her hands and her face flushed by the heat of the pan. She reads it too and at first no one speaks and then her mother puts her hand to her mouth as she repeats 'Oh my God', her hands first pulling at opposite ends of the tea towel as if she's trying to tear it apart then tightening it into a rope with which she might strangle someone. And she seems to hate her more than him because she's saying he's had the best of her, had it far too easy, and now he doesn't want the leftovers. There is coloured light touching her mother's feet but her words are flecked only by a bitterness and she uses the word shame twice before her father tells her to stop in a voice that is the closest to a shout that she has ever heard. And then they're still arguing while she slowly goes back up the stairs and climbs into a bed from which all the warmth has drained and so she tries to hug herself and by an effort of pure will doesn't allow herself to be sick. Then there is the slam of a car door and the sound of her father's car driving away. She wasn't sure but she thought the light in the painting looked like it was evening and she was glad because there would be no fullness of the day to stretch out ahead of her and that at least will be a mercy.

She knew now that she wouldn't cry. All her tears were released in the slow long hours of that day when her mother turned her back on her and left her to whatever misery she thought she deserved. So as she walked away through the crowds she was consoled by her anger and found in it sustenance and a strength that she knew had carried her in the past and might do so again.

He woke eager to get going, the knowledge of where he was already exercising some of its old power. Beside him Jack slept on, cocooned deep inside his white duvet, only a ragged spout of black hair sticking out like grass from a tousled fall of snow. It was still early: they had all day. There was no need to rush but then he remembered the capacity of teenagers to sleep and he deliberately stirred a little and lightly tapped the headboard. His son slept on and when he looked over he saw that he had rolled himself inside his duvet like a fat white cigarette.

There was no sound of his breathing, just a kind of strange snuffle every so often as if he was sniffing the quality of his sleep or hunting a dream truffle, and he remembered how the first time when as a baby he had slept through the night their physical pleasure had been shattered by an overwhelming fear and how they had both rushed to his cot, tormented by the worst of imaginings. That first night's unbroken sleep had been a long time coming – he remembered how a full night's sleep had become the most intense of desires and that sometimes when he had gone to work any horizontal surface was a temptation. He understood then that sleep deprivation could break a man, make him confess to anything that was asked of him.

He read his copy of Van Gogh's letters for an hour then showered and got himself ready, hopeful that the noise would waken his son, but although he continually glanced at the bed he couldn't detect any sign of him stirring. He went to the window but despite the hotel overlooking a canal the view afforded not much more than a brief glimpse of the street below and a mesh of ugly pipes and conduits. At least the day looked bright and clear and if he angled his head he could just about see blue sky. He felt hungry and was starting to worry that they would miss the breakfast that was included in the price he'd paid. For a second he took a malicious pleasure from imagining that he went out leaving Jack to stew but then felt shame at the idea of abandoning him in a strange city. For better or worse they would have to see the weekend out together and although it hadn't begun particularly well, it still represented the best chance in a long time to try and kickstart some better relationship, or at the very least to strike a better balance and find an equilibrium that would allow them to give and take just whatever each wished, without everything always feeling as if it were on the edge of disaster.

He needed to visit the Van Gogh Museum, look at a few pictures, gather some books that he might usefully – he didn't want to use the word plagiarise, even to himself – synthesise and use as the basis for some academic article that might postpone the arrival of the wolves at his door. He told himself he felt the same sense of invigoration that he always felt in this place and so his thoughts turned to his own painting. Stan had been right in one thing at least – it was too long since he had been creative and perhaps the time had come to galvanise that rusting part of himself into new life. Perhaps time to leave his old abstraction behind and branch out in a new direction. Momentarily fired by his own enthusiasm he wondered if in some way that still eluded him he could combine his research paper with this new work that already existed in his head even though it had neither subject matter nor form. And spurred on by this new surge of optimism he wanted Jack to waken so that they could get out and crest the wave of the day.

'Jack,' he whispered gently and without response. A little louder this time. 'Jack, it's time to get up if we're going to have breakfast.' The fat cigarette that was his son rolled slightly to one side and another tuft of hair puffed out, intensely black against the whiteness of the duvet cover. There was a louder snuffling noise and at last an arm worked itself free like a periscope from the tight burrow he had made of the bedclothes and briefly scanned the air before disappearing again.

'Jack, is there any chance of getting up soon – we don't want to miss our breakfast?'

He had tried to use the temptation of food but ultimately believed it had no guarantee of success because his son's biological clock ticked in ways that bore little connection with Greenwich Mean Time and the eating of meals could take place unpredictably. For all he knew Jack's clock was telling him it was the middle of the night. Perhaps his son's body was even telling him that it was winter and he should be hibernating in the dark cave of sleep. But Jack was saying something. The words were muffled and indecipherable but he was definitely speaking and as he went closer to the bed he realised he was asking what time it was. He glanced at his watch and then even though he had adjusted it on the plane added another hour to his answer. As more of his son's black head emerged like a seal's cautious appearance at an ice hole he felt a sudden burst of tenderness and had to stop himself sitting on the edge of the bed and stroking his hair. The way he did once before when he'd cried because he hadn't been selected for his primary school's football team after the trial game. Stroked it even though it appeared to have little effect until eventually his son had turned his face to the wall and sobbed as silently as he could. Then he had understood for the first time the terrible truth that you couldn't take away the pain the world gave your child and although each tear hurt him to the quick, he had been able to do nothing but sit and forlornly hope his presence would help it pass. Now as he watched his son unwind himself, a mummy come back to life and stripping away his bandages, he wanted to go to him and tell him that if it were only possible he would take all the pain of the past and all the pain that was still to come and press it on himself. And then he remembered the first time Jack had been stung by nettles and he had shown him how rubbing it with a dock leaf would ease it, and how that had been the best moment ever as a father, and he tried to hold its comfort.

'Jack,' he said and only into his child's name was he able to pour all the love he inexplicably and inexpressibly felt in that moment, 'how are you?'

'Fine.'

'That's good. Did you sleep OK?'

'OK.'

'That's good. So I didn't keep you awake?'

The answer was lost as Jack burrowed his head into the pillow and stifled a sneeze. In the corridor outside a trolley rattled and a nearby door opened and shut loudly.

'Well have a shower and get dressed and we'll have breakfast. My stomach thinks my throat has been cut.'

There was something unexpectedly awkward as his son rolled himself out of bed in a Kurt Cobain Teen Spirit T-shirt and underpants that sagged like a loose nappy round his bum and he tried to avoid looking at him, picking up his book from the bedside table and taking it to the chair at the window. He opened it at his bookmark, the memory of the thin whiteness of his son's body staring at him from the page. It was a letter to Theo dated 8th September 1888 and Vincent was talking about his new painting *The Night Café* which was the Café de la Gare where he had lodged for about five months. In it he described how he had tried to 'express the terrible passions of humanity' through his choice of colour. The phrase echoed in his head. What an incredibly bold intention, rooted deep in the hand and the heart, to express those 'terrible passions' in reds and greens, the bright brush of yellow. The tenderness he had felt in the moment for his son seeped further and into the world itself. If only even once he could paint those same passions, find the colour and the style to portray them, then everything would have been worthwhile and all his other failures would surely be absolved.

He thought of George in his skinny red flag of a shirt as it wove those patterns that mesmerised and left behind the twisted blood. He thought of the colours of the flowers strewing the hearse and the rain-washed road, the whiteness of Susan's dress that he glimpsed over his shoulder as she came towards him like the first soft snow of winter. All the colours of his life. In the church where he had been brought up, the front ice-blue fresco coped with a rainbow and bearing the gilded lettering of the text 'Worship the Lord in the Beauty of Holiness'. The sunlight stirring the red wine in the red communion glasses: the black weighted gowns of those being baptised to symbolise that they were dead to their old selves and born into their new.

There was too the first bright splatter paintings of their children that they proudly pinned on kitchen noticeboard and fridge, the ones that gave all parents hope that their children might be imbued with the blessing of talent that they themselves had missed, and, in the assurance of some acclaimed future, nourish the sustaining idea that they might be carried along in their offspring's slipstream of success. It was too early to give up on Jack – everyone was a mess as a teenager. Not to be a mess was probably more of a warning of future dysfunction than the other way round. And there was the music. There was infinite hope in his love of music and his attempts to start a band and perhaps seeing Dylan would spark something and encourage him to go and make his own, whatever type that might be.

As he listened to his son rattling round in the hollow soundbox of the bathroom he set his book down and remembered the first time he heard Dylan. Probably around the age Jack was now. His parents had bought him a record player – they probably came later to think of it as the Trojan horse they had unwittingly brought into their house – a simple red mono box that he would treasure for the next ten years and then he'd bought his first LP in the city-centre Gramophone Shop. A record player and one record. *Bob Dylan's Greatest Hits*. He could never hear the opening organ sounds and the ragged jangling chords of 'Like a Rolling Stone' and not be transported back to that moment when everything that was fixed and settled in a permanent dreary conformity seemed to shift and the world itself tilted on its axis. Nothing could ever be quite the same as it had been before. If Jack could find that awakening, the same sense of expectancy even though it felt deliciously reckless, almost dangerous, then perhaps his life would embrace the momentum to move itself in a new direction.

At last Jack emerged and said he was ready. They made the breakfast with fifteen minutes to spare and as he paused to give their room number Jack almost walked into his back, so intent was he on stepping in his shadow. At the buffet he filled his plate but watched his son lift the most meagre of helpings – two pieces of toast, a slice of ham and a small glass of orange juice.

'Is that all you want?'

'Yes.'

'Why don't you take one of those croissants – there's a chocolate one. Or take a yogurt or a bit of cheese.'

He answered with a shake of his head then asked, 'Do you have to take so much?'

'We've paid for it. They expect you to take what you want. And the more we eat now the later we'll need to buy something.'

'I don't want anything else,' he said, staring across the table at his father's plate with accusatory eyes.

'Fair enough but if you want anything else you can go up and get it, or if you like I'll go for you.'

'I don't want anything else,' he said again, spreading the butter carefully on his toast with both sides of his knife, making sure it went right to all the edges. He didn't eat the ham – there was something wrong with it.

'It's smoked, Jack.'

'Do you want it?'

'OK, give it here.'

With a light kiss of their two forks there was a delicate transfer of the ham that had deviated from his son's expectations by not being exactly the same as the one with which he was familiar. They both looked at it, Jack with a kind of accusation in his eyes, and then he ate it and when he did so he wanted to point his fork and tell his son that he should taste everything the world was good enough to offer him. But already he knew that he had to stop this, constantly constructing unspoken homilies and inflating every one of his son's idiosyncrasies into some symbolic significance. He had to try harder, make the best of things as they were, not always seeking in his head to construct something new.

'So, Jack, what would you like to do today?'

'I don't know. What do you want to do?'

'Well at some point I need to go to the Van Gogh Museum and pick up a few things. It won't take long. But apart from that we can do anything you want. Would you like to go to the Anne Frank house?'

'I'm not really interested in history.'

Immediately he cued the record on the turntable about the Holocaust and knowing history so that it could be stopped from happening again and was about to press play when he looked at Jack and stopped. Even though part of him wanted to reach across the table and grab him by the throat, shake into him the reality of six million dead, when he did stretch out his hand it was only to remove a morsel of toast that somehow clung to the side of his son's mouth. The act startled both of them, Jack pulling his head back as if about to be struck and him by the fact that his son should have thought that. In that moment he was intensely grateful that he had never hit him as a child, given him that memory to nurse into an adult resentment. They both stared at their now empty plates.

'I know a good market we could go to. We can walk there in about fifteen minutes.'

'A market? With food and stuff?'

'No, although there is some food it's just about every-thing under the sun. Clothes, records, junk – everything really. Lots of interesting stuff.'

'OK.'

The response stopped short of enthusiasm but at least it wasn't a rejection and so the day was starting with a glim-mer of possibilities. However, as they set off it was clear that Jack thought walking in Indian file was best and as they were mostly making their way along narrow pavements and negotiating other people and various obstacles it didn't rankle quite so much as it might have done. As they walked he pointed out things – the houses that were narrow because tax was based on frontage size, the pulleys that were used to get furniture inside. He knew in part he was talking to himself but he also wanted to convey to Jack something of the exhilarating sense of adventure that he had felt on those first visits. In response Jack stared at him blankly and then after a discourse about reclaiming land from the sea said flatly, 'Dad, stop telling me things.'

'Sorry.'

He tried to assuage his hurt feelings with an acknowl-edgement that he had harped on too much, tried too hard to help his son see things the way he had seen them. Let the boy breathe. Let the boy see things through his own eyes, take his own footsteps.

They reached the market, a warren of stalls selling new and second-hand clothes; old furniture and knick-knacks; the dismantled innards of radios, televisions and parts of computers; endless jewellery; CDs and DVDs, in some cases of doubtful legality; T-shirts with slogans and images of rock icons. Dreadlocked vendors sold all things African and Rastafarian flags with images of Bob Marley and over everything hovered the waft of fast food, the fibrous hessian smell of alternative clothing and the sweet scent of incense sticks. At first they wandered slowly through the thorough-fares and then at his heel he heard Jack say something. He paused and looked back at him to check that he had caught it correctly.

'Cool,' Jack said again.

It was the first unsolicited response his son had uttered since they arrived and he didn't know how to respond but he was sure that the one thing he wasn't going to do was tell him anything, or suffocate the moment with words, so he simply nodded his head and tried not to skip as he walked. Jack seemed particularly interested in jewellery, browsing over the displays and touching things lightly with his finger, and he realised that he was looking for something to give to Jasmine. Eventually he bought her a bracelet shaped like a snake and the girl who sold it treated him nicely and took lots of care in wrapping it, handing over a pretty little pack-age with an equally pretty smile. He seemed pleased with himself. Then there were more stalls to explore and they spent a lot of time at a hat seller's which offered all sorts including what looked like ex-Russian military fur hats. They tried everything on, studying themselves in the mirror until one or the other indicated with a shake of the head that the look wasn't right. There were other clothes stalls where Jack ran his hand along a line of leather jackets and he could tell that he was interested but unwilling to ask about the price.

'Do you want to try one on?' he asked, pointing to the rack. 'I'll sub you if you want but we need to haggle over whatever price he quotes us at the start.'

Jack wasn't sure but then the stall's owner lifted his head from his paper and offered a seemingly disinterested open-handed invitation to try on whatever he wanted before resuming his reading. Starting at the end of the rail he angled each one for inspection before quickly moving to the next. Then he reached one he liked and tried it on, giving him his coat and package to hold before looking at himself in the full-length mirror, uncertainty etched on his face. He was about to suggest that the sleeves were too long and the lining was ripped a little but stopped himself.

'What do you think?' Jack asked, looking at him as if his opinion was suddenly important.

'I think the sleeves are a bit long but leave it out and keep looking.'

Jack nodded and worked on through the rail until he came to a studded jacket. He lifted it out and leaned it back over the rail. 'Cool,' he said.

'Very cool,' he said as he watched his son trace the pattern of the studs. 'Try it for size.'

It was slightly big in the shoulders, bulking up his thinness, but apart from that it fitted well. They both knew it was the one.

'Don't appear too enthusiastic. Keep looking along the rail. I'll ask how much he's after.'

The answer came back, thirty euros, and he turned to Jack and told him to offer less. He hesitated and then asked if he would do it for him. Something made him shake his head.

'Offer him twenty and see what he says. Go on, he expects you to do it.'

Jack considered it, torn between his desire for the jacket and nervousness. As he approached the stallholder he felt as if he was watching again his son's Christmas-morning first bike ride, or first swim in the sea. When he looked back over his shoulder for reassurance he nodded him on and then there he was, offering twenty, and when greeted with a reply of twenty-five he handed over his money immediately and almost desperately as if the deal was in danger of falling through. As he put the jacket in the bag the vendor smiled over at him and he felt proud of his child as if in buying this jacket they had shared something good. The jacket was a badge. In his imagination it was timeless and could once have been worn by a young teddy boy or a punk and now it was the chosen gear of an Emo or Nemo or whatever mysterious sub-group Jack belonged to, like a baton passed in relay in the eternal race to be cool.

After the market they went to one of the hot-food stalls and had hot dogs and cans of Coke, standing like seasoned punters at the chest-high metal tables. When they had finished and were leaving Jack stopped at a sprawling bric-a-brac stall and started to inspect everything with delicate, precise care.

'I'm looking for a present for Mum,' he said as he finally settled on a small wooden box that was probably meant to store jewellery. When he was told the price he told the seller that it was too dear and then waited for a lower one with the air of a professional dealmaker.

A present for his mother. He tried to suppress a tiny pang of jealousy and as they walked back the way they'd come he told himself that the time they'd spent in the market was his. His and his alone. Stored away.

They had no real plan when they set out, despite Richard scrutinising his map as if organising an expedition, and were both surprised at how mild it was, the briskness of their walk keeping them pleasantly warm. They went first to one of her favourite places – the floating flower market on the Singel Canal – where she was always amazed by how many beautiful varieties were on display. Even now at this time of year it still offered a variety of choice and prices that were so reasonable in contrast to the shops at home which she always characterised by their predictable and narrow range, their workaday carnations and chrysanthemums, not to speak of the ugliness of most garage flowers. She enjoyed looking at the bonsai plants, the garden ornaments and the bulbs with their photographs that seemed to guarantee future bloom. They had an argument over whether they were allowed to bring bulbs back home but she believed they could and bought some dark purple, almost black tulips, intending to plant them in pots at the front of the house. It was getting late for planting but there was still time and the mild weather would help.

They went into the all-year-round Christmas shop and looked at the contents with both a personal and a professional eye, wondering whether there were any lines that might be good business for them. There was every conceivable item, ranging in price from a few euros to the incredibly expensive. She was drawn to the nativity scenes, some of them garish but others simply carved out of wood and delicately painted. She bought one of these – it was something she had always wanted and she thought her grandchildren would like it when they came to the house. After she paid for it she arranged to collect it later on in the morning when they were returning to the hotel.

She wanted this morning to follow a familiar pattern and although her mind often fast-forwarded she tried to stay calm. It was best to be occupied like this and Richard seemed relaxed, happy to follow her round shops and the places they had visited before. In the Chinese shop a few doors further on she bought small items as stocking fillers for the grandchildren – embroidered notebooks, silk purses, green alabaster horses – and a lacquered jewellery box for Judith. When she asked Richard if he would like anything, probably just to please her he picked a light-green cup with a lid and decorated with blue fish. She liked it and bought one to match so they would have a pair. Sometimes as they walked she looked at him and wanted to speak to him but couldn't find the words and mostly she believed that this thing was best kept out of words, that it would happen and then it would be over and never be spoken of. She felt comfortable in his company but as they passed the last flower boat she thought of Anka and his idea of setting her up in the local florist shop, then imagined it transformed from the dullness of its present self with beautiful flowers – delphiniums, anemones, peonies – and Anka with her blonde hair and blue eyes standing amidst them and smiling.

A clock tower chimed and she was cross for letting herself think in this way. And then Richard was pointing something out to her and for a second she was confused about the direction she should look, and then she saw it. There on a kind of open barge was a wedding party, the bride in a long white dress and with flowers in her hair, her bridesmaids sitting round her on chairs. She managed only a glimpse before the barge disappeared under the next bridge and out of sight and it made her think of her daughter and wonder when she too would find someone to love.

'Beats a horse and cart,' Richard said and she smiled, sorry that she hadn't been able to get a longer look.

They walked back and down Kalverstraat towards Dam Square but most of the more familiar chain stores held less interest for them and they looked at the other shoppers as much as the window displays.

'Do you remember the first time we came here with the children,' he asked, 'and the afternoon we thought we'd lost Judith?'

'Hard to forget. I'd started to panic and then there she was following pigeons off into the distance,' she said, flinching inside at the memory.

'Shows how easy it is to lose a child. Just a few seconds and they can be gone.'

'You'd never forgive yourself if it happened. It was because Adam had spilt his ice cream down his front and we were both looking after him.'

'And the time we went to Disney after hearing all those stupid stories about children being taken and sold in South America to childless couples,' he said, leaning into her arm slightly. 'And you insisted on them wearing those wristbands attached to us.'

'Better safe than sorry and I think the stories were true.'

'It's an urban myth, Marion. If kids went missing you'd be hearing about it because it'd be all over the news and television. The thing I remember most is the way the leads kept getting tangled as they tried to run all over the place, hyper. Like having a pack of hounds pulling you.'

She smiled at his description but it was also true that she had let so many parts of her life be governed, if not by fear, then by apprehension and anxiety. Even that trip to Disney. It was a weight that wearied her and she told herself that after this day she would throw it off and walk lighter, do what had to be done to free the future for them. The shared memory of the children was a tender moment between them and underlying his teasing playfulness was a gentleness that she valued in him. She could never be with anyone who was aggressive or any kind of threat to her or her children. He had been a good father, generous and tolerant, only working

194

up to formal rebukes of his children when she had considered it necessary and not dragging it out, or ever being petty or vindictive. She struggled to remember when he had ever displayed any form of anger to her and couldn't do so and thought that the worst she could say about him was that he was a little stuck in his ways and occasionally capable of being stubborn when he thought he was in the right. Did he desire her? She wasn't sure. The times when he came to her were not predictable or regular and she didn't know if it was less or more than couples who were married as long as they had been. And did he come out of desire or out of simple impersonal need? She wondered if any woman could ever know this, then wondered, too, if it really mattered so long as he came.

As they sat at the window of the café the sun set his face in sharp definition. The grey hairs at his temples were thickening and stretching ever higher, some of the frown lines on his forehead deepening. In places the years of working outdoors had blemished his skin slightly and on his right cheekbone there was a stippled cluster of red dots that she had never noticed before, like dots of rust on the leaf of a plant. The light seemed, too, to drain some of the colour from his eyes so that they were rendered pellucid, strangely lifeless. Suddenly she was struck by the fear that he might be ill and, reaching out her hand between the cups, laid it on the back of his. She was conscious of how little it covered, the broad fingers that outstretched hers.

'How are you feeling, Richard? You look a little tired. Are you all right? In yourself.'

'Have you been getting the health insurance policies out? I feel fine.'

'You'd always tell me if there was anything wrong, wouldn't you?'

'Of course but there's nothing wrong, Marion. Nothing I know about and it's good to get away like this – a change is as good as a rest. We should try and get away more often.'

'I'd like that,' she said, taking her hand back again, glad that the sun had weakened and almost faded.

'But you're not doing my health any good by bringing me in places like this and buying me chocolate cake.'

'You've some on the corner of your mouth.'

She watched him dab at it with a napkin and then had to direct him by pointing at the place on her own face, nodding when he had succeeded. The moment made him look boyish despite the slant of sun that a few seconds earlier had suddenly and surprisingly etched his age on his face. Was what she was going to do an act of unspeakable foolishness or the thing that would help both of them in their future lives? She had another pulse of doubt and then she remembered the young women in the gym punishing themselves by eternally trying to run towards what they wanted to be. How was this so very different? It seemed a shortcut, the pain not drawn out or even perhaps meaning so much as others might think, and what meaning did it really have except the meaning you chose to give it?

They walked on to Dam Square and later on had lunch in one of the cafés in a shopping precinct that they didn't remember from previous trips, built in the shell of an older building. On their journey back to the hotel they collected the nativity scene and she wondered what it would be like to sell nothing but Christmas goods all year round and wondered also how many of her trees had been bought in her absence. It was complicated to get the figures right, in knowing how to balance out harvesting and planting, how to meet the requirements to qualify for government grants. Sometimes she wondered if the grants were worth the laborious tedium of the paperwork. Before they went home she would tell him about the black Christmas trees. About the black Christmas trees and not going back to the gym. This would be a special Christmas and she looked forward with pleasure to having all her family back home and under one roof. There would be presents for everyone and a cheque for each of their children given inside a card. She, however, had always hated getting money at Christmas, no matter how penurious her finances. There was no mystery, no magic in money. You couldn't unwrap money or weigh it in your hands with touch and anticipation perfectly synchronised and even when that same anticipation proved an anticlimax it couldn't entirely erase the previous pleasure of imagining.

She would set the nativity scene on the hall table where it could also be seen from the living room. Although she wasn't religious she liked the idea of refinding some connection with that part of the celebration. In recent years as the stresses of the event seemed magnified and exacerbated she had begun to wonder if it was all worth it and privately to long for something simpler and more in keeping with the memories she had from the past. Often, too, she felt she was part of that pressure through their business. No one, apart from the fanatics, bought garden plants in December so it was necessary to supplement their normal trade with the sale of trees and Christmas fare but she wished that some of it could be less tacky. She had liked the nativity set because it wasn't over-elaborate and had a plain simplicity in its carved wooden figures, unlike some of the others which in her eyes looked like the garish, grotesque replication of some grotto. The grandchildren could play with the figures, rearrange the scene how they wished and nothing would get broken.

* * *

On their way to the Van Gogh Museum Jack stopped at a shop that sold all sorts of herbal and legal highs and he watched uncomfortably as his son pressed his face against the glass to read the content descriptions and the promised, mostly ecstatic, effects produced. It reminded him of the small amount of cannabis that Susan had found in his bedside table and the late-night phone-call summons to the house where he had found her on the edge of hysteria constructing a future image of their son as a professional smackhead. They had their confrontation with Jack in the kitchen while outside moths pinged themselves against the lighted windows and Jack was initially unrepentant and assumed a favoured default position that everyone did it, just as everyone illegally downloaded music, spent lots of time on their computers and got drunk every now and again. With Susan relentless in her pursuit of supplier and threatening to call the police and everyone just short of the FBI, he had eventually steered them both into a calm-bringing admission that it was really only an experiment and their son didn't have a habit or want to get into it big time. The price his mother had imposed was regular searches under the guise of cleaning and the equally regular leaving of newspaper articles on his desk about the brain-frying dangers of its use. So as Jack actually smudged the glass with his nose he felt an unease stirring and a relief that Susan wasn't there to see their son's interest.

That night after Jack had received their admonition and what they believed was wise parental counsel and skulked off to his bedroom with the body language of the aggrieved party, Susan had cried a little and thanked him for coming over. She had made them coffee and as of old they had sat at the kitchen table over which so much of the conversation of their lives had crossed. He had reached out a consoling hand to rest on her shoulder and she had patted the back of his hand and for a second he dared to hope but almost immediately she had stood up, excused by the need of a tissue.

'The drugs don't work, Jack,' he said lightly as he, too, examined the window's content, wondering if the promised highs were merely the product of imagination but momentarily admiring the caption writer's ability to euphemistically capture the supposed pleasure-enhancing qualities of the goods.

'What's that?' Jack asked, indicating something which took a few seconds of further pointing to locate.

'It's some kind of mushroom extract.'

'Weird.'

He didn't know whether Jack's 'weird' was a good or a bad thing but he deliberately glanced at his watch to try and register his desire to move on while privately wondering what psychoactives were.

'Probably mushes up your brain into a kind of fungus. I'd stick to mushroom soup out of a tin.'

'What's that?' This time he was pointing to some complex piece of piping that looked like it should belong in a science laboratory.

'I don't know, Jack, I really don't know.'

'Look – they have hemp lollipops,' he said, giggling, with his bobbing head in danger of bumping the glass.

He didn't know what to say so he repeated lifelessly, 'The drugs don't work.' Then as an afterthought, 'Life's got enough crazy things of its own to screw your head up without helping it.'

Jack turned and looked at him, his reflection angled on the glass in the winter sun so for a second it appeared as if there were two of him.

'You must have tried stuff when you came here. When you were young.'

'No I didn't and I suppose that makes me even more boring. I was never interested in any of this stuff; it just never appealed to me,' he answered, unsure if his son believed him and secretly wondering if his advice might have had greater resonance if it sprang from the well of experience, instead of, as he suspected, making him look like a dried-up puritan.

'All hippies smoked dope,' Jack said, stepping away from his reflection until he cancelled out his other self.

'I was a hippy only in my head and anyway I came at the end of all that stuff so I wasn't actually part of it.'

Jack's phone beeped a text message and for the next few minutes his thumb was the hammer on a rapidly firing gun. As he stood and watched he thought about how often his son was in remote but intimate communication with someone and couldn't decide whether it was a good or a bad thing. Then memories of how often at the same age he had felt cut off from others crowded in, and of the long slow nights in a box bedroom listening to singer-songwriter angst which had only served to intensify his own. When he had come the first time to Amsterdam there had been young people with guitars in Vondelpark playing Neil Young songs and crazy guys with bongo drums beating out endless rhythms. Jack's head was bent over the phone and his total concentration allowed him to look at his son unseen. The paleness of his skin against the forced blackness of his hair once again struck him as did his son's thinness and the delicacy of his hands. His own were clumpy, thick in the fingers, the tips almost square like chisels. He was also increasingly aware that his son seemed to suffer from occasional twitches and tics, inexplicable little physical stutters that came and went in the blink of an eye.

They walked on and as they headed back towards the Leidseplein he forced himself to concede that he probably was still a bit of an abstainer. And although he no longer cherished a religious faith perhaps it was the legacy of his childhood and all those years sitting looking at the text that spoke of the beauty of holiness and never being sure what was holy and what wasn't. So whether Jack believed him or not it was the truth and although he really wanted to, he knew he couldn't start to expound on all the things that gave him a high. Music, books, films and art in all its forms. That's what did it for him. And women of course although this was an area in which he would have been more than willing to be less abstemious if the opportunities had only presented themselves. There had been a girl of course – an American student from Chicago – with whom he had spent some time in exploring the city but it hadn't amounted to much more than two slightly nervous young people chastely clinging to each other momentarily in the face of the unfamiliar.

But as he turned away from Jack to afford him some privacy he still wondered what messages shot back and forth across the ether. Then it came back to him, the night as a small boy when he had arranged to signal with torches to his friend who lived in the next street and whose bedroom was just visible. At precisely eleven o'clock when they were supposed to be fast asleep they had flashed their torches in the darkness, thrilled briefly by the returning signals and transported for a little while to the world of the Famous Five or stories about spies, but then both realised that they had no code, no way of actually talking to each other and after a few minutes they had given up as the excitement slowly drained away. Still, there was something touchingly sentimental and poignant about the memory, the image of the torches flashing secretly and mysteriously through the darkness, across the sleeping gardens and the deserted streets.

'Is it much further?' Jack asked in a little boy's voice after they had walked on for a while in the face of a wind that was strengthening and becoming sharp-edged.

'About five minutes. Why don't you put your jacket on – it's getting chilly.'

'I'm all right,' he said, shrugging his shoulders as if to brush off the intimate touch of the cold. But the wind tousled his hair and flipped strands across one of his eyes.

And so they trudged on towards the open, windblown spaces of the Museumplein where a small demonstration of some sort was taking place with an assortment of streaming banners and flags and huddled groups of mostly young people. Close to the Van Gogh Museum there was a group of five men in ponchos playing 'Quanta La Mera' on pan pipes and a large sombrero on the ground to collect donations. It must have been an unsuccessful afternoon because the wind was able to move it before the restraining foot of one of the players trapped it in place. It was the first time he'd managed to enter the museum without having to join a queue but going through the doors he promised Jack that they wouldn't spend too long before moving on.

He increasingly liked the idea of writing something about Van Gogh who had single-handedly become an art industry and whose populist appeal had pushed him outside the snobbish parameters of art criticism. To academics he was the equivalent of *The Sound of Music* or an airport novel and he doubted whether anyone had recently deigned to sharpen their analytical sword on such a romanticised and commercialised subject. In art and art criticism obscurity was the password to the inner sanctums and he could think of no other area where the dividing line between talent and gibberish was so often uncertainly vague. If he was cynical, and he tried not to be, then this was the shadowlands in which the clever or even the wilfully exploitative might pitch their tent. The idea of making Van Gogh and Gauguin the subject of his proposed article was growing on him and seemed to be a smart piece of radicalism, so as he arranged with Jack that they would meet in the café in precisely one hour, he felt a surge of enthusiasm and a feeling that things might happen.

Because his time was limited he had already identified the paintings that were completed in the period when the two painters shared the Yellow House and so he set out in a methodical way to look at these, writing short notes in the little book he had brought with him. It really felt as if he was engaged in research and that despite its spontaneous and desperate origins, it could possibly amount to something and perhaps the talk with Stan, or rather the talk from Stan, might well have been in his best interests in awakening a new flourish of creative thought and work. But as the time wore on he became increasingly conscious that Jack was somewhere else and, as soon as that idea intruded, the genetic hardwiring of parenthood programmed his brain into reflex thoughts of potential risk, of Jack absconding, of kidnapping, of self-harm, of anything that would stir an accusatory sense of guilt at his supposed dereliction of duty. So quickly cramming in a few final paintings he pocketed his notebook and hurried to the café where he saw his son already ensconced with a Coke and his headphones in place, his legs stretched under the table and resting on the chair opposite. He was tearing a little sachet of sugar and puddling it with his finger, oblivious to his approach. There was no telling how long he'd been there but he guessed he hadn't spent much time looking at paintings and he felt annoyed and then just sad. Ignoring him he went to the counter and bought a coffee and a muffin then sat at the table beside him. Jack looked at him but didn't nod or remove his head-phones and for an irritated second he thought of taking his coffee and muffin to another table, possibly one that looked out over the Museumplein, and comforting himself with the sight of young people caring about something enough to wave a flag. But as he hesitated Jack removed his head-phones to ask him how much the muffin cost and without answering he pushed it across the table towards him and stared into his coffee.

'So what did you think of the paintings?' he asked, wishing he had brought some sugar to ease the unexpected bitterness of the coffee.

'They're OK. But I don't think he's that good a painter.'

'No?'

'He's OK but some of the stuff doesn't look that good.'

'Lots of other people thought that,' he said, watching his son prise the muffin apart into bits he could place in his mouth, then just as he was about to launch into the predict-able and weary only-sold-one-painting patter he stopped himself. 'So who do you think's a good painter then, Jack?'

'Me?'

'Yes, you do GCSE art in school so there must be some-one you think is good.'

He watched as Jack funnelled the last segment of the muffin into his mouth. Some crumbs fell to the table and mingled with the sugar. 'I don't know,' he said, shrugging a little.

'There must be someone you like.' It suddenly felt impor-tant that his son should say a name – almost any name would do so long as he expressed an opinion – and as he sipped his coffee he watched Jack's finger puddle in the sugar again.

'Roy Lichtenstein,' he said without any sense of enthusiasm.

'Roy Lichtenstein, right. Pop art. So you like Lichtenstein?'

Jack nodded as one of his hands started to fidget with the earpiece in what looked like a preliminary to putting it back in place.

'What else do you like, Jack?'

'Painters?'

'No, just anything. What do you like?'

'Why are you asking?'

'Because I'm interested.' And because he wanted to know where his son found some glimpse of joy and because he found it intensely comforting to think that there might be things in the world that pleased him and helped him be alive. But he saw the reluctance in his son's face to play this game where things would have to be revealed instead of shrouded in the protective fog of mystery. 'And if you don't tell me a few things I'm going to bore you to death by talking about Lichtenstein. So which of his paintings do you like?'

'*Whaam!*'

'It's my favourite, too. "I pressed the fire control . . . and ahead of me rockets blazed through the sky." Classic.'

'Music.'

'Did you listen to the Dylan stuff I taped for you?'

'No. We don't have a cassette player any more.'

'What happened to the one that used to be in the front room?'

'I sold it on eBay. Nobody uses cassette tapes any more. But I downloaded some tracks,' he said, as if that was compensation for selling something that didn't belong to him.

'Isn't that illegal?'

'The whole world does it. They're not going to be able to send the whole world to jail.' The familiar tone of exasperation puffed across the table like mushroom spores.

'I suppose they've worked that out and will pick on a few individuals.'

'Comics,' Jack said.

'Comics?'

'I like comics.'

'What type?'

'Japanese manga.'

'So when did you get interested in these?'

'About a year ago.' He stared at his fingerprint in the sugar. 'Just after you left.'

From outside came the muffled sound of voices chanting. He lifted his cup to his lips but didn't drink as he pondered what to say.

'Van Gogh went through a period where he was very influenced by Japanese things. You can see it in some of the paintings.' He set the cup down clumsily so that it rattled against the saucer. 'Are you angry that I left?'

'No.'

Jack shuffled a little on his chair, his body seeming to shrink into stiff angular lines while his eyes stayed fixed on the table.

'You'd be entitled to be angry. I screwed up.'

'Why did you?' he asked, his eyes fixing on him and blinking with something which he wasn't sure was anger or nervousness.

'Screw up?'

'Cheat on Mum.'

He was glad his cup was empty: the coffee had seemed to get stronger the more he drank. He glanced over Jack's shoulder where a mother was negotiating her child's reluctant legs into a highchair. He held the cup again this time in both hands, hoping in vain to feel even the memory of its heat. The child was struggling against its impending loss of freedom but the father momentarily distracted him with the rattle of a toy and in a second he was being strapped in and further mollified by the offer of what looked like a biscuit. It wasn't where he wanted to have this conversation. It seemed as if some event in the museum was ending and more families were arriving with the children carrying balloons and there was a rising tide of sound punctuated by the clatter of trays and the squeak of chairs being rearranged.

'I know I owe you an answer to that question and I'll do my best to give you it but I don't think this is a good place. Let's go somewhere else, somewhere we can talk.'

Jack didn't answer but stood up, carefully stowed his earphones and lifted the bag which contained his leather jacket with the blackness of the leather shining through the thinness of the plastic. When they got outside the protest had disappeared and instead couples walked dogs and groups of friends posed for photographs. On the temporary ice rink that had been created in the Museumplein figures were skating as if in a winter scene by Bruegel. But the painting that replaced it in his mind was that of the old man crying, as he remembered the blueness of his tunic, the yellow of the chair, and then he tried desperately to think of what he was going to say.

Nine

I N THE HOTEL ROOM she carefully unwrapped the nativity scene and arranged the figures on the table by the window. He teased her about not waiting until Christmas before playing with her present but she didn't answer and concentrated on finding the best place for each figure. She liked the wise men best, their hands outstretched with the gifts they had brought. How strange those gifts must have seemed in the poverty of a stable. It was almost time and her nervousness made her fumble with the final figures, then she glanced down into the square and scanned the people hurrying on their way. Her hand trembled a little as she placed the last figure. She was pleased with the presents she had bought for her family and already they had been wrapped and labelled – she had used different-coloured paper for each of her three children and her sons' families. The only remaining present was for her husband and she couldn't see past that afternoon or fully comprehend its future consequences to consider what such a present might be.

Faithfulness had never been demanding for her either as an obligation or as a commitment. She had never been with another man emotionally let alone physically and she couldn't believe that would ever change. There had been the sales rep a few years ago who had tried to flirt with her, complimented her a little too freely, but it had only made her feel awkward and she never knew whether his attentions were prompted by genuine feelings or part of his sales ploy. It had been flattering the first time but she'd been glad when he had moved on to another area. She turned from the window and looked at her husband who lolled on the edge of the bed while flicking through the television stations, his attention held by each for only a few seconds. It felt as if she was falling helplessly through a dream without the respite of wakening or the prospect of stepping into the clarity of a new day. She didn't trust herself to speak. He had found a rugby game on the television and he leant backwards supported by both his arms as he watched it. The room felt too warm again.

She tidied away a few tourist leaflets and an empty bottle of water. If she ever came back to Amsterdam she would buy flowers in the market for her room. Perhaps come in the summer and have so much choice. Tall stems of blue delphiniums – that's what she would have. She thought of Anka with her blue eyes. Thought of her standing amidst the flowers of the market with her arms open and the sun burnishing her blonde hair, remembered the laughter she had overheard and how it had stopped on her arrival. Now, too, she would step inside and make things the way she wanted them to be rather than wait for ever, the slave of uncertain time and circumstance. This was the moment and she couldn't put off speaking any longer, so going back to the window she brushed back the curtain with her hand and picked out faces in the square below.

'Richard, I'm just going out for a moment – there's something I'd like to take back home. For presents.'

'I thought you'd got everything already,' he said without taking his eyes off the screen.

'It's just a couple of boxes of handmade chocolates. I won't be long.'

'Are you sure? Why not just get them at the airport tomorrow?'

'I'd rather be sure I've got them.'

'Do you want me to come with you?' he asked, looking at her for the first time.

'No need – you stay and watch your rugby. I'll not be long.'

She picked up her coat and bag from the chair then hesitated.

'Don't be getting kidnapped or running off with a sailor,' he said, his face breaking into a smile.

She felt a sweep of love pass through her and a new and sharper uncertainty. She had to pass him to leave.

'There's not much chance of that. You can't get rid of me that easy,' she said and kissed him lightly on the forehead. He took her arms and for a second it felt as if he would pull her forward on to the bed but she stiffened her back and told him once more she wouldn't be long. At the door she turned again and spoke the words she had tried to rehearse but had failed to shape in any way that satisfied her, so now she simply let them stumble out to find their own freedom.

'Richard. I'm coming back because I love you. And I'm going because there's something I'd like you to have and it's all right and I want you to have it and then we can go back home and don't need to talk about it.'

She opened the door before the confusion on his face could find expression in words. As she quickly closed it she could hear him calling her name but she hurried on and took the lift. The Japanese couple were in it again, also going down to the foyer. They smiled at her and she returned it, hoping that they would think the flush on her face and the quickness of her breathing was caused by rushing. There was the same elaborate politeness over who should exit first until she gestured insistently and as she left she briefly caught her reflection, a blurred, slightly untidy woman whose coat collar was partly turned up and whose hair needed attention. She went to the ladies' – it seemed important to look her best – and brushed her hair and retouched her make-up. There was a young woman standing at the mirrored wall and she glanced furtively at her combing her hair with long sweeping strokes that made it look as if a light breeze had crept under it to gently lift the ends. She wanted to splash her face but stopped herself and turned to leave just as the young woman dropped the comb in her bag and gave her hair a final smooth with the palms of her hands.

In the foyer she glanced at the clock and then walked quickly to the hotel entrance. The woman was already there at the top of the steps. She recognised her right away – the photograph hadn't lied – and she shook her hand as she said her name. It seemed important to be formal and business-like. They took each other in as quickly as good manners would allow and then discreetly she gave her the envelope which was equally discreetly slipped into the pocket of a winter coat. Perhaps she was a little older than the photograph but not by much and if anything she was glad of that, just as she was glad that her appearance was not designed to attract attention or cause embarrassment. But suddenly real and in the flesh and no longer an image on a computer that could be closed with a click, the reality of the moment pressed against her with all its rawness. The Japanese couple passed them, their opened map fluttering momentarily in the breeze like a flag. She wavered. The Japanese woman glanced over her shoulder, a tiny shimmer of curiosity in her eyes before she turned again and pressed their map into submission. It was still possible to call the whole thing off and walk away. The money didn't matter. She no longer knew what did and in that moment couldn't be sure whether she moved inside a dream or had crossed over into madness. Perhaps it wasn't Richard who was ill but herself, slowly eaten away by some malevolent and malignant sickness that had marked her out, secretly pursuing her down the road of all her years.

'Are you sure?' Lastri asked her, laying her hand gently on her forearm.

It was the kindness that convinced her. And perhaps that's what it was – a kindness, a kindness given out of her love – and somehow in that act, she would be able to go on with her life, no longer looking over her shoulder or measuring herself against the mirror of every young woman who crossed their path. Let him have his invitation and let him know that she gave her blessing, gave it fully and with love.

'I'm sure,' she said as she handed over the room keycard. It, too, discreetly slipped into the pocket of the coat. They moved past each other on the steps. For a second she allowed herself to be pleased with her choice just as he had been pleased with the other gifts she had bought that morning – the thought she had put into the items. She watched as the young woman strode confidently to the hotel entrance, the black glossy fall of her ponytail clapping quick time to the rhythm of her movements.

'Lastri,' she called. The woman stopped, her outstretched hand frozen on the hotel's revolving door, and turned to look down at her. 'I never told you his name – his name is Richard and he's a good man.'

Lastri nodded quickly and then she was gone through the door and out of sight. She turned to the city, forcing herself to look it full in the face, and then she started to walk. She wished she was back in her forest early on a Sunday morning when most of the world was still asleep and the new day slowly sprang the scent of the trees into freedom. The previous Sunday there had been a thin mist filtering through the rows like smoke and the branches had been webbed and latticed with what looked like spun lace. Once she saw a fox, its red shiver suddenly slinking out of the long grass at the edge of the plantation. She tried to conjure the scent of the trees and the damp grass, sought to let it wash over her. There would be new planting and seedlings to be ordered. She thought of the tulip bulbs she had bought and wondered if they would really produce those almost-black flowers of the picture on the package. She thought of her daughter Judith and wondered if she would ever find love, or even if it was important for her to do so and if it was possible to construct a life that was happy even though it seemed untouched by it. She thought of anything that screened her from the thoughts she didn't want to have and was so preoccupied that once she almost stepped in front of a bicycle, only brought back to a consciousness of the present by the sharp ringing of its bell.

What did it matter, if it pleased him? What did it matter what other women might think? It would always be their secret and he would respect that silence because he knew how to be kind. And anyway they had no right to judge her because they weren't her and hadn't ever been her, or lived her life. And all that it mattered to her was what she allowed it to and she could control that better than she could control the anxiety, the constant apprehension of something that she couldn't fully define and so could never master. But she knew she would never be on that running machine trying to run towards a fantasy of herself, trying desperately to become someone that could never be realised, and that was a relief to her. She made herself take precise care when crossing roads – it would be such an embarrassing thing to have an accident, particularly if it was a collision with a bicycle. The day they had cycled to the caravan had been one of the happiest days of her life and if she could have stretched out her arms through the years she would have embraced the three girls who shared that adventure and told them what it meant to her. She knew they wouldn't judge her now and when she thought of poor Lillian taken before she even saw any of her three daughters married, she felt a sadness surge through the city streets as people hurried by, their sense of purpose suddenly rendered meaningless by the knowledge of what awaited them all. Lillian who made them all laugh with her funny stories and impersonations, Lillian who sometimes freewheeled her bike with her legs kicked out and angled like the arms of a compass. Lillian who had more life coursing through her than any of them, sunken of cheek and withered like the last leaf of autumn, desperately clinging to something that was being slowly shaken from her grasp. She wanted to claim her, give her back that day when the sun warmed their skin and they high-stepped in the sea, trying to lift their feet out of the broken, breaking waves that splashed white against their legs.

She crossed the bridge and saw the water fired by the red neon sign and then the shadowy people who sat on the terrace protected by smoked glass from the growing cold. It felt as it had done when she had looked down into the square and thought herself separated from the world outside by more than the glass. She thought of taking a canal trip but didn't want to sit amongst families and couples who would only serve to emphasise her solitariness. Once close to the end when she had gone to see Lillian she had been unable to stop herself crying even though she knew it was selfish and so had been comforted by a dying woman who told her that everything would be all right and who told her, too, that she was a terrible worrier. She thought of walking in the park but on impulse headed on, resisting the temptation to glance at her watch or turn back.

In the Museumplein she looked at the poorly decorated Christmas tree and then went to the temporary skating rink. She paused to watch the skaters score their movements in the ice. Some young girls had red plastic ice-hockey sticks and scooted a puck back and forwards trying to avoid the feet of those all around them. Parents held the hands of young children who took tentative steps as if learning to walk again. From where she stood it seemed as if the ice stretched almost into the museum itself. And at intervals the eye caught the weaving balletic movements of the experts, sometimes young, sometimes surprisingly old, who glided through the slow and the unskilled like ghosts in the winter sun, their motion formed by fragmenting particles of light. She wanted to join them, move amidst them on some volition other than that of her will, but she hadn't skated since the children were teenagers and even then she had never been more than mediocre. Judith had taken to it so easily that she put the boys' noses out of joint as they struggled to emulate her balanced confidence and Richard had to tell her off when she had started to tease them about their lack of speed. As she watched similar families on the ice she tried to call back into freshness the memory of her own family outings. And above all she wanted to be light, untrammelled with the weight of worries that tried to cling to her like a coat sodden with rain. A young child skated backwards, the proud turn of her head disdainful of obstacles, then spun in ever-diminishing circles of herself until she was a trembling blur of light. An elderly woman dressed all in black with a pinned-up cascade of white hair did slow elegant laps of the rink, her hands clasped behind her back as if ordered to be at ease. A younger man skated with one arm behind him, the other sawing the air into speed. She saw how everyone was occupied only with themselves, how their concentration preoccupied them, and that like everything in this city the only distinctions were the ones made by their own desires.

She felt reckless – she had come this far so why should she limit herself? And as her heart beat faster and everything in her head seemed to have loosened into a freefall of memories and impulse, she hired her skates from a young girl who helped her and seemed to think her desire to be on the ice was the most normal thing in the world, handing her the skates and taking her shoes as if she was serving her coffee or providing some other service characterised only by its normality.

Then for some reason she didn't understand she was thinking of Lillian and it felt as if she was watching her and with that knowledge she turned to the ice and pushed herself off. Nervous at first but then bolder, she glanced at the purple-pleated sky and told herself that she was skating, moving across the ice, and that she could do it and she could do it and not worry. There was no need to worry. Faster skaters shot past her but it didn't matter and she settled into a rhythm that felt as if it was enough to take her where she wanted and there was no need to look anywhere but forward.

'We could get bikes and ride in the park,' he said as they stood at the entrance gates.

'Dad, I'm not a child. I don't want to ride a bike. And I don't know why we have to come in here to talk.'

'Jack, this isn't easy for me and we can talk as we walk. I used to come here a lot. Only in those days I was desperate for someone to talk to because I was always on my own. But if we're going to talk then you need to walk beside me, not three steps behind.'

He kept his head looking in front but felt Jack draw level with him. And so they walked on as a phalanx of cyclists and solitary joggers flowed past them. The trees had lost their leaves and the buildings along the side of the park were starkly visible. He didn't know how to start and so he kept walking, waiting for the words to form inside his head. They passed close to the film museum where rollerbladers were slaloming in and out of plastic cones. He watched the seamless smoothness of their glides and felt his own stuttering awkwardness.

'I screwed up, Jack,' was how he started. He had already used the same words and in some way he wished they were enough, that they could encompass everything that needed to be said. Perhaps he could even add that he had screwed up but everyone did it, in the knowledge that in Jack's world this seemed to carry an all-encompassing potential for pardon, for excuse. But as he looked at the tightening face of his son and his narrowed laser eyes that seemed to want to see right through him, he knew instantly that pardon was to be withheld.

'I screwed up and I wish I hadn't. I'm sorry that everyone got hurt.'

'So if you're sorry why don't you tell Mum that and get back together like the way it was before? And then I wouldn't be looking at a dickhead like Gordon for a stepfather and having to go and live in some dosshouse in Spain.'

So it was the personal collateral damage that Jack was angry about, and to emphasise the depth of his feelings he threw an arm rigidly in the air as if he was chasing away some wild animal. They were standing in the middle of the road with joggers and cyclists streaming past on either side. As an overweight runner in a baggy tracksuit laboured by leaning increasingly and precariously forward he heard the broken struggle of his breathing. The jogger wore a black plastic armband that presumably held his phone or music but which looked like he was in mourning for his lost youth.

'It's not so simple as that, Jack,' he said, momentarily shocked by the intensity of his son's expression and voice, something he hadn't witnessed in a long while. 'Your mother and I had been drifting apart for some time – it wasn't anybody's fault, it was just one of those things that happens to people. And if you ask me why I can't give you an answer. I don't know. Sometimes stuff just happens. You must understand that as well as anyone.'

'I don't understand,' Jack insisted. 'Why did you not think of Mum or Caroline or me before you had it off with some slag you were only supposed to be teaching who was half your age?'

What could be worse in the world than to have the moral condemnation of your child? To be condemned without understanding or sympathy, to be condemned with no regard for hypocrisy or irony by a son who was speaking to him from a seemingly bottomless well of selfishness. He was truly lost for words and so in response he merely opened his arms in a gesture of surrender. But even that brought no respite.

'So you never once thought of Mum or us or anybody other than yourself?'

That's right, Jack, that's exactly how it happened. You come to a point in your life when you're weary of thinking of others and when for the very first time you can't think of anyone other than yourself and suddenly you want to refind who that self is, in the hope that it's a better, happier self than the one you find yourself with now. So yes, Jack, that's how it happened. Thinking of no one but myself. But he didn't know what to say and he knew already that the truth was not going to fix this broken thing so he simply held his arms further out from his side as if he was ready to take his son's best shot.

'And Gordon's a total tosspot!' Jack almost shouted, waving his hand as if the thought was buzzing round his head and could be chased away.

'Yes, he is, Jack.' But where once being able to confirm such a judgement would have given him satisfaction, now there was only the accentuated pain that he was the cause of the tosspot being inflicted on his family. So although conscious of its inadequacy as a response he added, 'I don't think your mother will marry him.'

'You don't know that. You don't know anything about her any more.'

He watched his son shuffle his feet as if he was about to take off but was uncertain about what direction to take. A middle-aged woman jogged past them with a dog on a lead, its tongue lolling from the side of its mouth.

'If there was anything I could do to make it up to your mother I would do it, Jack, because the one thing I know is that I never meant to hurt her. Not even for a moment did I mean to hurt her.'

'So why did she end up crying every night and coming up with some stupid, weird idea about going to live in Spain?'

'Your mother's moved on, Jack – she doesn't want me back. She wouldn't have me back even if I got down on bended knees and begged. Not even if I begged, Jack, because she wants a different life now and I'm not a big part of it any more.' And suddenly he thought of coming to this same place all those years ago and thinking he had stumbled into a Garden of Eden where the life-changing power of love was waiting to be unleashed and imagining how he would return some time in the future with the ones with whom he had found that manifestation of love. But now what he had brought here was a trail of debris, the scattered fallout from a love he had destroyed, and he knew he could never come back again without the memory of this moment imposing itself on what had gone before. He felt as if he was the serpent who had dealt in the forbidden fruit and was desperate to try and salvage something.

'You don't have to go to Spain if you don't want to, Jack. You can stay with me – I'll get us somewhere better to live. Somewhere you can have your own space.'

'I don't want to live with you. I don't want to live in Spain. You don't understand.'

But he did understand – his son wanted everything to be the way it was before, to get in some time machine and travel back to where he felt safe, back to a place for which he'd never really shown much outward affection. And it wasn't in his power to make that happen. But he knew that in this moment he was talking to a child, a hurting, needy child, who, if only he would let him, he would put his arms around and say that everything was going to be all right. Say it over and over again until they both believed it. And then he'd look for some dock leaf whose healing properties would be able to salve the pain. But nothing was going to happen as in the manual, as in the wish-it-better world. And he remembered the Van Gogh letter he had read that morning while Jack had slept, the one where he had written about trying to express the terrible passions of humanity, and as he looked at the deeply etched anger of his son's face he wondered what colour could ever hope to capture the passions that swirled there.

He didn't know what to say so he said it again, 'I screwed up, Jack. I screwed up.'

'What's the point of saying that if you don't do anything about it?' And now his son was pointing at him as if he was the child, the one needing moral instruction. Then suddenly, as if unsure what was best to do, he flung the bag containing the leather jacket at his feet and, turning, ran off, only the difference in his clothing preventing him from merging with the joggers.

'Jack! Jack!' he called but his son ran on and didn't look back. People were staring at him but he didn't care and it was his anger now that wanted words and as more faces turned towards him he heard himself shouting, 'Stuff happens, Jack! Stuff happens!' Then with his hand shaking he bent down and picked up the plastic bag, at the same time watching while his son disappeared into the fading light of the day.

He was frightened now, frightened of losing his son in a strange city, but he didn't know what to do and as he stood in the flight path of joggers he felt weighted and rooted to the spot. Jack had already disappeared and he knew there was no way he could catch up with him and, even if that had been possible, what could he say that would assuage his son's anger or convince him that he could make things return to the way he wanted? He had a key to their hotel room and probably after a while that was where he would return and perhaps it was no bad thing to let him have some time on his own, time to calm down and regain some equilibrium. But the bitterness of the moment pressed against him and the memory of his son's anger seemed to shape and colour everything he saw. He turned and walked back towards the entrance gates, and ideas, stupid, desperate ideas, flooded through him, so perhaps this was a time when their best chance of connecting was on the bedrock of their gender, and instead of the Dylan concert he should take his son to one of the coffee houses and smoke themselves into an accordance or hit a bar and drink themselves mutually forgiving. Perhaps there was too much thinking when what was needed was a sudden blast of some unmoderated indulgence that would breach the dam of what separated them.

But as he walked through the dropping dusk even the plastic bag with the leather jacket felt increasingly heavy and the hand that held it colder. And he wondered if he could tell Jack about his own father, how nothing ever passed between them except indifference, of how their parallel lives never touched or connected in any way except for those rituals demanded by convention. But what good would that do or any of the other stupid ideas his apprehension had conjured up? And what if Jack called his mother and told her he was on his own in Amsterdam and cried down the phone? That was something too terrible to be contemplated and would confirm for ever his hopeless inadequacy as a parent and a human being.

He had reached the entrance to the park and he paused and looked back at what he had once considered to be the green garden of a new and better world and he felt the loss of that and the loss of something else for which he had no name.

Ten

S HE WAS VERY CONFUSED now and unsure of what she should do. Going off like that made it look as if she was the one in the wrong, rather than Shannon. It was something her daughter might do in a strop but she had always been the one who stayed steady and dependable, patiently waiting for a return. She felt forced into a role with which she wasn't familiar and although at first it had been intensified by being in an unfamiliar city, at least now she knew that she could survive in it and that it wasn't going to consume her. Pausing for a few minutes to watch the skaters on the ice she thought of the painting of the girl reading the letter. By being painted the girl had been taken notice of by someone who saw something that was important, but when she thought back to the morning she had picked up his letter from the hall carpet, the back of her hand momentarily wearing a little transfer of colour, no one, apart briefly from her father, had been there to share all that it had meant. She felt the sudden bitterness of the loneliness that had been her lot on that day and despite whatever support a few close friends were later able to offer, it was a loneliness that had endured right through the pregnancy and even the birth itself, ebbing away only when her child was finally placed in her arms.

Shannon's secret and what she had told her in the restaurant felt as if that moment had been ripped away again and in its absence flowed the same almost overwhelming sense of loneliness, made even more acute by the belief that what she had been able to protect herself with had been lost for ever. She was cut once more by the sharp-edged unfairness of the world and was tempted to think that it was caused by something bad about her. She remembered the bracelet that rested in her pocket and wondered if this was her punishment but told herself that everything had already been set in place long before she had taken it. There was part of her, too, that believed that if she hadn't been given things fairly then it was not a crime to try and make amends for that unfairness. She would have done anything for Shannon, she had done everything that anyone could do to provide for her, and not just provide, but to give her the things she wanted whatever their cost and despite what she herself thought about their worth. So what was left for her now? Out on the ice mothers and fathers formed hand-held chains with their young children and skated in wavering lines. All she had was Shannon and now she felt that she no longer had even this, so what should she do? She walked on, conscious for the first time of the cold. She should go back and try to talk, see what could be sorted, what could be fixed even in the short term. The alternative she knew was to be left with nothing even though she understood that what they shared could never be restored to the way it was before.

Cars and trams and bicycles – she wondered what Marty would think of driving his taxi here, of the endless possibilities of being cut up, of the names he would have to call, the gestures he would have to make every day. She thought too of his self-invite and wondered if she had declined it too quickly. Beggars couldn't be choosers, she tried to tell herself, but a stronger voice refused to think of herself as ever begging. She had always held on to some residue of pride despite it all, held it tight even when she worked at jobs that the world considered menial. So she knew she wasn't going to give that up for Marty and not even for Shannon.

She stood on the edge of the pavement not quite sure which way she should be looking and deciding that she would wait to cross until the others standing beside her led the way.

'Taking time out?'

The Belfast accent made her jump a little. It wasn't what she expected to hear. It was the guy on the aeroplane and she tried not to blush at the memory of holding a stranger's hand.

'Do you want me to hold your hand or are you OK with roads?' he joked.

'I do roads OK,' she said. 'It's just planes freak me out.'

'If it's any consolation I don't do needles. A nurse comes anywhere near me with a needle and I start to feel faint. So where's the rest of the tribe?'

'Taking time out before they hit the bars tonight.'

'Before they hit the warpath. And you survived last night?'

'Just about, just about.' She kept her eyes on the road, suddenly wary of tripping on the tram rail. 'Where's your boy?'

'Gone off on his own for a while – I think he got fed up trailing round after his dad.'

They reached the opposite pavement and paused, both momentarily confused whether it signalled the end of their conversation.

'So you've been shopping,' she said, pointing at the plastic bag.

'It's Jack's – he got tired carrying it. It's a leather jacket he bought in the market. He actually managed to haggle for it.'

'Are you not worried about him being on his own?'

He looked at her and rubbed his hand across his mouth as if suddenly unsure whether to gag the words forming. She was sorry she had asked the question as now it sounded like she was suggesting he was a poor parent but she didn't know how to apologise without making it worse, so instead she said, 'He'll be fine,' and lifted her hand in a gesture that was meant to be a goodbye.

'We had a row,' he said. 'He's angry with me about family stuff.'

She hesitated. It was none of her business. She had more than enough of her own to worry about. He blew into his free hand to warm it and she was conscious again of how cold it was becoming.

'Family stuff is always complicated,' she said, shivering slightly at the thought of the cold as much as its reality. That was all she had to give him and she turned to make her way back to the hotel without being totally sure if she was heading in the right direction.

'I split with his mother. He blames me.' He was staring at the bag, not meeting her gaze.

'Kids always need someone to blame,' she said. 'So where did he go?'

'I guess back to the hotel. I'm not sure. At least your girl's too old for this kind of stuff.'

'Don't you believe it,' she said, shaking her head. 'Is your hotel far?'

'About fifteen minutes. Where are you staying?'

'Somewhere near the station. Bit of a dump really. It's this way, isn't it,' she said, pointing her hand vaguely.

'I'll walk with you – I can go part of that way.' He hesitated. 'If you like.'

She hesitated, too. It was getting darker and she wasn't entirely confident that she could find her way back. 'OK,' she said. 'It's getting colder.'

They crossed the bridge and the water below was beginning to strut with its painted decoration of neon. He talked to her light-heartedly about Amsterdam and she knew he was drawing a veil over what had happened with his son and she was glad because she didn't want to hear about his problems, knew that because he was a man he would present himself as the victim and she had no reserves of sympathy. Soon she would have to meet her own child and she didn't yet know what it was she would say or what might be said to her. He walked a little quickly but it helped warm her against the cold. A group of women appeared in what looked like traditional African dress, swirls of yellow and turquoise, coiled turbans on their heads and their arms laden with parcels and babies. A young woman cycled by with a child strapped in a seat behind her and a small dog in the basket in front. They passed a shop with exotic arrangements of flowers in tall glass vases and offices where women in elegant suits stood chatting at desks.

Then he was pointing out a place where you could get beautiful cakes and handmade chocolates and soon they were heading down a narrow pedestrianised street lined with shops. There their conversation dried up, hindered by the crowds and the noise, and she was glad not to have to make the effort. She sensed that he was too and wondered whether he regretted offering to show her the way back. After a short while and feeling the pressure of the silence she lied and told him that she thought she recognised where she was and she would be able to find her way.

He looked at her and let the plastic bag swing like a pendulum and she wasn't sure what he was thinking until he said, 'Can I show you something?' And then he was pointing the way to an arched oak doorway that nestled just off the street and, in a city that seemed to insist that anything might happen if you were prepared to let it, she felt that she had no other option but to follow him. And so in a few seconds she stepped from a modern shopping street into a kind of courtyard, intensely calm and quiet, where ancient houses nestled shoulder to shoulder round a green lawn and trees. It was like a magician's trick where something disappeared to be replaced by something completely different. She smiled and he smiled at her smiling.

'What is it?' she asked, not taking her eyes from it in case it disappeared.

'They're seventeenth- and eighteenth-century almshouses, homes which were provided for widows and the needy by the city's rich businessmen who probably thought it bought them a first-class ticket to heaven.'

'I'd like to live here,' she said. 'Can we walk round and look?' she asked.

'We can't go past those barriers – they insist on some privacy – but we can walk this way.' He pointed to what he said was the oldest house in the city.

'Beats the Housing Executive,' she said, still taking everything in. 'I wonder how many points you needed to qualify for one.'

'I don't know. You care for old people, don't you?'

'Yes, in a care home,' and then she realised that he assumed she was a nurse or someone medically trained and she liked the idea that he thought that. Thought it about her rather than the truth that she was someone who cleaned and made tea, someone who cleared up other people's mess.

She was suddenly conscious of music but wasn't sure where it was coming from. He had heard it too. In some of the windows of the houses lights glowed yellow.

'There's a very old church over here,' he said and she followed as he started to walk towards it.

'It's like a secret,' she said. 'A secret world.'

'The first time I saw it I didn't quite believe it. And so close to the street. I don't think most people even know it's here.'

It was something she would be able to describe to Mrs Hemmings, tell her just before she found her bracelet that must have dropped behind somewhere she hadn't quite decided on. The paintings, the secret square, she'd be able to recount everything and get her commendation for being a good pupil. She told herself that she was capable of knowing things, of learning new things, and as the music grew louder she realised that these were the photographs that could be set on a desk to tell the world that she was someone and to mark the life she had lived.

The door of the church was open and there was a choir inside rehearsing, an elderly white-haired man conducting them, the cuffs of his shirt open and his thin blue-veined wrists swaying back and forward as his hands caressed the air and occasionally pulled the voices to a halt. Then his right hand would peck the air insisting on some improvement. They stood in the doorway until an old woman gestured them inside and pointed to one of the pews. They looked at each other and then she made the decision for both of them and quietly scurried into the back pew of the small church. She hadn't been in a church since Shannon was christened and it felt strange and unsettling as if at any moment an unseen power might pass judgement on her for all her broken promises, or a voice would boom out telling her to leave. But then the singing started and the sound filled the space, pushing against the walls as if trying to break free from these constraints. It was like nothing she had ever heard and it was so real that it frightened her a little and she didn't know at first whether it was beautiful or terrible. She looked at her companion but he stared straight ahead, the white bag held tightly on his lap. He still wore a wedding ring and she wanted to tell him and tell the singers whose faces focused only on the old man conducting that she could have been a nurse. She wanted her voice to be part of theirs and she wanted to say that she could have been a nurse if things had been different. The music rose and fell and it wasn't thin or stretched but settled about her in thick rich layers and she felt swaddled in its folds like a child.

She watched the nurses every day, knew the ones who cared and those who didn't. It didn't look so hard. And once when old Mr Hatton had died she had been the one there at the end, the one holding his hand and telling him everything was going to be all right. She had been the one listening to his laboured breathing, the final struggle and then the sudden slow release into silence. She didn't recognise the music but it felt like a carol and parts of it half-remembered echoes of something that perhaps she had once heard long ago. When the nurse came and took his pulse she had just shaken her head at her and then looked at her as if to say that it was time for her to go and get on with something important like vacuuming the corridors. Afterwards when his daughter had arrived she had kicked up a stink that he hadn't been sent to the hospital and that she hadn't been there at the end, as if the death should have been time-tabled to suit her. It wasn't her place to say anything but she wanted to ask why she should think this when she hadn't taken the trouble to visit him more often. Then she had been called to the office for the daughter to ask questions about her father's final moments and all she could think of but had no words to explain was the quiet in the room that seemed to make the struggle of his breathing louder and then how there was no more struggle and only the silence. A silence that even now spread inside her head despite the clamour of the music and then she looked at her companion again and saw that he was crying and so she took his hand just as she had taken the hand of that dying man.

The music was very beautiful. He had lost his father without ever expressing his love or even gratitude, a gratitude that only now pressed against his consciousness as he remembered how his father, out of a labourer's wages, had provided for them and taken nothing for himself from the weekly pay packet except the few coins necessary to buy a paper and a bar of chocolate. No he hadn't even taken them but had handed over the little brown envelope every Friday night and got his meagre pocket money in return. This was the second time he had cried recently and it didn't feel any better than the first. There was too much of it that felt like sentimentality, a nostalgia for something he wasn't even sure had ever existed, so he wiped the few tears away and tried to stop. But the music continued to course through him and he sought to protect himself by insisting that his father hadn't tried hard enough to understand him, to understand that he was different and wanted to live in a different world. That was his punishment of course, the punishment to come to every son, as he became the father whose own son now turned his face away. There was no music, however beautiful, that could wipe away the bitterness of that.

He thought of his daughter Caroline who was training to survive the joys and terrors of the classroom and hoped that some at least of the thousands of children she would meet over the course of her career would be kind to her. He thought of Susan at this moment in a strange country contemplating the possibility of a new life and if he could say only one thing to her it would be that he wished with all his heart that she would find a life in which she could be happy and happier than he had ever been able to make her. And Jack, Jack for whom he was responsible – where was he now? In a foreign city where he didn't know a single soul with only his misery for company and he needed to go and find him. Find him just as soon as the music stopped. Find him as soon as he was sure he wasn't crying. He thought that if he were American he would return home and go into therapy, spill it all out in front of some stranger with a sincere face and ask them to put it all back together for him. Put it all back neatly in the box, shipshape and sorted. But he lived in Belfast so it was a question of catching himself on, pulling himself together and taking up a socially approved therapy such as drinking too much or trying desperately to have meaningless sex with people he didn't like but who were available for general medical care like first-aid boxes in public places.

The music slowly unpicked the stitching of memory and need and then he thought again of the painting of the old man crying. The blue clothes, the yellow chair, the bare floorboards, and he felt the fear of what he could become. He had reached an age when everything should be laid out in front of him with the only uncertainties those of health, the threescore and whatever, but now even his job in the college felt shadowed and precarious and he knew that if he didn't toe whatever was the currently fashionable line they would edge him out, or shunt him into some siding where he would be the first casualty of rationalisation in the next wave of cutbacks. He had to get his life back on track. Find Jack. Get his life back on track. Stop crying and get it back on track. And then the woman who sat beside him and whose name he wasn't quite sure he had remembered correctly was holding his hand. He stared straight ahead and wondered if she was frightened of churches as well as planes.

The journey back to the hotel was fraught and uncertain and if she hadn't been so cold she would have postponed it even longer. The warmth generated by the skating had long since dissipated. Everyone she passed seemed to have added a spring to their step in their desire to reach their destination but their pace only served to accentuate her reluctance to go back. Sometimes she met the eyes of women she passed and in every gaze she imagined she could see their judgement. Had she betrayed them, betrayed herself? She didn't know but told herself that she didn't care because what she had done was a secret between man and wife that was not to be the concern of anyone but them. She could never run fast enough to reach that perfect image of herself in the mirror – it wasn't going to happen and she didn't care about it any more. They would move on and never talk about this thing, and what was its meaning anyway? There was nothing in it, no betrayal, because she had made it happen and no hurt to her because whatever it was she felt now it was without any sense of loss or shock.

Only going on mattered now, pushing on like she had been able to do in the skating and finding a new balance that would carry them both over the surface of their lives.

She had sold her last black Christmas tree, sold her last piece of tat, run her last mile on the treadmill. When she got home she would investigate the possibility of expanding the plantation, perhaps even explore what grants were available for growing other types of trees. She had read somewhere that willow was increasingly used for a range of ecological purposes. There were lots of possibilities forming in her head. Future plans to be made, internet searches to be carried out. And when she was home she would lay out the nativity scene on the hall table, carefully set each person and creature in place. Arrange it all just like it must have happened in the story. And perhaps if she could find the right supplier that was the type of thing they could sell next Christmas and, if it wasn't too fanciful, turn the shop into something that had style and dignity with every piece of junk banished for ever. Somewhere mothers and fathers would bring their children and feel better even for a little while for having come.

As she drew closer to the hotel with its splashes of light she wished she could be home without the intervening night and the Sunday flight. She didn't know what would fill those hours and it made her nervous. In the square the linked lights seemed to tighten then lift a little like a necklace on a dancer. She soothed some calmness into her hair and smoothed her coat as she entered the foyer where the heat and noise confronted her suddenly and more forcefully than she had expected. An elderly couple was booking in and the wife kept turning round to glance at their luggage as if to ensure that no one was about to make off with it. The Japanese couple were perusing some tourist leaflets and coming out of the lifts were two young women dressed formally in black suits and carrying violin cases. The Japanese woman smiled at her and gave a slight bow. There was always something private and unspoken that passed between women that was unhindered by differences in age or nationality and for a second she was grateful that it still existed and that she still was part of it. She hesitated for a moment, pretending that she too would look at the leaflets, but then opening the top button of her coat she stepped into the waiting lift.

Eleven

H<small>E DELIBERATELY DIDN'T TAKE</small> the lift but slowly climbed the stairs hoping that the extra time this afforded would grant some greater certainty about what it was he should say. He was increasingly hopeful that Jack would be in the room but less sure about what state he would be in. The one thing he couldn't bear to anticipate was a continuation of what had gone before and that apprehension slowed his walk even more, so he was glad when on reaching their floor he had to momentarily stand aside to let a young woman pass him with her trolley of bed linen and towels. There were cleaning materials clumped in a plastic container clipped to the front and as she smiled the smile that staff give to guests he wondered how he was to clean up this mess. What was it he could do or say that would ever make it better? Opening the door with his card he was glad that already he could hear the sound of music and when he entered the room, dark apart from the television light, Jack was curled on the bed watching what looked like MTV.

Instinct told him that the worst thing he could do now was to do anything and so he simply set the bag with his son's leather jacket on the chair beside the television and, as Jack registered him in his peripheral vision, quietly asked,

'OK?' Almost imperceptibly his son nodded then curled a little tighter, one hand pressed between his head and the pillow. But it was enough and he felt a surge of relief shoot through him. Taking off his coat and shoes he stretched out on the bed and glanced at the foetal fold of his son's body. He remembered the music he had heard in the church and for a few seconds it blocked out what seemed like the frantic screech of guitars, the caterwauling of some stiff-limbed marionette of a singer. Ten years ago he would have reached out his arm and embraced his son but now there was no arm long enough to bridge the gap that the intervening years imposed between them, so he too curled on the bed and tried for a moment to let nothing but his own weariness flow through him. Almost at once he felt sleep coming on and knew there was nothing he could do to stop it.

But there was no respite in his dreams and at one moment he was confronted with an art-history examination upon which his job depended but for which he had done no revision, then in another he was wandering lost in Vondelpark unable to find the exit, while all around him young men and women raced past him in their running gear with mocking smiles and shouting directions he couldn't understand. Then he was back in the church of his childhood looking up at the blue tableau instructing him to 'Worship the Lord in the Beauty of Holiness' and a babble of voices telling him everything would be well if he could only find what this requisite beauty was, but the more he searched the more he struggled to understand its meaning.

When he woke some time later he felt a second's confusion about where he was and then in the gloom glanced towards his son who had loosened himself from the tightness of his shape and stretched into sleep. He had partly covered himself with the duvet and the now-silent television was a

238

splurge of psychedelic colour from some music video. Even though his watch told him that he had slept for over an hour part of him wanted to fall back on the pillow and plunge into an even deeper and dreamless sleep. But they had the concert that night even though he was unsure if Jack would go, and if Jack didn't go then he couldn't go either because he wouldn't leave him on his own again. He reached for his book of Van Gogh's letters but needed more light and he didn't want to switch one on, so instead turned his eyes to the coloured flickering of the television. All his life Van Gogh had longed for what he saw as the ideal happiness of a family. He'd offer him a swap, a family for the paintings, see how genuine his desire really was. Hang a family round his neck and see what that did to his art. But he knew it wasn't his family that carried the blame for what had happened to his own painting. His work was distinguished only by its meaninglessness – apart from a very few early years, had he ever truly believed in it? And if he didn't believe in it then how could he expect anyone else to do so? It all just felt part of the game, something in which you attired yourself to fulfil the obligations of the role, wrapping yourself in abstraction that you used to suggest an intellectual depth but whose purpose was to mask the deficiencies of technique. Not embarrassing deficiencies but insistent enough to whisper that whatever talent you had would never amount to what you wanted it to be. He looked across at Jack, saw that even in sleep his back seemed pulled taut like the stretched string of a bow and how he had burrowed and scissored his legs under the warmth of the duvet. For a moment he thought that the very best thing they could do was to climb into their beds and not wake until the morning and then take the plane home, but no sooner had he done so than his son started to stir, giving one of those curious snuffles that made him sound like a small sleep-sodden animal emerging from winter hibernation.

He knew he had to be patient, that trying to hurry him would produce the opposite effect, so to avoid letting his son know that he had been looking at him he turned on to his back and stared at the ceiling which wore a melded transfer of confused light from the outside streetlights and the television. Although it pained and confused him to admit it the Van Gogh paintings had disappointed him a little but he wasn't entirely sure why. Perhaps it was because there were too many of them with too much intensity of colour, too much intensity of feeling. And intensity of feeling was something he had decided that he didn't want any more about anything. Now he only wanted to step into the respite of the shadows, not to be constantly confronted with scrutiny and situations that required responses that were outside the comfortable range of what he knew best. So they were going to take the secret garden of education and lay it open to accountability and every aspect of his job was to be measured and analysed. He didn't think he had any chance of producing the research he had burbled on about and there was a limit to how long he could rely on Stan's friendship to protect him.

Jack shuffled his legs under the quilt and then shivered his shoulders as if he was thinking of waking. He couldn't even begin to predict what his son's mood would be when he woke but the relief that the storm seemed to have blown itself out didn't prevent him from feeling irked by the fact that he had been tried and found guilty of failure, when all his son's frequent screw-ups were met ultimately only by forgiveness. And what would be his sentence? Pushed to the margins of his son's later life, their relationship marked by increasing indifference and even embarrassment until the gaps between their functional encounters grew ever longer. He asked himself if it mattered, if in the long run it was better that way than rubbing each other raw over memories that couldn't be changed. He looked at his watch – there was still plenty of time and he lifted the book again but as he glanced at the shadowed blur of words he knew it couldn't be read. He needed glasses.

A week earlier a young woman, not much older than his daughter, had told him that he needed reading glasses. Another test he'd failed. He remembered the way she slipped the lenses into the heavy metal glasses with the flourish of the magician. 'Is it clearer with this one or with this one?' Sometimes he wasn't sure and then she gave him her gentle patience. Perhaps glasses would make him appear like a teacher. He had thought of asking her as an attempt at a joke but instead concentrated on trying to get his answers right. He remembered, too, how she had put her head close to his and shone her light in his eye, told him to look into it, and how it seemed as if she was gazing not into his eye but deep into his being, and how intimate it had felt. Perhaps glasses would change the way things looked. Perhaps everything would be clear.

'What time is it?' Jack asked, the back of his hand sandpapering his cheek.

'Six. Do you want to get something to eat in a while?'

'Yes, but not Burger King.'

'No, not Burger King. Do you want to go to the concert or would you rather give it a miss?'

'Go of course – isn't that why you came? To see Dylan – isn't that why you came?'

'Yes, but we don't have to. I know it's not exactly your cup of tea.'

'I don't mind. Most of the early stuff is shitty but some of the new stuff is OK.'

241

He wanted to say that most people thought it was the other way round but instead he switched on his bedside light and started to look for his shoes. Jack slithered past him into the bathroom, his clothes crimped and wrinkled, a tuft of his hair sticking up from his head like an aerial from a roof. After savouring the relief of having his son talking to him again he tried to kindle some excitement about the concert which in many ways was the late fulfilment of a long-standing ambition, but there were too many other thoughts pressing against his anticipation for it to be successful. Going to the window he looked down into the street where two girls riding tandem on a scooter were engaged in what looked like an animated conversation, one waving her arm to emphasise some point. In the bathroom he heard Jack flush the toilet and a few minutes later he emerged, the errant tufts of hair plastered back into place.

'Why don't you put your jacket on?' he said, pointing to the bag that still rested on the chair. 'It looks cold out there.' He saw his son's uncertainty, probably reluctant to be seen to acquiesce to any of his father's suggestions, however sensible. 'It's up to you,' he added, shrugging to provide the necessary leeway and to suggest personal indifference.

Jack considered, as if faced with a major decision, but then took the jacket out of the bag and put it on, letting his hood flop out over his collar. He was going to say that he looked good but decided that compliments would probably not be helpful and instead concentrated on getting his own coat on and ensuring he had the tickets safely stowed in an inside pocket.

'Let's get something to eat,' he said.

'Not that Burger King place,' Jack insisted again.

'No, somewhere different. Turn the television off.'

Jack aimed the remote like a gun as if he was shooting the television into silence. In the lift they both studied their reflections in the mirrored panel. He wondered if there would be other fathers with their sons at the concert engaging in what they probably considered a rite of passage and he was curious to see the make-up of the audience. Then as they left the hotel he concentrated on finding them somewhere to eat, knowing that it was pointless to ask Jack for a preference and knowing that if the evening was to have any prospect of success it had to start well. As they headed to the Leidseplein he felt Jack tugging his sleeve and indicating a Chinese place and surprised and relieved that the choice had been made for him he was happy to join the short queue at the counter. In the front window, open to the street, two women stir-fried in giant woks, the leaping, guttering blue flames from the gas rings glistening their faces with a sheen of sweat. Jack stood close to the counter staring intently at the closest young woman. Her hair, pulled back from her face, was a dark river glazed by the overhead lights and wisps of neon and on the bare forearm that worked the contents of the wok was a green tattoo which tailed off into mystery under the rolled sleeve of her black blouse. They both stood watching as her wrist frantically flicked and circled, finally shuffling the contents into a cardboard container before sluicing the wok and starting the next order. He persuaded Jack to order for them both and when he had given their name they took their place at one of the long benches and watched the street outside.

A stag party went by where all the men were dressed as Santa Claus, some of them ringing bells and singing 'Jingle Bells'. Soon it would be Christmas and that awareness stirred a new apprehension. Last year he had been allowed to have his dinner with Susan and his children but now they were

243

divorced and of course Gordon had arrived on the scene. Susan had always been vague about her boyfriend's marital status and he didn't doubt that he trailed some complex family baggage in his wake but what did that matter if they chose to spend their first Christmas together? Where that left him was precisely nowhere except celebrating on his own in a flat above a flower shop. He shivered a little and the prospect wasn't warmed by the possibility that as a parental trade-off Caroline and Jack might come to him on Boxing Day which he already imagined as a stilted embarrassment that would surely flounder on the ineptitude of his cooking and his children's furtive watch-glancing. One of the Santa gang who had lagged behind jogged past them, wearing reindeer horns that flashed red light at their tips and carrying a brown sack over his shoulder. As two young women in short skirts drew level he stopped them and gave them something out of his sack that made them squeal with embarrassed laughter. Jack sniggered.

'What did he give them?' he asked his son.

'You don't want to know,' Jack said, still smiling.

He was sure he didn't but grateful that it had made his son smile, something about which he had long since conceded failure. Their name was called and without being asked Jack clambered back over the bench to collect their food at the counter. He suddenly seemed more confident, his diffidence in a new environment easing a little, as if he was finding his feet, understanding how things worked. It was even possible that he would come to like this place if in a completely different way to his father.

The food was good and from time to time as they ate they watched the young woman with the wok, the jade green of her tattoo quivered into motion by the light and the dexterous speed of her body. He didn't know what his son was thinking but he thought if he sat there much longer he could fall in love with her and in his imagination he walked up to her and told her that he would look after her all the rest of her life and that she would never need to work again if she would only come home with him. Why could life not spin into something better on the most crazy of impulses, on chance, on placing all your chips on the most unlikely of outcomes? He listened to Jack slurping the last of his noodles and crushing the empty drinks can in his clenched fist. Why did he always have to do that with his empty cans? It made him look brutish and, whatever he was, he wasn't that. So in silent opposition he lifted his own empty can and held it as if studying it, rotating it slowly so he was able to inspect it from every angle.

The young woman paused to fix a clip in her hair, wipe her brow and drink from a bottle of water. To capture the frozen stillness of that momentary beauty for ever, to lift it from the chaos and transience of time – there was nothing he wouldn't have given to be able to achieve that. But without letting the thought linger he told himself that perhaps his future life would be happier if he admitted finally that he was not going to be that artist and the part he had been chosen to play was to support and advocate those who could. She turned to take her next order from the little row of squares of paper and then was lost to him as the queue at the counter thickened.

'We should have one of these in Belfast,' Jack said.

'Yes we should. There's a lot of things we should have that they have here.'

'If we had canals in Belfast there'd be old fridges and settees floating in them.'

'And bodies. Every morning a new body to be fished out.'

Jack didn't reply but to signal that he had finished his part in the conversation took his mobile out of his pocket and clicked his fingers over the keys. To his surprise, his son hadn't finished speaking.

'It's a rip-off what they charge you to use your phone,' he said as he held the mobile at arm's length in front of his face like a mirror. 'A total rip-off.'

'Love never comes cheap,' he said, regretting almost immediately his need to say things that sounded wise. But his son only glanced at him quizzically and said nothing before they got to their feet and eased past the queue, their passage made more awkward by the number of backpacks. As he stepped outside he glanced for a final time at the young woman with the wok and then he knew he was destined to spend the rest of his life falling in love with women he never spoke to and whose traverse across his heart lasted only long enough for him to feel the pain of their loss.

'Did you see her tattoo?' Jack asked. 'It's class.'

'Yes,' he answered, feeling guilty that his son had observed his gaze and so almost immediately he turned the conversation away from himself. 'You're not thinking of getting a tattoo, are you?'

'Might do. Coloured ones like hers are cool. You can get ones that are symbols and kind of ancient writing. I like them.'

He couldn't help himself – it was too important. 'The first rule of getting a tattoo is to get it where it's only visible when you want it to be.'

Jack merely shrugged a reply and then put in his earphones. So as they walked he was left to ponder what his son might choose to engrave on his body and he remembered the 'people are shit' he had printed on the white page of his arm. Perhaps the disguise of Latin or some hieroglyphic squiggles might ameliorate the impact of whatever inane or aggressive slogan his imagination was able to devise. He wondered what age you had to be to legally get a tattoo but realised it hardly mattered after it was done and then told himself that if Jack did go ahead and get one, he and his mother would be the ones paying for the laser removal ten years down the line. Every other person they passed seemed to have one, including a guy who sprouted green-leafed tendrils from some hidden plant clinging to the lattice of his neck.

The journey on the metro to the concert hall in the south-east of the city took less than half an hour and they arrived before the doors had been opened so they milled about aimlessly for a while as the crowds gathered and touts tried to do business in tickets and hawkers sold posters and other Dylan merchandise. There was a lot of smoking and the air was clotted and pungent with the smell of cannabis, sometimes sickly sweet, but sometimes reminding him of burnt grass. No one was dealing, everyone seemed to have brought their own and were sharing it openly with their friends. The assembling audience now forming an orderly queue, while not confined to a particular age group, inevitably revealed a sprinkling of bald men with ponytails. At one point the crowd cheered the arrival on a tandem of what looked like man and wife, both bedecked in tie-dye from head to foot, their long grey manes of hair held by red bandannas and, apart from the colour of their hair, looking like they had stepped out of a time machine that had brought them straight through the decades from Woodstock. They flashed peace signs at their audience and the driver honked a large horn perched on the handlebars of the bike which drew renewed, if ironic, cheers. He tried to tell himself that it felt counter-culture but there were too many things that jarred to allow himself to spark that nostalgia – the exorbitant price of the tickets for a start; the fact that the audience was so diverse in age and dress and so lacked any sense of cohesion or shared identity; their passive amenability to the instructions of the stewards; but mostly the fact of everything that had happened to the world in the intervening years. So he knew there was no flag of freedom flying, that most of those of a similar age to himself who had come there had momentarily slipped discreetly out of lives of quiet respectability and careers which were bound up with preserving the status quo and for whom all forms of change were shrouded in fear.

'You could get high just breathing,' Jack said, slipping his hood over his head, and he wasn't sure whether his son was expressing a moral objection or just sheltering from the coldness of the wind that was beginning to course round the hard edges of the building. Whatever the reason it made him look like a young monk, a novice, and he momentarily felt again that pleasing image that their journey to this city was an initiation, a sharing of what he had known and treasured in the past. Perhaps everything was not yet lost, perhaps those opening jangling organ chords could still hold the power to quicken and spin them both into some new orbit. He had to stop himself reaching out a hand and resting it on his son's shoulder and then another cheer rose from the throat of the crowd as the doors opened and suddenly they were moving forward when people started to progress through the security checks. He held on to Jack's arm as the queue suddenly took on a life of its own but he felt his son flinch away and so he dropped his hand.

She had left him at a point where all she had to do was follow the road and she would be back at her hotel. He had offered to take her all the way but she had declined, not wanting him to see the basic nature of her accommodation. When the time came for them to go in their separate directions there was a moment of awkward uncertainty and he stared over her shoulder then swung the plastic bag again so that he looked like a boy going home from school.

'Well thanks,' she said. 'I hope everything works out with Jack.'

'Thanks. It's Karen, isn't it?'

She nodded and waited for him to say whatever it was that he was reaching for.

'You make a good nurse, Karen. Thanks.'

And then he turned to hide his embarrassment and for a second she stood watching him go before she too turned and set off to find her daughter. But she didn't want to be a nurse any more. It was what she spent half her life doing – looking after other people, cleaning up their mess. Just once in her life she wanted someone to look after her, to nurse her with gentleness and kindness, put their arm round her and tell her that everything was all right. If such a person existed and if it was someone she could finally give herself to in trust, then she believed it was just possible that the hardness she knew had grown on her like a second skin might be softened. She had always thought of it as a protection but now she wondered if it was a barrier to whatever good might happen. She would lose her daughter one way or the other, whether through the physical separation of the coming marriage or through what would happen between them in the next hours. That awareness suddenly echoed again with loneliness and despite everything that she had thought before about being better on her own, she could not sentence herself to a life without love. There were people in the home who hardly ever had visitors but there were others who had someone who came faithfully and whose regular presence was a source of comfort. She thought too of the dying man whose hand she had held and she knew she didn't want to be old and alone.

She tried to think of what she would say to Shannon and with renewed shame she remembered hitting her. Perhaps her daughter wouldn't even want to speak to her. All her life she believed she'd had to pay a high price for her mistakes. And this one could be as big a grief as any that had gone before. But the shame was counter-balanced by the knowledge of how her daughter had betrayed her, of how she had planned to tell her in a strange city far from home of what she had schemed and hidden from her. She had no idea of what she would say and as she walked the events of the day splintered in her head then re-formed in sharp-edged, disconnected images – the pregnant girl reading the letter, the ice-skaters, the music in the church, a stranger's tears.

She noticed that as she got closer to where her hotel was the neighbourhood became seedier and a little run-down. There were some small restaurants that looked like customers never crossed their thresholds and a few boarded-up doorways. The cold was much more intense now and the faces of those who passed her looked pinched and pale. There were no Christmas lights here either and for the first time that day she felt a little apprehensive about being on her own. There was a slewed concertina of collapsed bicycles and out on the road two trams slithered alongside each other like mating snakes. From an approaching car ripped the bass beat off a pumped-up sound system. A man who passed looked at her and made her nervous but then momentarily glad that she could still, if not turn heads, attract a stranger's fleeting gaze. She didn't spend that much time on herself but Shannon's fixation with appearance had ensured that she had never been allowed to let herself go, even when she had no other motivation than to humour her daughter.

She remembered, too, how her own city had looked from the Craigantlet Hills on that night, stretched out below them and studded with amber pearls of light, how it had assumed a momentary beauty like a bride dressed on her wedding morning. She had almost forgotten how love could colour and shape the world. He had given her a metal ring from his van and she had thought herself lucky and nursed it as if it was the most valuable of diamonds. She had never had a wedding dress and after it was all over and the honeymoon started, she would try on Shannon's dress and no one would ever know but herself. In some ways it felt like hers because she had worked so many extra hours to earn the money to pay for it. Every flounce and frill, every stitch of embroidery was the result of her labour, of working in the kitchen in the home, of cleaning toilets and showers, of toiling in the laundry room. So she was entitled to try it on and for a moment at least to think that it was hers.

She was nearly there and almost sick with nervousness as she got closer. Then suddenly there was a young woman running to meet her. It was Shannon and her arms were outstretched but almost immediately she saw that it wasn't her daughter but Lorrie.

'Karen, thank God you're here.'

'What is it? Is it Shannon?' She felt the slime of sickness in her throat. 'What's wrong, Lorrie, tell me!' But the girl was starting to cry and she had to grab her arm and force her into a response while her own imagination rippled through ever-expanding terrors that left her desperate for an answer.

'Has something happened to Shannon? Lorrie, tell me. Tell me right now!' And she pushed the girl's arm again as if she was pressing her into a starting gear.

'She's been crying her eyes out all day and we've all been out looking for you. But we couldn't find you and Shannon was starting to say that something bad had happened to you. And she's really upset. And then an hour ago she said she was going to find you and she wouldn't let any of us go with her and we're all worried sick.'

So her daughter wasn't dead or in some hospital ward on a life-support machine. She was upset and she was somewhere in Amsterdam and looking for her. She must go and find her but first of all she released her grip on Lorrie's arm, tried to lightly brush away the print her grip had puddled on it, told her everything would be all right and then turned and set off into the night.

Twelve

S HE HESITATED AT THE door of their room, more nervous than she had ever felt at any time in their marriage
since their first night in the Slieve Donard Hotel with the sea
a grey featureless swathe outside their window and almost
indistinguishable from the sky that seemed to press it into a
stubborn stillness. Too nervous and shy to enjoy much more
than the comfort of the room and the knowledge that it
was just the soft rasp of the sea stretching away from them
outside. Only that one night before they caught a flight to
London where they found themselves in a cheap and cheer-
ful hotel near the British Museum. And somehow it was
easier in an unfamiliar place where no one knew anything
about them. Taking the boat on the river past all the sights
that they'd only ever seen on television. She was happy then,
filled with anticipation about the future.

Without being entirely sure why, she knocked on the
door before inserting the key-card. It didn't work first time
and she had to take it out and swipe it again. It still didn't
work – perhaps she was doing it the wrong way. Then there
was the click and she opened the door to find an empty
room. She looked at it carefully but in its neatness it was a
room without a story. She looked in the bathroom to find

it too how she had left it. Then there was the stirring of panic as different scenarios started to play themselves out, each one more fantastic than the one it replaced. She lifted the phone to ring the front desk but put it down again not knowing what it was she intended to say. Perhaps she had been scammed – it was the perfect opportunity for easy money and no likelihood of any comeback – and she felt both foolish and then for the first time in her life dangerously reckless. Who knew what might have happened or the potentially dangerous repercussions of her actions? She had to find him, assure herself that he was all right, and nothing beyond that mattered now to her as she hurried out of the room and towards the lift.

How could she ever forgive herself if she had brought danger to him or if she had been the cause of some terrible misfortune? Despite her frantic pressings of the buttons, the lift took a long time to come and she was glad that it was empty but it stopped at the floor below where no one was waiting and in her panic she pushed buttons randomly and impatiently in her desire to see the doors closed. But as if to punish her the lift stopped at each succeeding floor. The foyer was empty and as she headed to the front door, unsure of where it was she was heading, she heard her name called and he was standing in the entrance to the bar. He was staring at her, staring more intently at her than she could ever remember, and she felt herself flinching, as if she was suddenly exposed and unprotected.

'Marion, what in the name of God is going on? Have you lost your senses?' In the face of his unaccustomed anger she simply shook her head and knew she was going to cry. But he softened almost immediately. 'Are you all right, Marion? Are you . . . ?' He hesitated, obviously unsure of what word he wanted to use. 'Is there anything you want to tell me?'

She felt that if she tried to speak the tears would come and if they did she wasn't sure whether she would be able to stop them. He took her by the sleeve of her coat but not forcefully and led her to the corner table where he had a drink sitting. His outdoor coat was draped over the back of his seat. There were only a few other couples in the bar.

'That looks like whisky,' she said. 'You never drink whisky.'

'Tonight I am,' and as he guided her to a seat, 'and you're going to join me. I think we both need a drink.'

She didn't want him to leave her even to go as far as the bar as she stared at the honey-coloured glass. The bar was almost empty but it felt as if the faces in the photographs that lined the wall were all looking at her and she turned hers from their intrusive gaze and touched the coldness of his glass with her fingertips. He set a gin and tonic in front of her.

'Drink that and then we'll go upstairs and talk and I've no idea what it is you're going to say but you're scaring the hell out of me and it's scaring the hell out of me even more trying to imagine what it is you're going to say.' He cupped his glass and held it for a moment in front of his chest before finishing the contents.

'Richard . . .' she started, but he stopped her and told her it wasn't the right place and she was suddenly conscious of how important it was to him that things looked right and knew how much and how clumsily she had broken that precept. So she drank the gin and tonic and tried to avoid his scrutiny. She drank it more quickly than she should have but it seemed the first requirement of what she had already started to think of as her penance. As soon as she had finished he stood up and said they should go to their room. She hadn't eaten much during the day, the gin was swirling her head a little. The faces in the photographs were staring at her with accusatory eyes and then she felt the welcome slow burn of anger expiating the shame she was expected to feel.

'I don't want to go up to the room.'

'We can't talk here,' he said, looking round him as if they were the focus of the few people in the bar.

'Let's go out and walk. We can talk as we go.'

He nodded his thanks to the barman and took her arm again as if frightened that she might suddenly try to escape. When they reached the steps at the front door he slipped on his coat and as he did so he checked to see that the map was in his pocket. Instinctively she took it from him and stuffed it in hers.

'Let's just walk. We don't need a map.'

'What if we get lost?'

'Then we'll just ask someone. And I don't care if we get lost.'

'Marion, have you been smoking the wacky baccy or taken something you shouldn't have? You're really worrying me and never in my life am I going to understand what earlier was all about.'

She walked a few steps ahead of him not caring where they were heading and suddenly it struck her that she wouldn't be able to put it into simple words, that it was a tangled confusion inside her head, but she had to try and find some means of making sense of it for him, unravelling it for herself. But she wasn't ready and there was no easy way opening up for her or offering itself as the right road to take.

'Let's just walk a while and I'll try to explain but please, Richard, never once in all the time we've been married have you been angry with me and I've valued that more than you can ever know so if it's at all possible I want you to try not to be angry with me now.' The night suddenly seemed much colder than the earlier day had rendered probable and they were passed by people scurrying to their destination rather than walking. She stopped and looked him full in the face. 'Do you think that's possible because I don't think I can do it without that.'

'Marion, I'm worried sick about you, not angry. You go out and a young woman comes to the room and tells me that you've sent her and she's a . . .' he struggled incredulously to remember the word, ' "a present". What in the name of all that's holy am I supposed to think?'

'She was a present, I picked her for you. It was something I wanted to give you and then we'd go back home and everything would be the way it should be.'

'What sort of present is that? And what do you mean "the way it should be"? What's wrong with you, Marion? There must be something you're not telling me. Are you ill?'

She slipped her arm through his and steered them down a narrow side street – she wanted them to walk away from the possibility of crowds, wanted to take the canal side, but there were too many parked cars so instead they headed down the middle of the deserted street, the tall shadowy houses looming over them illuminated only in scattered random patterns.

'No, I'm not ill but there are things that are difficult to tell you and I don't know how to do it.'

In some of the basement flats lighted windows gave tantalisingly brief glimpses of interiors as increasingly conscious of the cold they walked faster, their heads involuntarily bowed a little by the sharp-edged wind. For some inexplicable reason she thought of the nativity scene she'd bought and her favourite part – the wise men bringing their gifts. She wanted to be in her own home again and arranging it on the hall table just as she had planned. She wanted to be on her computer where everything could be managed by the simple click of the mouse.

'And let me get this right,' he hesitated, 'I was supposed to have sex with this person whom I assume is a prostitute.'

She cringed at the ugliness of the word, blanched at the shame of having made him use it. The incredible dangerous foolishness of it reared up before her like a mountain that could never be climbed and which threatened to shadow everything that dared approach it. It was beyond explanation but she had to try.

'Yes, it was supposed to be something I gave you and to be private between us and never talked about again.'

'So I was supposed to do this thing and then we'd just go home and pretend it hadn't happened.'

She knew it sounded more and more deranged when he said it like that so she didn't answer and momentarily turned her head away towards the blackness of the canal that was salted sparsely with light.

'But why, Marion? Why? – that's what I want to know. What possible reason had you for doing this?' And as he said this he pulled her lightly back by the arm so that she was forced to stop walking and face him.

'Because you're not happy with me, because I'm not enough for you and because it's what you want.' It spilled out even before she knew she was going to say it and she was frightened by it and the uncertainty of where it might take them.

'And what put this in your head – that I'm not happy with you?'

She stared at him and his head was framed by the large lighted window of a room in one of the old canal houses where the walls were painted a soft yellow and a young woman was standing with a wine glass in her hand. She searched for what to say, unsure of how much she could tell him without tipping what existed between them into a new and more precarious balance. And as she struggled to reach an answer he spoke again.

'You think I don't love you, Marion?'

And she was momentarily angry that everything was to fall back on her, that she was the one who had to provide answers to every question.

'I know you love me, Richard, but for a long time what I think you love best is the settled comfort of it, of what we give to each other that helps us both get by and which is solid and dependable. But do you love me in a way that's more than that? I don't really know and perhaps you don't either.'

A bicycle was coming, its light a white, blinking strobe. They stepped over to the water's edge suddenly aware that they had been standing in the middle of the road.

'Marion, I don't know where any of this is coming from, or what it's all about, but it's shaking the life out of me and I don't understand any of it.'

But she was increasingly conscious that he hadn't yet said he loved her and she felt that if he were to do so now it would be too late. She didn't know if she could ever make him fully understand.

'You didn't like her?' she asked suddenly as she stared down at the light-stippled blackness of the water.

'I couldn't even tell you what she looked like and it doesn't matter what she looked like because I don't want to sleep with anyone except my wife. Except with you.' To emphasise the point he rested his hand on her shoulder. For a second she thought of shrugging it off but instead she turned her collar up as if to say that she could find her own warmth.

'Let's walk, Richard. Let's just walk.' And without waiting for a reply she set off again, this time on the same side of the street as the canal. More cyclists passed them, some with lights, some with none. 'I went skating today, on the Museumplein. I didn't think I would remember how to do it. I thought about when we took the children to the Ice Bowl and Judith took to it so quickly that the boys had their noses put out. I don't think she even fell once.'

He paused for a second as if unsure of where she was leading him then followed and when he spoke his voice came from behind her. 'Ice-skating, Marion? You went ice-skating? You've done some pretty strange things since we arrived here. Do you think you're having some sort of breakdown? Did you fall?'

'No I didn't, and I didn't bang my head if that's what you're thinking, and I'm not having a breakdown,' she said as he drew level but almost walking sideways and staring at her face.

'You asked the man in the chip shop about his family and you made me give him the money – you have to admit that was a bit weird.'

'I thought you understood why we gave him the money,' she said, meeting his stare with an intensity that she knew he wasn't used to and which she saw confused him. And now it was her turn to ask the questions. 'And why did we do it?'

He knew it was a test of some sort and she watched as he searched for the right answer.

'Because you felt sorry for him?' he ventured.

'I felt sorry for him but just the way I feel sorry for everyone in the world and that's not the reason we gave him the money.' Perhaps it was the drink she had taken too quickly or perhaps it was something else but she felt a new sense of release as she told him, 'We did it because it was the right thing to do, because it was kind and there isn't ever enough kindness.'

'There was no harm in it,' he said and she was aware that his voice was edged with appeasement.

'All my life I've tried to do the right thing and what happened this afternoon was me trying to do the right thing but sometimes even when that's what you're trying to do, it comes out wrong. I suppose sometimes it's hard to know what the right thing is. Do you understand?' Never in her life had she spoken like this and for a second she wasn't sure whether the voice was hers or belonged to someone else and there was a momentary sweetness in the freedom of not having to worry about what she might say next.

'I think so. But why did you think the girl was the right thing? Do you think I'm that sort of person?'

'You're a good person and when I thought of it I didn't think of it as a bad thing or that even for a second it would make you a bad person. It was just something I wanted you to have.'

'But why, Marion? In God's name, why?'

They paused at the end of the street to allow a taxi to pass. There was a young couple kissing in the back seat, sliding gratefully into a tighter embrace as the car cornered. Across the street bristled a small working-class bar, its lace-curtained, bevelled windows fogged with heat and music. It felt as if the whole city was shut indoors, warming itself on friendship and laughter, a world from which they had excluded themselves. She knew she owed it to them both to try and put it into words.

'Because, Richard, you like women and because I suppose I think that sooner or later you'll want to know the pleasure of one of them. And please don't say anything now that isn't true and I know, I know, that you wouldn't ever humiliate me or openly hurt me.'

'So you think I'm running round looking for other women?'

'Richard, that's not what I'm saying. This is very hard for me and the only thing I'm sure about is that after we've had this conversation I never want either of us to mention it ever again. Can you promise me that?' But as soon as she said it and had glanced at him to gauge his reaction, she knew he would promise anything that would bring her back to her senses, to the person he wanted her to be. She felt the need to force him towards some understanding so she pushed recklessly further. 'Tell me how you feel about Anka.'

'Anka?' He said it as if he had never heard of the name and in so doing only seemed to confirm what she already believed. 'She's a nice girl and Celina is too and a very good worker.'

'I know that, Richard,' she interrupted. It was important to her that he was honest – if they came this far and stopped at the edge, sooner or later they would topple into freefall. 'But what do you feel for her?'

'I don't feel what it is you're getting at – that's ridiculous. As if she'd be interested in an old man like me.'

'You're a handsome man and not so old – it's entirely possible she'd be interested in you – and your idea about the flower shop, what about that?'

When she played the trump card of the flower shop she felt a sense of triumph. In reply he took her hand, holding it and looking at it as if he was going to tell her fortune by reading her palm. 'I never told you this but Anka has a name for me – it's something like Wujek. It means "uncle", Marion. Uncle. That's how Anka sees me. As her uncle. I suppose you'd be happier if it was as her grandfather.'

'And the flower shop?'

'It just seemed a good idea. She's a hard worker, she'd make us money. But we'll bin that idea because I'm not going to do anything you're not happy with. And I'm not going to do anything crazy now or in the future because I'm very happy with what I've got and I don't want to lose it.'

She slipped her hand free from his and turned her face away. There was a mist seeping along the canal, softly smothering the small boats moored on the far side. It seemed to unfold and layer itself along the surface of the water then rise up round the buildings until edges and outlines blurred and the world was smoothed into an indistinguishable whole.

'I can't say it any plainer than that, Marion.'

'I think you could have,' she said and immediately felt she had been too hard on him. He had never found the words easy and if she was honest then neither had she, often telling herself that there were other and perhaps more meaningful ways to express what was felt. She wanted the mist to swallow her up, to soften the sharpness of her thoughts.

As they passed a bar an old man came through the door, releasing the interior's smell of smoke and beer, but what she wanted was the scent of those early-morning trees that she had brought into being and what she desired now was to be back in the world that was familiar to her. Perhaps Richard had been right and she was going through some kind of breakdown and whether he was right or wrong, nothing had worked out the way she had planned, so what was to be done? What was the way to retrace the steps that no longer felt as if they had brought her to where she wanted to be? Perhaps after all that young woman on the running machine had things better worked out than she had, perhaps she was gifted with a surer sense of direction than her own which stretched out uncertain and swaddled by the mist. She gave him her hand again in an offer of reconciliation and he took it without hesitation and perhaps that was enough, both now and for the future.

'I think we should go back,' he said, 'before this mist gets any worse and we end up falling into a canal.'

'Just a little bit longer.' She squeezed his hand and knew she was frightened to go back to the room, to be alone in that confined space where a third person would hover between them like a ghost.

And so they walked on, turning down unknown streets at random, their shoulders instinctively huddled closer against the cold. Without a map. Then after a period of wordless walking she started to turn them in a direction she believed would lead them back and reaching a main intersection they were startled by the sudden warning bell of a tram that clattered round a corner and clanked past in a blurry smear of yellow light.

'You need to have eyes in the back of your head in this city,' he announced and she knew that they had started to drift back into a world marked by familiar parameters and she wasn't sorry. It all felt too much now, a moment of madness that would sit in their shared memory until it either corroded itself with the rust of time or else would quicken into recurring life and, although never allowed to shape itself into words, would be seen and recognised in the eyes, be suddenly present in random moments of silence in a conversation. But despite her simple desire now for safety there was some insistent part of her that would not let it go, partly because she realised this was the only time when the thing that had lodged in her head for so long could find expression and that this was a door better not to have opened. But before it shut for ever she had to know. So as they gradually found themselves back in a vaguely recognisable part of the city she slowed their walk and tried to compose what she wanted to say. They had to step aside as a tight knot of football supporters lurched past in a clatter of hand-clapping chants, one of them waving a flag in slow, sweeping movements.

'You didn't think she was pretty?'

'I told you, Marion, I wasn't interested in how she looked.'

'But you must have looked at her, even for a second you must have looked and imagined it.'

'I don't know what you want me to say.' He shook his head slowly as if in exasperation.

'You must look at other women, Richard.'

'Of course I look, but looking and doing are two completely different things.'

'You must compare them to me when you look.' She knew it was cruel and without purpose to punish him like this but once again she felt the strangeness of the power the words gave her.

'No, I don't compare them to you and if I've done something bad or something that's hurt you then I'm sorry and all I know is that I didn't mean to. I know I didn't mean to, Marion.' And he swung her hand slightly forward before letting it fall again.

She believed him but said nothing as the hotel appeared in the distance. They were passing restaurants and bars that sat shoulder to shoulder and jostled for customers. Here the mist appeared to have been burnt away by the frenzied flare of light. There was loud disco music thumping from somewhere, a wavering modulation, its sharp descant of high notes piercing and tattooing the soft skin of the night. She thought she could hear Abba's 'Dancing Queen' playing somewhere. It was the only thing that felt faintly recognisable from everything that throbbed around them. She hadn't danced since their wedding reception when she had clung to the memorised movements Lillian had taught her the day before. Lillian who was the dancer and the most full of life of them all, Lillian whose death had shocked them and emptied something from their own lives.

'Do you feel you've missed out on something, Richard?'

'Like what?'

'You remember you told me you always regretted not going to the City Hall the night Clinton turned on the lights? Do you ever feel that all these people,' and she gestured vaguely with her free hand, 'have been invited to the party and you're on the outside looking in?'

'Marion, I'm sorry but I don't know any of the answers to these questions. Maybe I don't think about things enough, maybe I just think too much about going out and earning a living. When the children come at Christmas won't that be like a party and that's more than good enough for me?'

He loved his family, he loved her. She told herself it was enough. She wouldn't punish him any more; there would be no more questions. As they hurried across the road to the hotel, she noticed the Japanese couple a few steps in front, their raincoats bright against the night. They looked more like twin brother and sister and, following them up the steps, it suddenly seemed important to speak to them, to know something about them, because in a short while she would be returning to a life where such impulses would no longer be possible.

'Richard, ask them if they'd join us for a drink. It's too early to go up to the room.' She pressed his hand in persuasion and watched him trying to decide what was for the best and whether this was another inexplicable aberration. She squeezed his hand again before she let it go. He hesitated. She wanted to tell him that it seemed a sin on a night like this, and even after all that had happened between them, to surrender the moment without trying to be part of something other than themselves. It was her fault, all her fault that their life had slipped into nothing more than the predictable rhythm of work. Why couldn't it change? Why couldn't they learn to dance or go skating or one of a hundred other things? Why couldn't they discover new friends who would help bring them out of themselves?

Whatever her husband really felt, he approached them with a polite confidence, his arms stretched wide, and she recognised the boyish smile edged with shyness that had made him so attractive to her in those early days. The couple looked at each other, spoke a few words to one another in Japanese and then accepted their invite, and as Richard gestured them politely towards the bar the young woman smiled again at her. After sitting at a table they exchanged handshakes and first names. Richard got the drinks – the couple wanted Diet Cokes while they both ordered coffees, still feeling the chill of their walk. She felt slightly drunk even though she knew she couldn't be and part of her wanted to stretch out her arms across the table to these two strangers who smiled a lot and spoke in slow but adequate English and hold them tight. She wanted to press their friendship into the patina of her life. They told each other their names twice but no one quite mastered the others'. The woman might have been called Hina but she wasn't sure and they didn't manage to identify much more than the cities they came from and their respective jobs. So they came from Osaka and he was an engineer. She asked them how long they'd been married and learned that it was five years and when in return she told them how long she and Richard had been married they nodded repeatedly and smiled, in a bestowing of their congratulations. Then they talked about the weather while she looked at how beautiful the young woman's eyes were and how they seemed so ready to quicken into a smile and if it had been possible she would have had her tell her everything about her life, about her husband and whether she wanted children. But instead when an awkward silence settled she told them about her skating but had to mime it before they understood and she was rewarded with laughter. She wanted to talk all night, not to have to go to their room, but after a while and her giving them her email address, the couple bowed almost formally before saying goodnight.

They were left in their pocket of silence until Richard said, 'A nice couple. I'm not sure how much they understood.'

'Would you like to go to Japan some day?' she asked.

'I've never thought about it. It's a long way.'

'All those cherry-blossom trees. It's supposed to be beautiful.'

'Well then we better go.'

She looked at him to see if he was laughing at her but there was only seriousness in his face and then he drank from his cup of coffee and set it carefully back in its saucer in a way that said he was finished and she knew there was nothing now to detain them from the room. She thought of asking for another drink but knew it was pointless to postpone the inevitable any longer. Her eyes scanned the rows of photographs one last time but she did it so quickly that they blurred into one homogeneous whole like the school photographs the children brought home every few years where the entire school squeezed close together in tiered rows and where your own prodigy seemed to bleed into those all around them. In the lift he asked her if she was all right and he did it gently and genuinely with no trace of irritation or patronisation in his voice. She nodded that she was, afraid that if she spoke her voice would betray her nervousness, the sensation of everything falling away. She couldn't think of what she had done now without feeling that she had shamed something loose for them both so she tried to anchor herself by going over all the preparations she would have to carry out before Christmas, itemising the list of things to be done and finding a temporary comfort in those that were the most mundane.

In the room she hoped he would switch on the television but he went straight to the bathroom and closed the door. She turned off the brightness of the overhead light that felt too revealing and replaced it with the two bedside lamps, then despite herself she looked around again, bevelling everywhere with her hand, edging delicately with her fingers, looking for anything that deviated from her memory, for some trace of what might have been, only at the last second stopping herself from lifting the pillow to inhale its scent. Going to the window she looked out towards the square. The mist seemed to have breathed new life into itself and thickened again and it reminded her of that first night when the sea, a permanent watching presence, stretched grey and whispering outside their wedding room, echoing the murmuring of her heart.

'I think it's got worse,' she said when he came back, lightly tracing her fingertips along the glass as if to feel the mist outside.

He came and stood behind her, resting his hand on her shoulder. Down below the lights bloomed in soft-petalled buds of colour, trying in vain to blossom against the grey mist silently pressing itself on the world. He gently touched the back of her neck with his fingers, parting her hair to touch her skin. She didn't know what she felt in the moment except that the only thing of which she was sure was what she had to do in the future. And again she pressed the list into her consciousness believing that if she did it carelessly or vaguely in her imagination now, then she would get it wrong when the time came. She wanted him to speak to break the pressure of the silence which felt more than she could bear but he simply stood behind her and looked at the encroaching tide that seemed to flow up to the very shore of the room. She searched for what she could say, for what might finally drown the day in their memories, but no words would come and so she was glad when eventually he spoke.

'Marion, I have something I wanted to give you but I don't know if it's the right thing to do now or not. It's a present. A sort of present.'

Surely they had seen enough of presents to last them the very rest of their lives. Her fingers unintentionally squeaked the glass. He had stepped back, his hand slipping slowly and uncertainly from her neck.

'But you've already given me my presents,' she said, looking at the flush of self-consciousness that coloured his face.

'I thought it was something that you might like but I'm not sure now. Maybe it's stupid, maybe it's not the right thing any more.' He puffed his cheeks, holding his breath then blew it free in a long stream and as if releasing his doubt took a small black box from his pocket. 'It's a ring.'

'A ring?' she asked while taking the unopened box from his outstretched hand and letting it balance in her palm. 'A ring for me?'

'Sort of, but not exactly. It's for you but it's for me.'

She didn't understand but he took the box back and opened the lid, then angled it forward for her to see. It was a wedding ring. A man's broad, plain wedding ring.

'I thought it was high time I had one. Don't know why I never got one before.' His voice was more nervous than she could ever remember hearing it. It seemed fragile, beating against the tightening stillness of the room, and as the meaning of it coursed through her she struggled for words and could only stare at his face until he looked away. 'Perhaps I should have done it sooner and perhaps this is the wrong time for it. If it is I'll put it away and it can be something else we're going to forget.'

'It's the right time,' she said, brushing his cheek with the tips of her fingers, the way she had touched the coldness of the glass. 'I'm glad.' Her voice was a whisper and for a second she looked back to the window where the greyness smeared the glass and threatened to flow into the room itself. 'It's the right time.'

'That's good,' he said, his voice stronger than before.

She took the box again and, removing the ring, held it tightly in the pinch of her fingers then raised his hand and carefully slipped it on his finger. 'Where did you get it?' she asked.

'In Lunn's where we got yours. Seemed the right place to go.'

'Even after all these years?'

He sat on the edge of the bed and looked at it on his finger, moving his hand slowly to let it catch the light. She sat beside him and held her own hand out. 'Mine looks dull in comparison.'

'Does that mean you want a new one?'

'No, you never replace your wedding ring. For better or worse this is the only one.'

'Where did all those years go, Marion?' He half-turned to look at her. 'We've been happy most of the time, haven't we?'

She heard the uncertainty in his voice and leaning lightly against him said, 'Yes, Richard, I think we have.' Then there was only the slight rustle of their breathing. She glanced again at the window. 'Do you remember that first night in the Slieve Donard and our room looking out over the sea?'

'Of course I remember it. I think I was more frightened that night than any time in my life.'

'You were frightened?'

'The speech, that first dance and you know – all the rest.'

'There's a lot to worry about, a lot to get right. Young ones seem to take it in their stride nowadays. It was just a big day out for the boys. And as for Judith – there's no sign of it happening.'

'As long as she's happy.'

'As long as she's happy,' she echoed.

They sat in silence again and then she asked him to draw the curtains and as he did so she half-expected to hear the disappearing rasp and flow of the sea. On the table stood the nativity scene and the wise men offering their gifts. In the morning she would pack it carefully in her case, wrapping each figure in the soft tissue paper and snuggling it all between the protective softness of her clothes so that nothing got broken. He had given her a ring. If she had let herself, she would have constructed different reasons why he had done it but as she watched him vanquish the last chink of the outer world she told herself that he had given it and that was enough. Everything was enough – it was foolish of her to have looked for something more, for something that now seemed as nebulous and undefined as the mist slowly embracing the city in its languid arms. She thought again of Lillian who had everything taken from her so early and she knew she owed it to her and to herself to live, to hold on tightly to whatever it was she had. She would not be the one who would give it away or let it sift slowly like sand through her fingers. And there were things that she knew were no longer worthy of her care and how much of herself she had wasted in worrying about them. What would happen would happen. So after they had switched off their lights and he came to her, nervous and frightened like he had that very first time, she opened her arms to him and when in the final moments his breath streamed warm and needy against her face and she heard him whisper, 'Only you, only you,' she gently hushed him, over and over, until her whisper sounded like the ebb of some far-off sea.

Thirteen

As SHE WALKED THE cold wind began to slip like a silent thief between the buildings and she pulled her jacket tighter to stop it stealing the little warmth that was left to her and when she passed bars and restaurants, their windows steamed with heat, she envied those inside. She remembered the time Shannon had got lost as a child and the sense of terror it had produced as running from place to place, frantically calling her name, she tried to recall where she liked to play, all the time tormenting herself with thoughts of injury or kidnap. If that hadn't been enough there burned the fear that he might have taken her, come back into their lives and taken her for no other reason than he thought she was his. And as she sidestepped the two lurching drunks coming towards her, their arms round each other's shoulders so that they looked as if they were in a ragged three-legged race and about to sprawl forward at any moment, she was cut again by the thought that the very thing she feared had happened all these years later. She tried to remember how long Shannon had said she'd been seeing him but it was blunted by confusion and all that was sharp in her memory was their angry reflections in the mirror of the toilet and the look on her daughter's face when she had hit her.

One of the drunks saluted her but she kept on walking and part of her believed that even in this strange city there would be something that would finally lead her to her daughter, just like that time all those years ago when she had found her on the old disused train line under the bridge with her friend, making echoes with their voices. She had heard her before she saw her and at first there was the panic of thinking it was a cry of distress as her own voice intercut the childish echoes. Shannon's confusion and ultimate indifference to her concern, her childish insistence that she was having fun and didn't want to go home, that it was too early for bedtime and her anger as she had been led forcefully by the arm to the house, all came rushing back. It was all happening again – her daughter indifferent to her distress, not understanding how she had upset her, absorbed entirely by the echo of her own voice. Despite the sharpness of the memory part of her was already cynical about what Lorrie had told her and unconvinced by her description of Shannon's distress even though she desperately wanted it to be true. But it wasn't safe for her daughter to be alone in a foreign city at night and she needed to find her as quickly as she could, calm her and do whatever was necessary to get her back to the hotel.

All around her the city simmered with noisy life, the streets thronged with people intent on pleasure. She passed lots of groups, mostly of young women with their cigarettes held aloft like fire-flies in the night and shiny mobile phones pressed to their ears. There was the chattering clatter of their heels and despite the cold their primped bodies on show with their excited voices breaking against each other before shattering into laughter again and again. She passed the older couple she recognised from the plane, who in contrast to the young women walked hunched against the cold, seamed at the shoulder and locked into each other's silence. Hardly anyone walked alone and those who did strode out with a purpose that said that soon they too would be with the one they loved. Once again she felt conscious of her solitariness and she thought that this was not a place in which to be on your own.

She had no plan in her walking, just a belief that sooner or later she would find her daughter, and in her imagination she called her name and waited for her echoing voice to rise up above the clamour of the city but there was only a returning chaos of sound that coursed through the streets and flowed about her, indifferent to her growing concern. The same sense of loneliness she had felt after Shannon had told her renewed itself, framed in her memory like the painting of the girl reading the letter. After all these years he had returned and kidnapped her for no good reason that she could ever concede, other than the desire to lay claim to her as if she were a possession to be added to what was already his. He had always been someone who wanted to own things – she remembered how he had liked to walk past the moneyed houses in Cultra, how he had liked to talk big about the future. After he had left her she had seen him once, only once and by accident, in the city centre on a Saturday afternoon going into a shop and for no longer than a few seconds. But she had felt sick, sliding into a faintness which made her call her father in a breathless panic to come and collect her, never telling him what had happened and not going back into the city centre on that day for more than a year.

So how could she bring herself to look at him now, to watch him lead her child down the aisle? Perhaps Shannon would see sense, understand what it meant to her, but even as she tried to comfort herself with these possibilities, she knew with bitterness that there were other considerations for her daughter that were as compelling as her mother's feelings. So she kept on walking, trying to pick out her daughter's face from those streaming around her, and then just as she realised that the wind had dropped, she was aware of a mist softly smoking its way up from the canals and seeping into the side streets. It gave them a ghostly feeling as if they had become a spectral memory of what they had been during the day and she shivered and hurried on, frantically scanning the crowds, desperate to find her before the city was sealed in the mist and they were lost to each other for ever.

The sense of loneliness pressed against her as she thought of the old man dying, her presence at his side only by chance – perhaps at some other time she would have merely collected what she was required to and left him there to sleep. But she had known he was going to die and not just from his breathing but from something she had felt in the room, some emptiness that seemed to arch over him and which she couldn't put a name to. And despite it all, despite the elaborate show and the rituals of being a community, the home was the loneliest place she had ever been and if she didn't need the money she would pack it in. The ones who did the most talking about their families were the ones who saw them least, covering up absence with stories about how successful their sons or daughters were and how their business needed them at the helm more and more. Occasional fleeting visits to keep the conscience sweet were the order of the day and these were always the ones who complained the most, probably believing that pointing out supposed deficiencies in care was a substitute for more frequent attendance.

At least Mrs Hemmings had found a substitute for company, sending her letters to the newspapers and posting her comments. She remembered how proud of these she was and how she liked to tell her that she was part of 'an online community'. But loneliness wasn't confined to the residents and she thought of the time when in late afternoon in a small upstairs lounge, lit only by the light from the corridor, she had heard the quiet crying of one of the Filipino nurses curled in a corner armchair almost hidden in the shadows. She had hesitated at first, knowing the nurses kept themselves to themselves, speaking their own language to each other and sometimes seeming a little distant from the rest of the staff. But then she had gone over, only changing her mind when she saw the letter in her hand, and then quietly she had retraced her steps. Later she had heard from one of the other nurses that her mother was ill but she wasn't able to go home.

And now in a strange city where the sullen mist seemed suddenly patchy and unable to sustain itself, she too had a daughter who was crying for her. Well let her cry – she deserved every one of the tears – and no matter how many she shed she would never know what her mother had suffered. And let her cry whatever tears she felt were needed because now she would make her mother suffer it all over again.

She recognised some of the shops she had passed earlier with the guy from the plane and she wondered if he had found his son. So perhaps her photograph, her snapshot shaped and coloured only by hurt, wasn't so different after all, perhaps it was the one everyone had in their album but never showed anyone. And there was the shop that supposedly sold the most beautiful handmade chocolates – what did he think, that hers was a life that would be affected by this knowledge? That when she was at home she spent her time in search of such a shop? Perhaps she should ask the manager of her local Spar why he didn't sell such things. The bitterness of her loneliness had slowly dissolved itself and been replaced by self-pity, something early in her life she had understood was pointless and wasteful of the energy she needed just to keep going, but she told herself that she was entitled to hug it just a little while longer before she let it go. And there was the prospect of Christmas for it to feed on. It had already been decided that Shannon and Wade would go to his parents' on Christmas Day and come to her on Boxing Day, so she had volunteered to work in the home where the order of the day would be party hats and crackers, organised cheeriness and visitors arriving to play happy families in the afternoon, or just before teatime returning the relative they had signed out earlier like a book from the library. But the only certainty was that before the day was out the place would be a wash of tears with too many unravelling memories spooling out, too many longings for what didn't exist any more and couldn't exist ever again. Well she was paid to clean and serve and there would be more than enough of that to keep her busy until late at night so it wasn't her job to go around offering comfort. Let those whose job it was do it and then she realised that there wasn't anyone whose job it was, that despite the glossy brochures and all the big talk it wasn't in anyone's job description. She tried to spark a little consolation from the thought of the extra pay but it flared only briefly before being replaced by a new awareness of the night's unforgiving coldness.

She wanted to raise her head and before the mist filled her lungs shout her daughter's name across the city, shout and shout it so that they could both go home to whatever warmth might be found, but she knew if she were to do so the only echoes would be the stares and indifference of those around her. And then she saw her. Even at a distance she knew it was her and despite everything she smiled as getting closer she saw her daughter, oblivious to everything, inspecting the display in a shoe shop.

'You don't have enough shoes?'

'Mum!' she shouted, her face splintering like breaking glass and throwing her arms around her in the tightest of embraces so that the side of her face was curtained by the side of her daughter's hair and smeared heavily by her scent. 'Where have you been? I've been looking everywhere for you.' And so Shannon was speaking to her, the hot rush of her words pressing against her skin as if her mother was the missing child who had been the cause of concern.

'I've just been walking, looking at stuff, looking at paintings,' she said, patiently waiting for her embrace to loosen. 'Are you all right?'

'I was so worried about you – you've never gone off like that before and somewhere you don't even know.'

There was a novelty in hearing Shannon's concern but there were things that had to be said and so she gently prised her arms from round her neck then smoothed her daughter's frantic hair into calm. 'Shannon, I'm sorry I hit you.' The words weren't easy to say but she did her best to mean them and in response her daughter shook her head slowly from side to side as if she was refusing the apology.

'I deserved it,' she said, taking her mother's hands in her own but not looking her in the eye. She watched her bite her bottom lip and they both stepped back a little, perhaps equally shocked by the unaccustomed admission of guilt.

'Yes you did,' she said before the admission faded on her daughter's lips into the mist.

'I was going to tell you lots of times but I knew what you'd say and then I thought we'd be here and maybe it'd help me to do it and help us see things in a different way.'

'So just being in a plane for the first time and being some-where new would change the past and how I feel about everything?'

Shannon shivered – as always she wasn't wearing warm-enough clothes – and she shivered in reply.

'We need to go somewhere we can talk, somewhere out of the cold before we both freeze to death.'

She glanced around her but there was nowhere obvious and for a second she caught their reflection in a mirror in the shop window. They both seemed thin, pinched of face, her daughter's riot of hair shocked out of its normal pliant submission.

'Look,' she said, pointing. 'We both look as if we've been pulled through a hedge backwards.'

'It feels like it,' Shannon answered, thrown into a panic about her appearance, her hands pressing and plumping her hair and pulling up her collar.

'We need to walk and find somewhere before we freeze to death and there's no point going into one of those bars where you can't hear yourself talk. Are you hungry?'

'Looking at paintings? Where were you looking at paintings?'

'In the museum,' and her daughter's surprise annoyed her because it suggested she considered it something beyond her capacity and so she said, 'I'm not really hungry but we can get something if you want. Something that's not going to cost the earth.'

'Everything costs the earth when you turn it into euros. Some of the girls are all spent out.'

'And drunk out?'

'Mostly, but there's a couple who never reach the bottom of the bottle.'

'So are you hungry or not?'

'I could eat some chips. They call them *friet* and if you don't stop them they put mayonnaise on them. How gross is that?'

Hearing her daughter's voice assume a glib lilt of knowledge made her think of telling her the really important things that she had seen in the city, about the paintings with the light coming out of them and about the old houses hidden off the shopping street huddled tightly together like old books on a shelf, but she suddenly realised that these were things that she didn't want to share with anyone, things she wanted to add to her private store. The guy on the plane knew about paintings – if she saw him again perhaps she could ask him about the light. She looked round her at how the suddenly re-forming mist laced and layered itself around the neon lights as if trying to soothe them into softness. All her daughter's upset seemed temporary and shallow and she wondered what it was she would say to her as she pointed the way to where she remembered seeing a chippy in a side street just off a main thoroughfare. As they walked she felt Shannon link her arm.

There were only three small round tables and they sat at the one pushed tight into the corner and studied the menu before each finally deciding on a small portion of chips and two cans of Fanta. Shannon insisted on paying and she let her, staring at her daughter's back as she stood at the counter, her purse in her hand. Her back was straight and slender, making her look taller than she actually was – it would be easy for her to look good in her wedding dress and she saw the way the man behind the counter gave her his full attention and more smiles than he normally served. He called her back to give her an abundance of serviettes and the chance of another look and she heard a familiar voice in her head saying that she could have done better than Wade. Someone who could have offered her the possibility of breaking into a better way of life, someone with the energy to make something of himself. And she realised that Wade must have shared her secret and she thought with bitterness of all the times that she had made him meals and put him up. Of all the times he had sponged off her, taken her hospitality for granted and given nothing back.

'He asked me if we wanted mayonnaise,' she said, widening her eyes in mock horror while setting the chips and the drinks on the table. 'I got ketchup.'

'That's good. So how long have you been looking for me?'

'A couple of hours. We thought you'd be back earlier and we didn't realise you'd gone until we surfaced.'

'And that was pretty late, I suppose.'

'We were all pretty hung-over and I lost track of time and things. But we just thought you'd gone out for a look round this afternoon and would be back later. Then I got worried even though Martina said you'd be all right and maybe it was better if everyone had time to cool down.'

The chips were hot and tasted good. They ate them with the little wooden forks they'd been given and dipped them in the sauce. She saw that there was no sense of tension or apprehension in her daughter as from time to time her eyes flicked to the mirrored wall that faced them. Her casual assumption that everything was fixed between them angered her but she waited until that anger had shaped itself as calmly as she could muster into words.

'We need to talk, Shannon.'

'I know.' She dabbed delicately at the corners of her lightly sheened lips with her paper serviette.

'And I need you to tell me the truth. It's important now for both of us. No more lies.'

'I didn't tell you any lies,' she protested, her eyes widening with hurt.

'Not telling me that you had met your father was a lie and not telling me you had invited him to the wedding was one as well. You didn't think that these were things I was entitled to know?'

'I know you were entitled to know and I tried to tell you lots of times. But every time I couldn't at the last minute because I knew you'd go ballistic.' She drank from the can, hiding her face behind it for a second.

'And why do you think I'd have gone ballistic?'

'Because you hate him for running out on you all those years ago.'

She wanted to stretch her hands across the table, take her daughter's shoulders and shake her into the truth.

'Shannon, he didn't just run out on me – all those years ago he ran out on you, his child. Can't you understand that? And he stayed away all the time you were growing up. Not once did he want to know how you were doing, not once did he try to be part of your life.'

'I know that, Mum, I know he did a bad thing but . . .'

'And now he wants to walk you down the aisle and suddenly after all these years play your father.' Her anger was rising, she wanted to strike out at something, scatter everything off the table on to the floor. 'And that's all he'd be doing – playing being your father.'

There was a sequence of sniffles and then Shannon started to cry, her head bowed over the chips, her hair falling forward and curtaining her face. But she had no sympathy for her and didn't care that the man behind the counter was glancing at them. She spoke quietly to the top of her daughter's head that leaned submissively towards her, but it wasn't submission she wanted, it was understanding.

'All these years I struggled to look after you and take care of you and I did it with nothing from him and now he wants to turn up on the most important day of your life and waltz you down the aisle like he's never been away, that it's all been some sort of misunderstanding and this'll put it right. Well I don't think so, Shannon.'

She sat back on her seat, suddenly feeling empty inside. It was like the emptiness she had felt in the old man's room, arching over everything, draining the space of all its being. So she couldn't speak or register any emotion when her daughter looked up at her, brushed the hair back from her face and started to speak.

'You're right to be cross because I should have told you right at the start. But it wasn't easy and I wasn't sure what I was going to do so there wasn't any point that first time he spoke to me coming home and upsetting you if I wasn't ever going to see him again.' She moved the can of drink to a different spot on the table as if to give her more room for what she wanted to say. 'It was a Saturday afternoon, getting on to closing time, and I saw him looking at me but you get that sometimes, so I didn't pay any attention, and then he came up to the counter and bought something for his wife but I knew he didn't understand or care what it was he was buying. It happens every so often but he didn't look creepy or anything. Then right out of the blue he asked if he could speak to me after work finished and I was just about to tell him to get lost and call the supervisor when he said it. Just blurted it out – "Shannon, I'm your father but if you don't want to speak to me I'll understand and go away and never bother you again." Said he'd really like to speak to me. And he'd wait in the bar across the way.'

Her daughter's words were inside her, tearing at her, each one a hook pulling her from everything that served to weight her to herself, and all she could do was grip the edge of the rickety table that separated them and yet she didn't want her daughter to stop. She needed to hear it all so she didn't speak but nodded for her to go on.

'I didn't know what to do. I felt sick at first, my stomach turned right upside down, and then when I got over that I felt curious. All the times I've thought about him as a child, wondered what he was like, imagined stupid things and here he was and at first I was frightened, really frightened, and then I wanted to know, to ask him why he didn't want us. So I went.' She paused again to dab her lips, pressing the tissue gently against them with the tips of her fingers. 'And he was there in the bar and he was really pleased to see me and he kept asking if I was all right and how he didn't want to upset me so there was no pressure and I could leave any time I wanted and he'd understand.'

She listened to her daughter slip towards what she already knew would be some kind of all-too-easy accommodation and she was filled with a thrilled anticipation of terror. So she sipped slowly from her drink, holding it tightly and then, without meaning to, set it down too firmly so that everything on the table quivered a little before settling again. The seats beside them were taken by new customers and a loud babble of foreign language now threatened to drown out her daughter's voice that had started to flutter into a whisper like a moth trapped against glass.

'Well we just talked and he told me he was married – which I knew already – and that he had two children, a boy of thirteen and a girl of eleven. So I had a stepbrother and -sister I didn't know about.'

'Have you met them?' she asked, already knowing the answer from the edge of pride in her voice.

'Yes. They're nice kids.'

'You've been to his house then?' She could hardly bring herself to ask the question as more and more of what she had always held secure worked itself loose and slipped away from her.

'Yes.'

'And I suppose it's very nice.'

'It's on the King's Road.'

'So very nice?'

'Yes.' Suddenly Shannon looked uncomfortable, her eyes flitting round the other customers whose loud laughter clapped itself about their heads. 'I've only been a couple of times.'

'You've met his wife? And I'm sure she's happy to suddenly have a stepdaughter?'

'She's cool with it.'

'That's good,' she said, not trying to disguise her sarcasm.

'Maybe we should go somewhere else. If you've finished?'

'In a minute, Shannon. There's some things I need to know before we go anywhere,' she said, leaning closer across the table so that she didn't miss any of her daughter's answers. 'So when did you first meet him and how often were you seeing him?'

'That first time – the time he came to the store – was in January. The sales were on. We met every so often, went to his house a couple of times – that's all.'

She wanted to stretch her arms across the table and pull her daughter into sharper focus. Vagueness would only allow uncertainties to rattle round her head for longer than she could bear.

'How often? Once a month, twice a month, more?'

'Mum, what does it matter whether it was once or twice a month?'

Her face said she was weary of the questions but she didn't care about her daughter's weariness and if she had been able to maintain a secret for almost a year then she could have the decency to bear them now until she had answered every one.

'It matters to me, Shannon, everything matters to me, so how often did you see him?'

'I don't know,' and in her voice was a thin little whine of protest. 'No more than once a month, mostly he'd meet me after work and we'd have a drink and then he'd drive me home.'

'He drove you to the house?'

'Don't panic, he never came into the street, just left me off somewhere I could walk. Mum, let's go somewhere else.'

'In a minute.' Then she paused. 'And did he ask about me?'

'Just if you were all right but before you start we didn't spend the time talking about you. OK?'

'So what did you talk about all these times you were meeting him?'

Shannon leant back on her seat and pushed her finished tray of chips away from her as if they had nothing to do with her then wiped her fingers with the tissue, scrunched it and dropped it into the empty tray.

'I'll tell you if that's what you really want but not in here and not if you're going to go berserk over everything I say.'

'OK, we'll walk or find somewhere else. And I'm not going to go berserk,' but as soon as she had said it she didn't know whether she'd be able to keep her temper or not.

The man behind the counter called goodbye and told them to come again as they stepped into the night street and turned the corner to join the main thoroughfare that she knew was the start of their journey back to their hotel. As they set off she sensed the awkwardness between them and her daughter didn't link her arm as she had done earlier.

'So what do you think of Amsterdam?' Shannon asked, glancing at her across the self-conscious gap that separated them.

'It's beautiful.'

'Beautiful?' Her daughter's voice echoed with incredulity. 'I think it's a hole and these bloody bikes do my head in – everywhere you go you nearly get run over. And we saw the red-light area this afternoon. Just tacky and gross. I don't know why we didn't go somewhere else, somewhere closer and cheaper. Even Dublin would have been better than this dump or we could even have stayed in a Belfast hotel with a health spa.'

She resisted the temptation to remind her of her own opinion offered when the trip was announced and they walked in a laboured silence under the beaded strings of Christmas lights and those in the shapes of flowers and butterflies attached to the fronts of shops. Across a canal the complete outline of a house was illuminated and as they walked at an angle to it, it seemed to move and lend its light to its neighbours. Back home most houses had their trees and lights up for weeks and every year there were more and more families turning their homes into Santa's grotto with every single space of house and garden plastered with so many lights and illuminated figures that they could probably be seen from outer space. It was all a show, all a competition to be better than everyone else – she'd no time for it and she wondered if they felt so smug when their January electricity bills arrived. She remembered that Shannon had complained that their tree was too small and the decorations ugly. She wanted a tree dressed all in the same colour, in red or silver, like she had seen in a magazine, but never showed any inclination to do something about it herself, or spend some of her money in the store where she worked to make it possible.

Her daughter thought the city was ugly. Well she was glad because she didn't want to share the truth of it with her. So let her think that. She glanced at her as they walked, the gap between them just wide enough for both to know its meaning, and in that moment her daughter's beauty, the thing in which they both took so much pride, seemed suddenly a little tawdry, a little threadbare. She saw something of her own hardness in the face that was pinched and sharpened by the cold but there was something else she didn't like. She knew that she could never tell her daughter about the pictures with the light coming out of them, about the music in the church, and she realised for the first time that there were so many things she never shared with her child. She had said nothing about the dying man, or the missing bracelet, or what it was like to work in the home. And after what Shannon had kept hidden from her there would always be this distance between them even when it was over and they had made things up in whatever way was possible.

They walked quickly, from time to time glancing in at the doorways of some bars, but everywhere looked crowded and noisy and so they kept on and she wondered who would be the first to break and bridge the gap by linking arms. She told herself that it wouldn't be her as she constructed glossy images of his house, hurting herself by compiling unfavourable comparisons with theirs. He knew where she lived and so understood that she hadn't made anything of herself in terms of what would impress him. It couldn't be hidden either by a new wedding outfit which despite the money she had spent on it wouldn't ever make her look more than someone who was trying but who hadn't had enough to spend. She couldn't even console herself with her daughter's beauty because he would be able to claim at least half of that. It suddenly felt like the mist was in her eyes and throat.

In a short while they would be back at the hotel that was really only a cheap hostel. She had established a surer grasp of the city's geography now and knew that soon, in the company of the rest of the party, there would be no chance of hearing or saying what she needed. So she pulled her daughter by the arm and silently gestured that they should sit on one of the sheltered metal benches at a tram stop. It would do. There was no one else there. Shannon wiped the seat dismissively with one of the serviettes that she had carried with her but sat down, her hands stuffed deep into her thin jacket.

'So, Mum, ask me whatever it is you want to know and I'll tell you.' Her voice was stubborn, almost resentful.

She wanted to ask her how she could stick this knife in her heart, how it was that she had no idea of the pain and betrayal she had caused. She wanted to ask how her daughter could believe that she could go to the wedding and sit at a table with someone who had left her pregnant and abandoned her to the world's scorn with a scribbled note pushed through her door in the darkness. Part of her wanted to slap her again and she would have done it, if even for a second she believed that it would make her understand.

'Did he invite himself to the wedding or did you?'

'I invited him. But not for ages and ages. He wasn't going to come at first but I persuaded him. It wasn't easy.'

'But why, Shannon? Help me to understand why?' The pleading in her voice shocked her – it was not something she had ever heard before.

'Because he's my father and because he's sorry – he's really, really sorry. He said he behaved like a bastard and he's always regretted it. Says if it's not too late he wants to try and make up to me for it in any way he can.'

'And what about me – how's he going to make it up to me?'

'He knows he can't.'

'And how's he going to make it up to you after twenty years? Get in a time machine and travel back, make everything different?'

A bicycle went by with an old woman hunched over the handlebars and labouring a little. She heard the whirr of the wheels, the slow rasp of her breathing. Only the steady beam of her lamp's white light signalled any sense of conviction. As she watched she felt intense sympathy for her then an anger that life had to be such a struggle, that nothing was given easily to people like them. An idea came to her that if someone had been able to paint her that morning as she read his letter, the same way that someone had painted the young woman in the blue smock, then her daughter might have been able to understand. But she knew she would never even be the centre of one of the photographs that she looked at each morning, much less a painting. Shannon took her hands out of her pockets and blew into them, then with her eyes focused on the other side of the street said, 'He's giving me money.'

'Money?'

'A deposit for a house.'

'How much?' She shivered then started as a tram rattled round the corner, its warning bell a loud clang that seemed to echo inside her head. She felt sick. There was a shrill shunt and a wheeze of brakes as the tram stopped in front of them and people emerged from the opened doors. She glanced up at the illuminated faces behind the glass and saw them looking down at her. She turned her eyes away. There was no way of knowing what her daughter might say any more. The tram snaked into the mist and they were alone again.

'Twenty thousand pounds. He's giving us twenty thousand to put down as a deposit. He knows a builder who's doing some town houses out near Dundonald and we're getting first choice of a site. And they're turnkey which means everything's already done for you – the kitchen, floors and everything. All you have to do is put your furniture in.'

'And you think twenty thousand pounds makes everything all right?' She stared at her daughter but Shannon continued to keep her eyes fixed in front. 'Twenty thousand pounds – that's a thousand pounds for every year he wasn't there for you.' But as she said it she knew it was over. Shannon had been bought out and there was nothing she could put on the table to change that. She slumped back empty-handed against the glass and felt it cold on the back of her head. Faced with the hard currency and power of money, what could compete? All the years she had scrimped and saved, the years she went without, all the times she got up half-asleep in the middle of the night to look after her, even the nine lonely months she carried her – none of these could be traded in for a deposit on a house. And so everything she had given her daughter was in the past and it was her father who was to give her the future. She felt the sickness in her stomach again and knew she would have cried if that had been something allowed to herself. There seemed a special cruelty in that she had seen the wedding as her single chance of reward, of receiving public credit for having paid for so much and brought everything to its moment of success. It had pleased her that despite it all, despite being a single parent, people would acknowledge that she had done right by her daughter, that she had given her her big day. Now there was to be no reward and all that remained was to decide what it was she was going to do about the wedding. Her attendance was the only card she had left to play. As

293

she glanced at her daughter again she thought of making her choose between her presence and her father's and she cringed at the very use of the word father. To use it was to put them both on an equal footing and give him a status he had never earned.

'I don't forgive him,' Shannon said, looking at her for the first time. 'I'll never forgive him. What he did to you was terrible and no money can make that right.' She paused as if waiting for her mother to say something but she sat silently, unable to trust her voice. 'I know that, Mum, and I won't ever forget it. So don't ever think that.' She paused again, looking for a response.

'I'm glad,' she said in what sounded whispery and uncertain to her and like someone else's voice. Two young black boys in white tracksuits ambled past, inspecting them briefly before disappearing like twin ghosts into the mist. The sound of music seeped lazily in from the distance.

'I think he's sorry about what he did and wants to try and find a way to say that.'

'He's never said sorry to me.'

'And what would be the point of that, Mum, because you wouldn't accept it and you'd be angry that he's even said it! He knows that. You know that. And he said he wouldn't come to the wedding unless you allowed it.'

'But I don't allow it, Shannon.' Her voice was stronger now, renewed with the passion of her feelings but shaken by the shock of her daughter telling her something that she knew was true.

'I know you don't want it but I'm not asking for him, I'm asking for me and that's a big difference. I think he's probably not the same person you knew. He's good to his two children and I know he wasn't good to me but he's ashamed of that and I want to let him be a part of my life. So I'm asking you to let him come, to do it for me and because it's my day and I want him to be there even if he doesn't deserve it.'

'I can't, Shannon, I just can't.' She was pleading now. 'You have to understand.' She rested her hand on her daughter's hand, desperate for that understanding.

'I need you to do this for me, Mum. All my life you've done everything for me and this is the very last thing and the biggest thing.' Her daughter covered her hand with her own and held it tightly.

She had never heard her talk like this before. She wanted to pull her hand away and retreat into herself and what she had decided but the words tore at her and refused to let her go.

'I'm cold, Shannon, we should go back to the hotel. They'll be worrying about us.'

Her daughter leaned into her and spoke so close to her face that she felt her breath on her cheek bringing back to her all the times when she had nursed her, nursed her through illness and heartbreak. Shannon wanted her to nurse her now.

'Please, Mum.' And her voice was childlike, the child she had never turned her back on even when she was completely in the wrong. The child, too, she had felt guilty about all her life for giving her something less than everyone else had.

She wanted to push her away and hold on to whatever resolve had firmed itself in her mind but knew that if she pushed her away she would risk losing her for ever. She had already lost too many things in her life and although nothing would ever be the same between them, there had to be something left to help her make it through whatever the future would bring. The music sounded a little louder, vaguely familiar. It made her think of the music she had heard in the church. She knew it was over now and that she had lost, but a final remnant of pride stopped her giving what her daughter wanted without one final struggle.

'I'm going to think about it, Shannon. That's all I'm going to say. And no promises. You understand?'

But despite her words her daughter understood well enough and put her arms round her to hug her. Her only response was to lightly lay her hand on her daughter's arm, and for a second it felt as if the tightness of the embrace was choking her. She thought about the consequences of what she was about to agree to and it felt suffocating just as the now-thickening tides of mist seemed to be slowly choking the city's buildings and forcing them into some indistinct and lifeless form. So she would be changed and not in ways that she would have chosen and she was frightened by not knowing how those changes would shape her life or who she would have to be.

Shannon was talking quickly, rattling on about inconsequential things, but her voice washed meaninglessly over her to be lost in the spread and splay of her fears.

Then from out of the froth of her daughter's words she heard her say, 'Let's go, Mum,' and she was helping her off the bench, as if suddenly her mother had become an old woman. 'It's this way, isn't it?'

She had to look around her, momentarily confused about the right direction, but then pointed the way ahead. She felt her daughter's arm link her own and the firm lean of her shoulder, tried to listen to her renewed chatter as they walked, but it was as if her thoughts were intercut with the echo of Shannon's voice, just as her calls had been with the echoes under the tunnel on the day she thought she had lost her. What would she have done if she had lost her for ever then? How could she have gone on living? Her child had given her a purpose, a reason to do all the things that she had to do. Without her she would have become a ghost of herself, worn down by the purposelessness of her work and the weight of what the world asked of her. She glanced at the animated face of her daughter and was carried a little on the breaking wave of the happiness that had chased the coldness from her features. She saw the neon sign of their hotel reddening in the distance. Soon they would be back in the warmth. Already she could see a group of figures bunched on the front steps, their cigarettes glowing in the darkness. It would be the girls waiting for them.

She had given her daughter all that she could. He had given her something else, something that was easy to give. She told herself that her daughter would always know the difference between the two. But she understood too the power of money. And then she remembered that there was something else she could give her.

'Wait, Shannon, a second. I have something for you.' She looked at the surprise on her daughter's face, the too obvious, eager expectation, but nothing mattered now. 'It's not wrapped or anything but I hadn't time. I bought it for you in Amsterdam – it's not new, it's old – an antique. I don't know if you'll like it.'

She took the bracelet from her pocket and cradled it in the palm of her hand in the light of a shop window. Its value weighed heavily and made it shake a little. Even in that light the blue stones sparkled in their plaited ring of gold. Her daughter took it delicately and slowly, her eyes widening in a gradual consciousness of its worth. Her mouth formed a silent circle as she raised the bracelet level with her eyes as if not fully believing what she was holding.

'It's beautiful, it's really beautiful,' she said, giving little squeals of pleasure and then trying it on her wrist. She had to help her with the clasp, show her how it worked.

'But it must have cost a fortune.' She held her wrist up to the light and turned it as if she was giving the world a chance to admire it.

'I've been saving. I got a good price. So you like it?'

'It's absolutely gorgeous. Really classy. I love it, really love it. But where did you get it?'

'In an antique shop near the museum.'

Shannon hugged her again and again and for a second the bracelet almost caught in her hair. They rocked one another in a tight embrace and then with the bracelet still on her daughter's wrist they set off to cover the short distance that separated them from their hotel.

Fourteen

THEIR ALLOCATED SEATS, ALTHOUGH to one side of the stage, were reasonably placed, affording a clear view, and while the knowledge of how much they had cost still made him wince, what he mostly felt was a renewed sense of anticipation and excitement. Perhaps it was this that caused his trip as he started to funnel down their aisle and left him almost sprawling face first to the accompaniment of his son's loud snigger. A moment later Jack burrowed himself into his seat then sank so low that only his head was resting on its rim. The dark, bruised patina of the leather jacket contrasted with his youthfulness and his thin wrists spindled out of its wide sleeves. He thought Jack was underweight and he would have to talk to Susan about it but his concern for his son was replaced by thoughts of her in Spain with Gordon. The different country they were in, and almost certainly sleeping together in, generated an unwelcome sense of romantic adventure that despite his efforts to block them out was exacerbated by images of remote mountains and stone-built tavernas with simple but quaint and single-focused bedrooms whose windows looked out over sweeps of olive groves. He didn't think he would ever be able to imagine her with someone else without feeling this stab of pain, primed by a jealousy that he couldn't deny was the product of some primitive male possessiveness. He reminded himself again that the pain was deserved because he was the one who had betrayed her and there was no consolation in knowing that his Hallowe'en moment of madness had been such a damp squib, a complete and utter nothingness, spluttering his life into a cascading fall of ash.

He sneaked a look at his T-shirt underneath his coat that he had discreetly unbuttoned, with its 'You go your way, I'll go mine', and felt stupid and crass that its bitter irony had eluded him and that now he was wearing his shame in public. Glancing at his son whose spine seemed to have contracted into itself as if he had fallen from a great height he felt irritated by his posture and irritated by the fact that it was no longer possible to simply tell him to sit up.

'Are you comfortable, Jack?'

'Yes.'

'That's good. Do you think you'll be able to see all right?'

Jack turned his head to look at him then squirmed upright and looked again, his eyes fixed on his T-shirt.

'What are you wearing?'

'It's a T-shirt from way back. I thought I'd give it an outing.'

'What does it say?' he asked in a slow and exaggerated show of disbelief.

'You go your way, I'll go mine. It's got sentimental value,' he said, realising that he was apologising without meaning to.

Jack slumped back in his seat smiling to himself and giving his head one superior shake of incredulity. His son's reaction pleased him even though he realised that his only ability to make him smile or laugh was through tripping, or banging his head on something – some moment of clumsy slapstick – or by some aberration that confined the embarrassment to himself. But he didn't care and would take any humiliation, would tumble into a pile of horse manure if it guaranteed a smile – anything that cracked the frozen rictus that sometimes suggested his son's emotions were in rigor mortis. The smile also gave him encouragement to try conversation in the wait for the performance.

'Do you think your mother will really go to Spain?' He knew he was risking another eruption of blame but it was a risk he felt emboldened to take by a growing hope that Jack had vented part of what he needed and some at least of the danger had passed.

'Would you live in something that Gordon had built?'

'You don't like him much.'

'He's a complete and utter dickhead. What's there to like?'

'Your mother obviously sees something in him,' he said, desperately trying to resist the temptation to enthusiastically agree with his son because despite everything he felt a loyalty to Susan that included even her foibles.

'Mum's head's a total mess. I think she's having some kind of breakdown.'

'What makes you say that?'

'Gordon, obviously.' He lifted his arm slightly then let it fall again in seeming exasperation at his father's thickness. His thin wrist looked like the stick arm of a scarecrow. 'Maybe you haven't had to listen to him enough.'

'He's not great,' he conceded, reluctant to let the window of conversation close.

'Not great!' His voice dripped with scorn at his father's lack of insight. 'He's a total wanker. I hate him.'

His momentary confusion about whether his son should be using this type of language to his father, however justified, troubled him less than the intensity of his expression of hatred. This expression of hate he'd heard before, sometimes directed at the teacher he'd got into trouble over, a few times at some boy in school, that despite its superficial childishness was invested with something he found disturbing. There was no disputing the accuracy of his judgement of Gordon as a total wanker but he couldn't bear to hear the vehemence in his son's voice. It was as if he'd pressed all his frustration and all his self-hate and insecurities into one spew of words. He wanted to tell him that hatred was a corrosive, self-destructive thing best left to the suicide bomber and the fanatic, but he knew that his son blamed him for the appearance of Gordon and so he had to tread carefully if he was to avoid a meltdown like the one in the park.

'Your mother's too smart not to realise that before long. Perhaps she just needs him to lay a few bricks.'

'He couldn't lay an egg. He's a dead-brain no-hoper and if she takes up with him permanently then I'm out of there. Gone!' He raised his hand again, for some reason pointing it at the stage before letting it fall. The leather in the jacket seemed to stretch and crack a little as if aware of the seismic rage below its surface.

He didn't know what to say for fear of saying the wrong thing. He could only talk to his son when he wasn't there, or listening to his music through his earphones. He was filled with a sense of sadness that was also inexpressible. The only instinctive response was to put his arms round him and tell him that everything would be all right but knowing that, too, was impossible, he moved his hand closer to his son's arm then stopped short when Jack turned his body away as if intent on inspecting the far side of the hall. He was his father and yet he knew if he were to assume a wisdom with which to offer reassurance it would be fraudulent. And even if he tried the confessional and told him about crying at George's funeral he knew that it would come out wrong and stack up as just another exercise in competitive misery.

As always he wanted to take his son's pain but could find no way to do it. He formed an image in his head of lying beside Jack in two hospital beds with their bodies intravenously linked and everything that was poisonous and destructive in his son's system slowly draining into his. But there was nothing to console or assuage the sense of guilt that always wanted to make him believe that he had added to the mess his child was in. His child who thought people were shit and believed in UFOs and alien life forms. A mocking voice told him that communicating with an alien life form would be easier, less fraught with the possibility of failure, and he wanted to tell his son that he came in peace, that he didn't want to colonise him, or force him into slavery to things that he didn't believe in. He remembered when Jack was about ten the pleasure that they had both got out of his interest in magic and his delight at being able to master a few simple tricks that he had perfected from his Junior Magician's Outfit. Making things disappear behind cloth, identifying the right card – it had all given him so much smiling pleasure as they encouraged him with melodramatic gasps and wide eyes. Work a little magic now, Jack. Magic a little happiness for them both. Make the misery disappear.

The lights went down but it was only the warm-up band and there was nothing about their music that suggested any connection with the main act, everything sounding self-conscious and inconsequential, and he began to think that the concert would be a repeat of the Van Gogh visit. It wasn't a great start and two songs in he glanced at Jack to see that he was wearing his earphones and listening to his MP3. Despite the paucity of the music it seemed incredibly rude and then he was frightened by the thought that he might do it when Dylan was playing and risk the disapproval of the fanatics all around them who would see his son's actions as sacrilege. He didn't know what to do so he did nothing and hoped he would take them off when Dylan appeared.

The lead singer of the warm-up act sounded embarrassed as he introduced the songs as if he didn't really understand either why they were there. When they tried to kick a little ass it sounded half-hearted just like the applause that greeted it and he turned to Jack to tell him that they weren't very good even though he knew he couldn't be heard. One of his son's eyes was curtained by a drop of black hair that looked colour-coordinated with the black of his jacket. It would have pleased him to lean across and brush it lightly away. But instead he joined the polite applause when the set ended and then the emptying stage swarmed with roadies, tracking and testing, all of them conveying the good roadie ethos that their time on view should be as short and unobtrusive as possible, their dark clothes helping them blend into the backdrop. And for the first time he wished his son was somewhere else, with his mother and Gordon putting a spoke in their freewheeling loving wheels, or even back at home with Jasmine playing grown-ups. This was a special moment for him and he knew that it was going to be diminished by his son's presence, a constant mental distraction, and as he watched him take his euros out of his pocket and count them he thought of him as a moneychanger in the temple.

'Do you need any money?' he asked.

'No.'

'No thanks,' he said, unable not to give some vent to his irritation. 'No thanks.'

'No thanks.'

But his son's voice wasn't dripping with sarcasm and that surprise made him wonder if he and Susan should have been firmer, less accommodating, less ready to make allowances for everything. He thought of telling him to sit up but was unwilling to push his luck. And the talk of money reminded him that he hadn't yet bought any of his family their Christmas presents. The best thing to do with Jack was to ask him but it would probably sound as if he was trying to buy him. Perhaps there was something musical he could get him, a new guitar perhaps or an amp – he'd talk to Susan about it. In the past she had seemed to have an inside track to his thinking but he was unsure whether such a thing existed any more.

Jack appeared to be momentarily interested in what was happening on stage as roadies set guitars in place and tested microphones. He was sitting up and had taken his earphones out. Suddenly his face had assumed a childish curiosity.

'I'm really looking forward to this, Jack.'

'That's good.'

'He was such an important part of my growing up and such a big influence on so many things.'

'When you were a hippy?' His son was laughing at him but he didn't care.

'I thought I was. Like I said, I only played at it for a while.'

'And you never took drugs, not even once?' There was disbelief in his voice as he gave the subject a second going over.

'No, never, and if you really want to know I've never been drunk either.'

'Everybody's been drunk – you must have been some time.'

His son was scrutinising him, weighing up whether he was spinning him a line, and his unshaded eye narrowed and hardened as it tried to burrow into the truth. But it was important that he didn't make him think he was offering some Sunday-school lesson or holding himself up as a moral template by which he should live his life. At least for this moment Jack seemed interested in knowing this stuff and as the roadies finished their preparations it felt like the briefest of opportunities that he would regret not taking if he let it slip away.

'You know I grew up in the church and there were pretty strict rules about everything and what life was about was spiritual things, their idea of course of spiritual things. Now gradually I came to believe in other things, things that were spiritual but in a different type of way. Do you understand?'

'What sort of things – you don't go to church.'

'No, I don't. Things like art and music, I suppose.'

'You think they're religious?'

'Yes, in their own way. Anything that's to do with the spirit, the soul, or whatever you want to call it, is spiritual. When you play your music, your own stuff, you must feel sometimes that it's to do with your spirit, that it's coming from somewhere deep inside yourself.'

Jack nodded without much conviction but it didn't matter because he had his own animation now, the words spurred on by the intensity of memory and the need to explain himself, if not to his son, then to himself at least.

'Well, when I left all the church stuff behind and was in

306

what the church would call the world, then I didn't want some of those things the world offered.'

'Because you thought they were sinful or something?'

'No, I didn't think they were sinful, just that they hadn't any real meaning.'

'Maybe you were just scared or some kind of good boy,' he suggested but his voice wasn't completely laced with scorn.

'Maybe I was. Maybe you're right and I was just scared.'

'Scared of what? Getting into trouble?'

He paused as he tried to think of the answer. Around him the audience had started to rustle in anticipation. Someone let out a loud whoop.

'Scared of damaging something that was important.'

It was all mangled up in his head now and he didn't have the words to explain about the beauty of holiness that wouldn't make it sound embarrassing for both of them and inexpressibly wet and soppy for his son but just before he slumped back into his seat and admitted defeat, he said, 'So I ended up living in two worlds, neither one or the other. A kind of limbo.'

Then Jack was saying something to him, blowing away the smudge of hair from his eye as he spoke, but his words were lost in the roar of the crowd as the house lights went down and on to the still-shadowy stage strolled a series of undefined figures.

He heard himself clapping loudly, his heart racing on the pulse of having spoken to his son and having him listen, of being in a place and time which would help him know that the world he was trying to talk about was as real and tangible as the touching flesh of his palms. And there, after all those years there he was, inevitably smaller than antici- pated, wearing a black hat with a little feather in the band, black-suited like some Amish farmer, black-suited like a Victorian undertaker, and from the moment he stepped on the stage he wasn't really there but dissolved into particles of memory and re-formed in the iconic images from the albums, the most famous of the photographs. So in an instant he was the coy boyish figure with the upturned sheepskin collar and the corduroy beatnik cap, or with wild electric hair, the scarf, and the serious frown and hooded eyes, and now right before his eyes he metamorphosed into the freewheeling young man with the girl on his arm in the middle of a New York street huddling together against the cold. He couldn't look at him in those first few moments and see him in any way that was constant or confined to the tentative shape on stage that hadn't acknowledged them or taken his eyes from the organ at which he was standing. Instead he was watching a chameleon flicking his changes through the back pages of his memory, each image slowly dissolving into the next and nothing that could ever be gauged or bound in a fixity of time. And something was always hidden, always camouflaged so that the centre couldn't be fully known or commandeered, couldn't be set in stone, always changing. He found himself edging forward on the seat wanting to stand and he thought of Stan and wished he was there in the seat beside him and how they would both find some renewing flame from this experience that would fill their bellies with fire so together they could slay the policymakers and the accountants, the bureaucrats and the administrators whose stony philistine hearts had never known what it was to be alive like this. He felt high. High and almost happy. Even Jack looked alert, craning his head eagerly forward as if the electricity of the moment had flicked him into animated life like all those around them.

Then on the count-in of his head the band started to play and it was 'Maggie's Farm', the audience applauding their own talent for recognition, but immediately he knew there was something wrong, something wrong with the sound system. And then as he stared at Dylan who was standing sideways to the stage at the little organ that looked like something a kid would get for Christmas, he realised that what was wrong was indeed the sound, but the sound of the voice because what he was hearing was a distant, crumbling echo of what he knew. It was a rasping bear growl, grasping at the words from somewhere dropped far below the pitch of the melody, a hoarse bass counterpoint to the band's replication of the original. He looked at Jack, frightened to see some withering sneer of scorn, but his son was staring intently at the stage and all around them the audience was clapping and whooping its encouragement, singing along when he reached the refrain and everyone insisting they weren't going to work on Maggie's farm any more. But it sounded like a man singing into a beer bottle, half-spoken, half-sung, the familiar words slowly separating from the sound memory was playing in his head. He was shocked, immeasurably shocked – the voice was gravelled, shot to pieces – but he couldn't look away or relinquish any of the fascination he felt in the presence of this man he thought of as a shaman, the truest and most poetic chronicler of the age, of someone touched by genius. He struggled with his confusion as the songs tumbled out in the same, unbroken style, the band delivering the songs in their slick, effortless performance, buoying the singer up on the current of their playing, carrying him and creating little cameo spaces for him to fill.

He hadn't spoken to them yet and didn't look like he was going to and apart from a scrunch of the shoulders or a slight dip forward was almost motionless, a dark totemic figure blending with the backdrop. When he played 'Don't Think Twice, It's All Right' he reached for the harmonica for the first time but now there was no angry discordant blare of sound, just a vague contribution that got lost in the backing. He didn't know what to think. The music had always felt like the songlines of his life, mapping out and patterning his existence, but now each new tune felt nothing more than an historical artefact, devoid of meaning other than the one constructed by memory. Gradually he realised that it wasn't possible for him to hear anything independently so it no longer mattered about the voice because what he was hearing come tumbling out was the past.

And there he was with Stan marching with their rather superior, arty placard to Ravenhill rugby ground to protest against the appearance of the apartheid-era Springboks and there he was picketing the American consulate in Queen Street about their imperialist involvement in some South American country he couldn't remember. But he had never been a real radical – unlike Stan he had been too scared to try and invade the pitch that afternoon. It was more an infatuation with radical dreams that had his support – he was never a true believer in the reality of the politics, just fleetingly drawn to anything that seemed to offer a romantic sensibility, a seasonal Guevara T-shirt wearer, rather than a card-carrying signed-up member of anything. And when the Troubles arrived and there was no room for play politics any more he'd done what everyone else had done – dug a deep hole and climbed in. So he was only counter, only underground, only radical in his wishful imagination and there was no part of his life that he could ever think of as freewheeling. The closest he came to that, and inevitably in spirit rather than in body, was the first time he arrived in Amsterdam. His own summer of love – unreciprocated and unconsummated but a memory that was special to him and which in this concert hall felt like it had now reached a moment of finality. He thought it unlikely that he would ever return. If truth be told he'd spent his life working on Maggie's farm and as he listened to Dylan croak the start of another song that blurred almost seamlessly into the previous one, it seemed as if the city had cast him off for ever.

Perhaps he had been unworthy of it, perhaps it was just one more thing rooted in his own peculiar and only half-understood need and which he had constructed purely from his own desire. So now as the band seemed to be locked in an interminable blues rhythm that made them sound like a weekend backroom combo, he thought only of his family and how it was splitting and rippling ever further beyond his reach. He turned to Jack who for some reason he couldn't understand was engaged in what was happening on stage and hadn't put in his earphones or played with his mobile phone even once and as the song chugged to an ending his son was clapping with what appeared to be sincerity.

'All right, Jack?'

He couldn't hear him so leant over and spoke into his ear. 'All right, Jack?' It was the closest physically he had been to his son. Close enough to smell the leather of his jacket, close enough to catch that musty scent of his body. 'So what do you think?'

'Pretty good. For an old guy.'

He was going to reply when the opening chords of 'All Along the Watchtower' started up and he drew back. It was the opening chords of each song that came nearest to sparking some magic. He was pleased that Jack seemed to be enjoying it but he didn't understand why, when he'd no perfect and personal auditory memory to bolster the failings of the sound and with which to substitute the inadequacies of the voice. But then for all he knew, perhaps for someone more used to listening to the screaming Death Pixels this voice was a beautifully modulated baritone. And if he didn't think he'd return to Amsterdam then he suddenly realised with shock that he probably wouldn't listen to his Dylan records any more. He couldn't listen to them any more without replaying what he didn't want. Everything had been inalterably changed in his mind and the more he thought about it the more he realised that he'd damaged some part of himself by holding on too much to things that had reached their allocated span and should have been let go. He should never have gone to George's funeral – it seemed now like the moment when things had started to spin out of his control – and he shouldn't have come to see Dylan. He knew that there was a weakness at his core, a sentimentality that compelled him to find things to elevate and then cherish with his naive hope and admiration. Perhaps it would be truer and a better medicine for him if he listened to the Death Pixels, whoever they were and whatever they sounded like. Listened then spat them out. And the woman in the art college – he saw now that it had been nothing but a shameful bit of sentimentality, coloured by ego and weakness.

He was glad when the concert came to an end. He was looking at his watch but Jack was raucously clapping and at one point put his fingers in the sides of his mouth and emitted an ear-piercing whistle. His own enthusiasm was largely simulated and on a free choice he would have done without an encore, even thought of suggesting they went to avoid the rush, but as he registered the involvement on his son's face and the way it had flicked into a shape and expression he almost didn't recognise, he lent his loudest cheers to the demand for more. He stood up with the rest of the audience and shouted for more but didn't know what he wanted more of, until after the requisite wait Dylan returned to the stage with nothing more than a slight bow of his head but why didn't he speak, turn everything round and just speak to them, even if it was in clichés, telling them what a wonderful audience they were or making some minor expression of gratitude? Why didn't he come to the front of the stage and strap on his guitar and play it as loudly as he'd done that night in Manchester when someone in the audience had shouted 'Judas' at him and he'd responded angrily by turning up the volume? But instead he went back to the organ that was both an instrument and a prop to hide behind and in his own disappointment amidst the swelling appreciation all around him, he felt like he was the Judas who after all those years was betraying what he had once believed in. He tried to tell himself he felt lighter, no longer weighed down by the need to give his faith to anyone or anything. And he was going to do it, write the bloody paper on the Yellow House and get it published. There was an arts magazine out of Dublin with someone he knew from way back editing it and he'd write a couple of thousand words of abstract pseudo-intellectual rubbish. He'd tell Stan that it had to be shortened for the magazine and he'd have an impressive bibliography of books he'd never read including some psychobabble ones. He'd finally admit in public that he worked on Maggie's farm and he'd do what they all did which was to do and say anything that kept them safe from the new mandarins, the zealots, the administrative Stasi. And just as he felt the bitterness of his resolution he looked up to hear the unmistakable opening chords of 'Like a Rolling Stone' and even though they were almost drowned out by the crowd's roar that burst forth as if from one throat, and even if they were stripped down to their bare essentials, they still filled the hall and they washed over him as if coming for that very first time out of that tiny red box in his Belfast bedroom and despite all his conviction, his new resolution, he felt transfigured by the power of that memory, the light riddling through the clouded debris of the intervening years. He understood then that memories couldn't be ditched or simply thrown away like unwanted baggage and without them he would stand naked, shivering unprotected against the winds of the world. So even if that moment and all the other moments like it that had followed would later prove at best insubstantial, at worst illusory, then he couldn't deny them or their part in forming who he was. That at least he couldn't betray. And there was comfort in that until the words barking from Dylan's voice and the whispering descant of his own seemed to taunt him with their questions asking him how it felt to be on his own with no direction home. Then the comfort was edged with apprehension and the knowledge that unless he could divert the path his future imagination had shaped, it would lead inevitably to the painting of the old man. The colours of human passion flooded again through his consciousness in a counter-harmony with the music – the red of the mono record player, the vermilion of the front door of the home he had once shared, the black smudges of crows in the painting clamouring upwards against the yellow of the wheatfields and the blue peasant clothes of the old man as he wept on the yellow chair. The blackness of his son's hair.

He didn't hear any of the concluding songs but slumped back into his seat until it was all over and his son was asking him if he felt all right. For some reason, not least because it was true in a way, but also because his son's expression of almost concern carried a welcome and unfamiliar tone of caring, he told him he felt a little dizzy.

'It's because the music's loud,' Jack diagnosed without looking at him and instead focusing on his mobile phone. 'It'll wear off in a minute.'

'So what did you think of Dylan?'

'Pretty good. A bit like Kurt Cobain but not as good.'

'Kurt Cobain?' He couldn't quite believe what his son had said. 'But, Jack, he put a shotgun to his head and killed himself.' He felt dangerously out of kilter and momentarily indifferent to the delicate gauze of compromise on which his relationship with his son was normally stretched. 'So how's he like Kurt Cobain?'

In reply Jack fiddled with the buttons on his phone. All the house lights were up. The audience was streaming to the exits. He should have let it go but instead repeated his question, turning to stare at his son and disregarding the insistence he heard in his own voice.

'I don't know,' Jack said.

'You think Kurt Cobain is someone to look up to?'

'Yes.'

'But, Jack, he killed himself and he didn't care or think about the people who cared about him and loved him.' He should have shut up, knew he was only heading into some counterproductive cul-de-sac, but part of him didn't care any more. 'The bravest thing you can do in life is go on living.' His son's dismissive trawling through old messages on the phone only irritated him even further. 'Look at Dylan, always on the road, always performing when he could be sitting at home.' He knew he sounded ridiculous and even more so if he had succeeded in formulating something he was trying vainly to compose in his head about he who isn't busy being born is busy dying but he didn't succeed and instead said lamely, 'He might have made good music – I don't know – but he shouldn't have killed himself.'

'You can't say that – it's his life and he can do what he wants with it. You shouldn't judge him. Better to burn out than to rust.' He turned the phone over and over in his hand as if it was a worry stone.

And then something boiled over in him, an anger that had never been in the core of him but only glimpsed occasionally like a molten star on the distant rim of his universe, and before he knew what he was doing he had reached out and snatched his son's phone and was making a call.

'Hello, is that Kurt Cobain? Yes? Well you're an arsehole who didn't deserve all the talent that you'd been given and you should've been braver and stronger and set a better example.' Then as Jack grabbed his phone back he suddenly felt like the drunk in the bar talking about George and the shock sobered him into a temporary shame.

'It's not just Mum who's having a breakdown, you are as well. You've both completely lost the plot,' Jack snapped, ostentatiously examining his phone for damage then nurturing it reverently like someone who had just rescued a sacred object from the hands of an unbeliever. 'What's wrong with you?' he asked, scrutinising him with his one unblinkered eye.

'What's wrong with *you*?' he countered, throwing shame and caution to the wind.

'Nothing's wrong with me. What's wrong with *you*?'

It had the potential to ricochet back and forth for ever, trapped eternally in its own bitter motion, and reluctantly he conceded that it was futile, so instead of saying as he wanted to, 'What's wrong with me, Jack, is I'm pissed off and weary worrying about you – I want to worry about me for a while. In fact I'm pissed off worrying full stop and

I want everything to be all right, not brilliant, but just all right will do,' he simply said, 'I was a bit disappointed with Dylan.'

'He was OK. Maybe he's been on the road too long.'

He hoped he had heard some slight conciliation in Jack's voice but wasn't sure. The rows in front of them had all made their way up the aisles to the exits and they were left to stare at the roadies dismantling the equipment.

'I suppose your heroes are always bound to disappoint you sooner or later,' he offered, buttoning his coat and thinking that they should go. His son was right – he had lost the plot and wasn't even sure any more that there was a plot. He felt washed out, drained, stumbling along his own road too long and desperate to fall into some deep sleep.

They walked in silence to the metro stop. It was even colder now and he wished he was wearing something warmer under his coat. Jack put his hood up and he glanced at him with envy, then as a poor substitute turned up his collar.

'It's possible Cobain didn't kill himself,' Jack said, his disembodied words seeping from the shaded cave of his hood. 'They didn't find any fingerprints on the shotgun trigger. He could have been murdered.'

'Murdered?' So it was to be another exercise in conspiracy theory. 'Who would want to murder him?'

'Don't know. Maybe someone in the music business.'

'Or a drug dealer? He was a junkie, wasn't he?' he asked with the pleasure of feigned innocence.

'Don't know.'

'Yes, if I remember right I think he was hooked on heroin.'

'When he was only eight his parents divorced and he got screwed up,' Jack said with a throwaway casualness then bowed his head to his chest as if in prayer.

He was trumped by his son and they both knew it as they travelled back in silence to the centre of the city. So a future drugs habit, self-harm and any other deficiency of character were to be his and Susan's permanent responsibility. Their divorce was to be a lifetime free pass, an entitlement to access all areas of personal failure with no need for personal responsibility or guilt. He wanted to tell his son who sat with his face angled to the glass that people got divorced every day of the week, and sad and disorientating as it was, it didn't result in people putting shotguns to their heads, but what was the point? He knew by now that Jack needed to hug his misery tight and long enough until he found something else to replace it. And he could only hope that what he found to replace it was something that would do him good. Only part of his son's face was reflected in the glass and the world outside never formed itself into anything beyond a distorted blur. Just before they arrived back Jack turned his face from the window.

'Are you going back to the hotel?'

'You don't want to?'

'It's Saturday night and we could do something.'

'It's getting late and we've to get ready to go home tomorrow,' he said but finding a flicker of optimism in his son's use of the word 'we'. He was suddenly aware of how rarely it crossed his son's lips and so he was unwilling to pass on any opportunity that might help sustain what he was keen to interpret as reconciliation. 'What would you like to do?' It was their stop and they stepped out into the mist that surprised them both. 'Hell's bells, where did this come from? I've never seen this before – everything looks a bit weird. We need to make sure we don't get run over by something. Maybe we should just go back.'

'It's too early,' Jack insisted.

'So what is it you want to do?' But he knew from his son's mixture of hesitation and conviction that there was something already hatched in his head and he said, 'Jack, we're not going to a coffee shop if that's what you were thinking and as you have to be over eighteen they wouldn't even let you in.'

'I don't want to go to a coffee shop. I never said I wanted to go to a coffee shop.'

They both stared into the mist and his own eyes scanned the surrounding neon that looked like smeared watercolours, each diluted from its intensity and smudging aimlessly into one another. Jack shuffled a little then rubbed his foot across the pavement as if he was trying to erase some stain.

'I'd like to see the red-light district,' his embarrassment only half-hidden in his cowled shadow. 'Everyone in school says there's no point going to Amsterdam and not seeing it.'

His son's embarrassment was subsumed into his own. He didn't know what to say then realised it was just another part of everything he associated with the city being taken from him and arranged into a new shape. He struggled for an answer, believing now that some of his peculiar, spaced-out brand of puritanism was responsible for perpetuating the gap between them. He didn't want to go, never really wanted to go, but he suspected that to say no would serve only to reinforce the view of him he thought existed in his son's head of always being afraid, of being afraid of life. He understood the teenage curiosity but balked at having to facilitate it.

'What would your mum say if she were to know that's where we went?'

'She's not going to know because I'm not going to tell her and if you don't then she's not going to know.'

He didn't entirely trust his son's commitment to discretion and could imagine it becoming a future weapon in whatever lay ahead for them all.

'I don't think it's a good idea. It's a pretty miserable place.'

'We're only going to have a quick look,' Jack said, pulling his hood down to reveal his face and presumably his sincerity.

It was a stupid idea but the mist that seemed to float weightlessly on the undercurrents of the city seemed an appropriate mask if he agreed to the tour. And then it struck him that if he could resist his usual temptation to moralise and not talk about dignity or exploitation of women, if he could walk silently through this human zoo, then perhaps there would be forged something private between them, hewed out of an unspoken but shared awareness of the weakness of the flesh, an inescapable acknowledgement from his son of the flawed nature of their gender.

'A quick look and then back to the hotel,' he said, not totally convinced that he had made the right decision and knowing the way he said it made him sound like a Boy Scout leader. Jack nodded his agreement and off they started through the mist. He set a brisk pace partly to try and inject some warmth into his body and partly to get the episode over as quickly as possible. Already he was having reservations, with his imagination enthusiastically constructing ever more disastrous scenarios that no attempts at explanation could hope to rescue from Susan's wrath and Gordon's sniggers. His vague memory of where it was located proved correct and before long they were trailing behind other groups of gawping tourists through streets along the canals where the trees were mist-shrouded, their branches congealed into a grey amorphous whole. He felt more and more nervous, glancing at his son as they started to pass what he wanted to see. Everything looked lurid and pink, human beings wrapped up in black plastic, skin tones the colour of basted turkey. Curiously sexless, shrieking the impossibility of tenderness, everything spinning on the ugliness of money. He felt embarrassed and ashamed to have brought his child there and he was glad he had put his hood up again because it felt as if it might grant him protection. He wondered what he was thinking but didn't dare to ask. They paused to avoid a stag party and suddenly in their bellowing bravado and their horned desire to rut he understood the name. Jack had taken again to walking closely behind him and when he turned to check he was all right he saw his eyes flitting from place to place but he looked nervous rather than curious.

'I've seen enough,' Jack said and he felt his son's hand tugging lightly at his coat in a curiously childish way. 'There's not much point going on.'

'We'll go back then,' he answered, having to try really hard not to show how pleased and relieved he was. 'It's getting cold.' He shivered as if saying the words had exacerbated it but there was relief too flowing through him and a desperate desire not to believe that what would be the shared legacy of their trip would be these images. 'It's just a bit sad really.'

They headed back to Spui walking in silence, linked only by what he felt as a shared embarrassment, his son a step behind somewhere over his right shoulder, and then as they got closer to their hotel he realised that he didn't want them to return to their room with these images still clinging to them like burrs. It was as if the mist made the memory sharper by smothering the brightness of the city that might have served to replace them.

'Do you want something to eat?' he asked, stopping suddenly and warmed by the memory of the girl with the wok. 'An ice cream or something?'

'An ice cream?'

His son's incredulous intonation told him that he was about ten years too late with the suggestion. But he continued in similar vein. 'A hot chocolate?'

'Could we have a drink? A proper drink. It is Saturday night.'

'OK just the one.' This felt like a concession but a minor one and, after the last experience, less fraught with unwelcome consequences. They would have their first beer like father and son in a civilised way and perhaps they would talk like father and son should. He wasn't entirely hopeful but Jack's sulk had grown less evident over the course of the night and if he hit the right subject, didn't rile him, then perhaps words would pass between them. 'There's some nice bars over at the Spui and they're on the way to the hotel.'

The first two on the square looked packed to the gills and they moved on round the corner where they found one which although less plush had the invitation of music and someone singing Van Morrison's 'Moondance'. They eased by the clatter of people on their phones at the door and in through the entrance where it was hard to tell where the mist ended and the cigarette smoke began. The best they could do was squeeze on the end of a table running into one of the corners and which ended quite close to a make-shift stage where a young man was finishing the song to polite applause. When a waitress greeted them, and without asking Jack, he ordered them both a small beer. Looking around he wasn't sure that all the cigarettes were tobacco but he smiled at Jack who just stared back at him and when the two beers arrived they were both glad to be able to concentrate on their drinks.

The 'Moondance' singer was followed by two young po-faced women who turned 'Heart like a Wheel' into a monotone dirge and followed it with some song in Dutch whose tune he didn't recognise but which had all the sing-songy characteristics of a Eurovision entry. It was an open-mic evening and they sat in silence through a series of singers, some more talented than others but all receiving the audience's encouragement. There was a guy who looked like a fossilised hippy who was compering, announcing the performers in a mixture of Dutch and English, and then they appeared to run out of contributors. It was their chance to talk but he didn't know what to say and so they sat facing each other in silence until he thought of Christmas and asked Jack what he'd like.

'Nothing really,' he said, lifting his glass and sipping from it carefully.

'There must be something – it would be better if you told me so I don't get the wrong thing.'

'Don't know.'

'Well have a think about it.'

The ancient hippy was trying to urge some further contributions and for a crazy second he imagined the shade-wearing young Dylan from the Greenwich Village era ambling from the back of the bar to the stage and sitting on the high stool while he tuned his guitar and fiddled with the harmonica holder round his neck. But no one stood up even when the compère held up an acoustic guitar to the audience or when he started to walk through the tables picking out individuals to coax.

'Nirvana – it's a good name for a group,' he offered, trying to break the silence.

'Kurt Cobain was religious, that's why he chose it.'

'He was religious?'

'It means freedom from pain, suffering and the external world,' Jack said, his eyes fixed on the top of his beer.

'Right. Sort of Buddhist or something.'

He nodded and then glanced over his shoulder a couple of times as if he was looking for someone.

'What's wrong, Jack?'

'Nothing.'

Then as they both went back to concentrating on their beers the compère moved along their table, his exaggerated and jocular gestures of invitation falling on stony ground. When he reached their end of the table he rested his hand on Jack's shoulder and spoke to them in English asking if either of them wanted to perform.

'I will,' Jack said, swivelling in his chair to look up at the asker.

He was completely and utterly astonished and then filled with deep apprehension. How could Jack, who looked at the world from behind the screen of his hair, who wouldn't walk beside him, who felt the brush of embarrassment in the most normal of social situations, suddenly say that he was going to perform in front of strangers in a city he didn't know? It felt like an outburst of madness and he stared at his son's drink to confirm that he had only taken a few mouthfuls. Perhaps it had been spiked, perhaps he was high on the smoke.

'I don't think this is a good idea, Jack,' he said, shaking his head at the hippy in as parental a way as he could muster.

'Why not? Let the boy have his chance.'

His chance to humiliate himself in a memory that they would have to add to their already expanding share of

324

things best forgotten. He had felt that despite it all things were slowly edging towards a vaguely less confrontational place so he was desperate not to see them slide backwards. 'I don't think this is a good idea – you haven't got your own guitar or practised anything. Why don't you give it a miss and we'll get another beer?'

The hippy shrugged a dismissal of his words and without speaking Jack stepped sideways on to the stage, sat on the stool with his hair sliding forward and started to tune the guitar like he knew what he was doing and ignoring the applause of the audience and the occasional whoop. His own heart was pumping fear and he had to restrain himself from standing up and telling the audience that it had all been a mistake and dragging his son off the stage and out into the mist-filled streets. Then the hippy put his hand on Jack's shoulder and was asking him something and he flicked the hair back from his eyes and said something in reply.

'Ladies and gentlemen, it's Jack all the way from Ireland doing Nirvana's "Come As You Are".'

There was more applause and he knew it was too late and what was going to happen, could not be stopped, but he felt that without much encouragement he could be sick. The beer was sour in his mouth. Jack hadn't looked anywhere but the guitar and it felt as if they were standing together on the edge of a cliff about to topple over and then he started, his thin fingers strumming out a strong rhythm that some people clapped in recognition but which he didn't know. Then his voice came, high and swooping over the heavier, chunky chords, and at first he didn't recognise it as belonging to Jack – not fully powerful but not hesitant, not in a Belfast accent but not in an American one either, coming from some place he didn't know existed and which flowed through him, releasing a surge of relief and then of pride.

The voice wasn't as assuredly confident as the playing but was delivering as it deliberately slurred out the words about friendship and memory and parts he didn't catch or understand. The word 'memory' was repeated in the chorus and as Jack's voice strengthened he glanced up once, the pale moon of his face suddenly open and visible before he looked away.

Fifteen

THERE WAS STILL ONE thing she wanted to do before they went home and so she gently nudged her husband awake, ignoring his complaints about holidays supposed to be about resting, and when she heard the lightness in his voice she was relieved that at least in these first moments of a new day, she had no sense of anything being different to any other morning.

'Richard, I want to go bike riding. If we get up now, get our breakfast and pack we'll still have most of the morning before we need to go to the airport.'

'You're not serious, Marion. We haven't been on bicycles since I don't know when,' he said, rolling on to his side and shrugging the duvet round his shoulder. 'It's crazy out there – we don't want to get run over five minutes before we're due to go home.'

'Richard, I really want to and we can just ride in Vondelpark – it'll be safe there.'

She slipped out of the bed, put on her dressing gown and then went to the window, only opening it wide enough to peep out, holding the curtains tight as if she didn't want to risk the world peering in. Part of her expected the mist still to be lapping against the glass but in its place instead was a sharp-edged swathe of sunlight that washed across the square, cold to the eye.

'The sun's out so you've no excuses,' she said, turning to find him sitting up in the bed and looking at her. She wasn't sure if he was scrutinising her and whether it was apprehension she saw in his eyes. 'And if you do have an accident you can claim from one of those insurance policies you always rush to give our money to.'

'Are you sure?'

'Yes, I want to try it before we go back. I used to cycle when I was a girl.'

'And you think you'll remember how? I suppose if you remembered the skating there's a chance you just might.'

Whether out of a desire to humour a madwoman, or a genuine wish to please, she knew there wasn't much he would deny her and there were two more things that she would ask for but she would leave them until later in the day. She looked back at the square and there was still an air of slumber, of life being reluctant to start. Leaving the curtains slightly open she walked through the spindling spokes of trembling dust and lifted her watch from the bedside table.

'I get the message,' he said, glancing at his own. 'You use the bathroom first.' He ploughed a hand through the unkempt mesh of his hair then sank down again below the duvet.

She wondered if she should join him but what she should do seemed less important than what she wanted, as all the life of that far-off day when they rode their bikes to Groomsport and paddled in the sea held out its arms in a murmuring invitation that she knew she couldn't refuse. In the shower's heat she remembered how cold the water had been, squeezing out their high-stepping shrieks as it frothed around the mottled whiteness of their ankles. In the skating, too, she had found some lightness of being, momentarily casting off the weight of the things that troubled her, and she hoped the rest of the morning would give her that opportunity again.

At breakfast she looked for the Japanese couple but there was no sign of them. Ships in the night and it made her sad that their lives had developed without the comfort of close friends. Perhaps it had been the fault of the business and the fact that in the early stages at least it had consumed so much of their energy and time, so that nothing was quite as attractive as sitting in and doing nothing but stare at the television. But now she thought how good it would be if without formal invitations they had friends who called in, friends who just took a cup of tea and didn't need you to worry about how tidy the place was. Perhaps Richard found Anka and Celina and the others he worked with served this purpose and if that were true then now she only envied him the laughter she had heard that afternoon. She watched him at the buffet, studying everything but filling his plate modestly, thankfully resisting the temptation to think that he had to get his money's worth. The room itself was painstakingly elegant with its art deco features and lights, coloured-glass windows and even in the depths of winter flowers that were beautiful. But she was impatient to be outside in the morning light however cold it was. They had already packed and she had managed only with difficulty to get all her presents safely stored, having to farm some out to Richard's case who as always seemed able to travel lighter than her.

In the bike shop they had to leave a deposit of their passports and Richard bridled as she could see him imagining his nightmare of being trapped in the city for ever. But she didn't care and, after a perfunctory check that the saddles were adjusted to the right height and more detailed instructions about how to use the wheel locks that would prevent the bikes from being stolen, they set off down an almost empty street with the air crisp but less cold than it looked. She half-expected to see some trace of the mist, shovelled up like yesterday's snow or its spent residue still lazily layering the surface of the canals, but the city seemed sharpened into a new brightness. The lightness of traffic encouraged their confidence and within ten minutes they were cycling through the gates of the park.

It had already woken into life, its wide paths pulsing with walkers, cyclists, rollerbladers and above all joggers who mostly took the same circular route round the lakes, their expressions serious and focused, glancing at intervals at their watches, earphones hanging like stethoscopes as if permanently ready to check the beat of their pumping hearts. Some, mostly middle-aged, or even older, ran in what looked like clubs, sharing a pace, having conversations without ever glancing at each other. Richard made her lead and she just followed whatever path opened up, pleased at how relatively effortless the cycling was and how she felt they blended seamlessly into the flow of the city's people, people who wanted to stay well, people who wanted to remind themselves that they were alive. She was happy in the moment, no longer thinking of the past, and she knew if she lived in the city she would come here and be part of this shared life for as long as she would be able. Once an elderly ponytailed rollerblader put his hand lightly on her back and instructed her to keep to the right and as he scooted past she raised her hand in apology.

There was a simple pleasure in having no planned route but being able to follow whatever opened up in front and they passed an area where there was an outdoor stage and racked seating, a stretch of grass where a football game was already in progress and more small lakes where ducks browsed lazily. In a stretch where they found themselves momentarily alone Richard rode level with her and her eyes rested on the ring on his finger, its brightness reminding her of everything that had happened, until faced with incoming traffic he was forced to drop back.

After about an hour when they had ridden to all the park's various limits they stopped close to the tennis courts at a café which nestled at the water's edge. She watched the care with which he locked the wheels and then chained both bikes to the fence and she knew he was thinking about the passports. They were warm enough to sit outside with their coffees and enjoy the weak sun that was still doing its best to seep through the clouds. Their flushed faces made them smile and her legs still held the echo of the hour's cycling. From time to time he glanced over his shoulder to check the bicycles.

'Relax, no one's going to steal them.'

'Someone must steal them or they wouldn't give you a chain with each one.' She thought his breathing was a little heavy and asked was he all right.

'You have the advantage over me of doing all this sort of stuff in the gym. I might have to join you,' he said, smiling and hiding his embarrassment by lifting his cup and then replacing it on the saucer.

'Richard, I have something to tell you,' and as she saw the sudden apprehension in his face, 'don't worry it's not a big thing.' But he straightened his back on the chair as if preparing to take a blow. 'I'm not going back to the gym.' She waited for a response but for a moment he said nothing.

'Is that it?' He leaned slightly towards her and she could see the confusion in his face.

'That's it. It was very kind of you to get me it but I don't like it and I don't want to go back.'

'Why didn't you say?'

'I didn't want to hurt your feelings. But if we give them a bit of notice in writing we can cancel the direct debit or if you wanted we could get it switched to your name.'

'Marion, you should have said. I thought you might like it. You don't want to go just for the swimming and forget the rest?'

'No, it's not me and I'd rather not – if you don't mind.'

'Of course I don't mind and you should have said sooner. I'll cancel it as soon as I get home. Is that it?'

'No there's something else.' She felt for a second as if she was bullying him but this was the best time to tell him. 'After this year I don't want to sell any more black Christmas trees. I want to do all the Christmas ordering next year and I don't want us to sell any black trees or any of those fibre-optic ones either. I know they sell well but I hate them and think we should do a different type of stock that if we get it right will still make good money. You'll be pleased to know that that's it. Nothing more to spring on you.'

He was staring at her, leaning back on his chair, looking like he didn't believe her, trying to take all of her in, gauge what next unexpected thing might come tumbling out of her mouth.

'This has been one hell of a weekend, Marion. My head's starting to spin. I don't know what to say, or what you're going to say next. Where's all this coming from?'

'I don't know and I'm sorry but that's it – there's nothing more, I promise.' She wanted to reach out to him, hold the hand that had the ring, but knew he would be embarrassed if she stretched her hand across the table. 'At least I didn't make you go skating.'

'I suppose that's something.'

She was relieved when he half-smiled but he was still slowly shaking his head, whether in disbelief at what she had said or in confusion, so she said again, 'I promise you that there's nothing more.'

'And you haven't booked us plane flights to Japan or anything?'

'No, nothing else but I'd still like to go some day – but only if you wanted to.'

He was gazing over her shoulder into the distance. As she looked into his eyes she hoped above all that she hadn't shaken too many things, disturbed the most important elements that anchored them to the life they shared. She thought again that he seemed tired and felt regret that she hadn't noticed it before. Across the water a couple were exercising a dog, throwing it a ball to chase, and a mother was bent over her toddler delicately holding his arms as he took faltering steps towards the water's edge.

'So what is it you've got against black Christmas trees?'

'I just don't like them and it might sound stupid but I think it's a bit of bad luck stored up every time we sell one.'

'I don't know what's stupid and what's not any more. And Santa climbing up our chimney – does he have to go as well?'

'No, he can stay – our grandchildren will enjoy him. Will we have another cup of coffee before we head back?' And as he stood up and offered to get them she thanked him for coming on the bike ride.

'I enjoyed it. Maybe we should buy a couple of bikes when we get home, try to get fit. I was a bit out of puff keeping up with you a few times.'

'I don't think it would be the same at home; for a start there's not a bit of road that's flat,' she said as her eyes flitted across the water to the mother with her toddler. Then it was her husband she watched as he went inside to the counter to order. Perhaps he should cut back, reduce his working hours, and suddenly she was frightened of losing him. Another birthday had come and gone, another year struck off, and as always she thought of the day when they would sell the business and, although she didn't want to do it, thought of how that would also mean selling their house and moving somewhere else. She told herself that she must be prepared to do it when the opportunity came, that it might be good to find somewhere a bit smaller and easier to look after. With the profit from that downsizing and the sale of the business itself they would be comfortable in their retirement, have the time and the money to travel when and where they wanted. But, still, to leave the home where they had brought up their children she knew would be hard.

The excitement of a child's first steps. That and everything a house contained. She sipped the final dregs of coffee and then her eyes caught the upturned face of the mother and suddenly recognised it. She had looked at it so often on her computer. She knew she wasn't mistaken. The child was kicking up little flurries of dead leaves with its feet and then her mother put her hands under her arms – she couldn't tell at that distance whether it was a boy or girl wrapped in its warm clothes and wearing a yellow woollen hat, but somehow she sensed that it was a girl – and gently swung her towards the water. Swung her gently backwards and forwards then set her feet on the ground again. She watched with fascination, her heart beating a little faster at first before settling into a calmer rhythm. Just another mother and daughter in the park on a Sunday morning. Soon her own family would gather round her and she would give them the presents she had chosen with so much care and she would take theirs in turn.

As Richard returned she watched the mother and child turn from the water and make their way slowly towards the trees. He had spilled a little of the coffee into the saucers and apologised, setting one down then swapping it for the other one.

'Marion, I'm the one now who has something to tell you.'

She anxiously searched his face for what he was about to deliver. But she could only wait, the delay intensified by his pausing to sip his coffee and the sense it brought that he was preparing himself.

'Richard?'

'About a week ago Judith phoned me from France about coming home for Christmas . . .'

'She's not coming?' Her intense nervousness was already dissolving into disappointment.

'No, Marion, she's coming. It's just that she wants to bring someone, a friend.'

'She's bringing a boyfriend – why didn't you say?'

'She's bringing a girl, Marion. A girl called Elise.'

She looked across the lake for the mother and her child but they had disappeared into the trees.

'That's not a problem – it'll be nice to meet one of her friends.'

'Marion, I'm not entirely sure, because she was a bit vague about everything, but I think Elise is not exactly a friend so much as a girlfriend.' He drank again slowly from his cup while watching her over the rim.

'A girlfriend, as in a girlfriend?'

'I think so but she said she would explain everything when she came home, didn't want to do it over the phone. She says she's very nice – works as a primary schoolteacher.'

'Why did she tell you and not me?'

'I don't know, she just did, but let's play things by ear, not get too worked up or anything. And there isn't any point in asking me lots of questions because I don't know much more than I've told you. I'm sure she'll explain things properly whenever she comes home.'

So her daughter didn't believe her mother would be able to deal with what she had discovered about herself. She felt the pain of that and wondered if she had ever done anything deserving of it but could not believe that she had. She knew it was important not to look shocked or make a fuss and although she had never said anything to her husband it was an idea that had sometimes lingered in the back of her mind.

'Elise – that's a nice name. We'll need a present for her. It'll be hard when you don't know someone but we'll get something sorted. And we've plenty of room but we'll let Judith decide where's best.'

'Marion, as long as she's happy?'

'As long as she's happy.'

They sat talking about it and each hesitated before using the obvious word but when she did it first, it felt like they had taken a step forward and nothing felt shattered or pushed beyond what could be understood and accepted.

'As long as she's happy.'

'Yes, as long as she's happy.'

This was to be the mantra that would help them welcome their daughter home and open their house and family to her friend and as they walked back to their bikes her hurt and disappointment were softened by a sense of what felt like relief. Things could go forward now, nothing needed to be hidden or locked away in secret rooms. When she got home she would ring her and tell her how much she was looking forward to her coming back and how much she was looking

336

forward to meeting Elise. That would be all she would need to say. While he fiddled with the locks she stood searching through the trees for the two figures but they had gone and in their place other families strolled and played, their laughter and shouts lulling across the water.

When they got back on the bikes and pedalled off, for a few seconds the air crimped a cold mask against their faces which then dissolved again as they found a rhythm. It was time to go back but she deliberately cycled slowly and then waved him to take the lead. She didn't want it to end too quickly and so she let a gap open up between them. All around her streamed the life of the city. She passed a husband and wife with what looked like identical twins in a stroller, their pride inscribed on their faces; a man running with a large dog on a lead; two grey-haired elderly women shuffling along as if miraculously powered by the pistons of their stick arms. A young woman with a short skirt and thick tights overtook her effortlessly with only one hand on the handlebars, the other hand bunching her confusion of red hair. No one stared at her or looked at her in any way that made her uncomfortable and she was grateful for that. She felt part of the city's inexhaustible flow and as she cycled on she turned her head one last time to catch the winter sun trying to tease and burnish the still sleeping surface of the lake into a newness of life.

He knew it would be hours before Jack woke and so he left him a note to say that he had gone for a walk. There was a sad stillness about the city which intensified his feeling that this journey was a requiem. Like so many other things that he had held on to too long he would let it go and try to step into the future, if not with enthusiasm then with less of his instinctive reluctance and fear. He would stop deluding himself with his secret belief that Susan would take him back and do whatever demeaning and inane things were required to keep his job. He would start to paint again, not because he thought he would ever produce anything that would take the world's breath away, but because it would be good for him. And it was just possible that it might arouse some interest or respect on the part of his son. Nor was he going to paint those abstracts where he only half-understood what it was he was trying to do; instead he would find a new style that was part of his future. Perhaps he should do figurative work and as the weak winter sun tried to assert itself he warmed himself with images of painting beautiful women, of painting any women. The girl with the wok and the sloe-black shock of hair. Magic them into beautiful life and receive their gratitude for his artistry. The sun slipped away, momentarily shut out by clouds. Perhaps better to start with still life. A bowl of fruit. More readily available and less expensive. Consumable afterwards. He told himself that if he could stop dreaming of doing big things then just perhaps he could get small things right, things on which he could build if he were determined enough.

He paused to let a nearly empty tram scuttle past almost apologetic for disturbing the stillness of the morning. The sun sidled out again and he knew he wanted to walk in the park one last time – it was where he had first fallen in love with the city all those years ago and it would be somehow rude to leave for ever without saying a farewell. He crossed the bridge where down below a canal boat was making its first tourist trip of the day, its smattering of passengers ensconced below the glass canopy. It was one of the things he had never done because it was too touristy but he regretted not having seen the city from the water.

As he entered through the gates he tried to think of that first visit rather than Jack's angry tirade of blame and accusation. He was sorry his son hadn't been able to see this place in the same way that he once had but Jack would have different memories of the city to nurture, not least his performance in the bar, the reliving of which still flooded his father with pleasure, if also a nagging apprehension that it might be a tantalising glimpse of something that would be deliberately hidden to him once more. Afterwards Jack had shrugged it off as no big deal and, reading the closing-down signs that were being posted, he had thought it prudent to limit his delight to a few simple compliments. He had already worked out that understatement and emotional minimalism were the correct technique, that he should avoid rising on any tide of emotion or intensity. Chilled out – this was supposedly the nirvana of teenage aspiration; and despite the instruction his son had given him on at least two previous occasions to take a chill pill he had mostly – setting aside the phone call to Kurt Cobain – managed to display the required degree of chill. But as he walked through the thickening flurry of weekend joggers he remembered the passions that he had felt as a young man in this place, the flame of which had threatened to consume him with its intensity. Then the world spun only on the optimistic possibilities of what had been nothing more than wishful dreams but he told himself there was a fundamental human decency and dignity about them which could never be completely undermined by their hopeless naivety. So now these men and women who cycled and jogged around him had mostly only individualised, self-preserving dreams because they lived in different times and knew the terrors of the modern world no longer let those former fragile things exist. And yet despite it all, when they could have gone to a thousand different places, they came there to the park and although he hesitated, the word he wanted to use was religiously, to share in the pursuit of staying alive.

He thought of sitting on a bench and watching it all flow past but already he felt ashamed of his sedentary life, of all the times he let self-pity snag and snarl him into a sort of paralysis. So he kept on walking, only just resisting the desire to run because he knew how soon he would come to an embarrassing and wheezing stop. That was another thing he was going to change. He'd get a pair of running shoes or a bike and try to get fit – he'd get them the same time he got his reading glasses and he'd breathe and see anew. He wondered if there was somewhere in Belfast like this where he could join with others on a Sunday morning in a pursuit of this life. He'd never do it on his own – he needed the galvanising spur of the collective – remembering how he had always despised those solitary joggers a little, thinking that they all looked like masochistic self-haters running from their fear of death. He looked up to see a couple he recognised from the plane, riding on hired bikes. So it was contagious, it could be done, and in his overcoat and purposeless walk he felt as if he was lingering outside looking in.

He passed a lake with an ornamental bridge and one with a little pavilion that he'd never seen used. There was a game of football going on with the players wearing individual tops so the pitch looked like a constantly changing pattern of colour. On that first time he had played football with strangers, listened to music, talked to people from other countries. But now it would no longer be possible to think of this place without seeing Jack and all his anger spilling out, of the sight of him taking to his heels, or hearing his own voice calling after him until he disappeared into the gloom.

He passed the screened tennis courts where only the squeak of shoes and the regular *thwock* of balls being hit betrayed the games within. That was when he saw her at a distance and felt the pleasure of a familiar face amongst a city of strangers. She hadn't noticed him and he had the chance to observe her in detail and waiting close to the entrance to the café he wondered why she was always on her own.

She was walking quite slowly, clearly with no other purpose than to take everything in and pull the final pleasure out of her time in a city she didn't know. He guessed she was in her early forties and knew already that she was some kind of nurse. As she drew closer and the winter light laid bare her unmade face he gauged that her life had been one of work and there was something slightly poor in the clothes she wore, a sense that she had never spent much money on herself. There was, too, something indefinable about her that didn't blend in with where she was or the people around her but he was curious about her, about whatever it was that she always held back from view. And he found her pretty in a way that was quiet and not asking for anyone's praise. As he realised that she was happy to be unobserved, moving on the edge of everything around her, he felt as if he was spying on her but just as he resolved to drift away in a different direction she registered his presence and he raised his hand in an uncertain gesture of greeting.

'We can't go on meeting like this,' he said, hoping that she hadn't seen him watching her. 'I'm not following you, honestly.'

'Where's Jack?' As she came close he saw that there were already two little wisps of grey in her hair just above her ear. Her eyes were blue but darker than the colour of his son's.

'He's asleep and will be for a while. I've left him a note. I'm just getting some air before packing for home.' He didn't know why she always made him nervous and desperate to hide it by saying funny things. 'He could sleep for Ireland. But where's your girl? Have the tribe expelled you? You're always on your own.'

'Shannon's still getting her beauty sleep so I just thought I'd go for a walk rather than wait for everyone to wake up. I'm used to being up early so I find it hard to lie in and it's not helped when one of the girls I'm sharing with snores like a train.'

He was about to tell her that Jack had complained about his snoring but stopped at the last moment and then didn't know what to say. He rubbed his chin with his hand as the sounds of the tennis filtered out through the covered fence. He hesitated again.

'Would you like a coffee? There's a nice café just behind us.'

'I don't know. I'm just out for a bit of a walk. Getting my head showered.'

He accepted failure and tried to make it easier for her by saying that he understood and hoped that she would enjoy the rest of her walk then lifted his hand in another vague gesture, this time he presumed of farewell.

'OK.' She touched her hair in a way that made it look as if she was trying to make herself presentable for going into the café and so he smiled at her and knew he should take the lead, pointing out a table for them and asking what she would like. In answer she asked him what he was having and he suggested they could have coffees with milk and a couple of scones. She nodded, tried to give him money which he refused and going off to get them was conscious as he walked away that he was presenting a good view of his bald spot and not entirely sure she would be there when he got back. There were no scones so he returned with the coffee and a couple of little biscuits. She tried to pay again, pushing money across the table, but he pushed it back as if they were playing a game and to appease her said that she could get the next ones. She didn't look at him, instead concentrating on her cup, and he searched for things to say, already starting to think that he had made a mistake.

'So you're a nurse?'

'No, I just work in an old people's home. Cleaning and helping in the kitchen and stuff. I'm not a nurse.'

He wasn't sure why he apologised and then worried that it sounded as if he thought he had made some embarrassing mistake so he quickly asked her if she liked it.

'It's a job. Helps pay the bills. Old people's homes aren't the happiest places in the world.'

'No, I don't suppose so.'

'You do something with painting, don't you?'

'Yes, I teach at the art college, for my sins.'

'Is that a good job?'

'Pays the bills,' he said, hoping that she would smile but she looked serious, a bit nervous.

'And do you paint?'

'I do a bit,' he said, thinking that his future intentions were enough to render his answer true.

'What sort?' she asked, cupping the coffee in two hands as if she were frightened of dropping it.

'I used to do abstract stuff but I'm doing figurative work now.' She was looking at him as if still waiting for his answer. 'I'm painting people.'

'I looked at paintings yesterday in the Rijksmuseum.'

She had pronounced it Rix Museum but he didn't correct her. 'Did you see things you liked?'

'Lots of things. There was a picture of a girl reading a letter, a girl in a blue smock-type thing.'

'By Vermeer?'

'Yes. I liked it best.'

He asked why she liked it but she was non-committal and he didn't press her. And then she wondered how Jack was and he told her about his performance of the song in the bar and felt a little glow of pride as he recounted it. And he couldn't help himself inflate its significance as he suggested that everything was being turned around and all their problems getting sorted out but then almost immediately felt guilty.

'You're lucky,' she said, but without any apparent trace of resentment. 'Things aren't so straightforward with Shannon. She came out with a bit of a surprise herself.'

He waited for her to go on but she sat still and quiet, gently swirling what was left of her coffee. He tried not to stare at her and looked away to where a phalanx of cyclists passed under a canopy of bare branches.

'She doesn't want to go through with it – she's got cold feet?' he offered.

'No, she wants to go through with it all right. That's not the problem.'

But what the problem was didn't seem as if it was about to be revealed and as she set down her cup it felt as if he had intruded into something private and he felt clumsy, keen to find a way back out. 'Perhaps we should be getting back before our sleeping beauties wake up,' he said, tidying his part of the table.

'How do painters paint light?' she asked, looking at him directly for the first time. 'In some of the paintings it looked like there was light shining out of them.'

He was about to try and explain, his brain already collating ideas about sources and shadows, about layering and colour, but he stopped himself, aware that to play the expert now would only carry him even further away from her, and so instead he said, 'It's pretty complicated and sometimes I get it completely wrong. I'm not actually a very good painter, I just have to pretend to the students that I am.'

She smiled for the first time – fleetingly and mostly with her eyes but enough for him to take a chance and try again.

'So I suppose the wedding is costing you an arm and a leg.'

'Pretty much but it's all sorted and everything ready to go.'

'And you like whoever Shannon is marrying?'

'Wade? He's all right but what we think doesn't matter because they do whatever they want and leave us to pick up the pieces.'

He heard the edge of bitterness in her voice and felt it linger in the silence that settled. From the tennis courts burst a sudden shout of frustration followed by collective laughter.

'Jack has a girlfriend – she's called Jasmine and she looks like a Goth or something but if you say that to him or even refer to her as his girlfriend he gets annoyed like you've insulted him or you're a complete idiot.' He thought of trying to describe Jasmine's appearance in a way that would be funny but caught the expression on her face and let it go.

'They break your hearts, don't they?' she said, her voice dropping to not more than a whisper.

'Yes, they do.'

'It's the price you pay for loving them so much.'

He nodded, knowing that she was talking to herself and the best thing he could do was to give her the space to say what it was she needed, but there was only a stretching silence while she stared at the table and ran her hand over its surface as if she was reading something in Braille.

Her whole body was tuned to waking early, an alarm clock that she could no longer turn off, and it was totally indifferent to the fact that she was in a foreign city and in a room with two of Shannon's friends, one of whom snored with a determined insistence that eventually used up all her goodwill and made her want to place a pillow over her face with its open pout of a mouth and her swelling chest that looked like it was rising up and down on a high tide. She couldn't stick it any longer and got washed and dressed, not bothering with make-up or doing much more than pushing a comb through her hair. She would go for a walk and be back before everyone had woken. They half-expected it of her now and she had already got some stick about going to look at paintings, about going to a museum on a hen do, but mostly they trod carefully around her and when they had spoken to her it was to tell her how beautiful the bracelet was and one or two had even offered private sympathy, suggesting that they thought what Shannon had done was out of order. But such sympathy hadn't helped and she felt angry that her daughter hadn't told her in the privacy of home and prevented the whole world from sharing the knowledge of her deceit. Now the gossips would have a field day and every one of them would believe that their relationship wasn't close and whatever happened on the wedding day would be overshadowed by this story.

Remembering the previous night she had put on a T-shirt under her blouse but when she stepped into the quiet street she realised that it wasn't so cold, with pockets of brightness in the sky and no trace of wind or mist. When she passed the spot where she had given Shannon the bracelet she felt the guilt of it – she had never taken anything before that was valuable. So now love had made a fool of her and made a thief out of her as well. She wanted to take it back but knew she couldn't – Shannon had rushed in to show it off to everyone and it was obvious how much she liked it. She was suddenly frightened as she imagined her daughter wanting to wear it on her wedding day and it being visible in the photographs. She didn't know what she should do – she had acted on the impulse of the moment, given it in a pathetic attempt to compete with his splash of money, and in so doing she had made herself bound once more to him.

She looked for the courtyard of old houses but it seemed to have disappeared, almost as if it had never existed, and so she just kept walking and trying to decide what it was she had to do. The city was still half-asleep but there wasn't the thick early-morning greyness that sometimes she believed she could taste in her mouth when she went to work at home. So many things were different here and in a way that she liked, for the first time making her reluctant to go back. Only the street cleaners, with their brushes and whirring machines sweeping away the debris of another Saturday night, echoed her own city. They joked amongst themselves in those thick gargling voices she had become familiar with and their gold neck chains glinted in the light. As she crossed a bridge she stopped to watch a small boat arrow-heading the water with two young children sitting fidgeting excitedly behind their father's standing stillness. She studied the rows of silent houses, waiting until the water calmed itself again.

By now she understood the basic layout of the city centre and there were signs at intervals pointing out the things that a stranger like her might want to find. She wondered if there would still be ice-skating in the square close to the museum but on the way there she ventured into the park to find what seemed like half the city engaged in physical activity. If she stood out it was only because she didn't obviously share their seriousness of purpose, or didn't have a small child to wheel, or a dog on a lead, and so she walked a little faster and tried to assume some of that same purpose because she wanted to fit in, to be an anonymous part of the whole. It felt like these people all around her owned this place whereas at home, and she didn't think it was just about the absence of money, she always felt as if she was an admitted visitor.

At intervals the sun broke through and she felt it however weakly on her skin as she took a path round a lake, carefully keeping to the side to avoid cyclists and the faster runners. A few of the trees still had a smattering of stubborn leaves but most were blown bare with what had been discarded forming a thick mulch between the evergreen shrubs. She walked on and with each step she pondered what it was she was going to do about the wedding. All around her stretched the freedom of space but her head felt as if it was tightening and constricting round this single decision and in that concentration she didn't notice him until he was speaking to her, and then it was too late to walk in a different direction or pretend she hadn't seen him. When he spoke and asked her questions she found it difficult to reply at first as she was suddenly and unexpectedly pulled from the thoughts that seemed so strong that it felt as if they must be printed on her face. He offered her a coffee. Why? What did he want? She thought of Marty's request for one and wondered if the offer was all about something else. She knew already by the way he spoke and the way he dressed that he belonged to a different class and that made her feel vulnerable and think that if he had any interest in her other than as people from the same city meeting in a foreign one, then it was wrapped up in motives that she didn't trust and she wasn't some creature in a zoo to satisfy whatever passing curiosity he had. So she hesitated at first, sidestepping him with a vague refusal, but he didn't try to persuade her and then she remembered him crying in the church and she stared at him again and something told her that this was someone who wasn't good at hiding things, who wouldn't be good at disguising his intentions, and so if she needed to shut the door she would have plenty of time and warning.

'OK,' she said with a deliberate edge of non-commitment, looking over his shoulder to check if she was about to enter somewhere that would make her nervous, but there were simple tables and chairs, some of them close to the water's edge where ducks circled aimlessly, dipping their heads below the surface as they moved. He refused her money for the coffee and it made her feel as if there was something wrong with it, as if it wasn't as good as his. When he walked away she tried to gauge his age and watched him as he put up a hand to trace the circumference of his baldness. Somewhere in his early fifties perhaps. Soft hands that said he was a stranger to physical work. Divorced. She wondered if she should ask about the light in the paintings. There were lots of questions she wanted to ask about the paintings but was frightened to reveal how many things she didn't know and then she was angry with herself for caring and wasn't going to endure the misery of pretending. In that instant she decided that if he were interested in her it would have to be as she really was and not as he imagined, so when he returned with the coffees and asked her if she was a nurse she told him the truth and was glad.

For a second when he asked her if she liked her work she was tempted to tell him about some of the things she had to do, what exactly she had to clean, about the residents who had to be helped in the toilet, about the scraping of the plates after meals. Tell him in a way that would let him understand and see how long he thought he should be sitting in Amsterdam with her on a winter's morning drinking coffee. See how long that held some sense of charm for him. And she didn't believe him about Jack all being sorted – she had seen enough and understood enough about her own child to grasp that there was no magic wand to make everything all right. He would find that out for himself soon if he didn't already know it.

He asked her about the paintings and she told him about the girl reading the letter. Perhaps she could use him to tell her things but when she asked about painting light he didn't give her a proper answer and she assumed that it was because he didn't think she was bright enough to understand it. And he was looking at her, not in a rude way but looking at her closely, and suddenly she remembered that she hadn't any make-up on. Lifting the cup of coffee in both hands she used it to screen her face. He asked her about the wedding and for a moment she thought of telling him, thinking that the sympathy of even a stranger would comfort, but then measured it against the sense of shame she would feel about revealing her daughter's deception and knew it would be a poor exchange. But she was grateful that he didn't press and seemed to know when to let things go and she looked at him again and thought it might just have been possible if he had lived in her world – been the doorman of the offices where she cleaned, or the person who drove their taxi home – it might just have been possible for her to like him. She wasn't sure. He spoke about his son, trying to amuse her, and the fact that he did that made her grateful.

'They break your hearts, don't they?' she said, surprised at the pain the words brought.

'Yes, they do,' he agreed and in the way he spoke she knew that he had understood what it meant for her to say it.

'It's the price you pay for loving them so much.'

He sat in silence. She stared at their empty cups for a long time, felt the cold surface of the table with her fingers and then she told him everything.

Sixteen

THE LANDSCAPE UNFOLDING ON the way to the airport held little echo of the city's heart as they passed through anonymous suburbs, then areas of light industry and commercial operations which shared the same sense of impersonal dislocation that the view from airport trains helps to generate. Even his son, who always insisted on the window seat as if still the natural right of the child, looked bored, with his head skewered into the corner of the seat and his eyes partly screened from the light. Jack had packed the leather jacket in his bag and reverted to just his black hoodie and he wondered whether the prospect of returning home had prompted him to bunker down in familiar defences. And perhaps it was that prospect, and whatever feelings it kickstarted, that had sent him retreating into what he now thought of as his son's default mode, so he had withdrawn into a non-communicative blankness where his father's emotional Geiger counter registered nothing at all.

Only the occasional small canal complete with barge or a drainage channel suggested the country they were rushing through and as Jack determinedly inserted his earphones and flicked through his playlists he couldn't help but glance at him and wondered what void had opened up again. He told himself that it was an emptiness born of teenage angst that would in time fill with things that would nurture and comfort. And there was the song in the bar to hold on to and which continued to offer the possibility of hope. But as his son reached up his hand to secure the earphone he caught the faded lattice of scratches on his wrist and he couldn't help but think of Cobain, destroyed by his pain and fear, his inability despite everything that he had to dam the widening breach inside. The shiver of that fear made him talk silently to his son and without meaning to his hand moved sideways as if underscoring his unspoken words as he said, so please, Jack, don't scare the hell out of your parents with this crap, please don't ever hurt yourself in any way, just try to be happy however hard that is and please don't think that it's glamorous or heroic or anything other than sad and a giving up. But the words were no use and all he had done was scare himself and the landscape fleeting past the window brought no relief with its flat, featureless topography that was imbued only with a sense of the year's light draining away.

A young woman walked through the carriage, her dress sloppy and unattractive and more suited to summer than winter, her bare legs streaked with an uneven fake tan that made them look as if they had been smeared by acid rain rather than the sun. She was one of the Belfast Indians and then he felt a little ashamed for his snobbish judgements because he knew she had come with Karen and he didn't want those kind of ideas to carry over to her. He had been sorry for her when she had confided her story and hoped he had conveyed that sympathy effectively because all the time she had been talking he understood how much it was costing her to tell him about the man who had deserted her. He tried to think back to it in the need to convince himself that he hadn't repaid her confidence with bland platitudes but wasn't sure. And at the end of the day he told himself that however much she had been hurt by her daughter, what she was worried about wasn't as fraught as the place they found themselves with Jack, which at regular intervals felt as if they were tottering on the edge of some abyss. Perhaps he was exaggerating, getting it all out of proportion, and they were just temporarily in the trough of a teenage wave that soon their son would crest and move steadily and safely on.

He thought too of this stranger whose path had crossed his in curious ways. He thought he liked her but wasn't sure and despite how often he told himself that he wasn't a snob he was aware that she wasn't well educated and came from a class that he had long since left. Although he tried to pretend that none of these things mattered he couldn't help being conscious that he didn't like some of the clothes she wore and her daughter and her friends were a bit of a nightmare. And anyway what gave him the right to assume that she might be interested in him? After she had told him everything in the café she had been embarrassed, made her excuses and left and he had realised that he could have been anyone willing to be the sympathetic listener. He tried unsuccessfully to catch his reflection in the glass but knew already that he was older than her, a bit worn and frayed at the edges and with declining prospects. Jack squirmed in the seat as if scratching his back. He was increasingly becoming a boy of tics and involuntary movements as if sparked by some inner electricity at curious odds with the comatose exterior. If his father ventured into some new romance and seemed to confirm the closure of his parents' relationship there was no way of telling how he would react. And anyway in his own current state of emotional confusion it would be madness for him to stumble into some new attempt at romance, the very thing that had brought him to this quandary. He was in a place and time when he needed to focus on his painting and concentrate on keeping his job.

'I'm hungry.'

He was so far away in his own thoughts that the voice took a few seconds to register as his son's who after having spoken had turned his face full to the glass.

'How much longer does it take?'

'About ten minutes. We can get something to eat at the airport.' He was amazed how in terms of having his bodily needs met his son could revert to childhood in the blink of an eye without any evident consciousness of irony. These were the first words he had spoken during the journey. He had momentarily taken one earphone out.

'So what did you think of Amsterdam?'

'It was all right.' A positive which as he anticipated immediately needed to be countered by a negative. 'It's not as good as New York.'

'You've never been to New York.'

'Everyone who has says it's class.' He put his earphones back in.

So Amsterdam wasn't as good as New York, Dylan wasn't as good as Cobain. It was fair enough, he supposed. Your father's choices could never be as good as your own – it was the natural process of life.

They were arriving at the airport now and after getting off the train they joined the queue at the escalator and although he didn't see her he clocked some of the Belfast girls at the top. One of them was carrying a pair of large red wooden clogs, another was wearing an orange Dutch football shirt; all clutched bottles of water carried, he imagined, in an attempt to dilute the alcohol swimming through their bodies. He hoped he wouldn't meet her directly or have to sit close to her on the plane, guessing that it would be embarrassing for them both. He was grateful that there was no sign of the girls at the check-in and suspected that they had got waylaid at one of the shops. He hurried Jack through security, telling him that they would get something to eat as soon as they reached the departure area.

He needed to go to the toilet first and told Jack to hold their hand luggage, pleased to see his twitch of nervousness at being left on his own, but when he returned his son was talking to Karen, nodding his head at whatever she was asking him and looking slightly embarrassed and suddenly boyish again.

It was Jack, standing on his own, his pale face white as paper smudged by the inky black of his clothes. He seemed nervous, even a little scared, shooting furtive glances at the people hurrying past him, even though his assumed posture was trying to suggest nonchalance, even indifference.

'Hi Jack,' she said, 'managed to lose your dad?'

He blushed a little colour into his face then said he was in the loo, pointing over his shoulder as if he felt the need to convince her of the truth of his statement.

'You have a good time?' she asked, glancing over to where her daughter's friends had ensconced themselves on a row of plastic seats, the floor space round their feet suddenly awash with a debris of bags and possessions.

'Yes.'

'Buy anything interesting?'

'Just a leather jacket – I got it in a market.' He blew a wisp of hair upwards as if the conversation was taking his breath away.

'That lot over there have bought half of Amsterdam and mostly the biggest load of junk you could ever see.'

He blinked his eyes rapidly then as he rubbed his cheek she caught the fading scratches on his wrist.

'I don't like flying,' she said. 'But you're OK, aren't you?'

He nodded and she noticed his pale blue eyes. He could be a handsome boy if he wanted. He still had two parents, two parents with money – what had he to screw himself up over? Now his father was coming but he paused to look at one of the information screens. She watched him over Jack's shoulder as he narrowed his eyes to peer at the monitor. He looked like a man who needed glasses. He hadn't registered her yet and so she told Jack she'd see him and then for some reason touched him lightly on the shoulder the way as a mother she might have touched her own child.

She found a seat at the end of the row and within a few minutes was given the job of looking after everyone's belongings while they went off to spend the last of their money. The screens told them they had to wait in the departure lounge before proceeding to their gate and she was glad because it delayed the moment when she would have to see the plane and once again be filled with alarm and confusion at how something made from the heaviness of metal could lift itself high in the air and then stay there. She told herself that the first time had to be the worst and that this return flight would be easier to endure. But she knew too that she didn't want to go home and have to go through the humiliation of the wedding, to have to share the day with someone whom the thought of having to meet almost made her feel physically sick. But it was the price she would have to pay and suddenly love felt like the worst kind of debt that would hang over her all her life and have to be repaid every single day until it bled her dry.

There were other things that she knew as well. She was going to pack in the home and try and get a job on the tills at Asda and it wasn't just because of the bracelet – something that she had to find a way of resolving – but because she'd had enough and because it was a place that always made you feel worse than you already felt. She'd seen a programme on television about SAD and that was what the home inflicted on her, depriving her of whatever warmth she had been able to gather in herself, not just through all the things she had to do but because every day you had to look at your own end. And would Shannon be a faithful caller, bringing her grandchildren on her regular visits? She couldn't imagine it.

There was one other thing she was certain of, and it was that she would return to this city some time in the future. Probably on her own – she knew she could do it, that there was nothing to be frightened of, apart from the plane and perhaps there was a pill she could take that would help blank out the fear. She wanted to experience it all again and this time in summer. She wanted to exist in a different life and even for a little while in her imagination live in one of those old houses in the hidden square. It was a secret she felt she shared, a good secret and one that was better even than any of the photographs on the desks she cleaned.

He was sitting with Jack several rows away facing her but far enough not to make easy eye contact. Some of the girls returned with coffees and sandwiches but none had thought to bring her anything. There was no sign of Shannon. She couldn't imagine Jack who couldn't stand straight and look her in the eye performing in the bar and she wondered if his father had made it up to make himself feel better. They didn't really resemble each other as they sat like two strangers with an empty seat between them. She wondered what his wife looked like and what had gone wrong for them. If he had been the one who cheated. Despite her determination she wondered, too, if in time enough desperation would build up to allow her to ask Marty in for the cup of coffee he was always angling for. She told herself that if she did she was finished, would have traded in whatever was left of her self-respect, but she knew nothing about the future was certain any more.

As always he had got them there much too early, rhyming out his motto that it was better to be safe than sorry. They had arrived even before the check-in desk was open and she begrudged the wasted time that could have been spent in the city itself. When they eventually made it through to the departure lounge they had toured the shops each on their own while the other watched their hand luggage and kept their seats. She had brought him a coffee and a croissant and as they waited she tried to tell herself that everything had slipped back into place and if nothing was ever said they could curtain it with the normal rhythms of their lives. But already there were little spaces of silence settling as they were excluded from some of the normal reflections on their trip that might otherwise have served them. Nor had either of them mentioned Judith and her coming visit, almost as if each had privately resolved not to venture outside the comfortable parameters of the familiar life they shared.

'Would you like anything else?' she asked as he finished his coffee.

'To be home without the trouble of getting there.'

'Why don't you go and buy chocolate for Anka and Celina?'

'I hadn't thought but I suppose I could. Do you think I should?'

'Why not? Use up some of those euros you've left.'

She was glad when he ambled slowly away towards the shop and she was left on her own. Without the struggle for conversation she was able to once again itemise the most important things that needed doing in the few remaining weeks before Christmas, glad that there was so much that needed her attention. The girls from Belfast straggled by her and she smiled inwardly at their bedraggled, weary state which contrasted so much with the excited clamour they had generated on the outward journey. One of them was getting married – she couldn't remember which one now – but she wished her luck, hoped that it would bring her happiness. She remembered the boat with the wedding party, the bride in the brightest of white and flowers in her hair. Then as the boat vanished under the bridge there came in its wake a slow procession of the city's inhabitants, each one coming out of the previous night's mist like a ghost but then forming in her memory as real as the travellers scuttling past her. The shopkeeper whose family was still in Africa; the Japanese couple with whom they shared a drink; a woman standing at the top of the hotel steps and then a mother with her child; and with them the nameless, half-remembered faces of all those who ran and cycled in the park, who played with their children or walked their dogs. All of them she was leaving behind, all of them she was taking with her. And she was part of it and whatever else might be taken from her this could never be taken away. The city had given her that at least.

He watched her stand up as the young women arrived back, each showing the others their final purchases with curious faces peering childlike into the bottom of bags. He wondered what it was that always seemed to separate her from the rest because a few moments later she walked off. He looked at the slumped Jack, who once again had deboned himself where all the parts and limbs of his body seemed to have congealed into a homogeneous whole, and wondered how the fast food they had both just consumed had any chance of finding its way to his stomach, or being digested.

'I'm going to get a coffee, do you want anything?'

'A Coke, please.'

'I'll not be long.'

He pressed his coat smooth and headed off in the direction she had gone, quickly stepping out past the shops selling expensive souvenirs and past the upmarket clothes and handbag outlets until he caught her a little way ahead, looking at a window display. But as soon as he saw her he hesitated. This was an impulse, a dangerous impulse, and he knew already that impulses were sometimes the key that opened the door to disaster but although he tried to tell himself that the strength of its pull should assuage his rising doubt, he couldn't bring himself to fully trust it. So he paused and pretended to look in one of the shop's windows then made himself glance at her and reminded himself once again that he didn't like some of her clothes, that her shoes were ugly, that she pronounced Rijksmuseum wrong. When he thought she was going to look back in his direction he pressed his attention to the contents of the window and found himself staring at expensive lingerie. Then to his horror he saw that she was walking towards him but it was too late to move away so he simply turned his back to the window and stood as if waiting for someone and tried not to look embarrassed.

'Did you see anything you liked?'

'I was just looking for a coffee and a Coke for Jack.'

'I don't think you'll get them here,' she said, smiling and studying the display.

'No. I think there's something further on.' He pointed vaguely forward while he imagined his face was the same colour as he had painted his old front door and which his wife had called pillar-box red.

'I owe you a coffee. If you like.'

'Thanks but I don't want to put you to any trouble.'

'OK.'

She wasn't going to try and persuade him. He didn't know what to do. She was turning away.

'Thanks, I will.'

They walked on to where there was a café and staked a claim at two seats. She tried to persuade him to take something with his coffee but he refused and then as she went to the counter realised it would have been better if he had accepted her offer. He didn't know what he was doing there and in a flutter of panic thought of making his escape but knew the shared plane flight made it impossible. He watched her hold her purse tightly in both hands as if someone might steal it and felt as if he was stumbling down a path which he had no idea where it would lead. Part of him believed that he would be better now on his own, unencumbered by complications and able to focus on his family and his job. Then for some reason he remembered the flowers left strewing the rain-washed road after George's hearse had passed, the way the wind stirred the petals, the way his tears had started. The brightness of the flowers against the grey slick of the road. And he remembered the night from childhood when they had shone their torches across the back gardens that had no fluent, coded message but which with every flickering stutter broke the silent bonds of loneliness. She was coming back now, all her attention focused on the two cups, her purse tucked under her arm. She was a good nurse. A good hand-holder. He thought of Dylan's voice straining to reach the memory of youth, the way time slowly takes everything away, of George as that young untouchable man moving like a spirit in his own element and scorning age and death that trailed mesmerised and club-footed somewhere in his distant wake. What did it matter if the impulse proved untrue? What did it matter if sometimes it led you to a place different to the one you intended? So as she set the cups down but even before she had the chance to sit he heard himself say, 'I'd like to paint you.'

He wanted to paint her. It had to be something pervy. She thought of the lingerie shop. It was just a middle-class version of Marty's cup of coffee. But she didn't know what to say so at first she simply sipped from her cup. Then as he patiently waited for her answer, 'You'd like to paint me?'

'Yes, I'm going to paint figuratively – I'm going to paint people.'

'You want me to model for you?' She was pleased that she had found the right word and in it expressed what was foremost in her mind.

'I want you to sit for me.'

She didn't know what the difference was between sitting and modelling and soon she would have to get to the heart of the matter and understand whether he intended her to take her clothes off but she didn't want to embarrass herself before it was necessary. So instead she asked, 'Why do you want to paint me?'

'Because . . .' he hesitated and in that second she understood that if he said she was beautiful she would know for sure that he was a liar and not to be trusted, 'you have a face with a lot of life in it, full of whatever life you've lived, and I'd like to capture it.'

She wasn't sure whether she felt disappointed or relieved. It felt like a place she hadn't been before, as if she was sitting at one of the desks she cleaned, or in the church again listening to the music. She sipped her coffee and winced at its bitterness. He hadn't touched his. Her face? She remembered the time in school when the photographer had come and then the different sizes of prints sent home in a cellophane package with her portrait visible, but her mother had sent them all back saying they had plenty of photographs and didn't need any more. She had been the only girl in the class who had returned them. Her face? She remembered how it had looked in the toilets' mirror when Shannon had revealed her secret. And how would her face look when she watched him walk her child down the aisle? In the unforgiving mirror of her imagination it felt like a face with its own special share of pain's ugliness. But perhaps this was her chance and he could somehow paint her with light in the picture, the way she had seen in the museum.

'I don't have to take my clothes off?' she asked, hiding her embarrassment in directness.

'No you don't, absolutely you don't.'

She looked at him openly. He was slowly shaking his head as if it was important to him that he confirmed what he had just said as the truth. She looked at him again. He had held her hand on the plane, she had held his in the church. In some important way that made them equal.

'OK,' she said and as he smiled and nodded his pleasure, 'but can you paint me reading a letter?'

*   *   *

They would land very soon. She wondered how things would feel between them when they were back in their familiar surroundings even though she had already made him promise that he would never talk about it again. She believed that there was too much talking about things in the modern world when mostly it was just best for everyone to keep things private. More than anything she hated those television programmes where families blurted out their most intimate secrets and the audience took sides like spectators in a Roman arena giving their thumbs up or down to the protagonists. That was why they would welcome Judith home as they had always done and why they would welcome her friend Elise in the same way without the need to make a show or do anything that was false or just for effect. His capacity for discretion was one of the things she admired and valued and as he read the flight magazine she glanced at the wedding ring and believed he would never embarrass her with this mad thing she had done, was probably by now able to corral it inside some vague belief that it was the product of the menopause or some other unspecified female ailment. And what did the ring mean? It should have pleased her, rendered everything all right, but she wasn't sure – there was something of the staged about it. She couldn't be sure, she could never be sure, but uncertainty didn't matter any more and she would never let it torment her again. 'Only you, only you' – it was what men said and when they said it, it was always true, and if it was true when he said it she told herself that the rest didn't matter to her any more, because in the morning she would get up early and walk in the plantation and the trees would herald her presence by releasing the scent that would fill the air with its precious gift. A gift to her alone. In her anticipation she already felt anointed with a new lightness and when he looked at her and smiled she took his offered hand in hers, let it rest in her lap and felt no heaviness.

She sat beside Shannon, her whole body stiffening as the plane climbed but she didn't take her daughter's hand, deciding that this was something she had to deal with on her own if she were to make other journeys. When they were up she was able to relax a little and deliberately occupied herself with the magazine, rapidly scanning and flicking the pages. She had his phone number in her bag – he had written it on a napkin at the café and after he'd done it they'd realised they didn't know each other's surname. He had used a proper pen, not a fountain pen but a proper pen that looked expensive, and she had watched the way his hand held it and moved across the paper. She hadn't given him her number and he hadn't asked so everything was up to her and she welcomed that. There'd be time to think about it after the wedding had come and gone. She didn't know if she'd ever phone but she did know she wouldn't be his model and wouldn't be his nurse. She was sure of that.

She glanced at her daughter looking at the duty free and wondered how much money they had already spent on this weekend and how much had been wasted and then she realised that she didn't care. Despite what she had felt before she came, the trip had shown her things she had never seen, things she hadn't even known existed and which now sat in her memory as her own photographs, and she felt proud of that and proud that a man wanted to paint her face. For a second she thought of telling Shannon but stopped herself. Her daughter spent her day painting women's faces with make-up and trying to sell them things they didn't need but she would laugh and think her off her head if she told her what he'd asked. This would be her own secret and even if it never happened it too would be part of her, just as all the other things she had seen and experienced were part of her and which no one could ever take away.

She wanted him to paint her reading a letter but hadn't explained why. There were worse things that she could have asked for and there was plenty of historical precedence. But while he was pleased that she'd agreed he didn't fully believe that both of them would go through with it. He thought it likely that one would change their mind but wasn't sure which of them it would be. At least he had tried and he told himself that it was better to try rather than just give up and take refuge in self-pity. He looked at Jack who was busily scanning the skies for signs of alien life. On his tray sat a little scrunched-up can of Coke and a mysteriously large amount of paper debris from a very small pack of biscuits which they dutifully passed to the stewardess who was collecting rubbish in a black bin bag as they started to prepare for landing. His son's face was close enough to the glass for his nose to touch it and the entire world he scrutinised so carefully was part of a malevolent conspiracy, designed to deceive the gullible and protect the faceless nameless mandarins who ruled the world. But in its reality, or its unreality, was it very different from any of the illusions he had nurtured so ardently throughout his life? Everyone clung to something, everyone was needy. He felt a sudden desire to stroke the back of Jack's hair but his raised hand hung motionless in the space between them and for a second as he held it there, it felt like he was in a courtroom and he was promising that he would tell him nothing but the truth. But it was a promise on which he knew he couldn't deliver because he didn't know what the truth was any more except that it was constantly coloured and changed by the refraction of light. So what could he give Jack that was true? He lowered his hand and slumped back into his seat already beginning to feel the encroaching bitterness of failure. He opened his book of letters but closed it again, his eyes struggling to read the print in the dimmed light. Then, as the plane shuddered a little, he remembered the young woman, the optician who had tested his eyes. What was it she had said to him? What was it she had told him to do? Look into my light – that was what she had said. Look into my light. And he knew that was what he must find a way to say to his son but find a way that didn't use the meaninglessness of words. It wasn't ever going to be a beacon that would blaze his son's path painlessly through the confusion of life, but let him look into his father's light, however small a spark of grace or holiness still smouldered there amidst the ash, and despite everything that had happened, use it to guide his faltering steps through the darkness until he found his own direction. Look into my light, Jack. There was the grinding sound of the wheels unfolding. They were coming in to land, the airport building lights clearly visible in the distance. Rain was falling. He touched his son's head and watched him slowly turn to face him, his pale blue eyes curious and a little startled.

The pilot had already warned them about the weather and when they came out of the plane they were greeted by rain and wind that made some of the Indians shriek and squeal and everyone hurried the short distance to the terminal building, some people holding newspapers over their heads. They went up a flight of steps and along a narrow corridor when suddenly they ground to a halt. A voice was speaking to them but he couldn't catch the words. People were looking at each other asking what was happening as three men in white shirts appeared, each shaven-headed, each a physical echo of the other and with authority stamped across their wide brows. They were coming down the line of passengers and directing them to stand in single file against the wall using slow deliberate gestures with their hands as if they were controlling nervous cattle. They had a kind of basic uniform but he wasn't sure if they were police or customs officers. They weren't smiling.

'Son, take those earphones off please,' one said to Jack, the 'please' mitigated by the irritated tone of voice.

He approached with impatience written over his face because Jack, not having heard him, had failed to respond. Before the shaven-headed man could come any closer he took them out of his son's ears himself and then they were being addressed by another of the white shirts. They were to stand still and stay in line facing the front. It would only take a few minutes and then they would be able to go. But there was still no explanation of what was about to happen and so they stood there passive and nervous in the face of this assertive authority. A dog appeared – a nondescript-looking thing, with a pug-ugly face and its tail wagging excitedly as if it had been let out to play after being cooped up too long. He realised it was a dog trained to sniff out drugs and felt a little angry that they were being subjected to this indiscriminate inspection. There were old people and children as well as whatever potential drug mules.

'Welcome home,' he said to Jack but was immediately instructed to stop talking by the first white shirt.

The dog was making its way along the line. People angled themselves out of position to watch its progress. It was getting closer. He wondered if they'd had some tip-off about the flight. And then suddenly it was rushing round their legs and barking insistently, its tail oscillating in a spasm of excitement. Barking and barking, especially at Jack. He put his hand on his son's shoulder – the time when he'd run off and been on his own. Please God he hadn't bought stuff.

'Jack? Tell me you haven't.'

'Stop talking.'

'No I haven't,' and his son's tone of hurt anger made him believe him.

It had to be the smoke from the concert, the smoke from the bar that had now identified them as drug dealers in the tiny olfactory brain of the dog. All heads were turned towards his son. The eyes of the white shirts were narrowing into slits of accusation and enforcement. And then Jack looked down at the dog that was barking and scampering round his feet and started to bark back, quietly at first but then with more enthusiasm. The dog was going crazy. It looked as if it was thinking of biting.

'Please, Jack, don't.'

'Stop that!'

But he didn't stop and the second white shirt who had just shouted was approaching him with aggressive intent. People were fanning forward out of the line to get a better look. There was the sound of someone laughing. And then he stood closer to his son, his outstretched arm shielding him as he looked down at the little Cerberus whose job it was to guard this underworld, and suddenly despite all the warnings, the restraining voices in his head, he too was barking. Every good reason in the world to stop and at worst *Midnight Express* already screening in his head, at best the imagined indignities of a full body search in some strip-lit cell, but he had no choice because in that moment he knew that love was the price that had to be paid for bringing a child into the world. And because he understood that now, he was barking at the dog, barking at the shirts, barking at the darkness of the underworld, his voice and his son's imperfect echoes of each other before they finally submitted, together, to the silence.

ALSO AVAILABLE BY DAVID PARK

ORANGES FROM SPAIN

Oranges from Spain is a collection of stories about of the trials of growing up in a community where tension, confusion and violence hold sway. Here, among other tales, a youthful seaside romance crosses the religious divide, a gang takes turns at the wheel of a stolen car, and an exceptional student stirs the resentment of her troubled teacher.

Set in Northern Ireland against the background of the Troubles, these vignettes capture the spirit of adolescence in difficult times.

'Writing I can only describe as magnificent'
IRISH TIMES

'One could recommend these stories for their author's formal dexterity alone: what raises them above the common ruck, however, is his ear for the murmurs of the heart'
DAILY TELEGRAPH

'David Park writes beautifully about growing up in Belfast – of childhoods under God and the gun. Somehow, against all the odds, his stories are gentle, vivid, life-affirming'
CHRISTOPHER HOPE

B L O O M S B U R Y

THE HEALING

Winner of The Authors' Club First Novel Award

A man is shot dead before the eyes of his young son as they work together in the fields near their home. Another victim of the violence in Northern Ireland. In the city, a confused and frightened old man grieves for his own loss and for the shattered world around him.

When the boy's life becomes entwined with his own, the old man believes he has found at last in the silent child the instrument of healing.

'Deserves to be numbered among the finest first novels of this or any other year'
THE TIMES

'A beautifully written story . . . sheer magically descriptive writing . . . the beauty of Park's work lies in the simplicity of the telling, the exquisiteness of his language and a blazing tension'
IRISH INDEPENDENT

'Park brings his celebration of language, and humanity, to every page'
DAILY MAIL

BLOOMSBURY

THE BIG SNOW

Belfast, 1963: unprecedented snowfall smothers and muffles the city and its inhabitants. In a house with windows flung defiantly open, a wife dies before her husband can make his confession. Elsewhere, an old woman searches desperately for a wedding dress in her dream of love. And in the very heart of the city, the purity of snow is tainted by the murder of a girl and as one man begins to unravel the dark secrets of the city, he knows he is in a race against time to find the murderer before the snow melts. With insight and compassion David Park peers into the souls of these ordinary people battling their secrets and desires.

'A writer of startling grace and integrity...Park's characters burn like the candles they light against [the dark], shivering but bright'
DAILY TELEGRAPH

'Bewitching...If you liked Ian McEwan's *Atonement*, you will adore this'
DAILY MAIL

'Luminously written...intense and extraordinarily compelling'
THE TIMES

BLOOMSBURY

SWALLOWING THE SUN

Shortlisted for Irish Novel of the Year

Having survived a brutal childhood in the heart of Belfast, Martin has built a life that he never imagined, and always fears he does not deserve. He has a devoted wife, a son and a daughter whose academic success is launching her out of her proud father's orbit.

Returning home one night to find police cars waiting, he thinks his sins have finally caught up with him, but instead the news is wholly unexpected; a senseless and devastating tragedy. And in the face of the trauma, which tears his fragile family apart, Martin finds that the violence of his past has not gone but is merely dormant; its call must be answered.

'It establishes beyond doubt that David Park is one of the most gifted writers in contemporary Ireland'
IRISH TIMES

'Technically brilliant and emotionally powerful, *Swallowing the Sun* thrills even as it breaks your heart'
GLENN PATTERSON

'Park writes prose of gravity and grace, full of great looping rhythms and subtly recurring motifs . . . it is hard to think of a more skilful contemporary Irish novelist'
JOSEPH O'CONNOR, GUARDIAN

BLOOMSBURY

THE TRUTH COMMISSIONER

Shortlisted for the Irish Novel of the Year Award
Winner of the Christopher Ewart-Biggs Prize

In a society trying to heal the scars of the past with the salve of truth and reconciliation, four men's lives become linked in a way they could never have imagined. Henry Stanfield, the newly arrived Truth Commissioner, Francis Gilroy, recently appointed government minister, retired detective James Fenton and father-to-be Danny share a secret from their past that threatens to destroy the lives they have painstakingly built in the present.

'Edgy and compelling . . . yields moments of heart-shivering beauty . . . a magnificent and important book'
JOSEPH O'CONNOR, GUARDIAN

'A fine, crafted novel, but it is also an important book . . . He sets out to examine what it means to be alive – and does so in fictions that are subtle, understated, not without a hint of menace and always courageous'
EILEEN BATTERSBY, IRISH TIMES

'We're reminded that with writers like David Park, the novel can itself be a kind of truth commission'
NEW YORK TIMES